Praise for *New York Times* bestselling author RaeAnne Thayne

"RaeAnne Thayne gets better with every book."
—Robyn Carr, #1 *New York Times* bestselling author

"[Thayne] engages the reader's heart and emotions, inspiring hope and the belief that miracles are possible."
—#1 *New York Times* bestselling author
Debbie Macomber

"RaeAnne Thayne is quickly becoming one of my favorite authors…. Once you start reading, you aren't going to be able to stop."
—*Fresh Fiction*

Praise for *USA TODAY* bestselling author Michelle Major

"*The Magnolia Sisters* is sheer delight, filled with humor, warmth and heart…. I loved everything about it."
—*New York Times* bestselling author RaeAnne Thayne

"Ingeniously funny and poignantly heartbreaking page-turner… Major handles her unforgettable characters' issues with compassion and finesse."
—*RT Book Reviews* on *Suddenly a Father*,
4.5 stars, Top Pick!

RaeAnne Thayne finds inspiration in the beautiful northern Utah mountains, where the *New York Times* and *USA TODAY* bestselling author lives with her husband and three children. Her books have won numerous honors, including RITA® Award nominations from Romance Writers of America and a Career Achievement Award from *RT Book Reviews*. RaeAnne loves to hear from readers and can be contacted through her website, www.raeannethayne.com.

Michelle Major grew up in Ohio but dreamed of living in the mountains. Soon after graduating with a degree in journalism, she pointed her car west and settled in Colorado. Her life and house are filled with one great husband, two beautiful kids, a few furry pets and several well-behaved reptiles. She's grateful to have found her passion writing stories with happy endings. Michelle loves to hear from her readers at www.michellemajor.com.

New York Times Bestselling Author

RaeAnne THAYNE

A SOLDIER'S SECRET

**HARLEQUIN
BESTSELLING
AUTHOR
COLLECTION**

HARLEQUIN®
BESTSELLING
AUTHOR
COLLECTION

Recycling programs
for this product may
not exist in your area.

ISBN-13: 978-1-335-74499-9

A Soldier's Secret
First published in 2008. This edition published in 2022.
Copyright © 2008 by RaeAnne Thayne

Suddenly a Father
First published in 2015. This edition published in 2022.
Copyright © 2015 by Michelle Major

For questions and comments about the quality of this book,
please contact us at CustomerService@Harlequin.com.

Harlequin Enterprises ULC
22 Adelaide St. West, 41st Floor
Toronto, Ontario M5H 4E3, Canada
www.Harlequin.com

Printed in U.S.A.

CONTENTS

A SOLDIER'S SECRET

RaeAnne Thayne

To my brothers, Maj. Brad Robinson, US Air Force, and high school teacher and coach Mike Robinson. Both of you are heroes!

CHAPTER ONE

LIGHTS WERE ON in her attic—lights that definitely hadn't been gleaming when she left that morning.

A cold early March breeze blew off the ocean, sending dead leaves skittering across the road in front of her headlights and twisting and yanking the boughs of the Sitka spruce around Brambleberry House as Anna Galvez pulled into the driveway, behind an unfamiliar vehicle.

The lights and the vehicle could only mean one thing.

Her new tenant had arrived.

She sighed. She *so* didn't need this right now. Exhaustion pressed on her shoulders with heavy, punishing hands and she wanted nothing but to slip into a warm bath with a mind-numbing glass of wine.

The day had been beyond ghastly. She could imagine few activities more miserable than spending an entire humiliating day sitting in a Lincoln City courtroom being confronted with the unavoidable evidence of her own stupidity.

And now, despite her battered ego and fragile psyche, she had to go inside and make nice with a stranger who wouldn't even be renting the top floor of Brambleberry House if not for the tangled financial mess that stupidity had caused.

In the backseat, Conan gave one sharp bark, though she didn't know if he was anxious at the unfamiliar vehicle parked in front of them or just needed to answer the call of nature.

Since they had been driving for an hour, she opted for the latter and hurried out into the wet cold to open the sliding door of her minivan. The big shaggy beast she inherited nearly a year earlier, along with the rambling Victorian in front of her, leaped out in one powerful lunge.

Tail wagging, he rushed immediately to sniff around the SUV that dared to enter his territory without his permission. He lifted his leg before she could kick-start her brain and Anna winced.

"Conan, get away from there," she called sternly. He sent her a quizzical look, then gave a disgruntled snort before lowering his leg and heading to one of his favorite trees instead.

She really hoped her new tenant didn't mind dogs.

She hated the idea of a stranger in Sage's apartment. If she had her way, she would keep it empty, even though Sage and her husband and stepdaughter had their own beach house now a half mile down the shore for their frequent visits to Cannon Beach from their San Francisco home.

But after Anna vehemently refused to accept financial help from Sage and Eben, Sage had insisted she at least rent out her apartment to help defray costs.

The two of them were co-owners of the house and Sage's opinion certainly had weight. Besides, Anna was nothing if not practical. The apartment was empty, she had a fierce, unavoidable need for income and she knew many people were willing to pay a premium for furnished beachfront living space.

Army Lieutenant Harry Maxwell among them.

She gazed up at the lights cutting through the twilight from the third-story window. She was going to have to go up there and welcome him to Brambleberry House. No question. It was the right thing to do, even if the long, exhausting day in that courtroom had left her as bedraggled and wrung-out as one of Conan's tennis balls after a good hard game of fetch on the beach.

She might want to do nothing but climb into her bed, yank the covers over her head and weep for her shattered dreams and her own stupidity, but she had to put all that aside for now and do the polite thing.

She grabbed her laptop case from the passenger seat just as her cell phone rang. Anna swallowed a groan when she saw the name and phone number.

She wasn't sure what was worse—making nice with a stranger now living in her home or being forced to carry on a conversation with the bubbly real estate agent who had facilitated the whole deal.

With grim resignation, she opened her phone and connected the call. "Anna Galvez speaking."

"Anna! It's Tracy Harder!"

Even if she hadn't already noted Tracy's information on the caller ID, she would have recognized the other woman's perky enthusiasm in an instant.

"So have you seen him yet?" Tracy asked.

Anna screwed her eyes shut as if she could just make those upstairs lights—and Tracy—disappear. "I just pulled up to the house, Tracy. I've been in Lincoln City all day. I haven't had a chance to even walk into the house yet. So, no, I haven't seen him. I'm planning to go up to say hello in a moment."

"You are the luckiest woman in town right now. I mean it! You have absolutely *no* idea."

"You're right," she said, unable to keep the dry note out of her voice. "But I'm willing to bet you're about to enlighten me."

Tracy gave a low, sultry laugh. "I know we didn't mention a finder's fee on top of my usual property management commission, but you just might want to kick a bonus over my way after you meet him. The man is gorgeous. Yum, that's all I have to say. *Yum!*"

Just what she needed. A player who would probably be entertaining a long string of model types at all hours of the day and night. "As long as he pays his rent on time and only needs a two-month lease, I don't care what he looks like."

"That's because you haven't met him yet. How much longer will Julia Blair and her kids be renting the second floor? I might be interested when she moves out— I'd love to be beneath that man."

Anna couldn't help her groan, both at Tracy's not so subtle sexual innuendo and at the idea of the real estate agent's wild boys living in the second-floor apartment.

"Julia and Will aren't getting married until June," she answered. With any luck, Lieutenant Maxwell would be long gone by then, leaving behind only his nice fat rental check.

"When she moves out, let me know. That might be a good time for us to talk about a more long-term solution to Brambleberry House. You can't keep taking in temporary renters to pay for the repairs on it. The place is a black hole that will suck away every penny you have."

Didn't she just know it? Anna let herself in the front door, noting that the paint on the porch was starting to crack and peel.

Replacing the furnace the month before had taken just about her last dime of discretionary income—not that she had much of that, as she tried to shore up her faltering business amid scandal and chicanery. The house needed a new roof, which was going to cost more than buying a brand-new car.

"Now listen," Tracy went on in her ear as Anna opened the door to her apartment to set down her laptop, Conan on her heels. "I told you I've got several fabulous potential buyers on the hook with both the cash and the interest in a great old Victorian on the coast. You need to think about it, Anna. I mean it."

"I guess I didn't realize there was such a market for big black holes these day."

Tracy laughed. "When you have enough money, no hole is too big or too black."

And when you had none, even a pothole could feel like an insurmountable obstacle. Anna swallowed another sigh. "I appreciate the offer and your help finding a tenant for the attic apartment."

"But you're not interested in selling." Tracy's voice was resigned.

"Not right now."

"You're as stubborn as Abigail was. I'm telling you, Anna, you're sitting on a gold mine."

"I know." She sat down in Abigail's favorite armchair. "But for now it's my gold mine. Mine and Sage's."

"All right, but when you change your mind, you know where to find me. And I want you to call me after you meet our Lieutenant Maxwell."

As far as Anna was concerned, the man wasn't *our* anything. Tracy was welcome to him. "Thanks again for dealing with the details of the rental agreement," she answered. "I'll let you know how things are going in a week or two. 'Bye, Tracy."

She ended the call and set down her phone, then leaned her head back against the floral upholstery. Conan sat beside her and, like the master manipulator he was, nudged one of her hands off the armrest and onto his head.

She scratched him between the ears for a moment, trying to let the peace she usually found at Brambleberry House seep through her. After a few moments— just when her eyelids were drifting closed—Conan slid away from her and moved to the door. He planted his haunches there and watched her expectantly.

"Yeah, I know, already," she grumbled. "I plan to go upstairs and say hello. I don't need you nagging me about it. I just need a minute to work up to it."

Still, she climbed out of the chair. After a check in the mirror above the hall tree, she did a quick repair of her French twist, grabbed Conan's leash off the hook by the door and put it on him, then headed up the stairs to meet her new neighbor.

As she trailed her fingers on the railing worn smooth by a hundred years of Dandridge hands, she reviewed what she knew about the man. Though Tracy had handled the details, Anna knew Lieutenant Maxwell had impeccable references.

He was an army helicopter pilot who had just served two tours of duty in the Middle East. He was currently on medical leave, recovering from injuries sustained in a hard landing in the midst of enemy fire.

He was single, thirty-five years old and willing to pay a great deal of money to rent her attic for only a few months.

When Tracy told her his background, Anna wanted to reduce the rent. She was squeamish about charging full price to an injured war veteran, but he refused to accept any concession.

Fine, she thought now as she paused on the third-floor landing. But she could still be gracious and welcoming to the man and hope that he would find the healing and peace at Brambleberry House that she usually did.

Outside his door, the scent of freesia curled around her and she closed her eyes for a moment, missing Abigail with a fierce ache. Conan didn't let her wallow in it. He gave a sharp bark and started wagging his tail furiously.

With a sigh, Anna knocked on the door. A moment later, it swung open and she forgot all about being kind and welcoming.

Tracy had told the God's-honest truth.

Yum.

Lieutenant Maxwell was tall—perhaps six-two—with hair the color of aged whiskey and chiseled, lean features. He wore a burgundy cotton shirt and faded jeans with a small, fraying hole below the knee.

He had a small scar on the outside of his right eye that only made him look vaguely piratelike and his right arm was encased in a dark blue sling.

The man was definitely gorgeous, but there was something more to it. If she had passed him on the street, she would have called him compelling, especially his eyes. She gazed into their hazel depths and felt an odd tug of recognition. For a brief, flickering moment, he seemed so familiar she wondered if they had met before.

The question registered for all of maybe two seconds before Conan suddenly began barking an enthusiastic welcome and lunged for Lieutenant Maxwell as if they were lifelong friends.

"Conan, sit," she ordered, disconcerted by her dog's reaction. He wasn't one for jumping all over strangers. Despite his moods and his uncanny intelligence, Conan was usually well-mannered, but just now he strained against the leash as if he wanted to knock her new tenant to the ground and lick his face off.

"Sit!" she ordered, more sternly this time. Conan gave her a disgruntled look, then plopped his butt to the floor.

"Good dog. I'm sorry," she said, feeling flustered. "Hi. You must be Harry Maxwell, right?"

Something flashed in his eyes, too quickly for her to identify it, but she thought he looked uncomfortable.

After a moment, he nodded. "Yeah."

With that single syllable, he sounded as cold and remote as Tillamook Rock. She blinked, not quite sure how to respond. He obviously didn't want to be best friends here, he was only renting her empty apartment, she re-minded herself.

Despite Conan's sudden ardor, it was probably better all the way around if they all maintained a careful distance during the duration of Harry Maxwell's rental agreement. He was only here for a short time and then he would probably head back to active duty. No need for unnecessarily messy entanglements.

Taking her cue from his own reaction, she forced her voice to be brisk, professional. "I'm Anna Galvez, one of the owners of Brambleberry House. This is my dog, Conan. I don't know what's come over him. I'm sorry. He's not usually so…ardent…with strangers. Every once in a while he greets somebody like an old friend. I can't explain it but I'm very sorry if his exuberance makes you uncomfortable."

He unbent enough to reach down and scratch the dog's chin, which had the beast's tail thumping against the floor in ecstasy.

"Conan? Like the barbarian?" he asked.

"Actually, like the talk-show host. It's a long story."

One he obviously wasn't interested in hearing about, if the remote expression on his handsome features was any indication.

She tugged Conan's leash when he tried to wrap himself around the soldier's legs and after another disgruntled moment, the dog condescended enough to sit beside her. "I'm sorry I wasn't here when you arrived so I could show you around. I wasn't expecting you for a day or two."

"My plans changed. I was released from the military hospital a few days earlier than I expected. Since I didn't have anywhere else to go right now, I decided to head out here."

How sad, she thought. Didn't he have any family eager to give him a hero's welcome?

"Since I was early, I planned to get a hotel room for a couple days," he added, "but the property management company said the apartment was ready and available."

"It is. Everything's fine. I'm just sorry I wasn't here."

"The real estate agent handled everything."

Not everything Tracy probably *wanted* to handle, Anna mused, then was slightly ashamed of herself for the base thought.

This whole situation felt so awkward, so out of her comfort zone.

"You were able to find everything you needed?" she asked. "Towels, sheets, whatever?"

He shrugged. "So far."

"The kitchen is fully stocked with cookware and so forth but if you can't find something, let me know."

"I'll do that."

Despite his terse responses, Anna was disconcerted by her awareness of him. He was so big, so overwhelmingly male. She would be glad when the few months were up, though apparently Conan was infatuated with the man.

She had a sudden fierce wish that Tracy had found a nice older lady to rent the attic apartment to, but somehow she doubted too many older ladies were interested in climbing forty steps to get to their apartment.

Thinking of the steps reminded her of his injury and she nodded toward the sling on his shoulder. "I'm really sorry I wasn't here to help you carry up boxes. I guess you managed all right."

"I don't have much. A duffel and a suitcase. I'm only here for a short time."

"I know, but it's still two long flights of stairs."

She thought annoyance flickered in his eyes, as if he didn't like being reminded of his injury, but he quickly hid it.

"I handled things," he said.

"Well, if you ever need help carrying groceries up or anything or if you would just like the name of a good doctor around here, just let me know."

"I'm fine. I don't need anything. Just a quiet place to hang for a while until I'm fit to return to my unit."

She had the impression Lieutenant Harry Maxwell wasn't a man who liked being in any kind of position to need help. She supposed she probably shouldn't be holding her breath waiting for him to ask for it.

"I'm afraid I can't promise you complete quiet. Conan is mostly well-behaved but he does bark once in a while. I should also warn you if Tracy didn't mention it that there are children living in the second-floor apartment. Seven-year-old twins."

"They bark, too?"

She searched his face for any sign of a sense of humor but his expression revealed nothing. Still, she couldn't help smiling. "No, but they can be a little… energetic…at times. Mostly in the afternoons. They're gone most of the day at school and then they're usually pretty quiet in the evenings."

"That's something, then."

"In any case, they won't be here at all for several days. Their mother, Julia, is a teacher. Since they're all out of school right now for spring break, they've gone back to visit her family."

Before Lieutenant Maxwell could respond, Conan broke free of both the *sit* command and her hold on the leash and lunged for him again, dancing around his legs with excitement.

Anna reached for him again. "Conan, stop it right now. That's enough! I'm so sorry," she said to her new tenant, flustered at the negative impression they must be making.

"No worries. I'm not completely helpless. I think I can still manage to handle one high-strung mutt."

"Conan is not like most dogs," she muttered. "Most of the time we forget he even *is* a canine."

"The dog breath doesn't give him away?"

She smiled at his dry tone. So some sense of humor did lurk under that tough shell. That was a good sign. Brambleberry House and all its quirks demanded a strong constitution of its occupants.

"There is that," she answered. "We'll get out of your way and let you settle in. Again, if you need anything, don't hesitate to call. My phone number is right next to the phone or you can just call down the stairs and I'll usually hear you."

"I'll do that," he murmured, his mouth lifting slightly from its austere lines into what almost passed for a smile.

Just that minimal smile sent her pulse racing. With effort, she wrenched her gaze away from the dangerously masculine appeal of his features and tugged a reluctant Conan behind her as she headed back down the stairs.

Nerves zinging through her, Anna cursed to herself as she let herself back in to her apartment. She did *not* need this right now, she reminded herself sternly.

Her life was already a snarl of complications. She certainly didn't need to add into the mix a wounded war hero with gorgeous eyes, lean features and a mouth that looked made for trouble.

HE FORGOT ABOUT the damn dog.

Max shut the door behind the two of them—Anna Galvez and Conan. His last glimpse of the dog was of him quivering with a mix of excitement and friendly welcome and a bit of *why-aren't-you-happier-to-see-me?* confusion as she yanked his leash to tug him behind her down the stairs.

It had been shortsighted of him not to think of Abigail's mutt and his possible reaction to seeing Max again. He hadn't even given Conan a single thought—just more evidence of how completely the news of Abigail's death had knocked him off his pins.

The dog had only been a pup the last time he'd seen him before he shipped to the Middle East for his first tour of duty. During those last few days he had spent at Brambleberry House, Max had played hard with Conan. They'd run for miles on the beach, hiked up and down the coast range and played hours of fetch in the yard.

Had it really been four years? That was the last time

he had had a chance to spend any length of time here, a realization that caused him no small amount of guilt.

Conan should have been one of the first things on his mind after he found out about Abigail's death—several months after the fact. He could only blame his injuries and the long months of recovery for sending any thoughts of the dog scattering. It looked as if he was well-fed and taken care of. He supposed he had to give points to the woman—Anna Galvez—for that, at least.

He wasn't willing to concede victory to her, simply because she seemed affectionate to Abigail's mutt.

Anna Galvez. Now there was a strange woman, at least on first impressions. He couldn't quite get a handle on her. She was starchy and stiff, with her hair scraped back in a knot and the almost-masculine business suit and skirt she wore.

He would have considered her completely unappealing, except when she smiled, her entire face lit up as if somebody had just turned on a thousand-watt spotlight and aimed it right at her.

Only then did he notice her glossy dark hair, the huge, thick-lashed eyes, the high, elegant cheekbones. Underneath the layers of starch, she was a beautiful woman, he had realized with surprise, one that in other circumstances he might be interested in pursuing.

Didn't matter. She could be a supermodel and it wouldn't make a damn bit of difference to him. He had to focus on the two important things in his life right now—healing his shattered arm and digging for information.

He wasn't looking to make friends, he wasn't here

to win any popularity contests, and he certainly wasn't interested in a quick fling with one of the women of Brambleberry House.

CHAPTER TWO

SHE COULD NEVER get enough of the coast.

Anna walked along the shore early the next morning while Conan jumped around in the sand, chasing grebes and dancing through the baby breakers.

The cool March wind whipped the waves into a froth and tangled her hair, making her grateful for the gloves and hat Abigail had knitted her last year. Offshore, the seastacks stood sturdy and resolute against the sea and overhead gulls wheeled and dived in the pale, early morning sky.

It all seemed worlds away from growing up in the high desert valleys of Utah but she loved it here. After four years of living in Oregon, she still felt incredibly blessed to be able to wake up to the soft music of the sea every single day.

Abigail had loved beachcombing in the mornings. She knew every inlet, every cliff, every tide table. She could spot a California gray whale's spout from a mile away during the migration season and could identify every bird and most of the sea life nearly as well as Sage, who was a biologist and naturalist by profession.

Oh, Anna missed Abigail. She could hardly believe it had been nearly a year since her friend's death. She still sometimes found herself in By-the-Wind—the book and gift store in town she first managed for Abigail and then purchased from her—looking out the window and expecting Abigail to stop by on one of her regular visits.

I know the store is yours now but you can't blame an old woman for wanting to check on things now and again, Abigail would say with that mischievous smile of hers.

Anna's circumstances had taken a dramatic shift since Abigail's death. She had been living in a small two-room apartment in Seaside and driving down every day to work in the store. Now she lived in the most gorgeous house on the north coast and had made two dear friends in the process.

She smiled, thinking of Sage and Julia and the changes in all their lives the past year. When she first met Sage, right after the two of them inherited Brambleberry House, she had thought she would never have anything in common with the other woman. Sage was a vegetarian, a save-the-planet sort, and Anna was, well, focused on her business.

But they had developed an unlikely friendship. Then when Julia moved into the second-floor apartment the next fall with her darling twins, Anna and Sage had both been immediately drawn to her. Many late-night gabfests later, both women felt like the sisters she had always wanted.

Now Sage was married to Eben Spencer and had a new stepdaughter, and Julia was engaged to Will Garrett and would be marrying him as soon as school was out in June, then moving out to live in his house only a few doors down from Brambleberry House.

Both of them were deliriously happy, and Anna was thrilled for them. They were wonderful women who deserved happiness and had found it with two men she was enormously fond of.

If their happy endings only served to emphasize the mess she had made of her own life, she supposed she only had herself to blame.

She sighed, thinking of Grayson Fletcher and her own stupidity and the tangled mess he had left behind.

She supposed one bright spot from the latest fiasco in her love life was that Julia and Sage seemed to have put any matchmaking efforts on hiatus. They must have accepted the grim truth that had become painfully obvious to her—she had absolutely no judgment when it came to men.

She trusted the wrong ones. She had been making the same mistake since the time she fell hard for Todd Ashman in second grade, who gave her underdog pushes on the playground as well as her first kiss, a sloppy affair on the cheek. Todd told her he loved her then conned her out of her milk money for a week. She would probably still be paying him if her brothers hadn't found out and made the little weasel leave her alone.

She sighed as Conan sniffed a coiled ball of seaweed and twigs and grasses formed by the rolling action of the sea. That milk money had been the first of several things she had let men take from her.

Her pride. Her self-respect. Her reputation.

If she needed further proof, she only had to think about her schedule for the rest of the day. In a few hours, she was in for the dubious joy of spending another delightful day sitting in that Lincoln City court-room while Grayson Fletcher provided unavoidable evidence of her overwhelming stupidity in business and in men.

She jerked her mind away from that painful route. She wasn't allowed to think about her mistakes on these morning walks with Conan. They were supposed to be therapy, her way to soothe her soul, to recharge her energy for the day ahead. She would defeat the entire purpose by spending the entire time looking back and cataloguing all her faults.

She forced herself to breathe deeply, inhaling the mingled scents of the sea and sand and early spring. Since Sage had married and moved out and she'd taken over sole responsibility of Conan's morning walks, she had come to truly savor and appreciate the diversity of coastal mornings. From rainy and cold to unseason-ably warm to so brilliantly clear she could swear she could see the curve of the earth offshore.

Each reminded her of how blessed she was to live here. Cannon Beach had become her home. She had never intended it to happen, had only escaped here after her first major romantic debacle, looking for a place far away from her rural Utah home to lick her wounds and hide away from all her friends and family.

She had another mess on her hands now, complete with all the public humiliation she could endure. This time she wasn't about to run. Cannon Beach was her home, no matter what, and she couldn't imagine liv-ing anywhere else.

They had walked only a mile south from Bramble-berry House when Conan suddenly barked with excitement. Anna shifted her gaze from the fascination of the ocean to see a runner approaching them, heading in the direction they had come.

Conan became increasingly animated the closer the runner approached, until it was all Anna could do to hang on to his leash.

She guessed his identity even before he was close enough for her to see clearly. The curious one-handed gait was a clear giveaway but his long, lean strength and brown hair was distinctive enough she was quite certain she would have figured out it was Harry Maxwell long before she could spy the sling on his arm.

To her annoyance, her stomach did an uncomfortable little twirl as he drew closer. The man was just too darn good-looking, with those lean, masculine features and the intense hazel eyes. It didn't help that he somehow looked rakishly gorgeous with his arm in a sling. An injured warrior still soldiering on.

She told herself she would have preferred things if he just kept on running but Conan made that impossible, barking and straining at his leash with such eager enthusiasm that Lieutenant Maxwell couldn't help but stop to greet him.

Maybe he wasn't quite the dour, humorless man he had appeared the day before, she thought as he scratched Conan's favorite spot, just above his shoulders. Nobody could be all bad if they were so intuitive with animals, she decided.

Only after he had sufficiently given the love to Conan did he turn in her direction.

"Morning," he said, a weird flash of what almost looked like unease in his eyes. Why would he possibly seem uncomfortable with her? She wasn't the one who practically oozed sex appeal this early in the morning.

"Hi," she answered. "Should you be doing that?"

He raised one dark eyebrow. "Petting your dog?"

"No. Running. I just wondered if all the jostling bothers your arm."

His mouth tightened a little and she had the impression again that he didn't like discussing his injury. "I hate the sling but it does a good job of keeping it from being shaken around when I'm doing anything remotely strenuous."

"It must still be uncomfortable, though."

"I'm fine."

Back off, in other words. His curtness was a clear signal she had overstepped.

"I'm sorry. Not my business, is it?"

He sighed. "I'm the one who's sorry. I'm a little frustrated at the whole thing. I'm not a very good patient and I'm afraid I don't handle limitations on my activities very well."

She sensed that was information he didn't share easily and though she knew he was only being polite she was still touched that he would confide in her. "I'm not a good patient, either. If I were in your shoes, I would be more than just a little frustrated."

Some of the stiffness seemed to ease from his posture. "Well, it's a whole lot more fun flying a helicopter than riding a hospital bed, I can tell you that much."

They lapsed into silence and she would have expected him to resume his jog but he seemed content to pet Conan and gaze out at the seething, churning waves.

It hardly seemed fair that, even injured as he was and just out of rehab, he didn't seem at all winded from the run. She would have been gasping for breath and ready for a little oxygen infusion.

"It looks like it's shaping up to be a gorgeous day, doesn't it?" she said. "Forecasters are saying we should have clear and sunny weather for the next few days. You picked a great time of year to visit Cannon Beach."

"That's good."

"I don't know if you've had a chance to notice this yet but on one of the bookshelves in the living room, I left you a welcome packet. I forgot to mention it when I stopped to say hello last night."

"I didn't see it. What kind of welcome packet?"

"Not much. Just a loose-leaf notebook, really, with some local sightseeing information. Maps of the area, trail guides, tide tables. I've also included several menus from my favorite restaurants if you want to try some of the local cuisine, as well as a couple of guidebooks from my store."

She had spent an entire evening gathering and collating the information, printing out pages from the Internet and marking some of her favorite spots in the guide books. All right, it was a nerdy, overachiever thing to do, she realized now as she stood next to this man who simmered with such blatant male energy.

She really needed to get a life.

Still, he didn't look displeased by the effort. If she didn't know better, she would suspect him of being perilously close to a surprised smile. "Thank you. That was…nice."

She made a face. "A little over-the-top, I know.

Sorry. I tend to be a bit obsessive about those kinds of things."

"No, it sounds perfect. I'll be sure to look through it as soon as I get a chance. Maybe you can tell me the best place for breakfast around here. I haven't had much chance to go shopping."

"The Lazy Susan is always great or any of the B and Bs, really."

Or you could invite him to breakfast.

The thought whispered through her mind and she blinked, wondering where in the world it came from. That just wasn't the sort of thing she did. Now, Abigail would have done it in a heartbeat, and Sage probably would have as well, but Anna wasn't nearly as audacious.

But the thought persisted, growing stronger and stronger. Finally the words seemed to just blurt from her mouth. "Look, I'd be happy to fix something for you. I was in the mood for French toast anyway and it's silly to make it just for me."

He stared at her for a long moment, his eyes wide with surprise. The silence dragged on a painfully long time, until heat soaked her cheeks and she wanted to dive into the cold waves to escape.

"Sorry. Forget it. Stupid suggestion."

"No. No, it wasn't. I was just surprised, that's all. Breakfast would be great, if you're sure it's not too much trouble."

"Not at all. Can you give me about forty-five minutes to finish with Conan's morning walk?"

"No problem. That will give me a chance to finish my run and take a shower."

Now there was a visual she didn't need etched into her brain like acid on glass. She let out a breath. "Great. I'll see you then."

With a wave of his arm, sling and all, he headed back up the beach toward Brambleberry House.

With strict discipline, she forced herself not to watch after him. Instead, she gripped Conan's leash tightly so he wouldn't follow his new best friend and forced him to come with her by walking with firm determination in the other direction.

What just happened there? She had to be completely insane. Temporarily possessed by the spirit of Abigail that Sage and Julia seemed convinced still lingered at Brambleberry House.

She faced what was undoubtedly shaping up to be another miserable day sitting in the courtroom listening to more evidence of her own foolishness. And because she felt compelled to attend every moment of the trial, she had tons of work awaiting her at both the Cannon Beach and Lincoln City stores.

So what was she thinking? She had absolutely no business inviting a sexy injured war veteran to breakfast.

Remember your abysmal judgment when it comes to men, she reminded herself sternly.

It was just breakfast, though. He was her tenant and it was her duty to get to know the man living upstairs in her home. She was just being a responsible landlady.

Still, she couldn't control the excited little bump of anticipation. Nor could she ignore the realization that she was looking forward to the day more than she had anything else since before Christmas, when everything safe and secure she thought she had built for herself crashed apart like a house built on the shifting, unstable sands of Cannon Beach.

This might be easier than he thought.

Fresh from the shower, Max pulled a shirt out of his duffel, grateful it was at least moderately unwrinkled. It wouldn't hurt to make a good impression on his new landlady. So far she didn't seem suspicious of him—he doubted she would have invited him to breakfast otherwise.

Now *there* was an odd turn of events. He had to admit, he was puzzled as all hell by the invitation. Why had she issued it? And so reluctantly, too. She had looked as shocked by it as he had been.

The woman baffled him. She seemed a contradiction. Yesterday she had been all prim and proper in her business suit, today she had appeared fresh and lovely as a spring morning and far too young to own a seaside mansion and two businesses.

He didn't understand her yet. But he would, he vowed.

Not so difficult to puzzle out had been his own reaction to her. When he had seen her walking and had recognized Conan, he had been stunned and more than a little disconcerted by the instant heat pooling in his gut.

Rather inconvenient, that surge of lust. His unwilling attraction to Anna Galvez. He would no doubt have a much easier time focusing on his goal without that particular complication.

How, exactly, was he supposed to figure out if Ms. Galvez had conned a sweet old lady when he couldn't seem to wrap his feeble male brain around anything but pulling all that thick, glossy hair out of its constraints, burying his fingers in it and devouring her mouth with his?

He yanked off the pain-in-the-ass waterproof covering he had to use to protect his most recent cast from yet another reconstructive surgery and carefully eased his arm through the sleeve of the shirt. He was almost—but not quite—accustomed to the pain that still buzzed across his nerve endings whenever he moved the arm.

It wasn't as bad as it used to be. After more than a dozen surgeries in six months, he could have a little mobility now without scorching agony.

He had to admit, he couldn't say he was completely sorry about his unexpected attraction to Anna Galvez. In some ways it was even a relief. He hadn't been able to summon even a speck of interest in a woman since the crash, not even to flirt with the pretty army nurses at the hospital in Germany and then later at Walter Reed.

He had worried that something internal might have been permanently damaged in the crash, since what he had always considered a relatively healthy libido seemed to have dried up like a wadi in a sandstorm.

He had even swallowed his pride and asked one of the doctors about it just before his discharge and had been told not to worry about it. He'd been assured that his body had only been a little busy trying to heal, just as his mind had been struggling with his guilt over the deaths of two members of his flight crew.

When the time was right, he'd been told, all the plumbing would probably work just as it had before.

It might be inconvenient that he was attracted to Anna Galvez, inconvenient and more than a little odd, since he had never been attracted to the prim, focused sort of woman before, but he couldn't truly say he was sorry about it.

And if he needed a reminder of why he couldn't pursue the attraction, he only needed to look around him at the familiar walls of Brambleberry House.

For all he knew, Anna Galvez was the sneaky, conniving swindler his mother believed her to be, working her wiles to gull his elderly aunt out of this house and its contents, all the valuable antiques and keepsakes that had been in his father's family for generations.

He wouldn't know until he had run a little reconnaissance here to see where things stood.

His father had been the only child of Abigail's solitary sibling, her sister Suzanna, which made Max Abigail's only living relative.

Though he hadn't really given it much thought—mostly because he didn't like thinking about his beloved great-aunt's inevitable passing—he supposed he had always expected to inherit Brambleberry House someday.

Finding out she had left the house to two strangers had been more than a little bit surprising.

She must not have loved you enough.

The thought slithered through his mind, cold and mean, but he pushed it away. Abigail had loved him. He could never doubt that. For some inexplicable reason, she had decided to give the house to two strangers and he was determined to find out why.

And this morning provided a perfect opportunity to give Anna Galvez a little closer scrutiny, so he'd better get on with things.

Buttoning a shirt with one good hand genuinely sucked, he had discovered over the last six months, but it wasn't nearly as tough as trying to maneuver an arm that didn't want to cooperate through the unwieldy holes in a T-shirt or, heaven forbid, a long-sleeved sweater, so he persevered.

When he finished, he put the blasted sling on again, ran a comb through his hair awkwardly with his left hand, then headed for the stairs, his hand on the banister he remembered Abigail waxing to a lustrous sheen just so he could slide down it when he was a boy.

Delicious smells greeted him the moment he headed downstairs—coffee, bacon, hash browns and something sweet and yeasty. His stomach rumbled but he reminded himself he was a soldier, trained to withstand temptation.

No matter how seemingly irresistible.

He paused outside Abigail's door, a little astounded at the sudden nerves zinging through him.

It was one thing to inhabit the top floor of Brambleberry House. It was quite another, he discovered, to return to Abigail's private sanctuary, the place he had loved so dearly.

The rooms beyond this door had been his haven when he was a kid. The one safe anchor in a tumultuous, unstable childhood—not the house, he supposed, as much as the woman who had been so much a part of it.

No matter what might be happening in his regular life—whether his mother was between husbands or flushed with the glow of new love that made her forget his existence or at the bitter, ugly end of another marriage—Abigail had always represented safety and security to him.

She had been fun and kind and loving and he had craved his visits here like a drunk needed rotgut. He had looked forward to the two weeks his mother allowed him with fierce anticipation the other fifty weeks of the year. Whenever he walked through this door, he had felt instantly wrapped in warm, loving arms.

And now a stranger lived here. A woman who had somehow managed to convince an old woman to leave her this house.

No matter how lovely Anna Galvez might be, he couldn't forget that she had usurped Abigail's place in this house.

It was hers now and he damn well intended to find out why.

He drew in a deep breath, adjusted his sling one more time, then reached out to knock on Abigail's door.

CHAPTER THREE

SHE OPENED THE door wearing one of his aunt's old ruffled bib aprons.

He recognized it instantly, pink flowers and all, and had a sudden image of Abigail in the kitchen, bedecked with jewels as always, grinning and telling jokes as she cooked up a batch of her famous French toast that dripped with caramel and brown sugar and pralines.

He had to admit he found the dichotomy a little disconcerting. Whether Anna was a con artist or simply a modern businesswoman, he wouldn't have expected her to be wearing something so softly worn and old-fashioned.

He doubted Abigail had ever looked quite as appealing in that apron. Anna Galvez's skin had a rosy glow to it and the friendly pink flowers made her look exotically beautiful in contrast.

"Good morning again," she said, her smile polite, perhaps even a little distant.

Maybe he ought to forget this whole thing, he thought. Just head back out the door and up the stairs. He could always grab a granola bar and a cola for breakfast.

He wasn't sure he was ready to face Abigail's apartment just yet, and especially not with this woman looking on.

"Something smells delicious in here, like you've gone to a whole lot of work. I hope this isn't a big inconvenience for you."

Her smile seemed a little warmer. "Not at all. I enjoy cooking, I just don't get the chance very often. Come in."

She held the door open for him and he couldn't figure out a gracious way to back out. Doing his best to hide his sudden reluctance, he stepped through the threshold.

He shouldn't have worried.

Nothing was as he remembered. When Abigail was alive, these rooms had been funky and cluttered, much like his aunt, with shelves piled high with everything from pieces of driftwood to beautifully crafted art pottery to cheap plastic garage-sale trinkets.

Abigail had possessed her own sense of style. If she liked something, she had no compunction about displaying it. And she had liked a wide variety of things.

The fussy wallpaper he remembered was gone and the room had been painted a crisp, clean white. Even more significant, a few of the major walls had been removed to open up the space. The thick, dramatic trim around the windows and ceiling was still there and nothing jarred with the historic tone of the house but he had to admit the space looked much brighter. Cleaner.

Elegant, even.

He had only a moment to absorb the changes before a plaintive whine echoed through the space. He followed the sound and discovered Conan just on the other side of the long sofa that was canted across the living room.

The dog gazed at him with longing in his eyes and though he practically knocked the sofa cushions off with his quivering, he made no move to lunge at him.

Max blinked at the canine. "All right. What's with the dog? Did somebody glue his haunches to the sofa?"

She made a face. "No. We're working on obedience. I gave him a strict *sit-stay* command before I opened the door. I'm afraid it's not going to last, as much as he wants to be good. I'm sorry."

"I don't mind. I like dogs."

He particularly liked this one and had since Conan was a pup Abigail had rescued from the pound, though he certainly couldn't tell her that.

She took pity on the dog and released him from the position with a simple "Okay."

Conan immediately rushed for Max, nudging at him with that big furry red-gold head, just as a timer sounded through the room.

"Perfect. That's everything. Do you mind eating in the kitchen? I have a great view of the ocean from there."

"Not at all."

He didn't add that Abigail's small kitchen, busy and cluttered as it was, had always been his favorite room of the house, the very essence of what made Bramble-berry House so very appealing.

He found the small round table set with Abigail's rose-covered china and sunny yellow napkins. A vase of fresh flowers sent sweet smells to mingle with the delicious culinary scents.

"Can I do anything?"

"No, everything's all finished. I just need to pull it from the oven. You can go ahead and sit down."

He sat at one of the place settings where he had a beautiful view of the sand and the sea and the haystacks offshore. He poured coffee for both of them while Conan perched at his feet and he could swear the dog was grinning at him with male camaraderie, as if they shared some secret.

Which, of course, they did.

In a moment, Anna returned to the table with a casserole dish. She set it down then removed covers from the other plates on the table and his mouth watered again at the crispy strips of bacon and mound of scrambled eggs.

"This is enough to feed my entire platoon, ma'am."

She grimaced. "I haven't cooked for anyone else in a while. I'm afraid I got a little carried away. I hope you're hungry."

"Starving, actually."

He was astonished to find it was true. The sea air must be agreeing with him. He'd lost twenty pounds in the hospital and though the doctors had been strictly urging him to do something about putting it back on, he hadn't been able to work up much enthusiasm to eat anything.

Nice to know *all* his appetites seemed to be returning.

He took several slices of bacon and a hefty mound of scrambled eggs then scooped some of the sweet-smelling concoction from the glass casserole dish.

The moment he lifted the fork to his mouth, a hundred memories came flooding back of other mornings spent in this kitchen, eating this very thing for breakfast. It had been his favorite as long as he could remember and he had always asked for it.

"This is—" *Aunt Abigail's famous French toast,* he almost said, but caught himself just in time. "Delicious. Really delicious."

When she smiled, she looked almost as delectable as the thick, caramel-covered toast, and just as edible. "Thank you. It was a specialty of a dear friend of mine. Every time I make it, it reminds me of her."

He slanted her a searching look across the table. She sounded sincere—maybe *too* sincere. He wanted to take her apparent affection for Abigail at face value but he couldn't help wondering if his cover had been blown. For all he knew, she had seen a picture of him in Abigail's things and guessed why he was here.

If she truly were a con artist and knew he was Abigail's nephew come to check things out, wouldn't she lay it on thick about how much she adored his aunt to allay his suspicions?

"That's nice," he finally said. "It sounds like you cared about her a lot."

She didn't answer for several seconds, long enough that he wondered if she were being deliberately evasive. He felt as if he were tap-dancing through a damn minefield.

"I did," she finally answered.

Conan whined a little and settled his chin on his forepaws, just as if he somehow understood exactly whom they were talking about and still missed Abigail.

Impossible, Max thought. The dog was smart but not *that* smart.

"I've heard horror stories about army food," Anna said, changing the subject. "Is it as awful as they say?"

Even as he applied himself to the delicious breakfast, his mind couldn't seem to stop shifting through the nuances and implications of every word she said and he wondered why she suddenly seemed reluctant to discuss Abigail after she had been the one to bring her into the conversation. Still, he decided not to push her. He would let her play things her way for now while he tried to figure out the angles.

"Army food's not bad," he said, focusing on her question. "Army hospital food, that's another story. This is gourmet dining to me after the last few months."

"How long were you in the hospital?"

Just as she didn't want to talk about Abigail, he sure as hell didn't want to discuss his time in the hospital.

"Too damn long," he answered, then because his voice sounded so harsh, he tried to amend his tone. "Six months, on and off, with rehab and surgeries and everything."

Her eyes widened and she set down her own fork. "Oh, my word! Tracy—the real estate agent with the property management company—told me you had been hurt in Iraq but I had no idea your injuries were so severe!"

He fidgeted a little, wishing they hadn't landed on this topic. He hated thinking about the crash or his injuries—or the future that stretched out ahead of him, darkly uncertain.

"I wasn't in the hospital the entire time. A month

the first time, mostly in the burn unit, but I needed several surgeries after that to repair my shoulder and arm then skin grafts and so on. All of it took time. And then I picked up a staph infection in the meantime and that meant another few weeks in the hospital. Throw in a month or so of rehab before they'd release me and here we are."

"Oh, I'm so sorry. It sounds truly awful."

He chewed a mouthful of fluffy scrambled eggs that suddenly tasted like foam peanuts. He knew he was lucky to make it out alive after the fiery hard landing. That inescapable fact had been drilled into his head constantly since the crash, by himself and by those around him.

For several tense moments after they had been hit by a rocket-fired grenade as they were picking up an injured soldier that October day to medevac, he had been quite certain this was the end for him and for the four others on his Black Hawk.

He thought he was going to be a grim statistic, another one of those poor bastards who bit it just a week before their tour ended and they were due to head home.

But somehow he had survived. Two of his crew hadn't been so lucky, despite his frantic efforts and those of the other surviving crew member. They had saved the injured Humvee driver, so that was something.

That first month had been a blur, especially the first few days after the crash. The medical transport to Kuwait and then to Germany, the excruciating pain from his shattered arm and shoulder and from the second-and third-degree burns on the right side of his body…and the even more excruciating anguish that still cramped in his gut when he thought about his lost crew members.

He was aware, suddenly, that Conan had risen from the floor to sit beside him, resting his chin on Max's thigh.

He found enormous comfort from the soft, furry weight and from the surprising compassion in the dog's eyes.

"How are you now?" Anna asked. "Have the doctors given you an estimate of what kind of recovery you're looking at?"

"It's all a waiting game right now to see how things heal after the last surgery." He raised his arm with the cast. "I've got to wear this for another month."

"I can't imagine how frustrating that must be for you. I don't know about you, but I'm not the most patient person in the world. I'm afraid I would want results immediately."

They definitely had that much in common. Though his instincts warned him to filter every word through his suspicions about her, he had to admit he found her concern rather sweet and unexpected.

"I do," he admitted. "But I was in the hospital long enough to see exactly what happened to those who tried to rush the healing process. Several of them pushed too hard and ended up right back where they started, in much worse shape. I won't let that happen. It will take as long as it takes."

"Smart words," she said with an odd look and only then did he realize that it had been one of his aunt's favorite phrases, whether she was talking about the time it took for cookies to bake or for the berries to pop out on her raspberry canes out back.

He quickly tried to turn the conversation back to her. "What about you? For a woman who claims she's impatient for results, you've picked a major project here, renovating this big house on your own."

"Brambleberry House belonged to a dear friend of mine. Actually, the one whose French toast recipe you're eating." She smiled a little. "When she died last year, she left it to me and to another of her lost sheep, Sage Benedetto. Sage Benedetto-Spencer, actually. She's married now and lives in San Francisco with her husband and stepdaughter. In fact, you're living in what used to be her apartment."

He knew all about Sage. He'd been hearing about her for years from Abigail. When his aunt told him she had taken on a new tenant for the empty third floor several years ago, he had instantly been suspicious and had run a full background check on the woman, though he hadn't revealed that information to Abigail.

Nothing untoward had showed up. She worked at the nature center in town and had seemed to be exactly as she appeared, a hardworking biologist in need of a clean place to live.

But five years later, she was now one of the owners of that clean abode—and she had recently married into money.

That in itself had raised his suspicions. Maybe she and Anna had a whole racket going on. First they conned Abigail, then Sage set her sights on Eben Spencer and tricked him into marrying her. What other explanation could there be? Why would a hotel magnate like Spencer marry a hippie nature girl like Sage Benedetto?

"So you live down here and rent out the top two floors?"

She sipped her coffee. "For now. It's a lot of space for one woman and the upkeep on the place isn't cheap. I had to replace the heating system this year, which took a huge chunk out of the remodeling budget."

There was one element of this whole thing that didn't jibe with his mother's speculation that they were gold-digging scam artists, Max admitted. If they were only in this for the money, wouldn't they have flipped the house, taken their equity and split Cannon Beach?

It didn't make sense and made him more inclined to believe she and Sage Benedetto truly had cared for Abigail, though he wasn't ready to concede anything at this point.

"The real estate agent who arranged the rental agreement with me mentioned you own a couple of shops on the coast but she didn't go into detail."

If he hadn't been watching her so carefully, he might have missed the sudden glumness in her eyes or the subtle tightening of her lovely, exotic features.

He had obviously touched on a sore subject, and from his preliminary Internet search of her and Sage, he was quite certain he knew why.

"Yes," she finally said, stirring her scrambled eggs around on her plate. "My store here in town is near the post office. It's called By-the-Wind Books and Gifts."

"By-the-Wind? Like the jellyfish?" he asked.

"Right. By-the-wind sailors. My friend Abigail

loved them. The store was hers and she named it after a crosswind one year sent hundreds of thousands of them washing up on the shore of Cannon Beach. I started out managing the store for her when I first came to town. A few years ago when she hit seventy-eight she decided she was ready to slow down a little, so I made an offer for the store and she sold it to me."

Abigail had adored her store as much as she loved this house. She wasn't the most savvy of business-women but she loved any excuse to engage a stranger in conversation.

"So you've opened a second store now," he asked.

She shifted in her seat, her hands clenching and un-clenching around the napkin in her lap. "Yes. Last summer I opened one in Lincoln City. By-the-Wind Two."

She didn't seem nearly as eager to talk about her second store and he found her reaction interesting and filed it away to add to his growing impressions about Anna Galvez.

He had limited information about the situation but his Internet search had turned up several hits from the Lincoln City newspaper about her store manager being arrested some months ago and charged with embezzle-ment and credit card fraud.

Max knew from his research that the man was cur-rently on trial. He didn't, however, have any idea at all if Anna was the innocent victim the newspapers had portrayed or if she perhaps had deeper involve-ment in the fraud.

Before coming back to Brambleberry House, he had been all too willing to believe she might have been involved, that she had managed to find a convenient way to turn her manager into the scapegoat.

It was a little harder to believe that when he was sitting across the table from her and could smell the delicate scent of her drifting across the table, when he could feel the warmth of her just a few feet away, when he could reach out and touch the softness of her skin…

He jerked his mind from that dangerous road. "You must be doing well if you've got two stores. Any plans to expand to a third? Maybe up north in Astoria or farther south in Newport?"

"No. Not anytime in the near future. Or even in the not-so-near future." She forced a smile that stopped just short of genuine. "Would you like more French toast?"

He decided to allow her to sidetrack him for now, though he wasn't at all finished with this line of questioning. Instead, he served up another slice of the French pastry.

Being here in this kitchen like this was oddly surreal and he almost expected Abigail to bustle in from another part of the house with her smile gleaming even above the mounds of jewelry she always wore.

She wouldn't be bustling in from anywhere, he reminded himself. Grief clawed at him again, the overwhelming sense of loss that seemed so much more acute here in this house.

Oh, he missed her.

He suddenly felt a weird brush of something against his cheek and he had a sudden hideous fear he might be crying. He did a quick finger-sweep but didn't feel any wetness. But he was quite certain he smelled something flowery and sweet.

Out of nowhere, the dog suddenly wagged his tail and gave one happy bark. Max thought he saw something out of the corner of his gaze but when he turned around he saw only a curtain fluttering in the other room from one of the house's famous drafts.

He turned back to find Anna Galvez watching him, her eyes wary and concerned at the same time.

"Is everything okay, Lieutenant Maxwell?" she asked.

He shook off the weird sensation, certain he must just be tired and a little overwhelmed about being back here.

Lieutenant Maxwell, she had called him. Discomfort burned under his skin at the fake name. This whole thing just felt wrong somehow, especially sitting here in Abigail's kitchen. He wanted to just tell her the truth but some instinct held him back. Not yet. He would let the situation play out a little longer, see what she did.

But he couldn't have her calling him another man's name, he decided. "You don't have to call me Lieutenant Maxwell. You can call me Max. That's what most people do."

A puzzled frown played around that luscious mouth. "They call you Max and not Harry?"

"Um, yeah. It's a military thing. Nicknames, you know?"

The explanation sounded lame, even to him, but she appeared to buy it without blinking. In fact, she gifted him with a particular sweet smile. "All right. Max it is. You may, of course, call me Anna."

He absolutely was *not* going to let himself get lost in that smile, no matter his inclination, so he forced himself to continue with his subtle interrogation. "Are you from around here?"

She shook her head. "I grew up in a small town in the mountains of Utah."

He raised an eyebrow, certain he hadn't unearthed that little tidbit of information in his research. "Utah seems like a long way from here. What brought you to the Oregon coast?"

Her eyes took on that evasive film again. "Oh, you know. I was ready for a change. Wanted to stretch my wings a little. That sort of thing."

He had become pretty good over the years at picking up when someone wasn't being completely honest with him and his lie radar was suddenly blinking like crazy.

She was hiding something and he wanted to know what.

"Do you have family back in Utah still?"

The tension in her shoulders eased a little. "Two of my older brothers are still close to Moose Springs. That's where we grew up. One's the sheriff, actually. The other is a contractor, then I have one other brother who's a research scientist in Costa Rica."

"No sisters?"

"Just brothers. I'm the baby."

"You were probably spoiled rotten, right?"

Her laugh was so infectious that even Conan looked up and grinned. "More like endlessly tormented. I was always excluded from their cool boy stuff like campouts and fishing trips. Being the only girl and the youngest Galvez was a double curse, one I'm still trying to figure out how to break."

This, at least, was genuine. She glowed when she

talked about her family—her eyes seemed brighter, her features more animated. She looked so delicious, it was all he could do not to reach across the table and kiss her right here over his aunt's French toast.

Her next words quickly quashed the bloom of desire better than a cold Oregon downpour.

"What about you?" she asked. "Do you have family somewhere?"

How could he answer that without giving away his identity? He decided to stick to the bare facts and hope Abigail hadn't talked about his particular twisted branch of the family tree.

"My father died when I was too young to remember him. My mother remarried several times so I've got a few stepbrothers and stepsisters scattered here and there but that's it."

He didn't add that he didn't even know some of their names since none of the marriages had lasted long.

"So where's home?" she asked.

"Right now it's two flights of stairs above you."

She made a face. "What about before you moved upstairs?"

Brambleberry House was the place he had always considered home, even though he only spent a week or two here each year. Life with his mother had never been exactly stable as she moved from boyfriend to boyfriend, husband to husband. Before he had been sent to military school when he was thirteen, he had attended a dozen different schools.

Abigail had been the rock in his insecure existence. But he certainly couldn't tell that to Anna Galvez. Instead, he shrugged.

"I'm career army, ma'am. I'm based out of Virginia but I've been in the Middle East for two tours of duty. I've been there the last four years. That feels as much home as anywhere else, I guess."

CHAPTER FOUR

Oh, the poor man.

Imagine considering some military base a home. She couldn't quite fathom it and she felt enormously blessed suddenly for her safe, happy childhood.

Her family might have been what most people would consider dirt-poor. Her parents were illegal immigrants who had tried to live below the radar. As a result, her father had never been paid his full worth and when he had been killed in a construction accident, the company he worked for had used his illegal immigrant status as an excuse not to pay any compensation to his widow or children.

Yes, her family might not have had much when she was a kid but she had never lived a single moment of her childhood when she didn't feel her home was a sanctuary where she could always be certain she would find love and acceptance.

Later, maybe, she had come to doubt her worth, but none of that stemmed from her girlhood.

And now she had Brambleberry House to return to at the end of the day. No matter how stressful her life might seem sometimes, this house welcomed her back every night, solid and strong and immovable.

It saddened her to think of Harry Maxwell moving

from place to place with the military, never having anything to anchor him in place.

"I suppose if you had a wife and children, you would probably be recovering with them instead of at some drafty rented house on the Oregon shore."

"No wife, no kids. Never married." He paused, giving her a careful look. "What about you?"

She had always wanted a big, rambunctious family just like the one she'd known as a girl but those childhood dreams spun in the tiny bedroom of that Moose Springs house seemed far away now.

Her life hadn't worked out at all the way she planned. And though there were a few things in her life she wouldn't mind a do-over on—especially more recent events—she couldn't regret all the paths she had followed that had led her to this place.

"Same goes. I was engaged once but…it didn't work out."

Before he could respond, Conan lumbered to his feet and headed for the door.

"That's a signal," she said with a smile. "Time for him to go out and if I don't move on it, we'll all be sorry. Excuse me, won't you?"

Though he had a doggie door to use when she wasn't home, Conan much preferred to be waited on and to go out through the regular door like the rest of the higher beings. She opened her apartment door and then the main door into the house for him and watched him bound eagerly to his favorite corner of the yard.

When she returned to the kitchen, she found Lieutenant Maxwell clearing dishes from the table.

"That was delicious. It was very kind of you to invite me. A little unexpected, but kind nonetheless."

"You're welcome. I'll be honest, it's not the sort of thing I usually do but…well, it *is* the sort of thing Abigail would have done. She was always striking up conversations with people and taking them to lunch or whatever. I had the strangest feeling this morning on the beach that she would want me to invite you to breakfast."

She heard the absurdity of her own words and made a face. "That probably sounds completely insane to you."

"Not completely," he murmured.

"No, it is. But I'm not sorry. I enjoyed making breakfast and I suppose it's only fitting that I know at least a little about the person living upstairs. At least now you don't feel like a stranger."

"Well, I appreciate the effort and the French toast. It's been…a long time since I've had anything as good."

He gave her a hesitant smile and at the sight of it on those solemnly handsome features, her stomach seemed to do a long, slow roll.

Oh, bad idea. She had no business at all being attracted to the man. He was her tenant, and a temporary one at that. Beyond that, the timing was abysmal. She had far too much on her plate right now trying to save By-the-Wind Two and see that Grayson Fletcher received well-deserved justice. She couldn't afford any distractions, especially not one as tempting as Lieutenant Harry Maxwell.

"I'm glad you enjoyed it," she said, forcing her voice to be brisk and businesslike.

Conan came back inside before he could answer. He headed straight for the lieutenant, who reached down to pet him. The absent gesture reminded her of another detail she meant to discuss with him.

"I'm afraid I'm going to be tied up in Lincoln City most of today. Some days I can take Conan with me since I have arrangements with a kennel in town but they were full today so he has to stay home. I hope he doesn't make a pest of himself."

"I doubt he'll bother me."

"With the dog door, he can come as he likes. I should probably tell you, he thinks he owns the house. He's used to going up the stairs to visit either Sage when she lived here or Julia and the twins. If he whines outside your door, just send him back downstairs."

"He won't bother me. If he whines, I'll invite him inside. He's welcome to hang out upstairs. I don't mind the company."

He petted the dog with an unfeigned affection that warmed her, though she knew it shouldn't. Most people liked Conan, though Grayson Fletcher never had. That in itself should have been all the red flags she needed that the man was trouble.

"Well, don't feel obligated to entertain him. I would just ask that you close the gate behind you if you leave so he can't leave the yard. He tends to take off if there's a stray cat in the neighborhood."

"I'll do that." He paused. "Would you have any objection if I take Conan along if I go anywhere? He kind of reminds me of a…dog I once knew."

At the sound of his name, the dog barked eagerly, his tail wagging a mile a minute.

Conan would adore any outing, she knew, but she couldn't contain a few misgivings.

"Conan can be a little energetic when he wants to be. Are you certain you can restrain him on the leash if he decides to take off after a squirrel or something?"

"Because of this, you mean?" he asked stiffly, gesturing to the sling. "My other arm still works fine."

She nodded, feeling foolish. "Of course. In that case, I'm sure Conan would love to go along with you anywhere. He loves riding in the car and he's crazy about any excuse to get some exercise. I'm afraid my schedule doesn't allow me to give him as much as he would like. Here, let me grab his leash for you just in case."

She headed for the hook by the door but Conan had heard the magic word—*leash*—and he bounded in front of her, nearly dancing out of his fur with excitement.

Caught off balance by seventy-five pounds of dog suddenly in her way, she stumbled a little and would have fallen into an ignominious heap if Lieutenant Maxwell hadn't reached out with his uninjured arm to help steady her.

Instant heat leaped through her, wild and shocking. She was painfully cognizant of the hard male strength of him, of his mouth just inches away, of those hazel eyes watching her with a glittery expression.

She didn't think she had ever, in her entire existence, been so physically aware of a man. Of his scent, fresh-washed and clean, of the muscles that held her so securely, of the strong curve of his jawline.

She might have stayed there half the morning, caught in the odd lassitude seeping through her, except she suddenly was quite certain she smelled freesia as she had earlier during breakfast.

The scent eddied around them, subtle and sweet, but it was enough to break the spell.

She jerked away from him before she could do something abysmally stupid like kiss the man.

"I'm sorry," she exclaimed. "I'm so clumsy sometimes. Are you all right? Did I hurt you?"

A muscle worked in his jaw, though that strange light lingered in his eyes. "I'm not breakable, Anna. Don't worry about it."

Despite his words, she was quite certain she saw lines of pain bracketing his mouth. With three older brothers, though, she had learned enough about the male psyche to sense he wouldn't appreciate her concern.

She let out a long breath. This had to be the strangest morning of her life.

"Here's the leash," she said. "If you decide to take Conan with you, just call his name and rattle this outside my door and he should come running in an instant."

He nodded. For a moment, she thought he might say something about the surge of heat between them just now, but then he seemed to change his mind.

"Thanks again for breakfast," he said. "I would offer to return the favor but I'm afraid you'd end up with cold cereal."

She managed a smile, though she was certain it wasn't much of one. He gazed at her for a long moment, his features unreadable, then he headed for the door.

Conan danced around behind him, his attention

glued to the leash, but she managed to close the door before the dog could escape to follow him up the stairs.

He whined and slumped against the door and she leaned against it, absently rubbing the dog's ears as that freesia scent drifted through the apartment again.

"Cut it out, Abigail," she spoke aloud. Lieutenant Maxwell would surely think she was crazy if he heard her talking to a woman who had been dead nearly a year.

Still, there had been that strange moment at breakfast when she had been almost positive he sensed something in the kitchen. His eyes had widened and he had seemed almost disconcerted.

Ridiculous. There had been nothing there for him to sense. Abigail was gone, as much as she might wish otherwise. She was just too prosaic to believe Sage and Julia's theory that their friend still lingered here at Brambleberry House.

And even if she did buy the theory, why would Abigail possibly make herself known to Harry Maxwell? It made no sense.

Sage believed Abigail had played a hand in her relationship with Eben, that she had carefully orchestrated events so they would both finally be forced to admit they belonged together.

Though Julia didn't take things quite that far, she also seemed to believe Abigail had helped her and Will find their happily-ever-after.

But Abigail had never even met Harry Maxwell. Why on earth would she want to hook him up with Anna?

She heard the ludicrous direction of her thoughts

and shook her head. She had far too much to do today to spend any more time speculating on the motives of an imaginary matchmaking ghost.

She wasn't about to let herself fall prey to any beyond-the-grave romantic maneuvering between her and a certain wounded soldier with tired, suspicious eyes.

MAX RETURNED TO his third-floor aerie to be greeted by his cell phone belting out his mother's ringtone.

He winced and made a mental note to change it before she caught wind of the song one of his bunkmates at Walter Reed had programmed as a joke after Meredith's single visit to see him in the six months after the crash.

His mother wouldn't be thrilled to know he heard Heart singing "Barracuda" every time she called.

When he was on painkillers, he had found it mildly amusing—mostly because it was right on the money. Now he just found it rather sad. For much the same reason.

He thought about ignoring her but he knew Meredith well enough to be sure she would simply keep calling him until he grew tired of putting her off, so he finally picked it up.

With a sigh, he opened his phone. "Hi, Mom," he greeted, feeling slightly childish in the knowledge that he only used the word because he knew it annoyed her.

She had been insisting since several years before he hit adolescence that he must call her Meredith but he still stubbornly refused.

"Where were you, Maxwell? I've been calling you

for an hour." Her voice had that prim, tight tone he hated.

"I was at breakfast. I must have left my phone here."

He decided to keep to himself the information that he was downstairs eating Abigail's French toast with Anna Galvez.

"You said you would call me when you arrived."

"You're right. That's what I said."

He left his sentence hanging between them, yet another strategy he had learned early in his dealings with her mother. She wouldn't listen to explanations anyway so he might as well save them both the time and energy of offering.

The silence dragged on but he held his ground. Finally she heaved a long-suffering sigh and surrendered.

"What have you found?" she asked. "Have those women gutted the house and sold everything in it?"

He gazed around at the apartment with its new coat of paint and kitchen cabinets and he thought of the downstairs apartment, with its spacious new floor plan.

"I wouldn't exactly say that."

"Brambleberry House was filled with priceless antiques. Some of them were family heirlooms that should have gone to you. I can't believe Abigail didn't do a better job of preserving them for you. You're her only living relative and those family items should be yours."

Since she had backed down first, he let her ramble on about the injustice of it all—as if Meredith cared about anyone's history beyond her own.

"I was apparently mistaken to let you visit her all those summers. When I think of the expense and time involved in sending you there, I just get furious all over again."

He happened to know Abigail had paid for every plane ticket and Meredith had looked on those two weeks as her vacation from the ordeal of motherhood but he decided to let that one slide, too.

"She must have been crazy at the end," Meredith finally wound down to say. "That's the only explanation that makes sense. Why else would she leave the house to a couple of strangers when she could have left it to her favorite—and only—nephew?"

"We've had this conversation before," he said slowly. "I can't answer that, Mom."

"What do you intend to do, then? Have you spoken with an attorney yet about contesting the will?"

"It's been nearly a year since Abigail died. I can't just show up out of nowhere and start fighting over the house."

He didn't need Brambleberry House. What did he care about some decaying old house on the coast? He certainly didn't need any inheritance from Abigail. His father had been a wealthy, successful land developer.

Though he died suddenly, he had been conscientious—or perhaps grimly aware of his wife's expensive habits. He had left his young son an inviolable trust fund that Meredith couldn't touch.

Through wise investments over the years, Max had parlayed that inheritance into more money than one man—or ten—could spend in a lifetime.

The money didn't matter to him. Abigail did. She had been his rock through childhood and he owed her at least some token effort to make sure she had been competent in her last wishes.

"You most certainly can fight over it! That house should belong to you, Maxwell. You're entitled to it."

He rolled his eyes. "I'm not entitled to anything."

"That's nonsense," Meredith snapped. "You have far more claim on Brambleberry House than a couple of grubby little gold diggers. Did you contact Abigail's attorney yet?"

He sighed, ready to pull the old bad-connection bit so he could end the call. "I've been in town less than twenty-four hours, Mom. I haven't had a chance yet."

"You have to swear you'll contact me the moment you know anything. The very *moment.*"

He had a fleeting, futile wish that his mother had been as concerned when her son was shot down by enemy fire as she apparently was about two strangers inheriting a house she had despised.

The moment the thought registered, he pushed it quickly away. He had made peace a long time ago with the reality that his mother had a toxic, self-absorbed personality.

He couldn't change that at thirty-five any more than he had been able to when he was eight.

For the most part, both of them rubbed together tolerably well as long as they were able to stay out of the other's way.

"I'll do that. Goodbye, Mom."

He hung up a second later and gazed at the phone for a long moment, aware she hadn't once asked about his arm. Just like Meredith. She preferred to pretend anything inconvenient or unpleasant just didn't exist in her perfect little world.

If Brambleberry House had been some worthless shack somewhere, she wouldn't have given a damn about it. She certainly wouldn't have bothered to push him so hard to check into the situation.

And he likely would have ignored her diatribes about the house if not for his own sense of, well, *hurt* that Abigail hadn't bothered to leave him so much as a teacup in her will.

It made no sense to him. She had loved him. Her Jamie, she called him, a nickname he had rolled his eyes at. James had been his father's name and it was his middle name. Abigail seemed to get a kick out of being the only one to ever call him that.

They had carried on a lively e-mail correspondence no matter where he was stationed and he thought she might have mentioned sometime in all that some reason why she was cutting him out of her will.

He had allowed his mother to half convince him Sage Benedetto and Anna Galvez must have somehow finagled their way into Abigail's world and conned her into leaving the house and its contents to them. It now seemed a silly notion. Abigail had been sharp as a tack. She would have seen through obvious gold-digging.

But she was also very softhearted. Perhaps the women had played on her sympathy somehow.

Or maybe she just had come to love two strangers more than she loved her own nephew.

He sighed, disgusted with the pathetic, self-pitying direction of his thoughts.

After spending the last hour with Anna Galvez, he

wasn't sure what to think. She seemed a woman of many contradictions. Tough, hard-as-nails business-woman one moment, softly feminine chef with an edge of vulnerability the next.

It could all be an act, he reminded himself. Still, he couldn't deny his attraction to her. She was a lovely woman and he was instinctively drawn to her.

Under other circumstances, he might have even liked her.

He heard a vehicle start up below and moved to the window overlooking the driveway. He saw her white, rather bland minivan carefully back out of the drive-way then head south toward Lincoln City.

The woman was a mystery, one he was suddenly eager to solve.

CHAPTER FIVE

This was a stupid idea.

Just after noon, Max slipped into the condiment aisle of the small grocery store in town, cursing his bad luck—and whatever idiotic impulse had led him to ever think he could get away with assuming a false identity in this town.

He must have been suffering the lingering effects of the damn painkillers. That was the only explanation that made sense.

It had seemed like such a simple plan. Just slip into town incognito, then back out again without anybody paying him any mind.

The idea should have worked. Cannon Beach was a tourist town, after all, and he figured he would be considered just one more tourist.

He had forgotten his aunt had known every permanent resident in town. Scratch that. Abigail probably had known every single person along the entire northern coast.

He felt ridiculous, hovering among the ketchup and steak sauce and salad dressing bottles. He peeked around the corner again, trying to figure out how he could get out of the store without being caught by the woman with the short, steel-gray hair and trendy tor-toiseshell glasses.

Betsy Wardle had been one of Abigail's closest friends. He knew the two of them used to play Bunco on a regular basis. If Betsy recognized him, the entire jig would be up.

He had met her several times before, as recently as four years earlier, the last time he stayed with his aunt.

He couldn't see any way to avoid having her recognize him now. The worst of it was, Betsy was an inveterate gossip. Word would be out all over town that Abigail's nephew was back, and of course that word would be quick to travel in Anna's direction.

He had two choices, as he saw it. He could either leave his half-full grocery cart right here and do his best to hightail it out of the store without being caught or he could just play duck-and-run and try to avoid her until she paid for her groceries and left.

He shoved on his sunglasses and averted his face just in time as she rounded the corner with her cart. He pushed past her, hoping like hell she was too busy picking out gourmet mustard to pay him any attention.

To be on the safe side, he turned in the direction she had just come and would have headed several aisles away but he suddenly heard an even more dreaded sound than Betsy Wardle's soft southern drawl.

Anna Galvez was suddenly greeting the older woman with warm friendliness.

He groaned and closed his eyes. Exactly the last person he needed to see right now when Betsy could expose him at any second. What was she doing here? Wasn't she supposed to be in Lincoln City right now?

He definitely needed to figure out a way out of here fast. He started to head toward the door when Betsy's words stopped him and he paused, pretending to compare the nutritional content of two different kinds of soy chips while he listened to their conversation one aisle over.

"How is your court case going against that awful man?" Betsy was asking.

"Who knows?" Anna answered with a discouraged-sounding sigh.

"The whole thing is terrible. Unconscionable. That's what I say. I just can't believe that man would work so hard to gain your trust and then take advantage of a darling girl like you. It's just not fair."

"Oh, Betsy. Thank you. I appreciate the support of you and Abigail's other friends. It means the world to me."

He wished he could see through the aisle to read her expression. She sounded sincere but he couldn't tell just by hearing her voice.

"I know I've told you this before and you've turned me down but I mean it. If you need me to testify on your behalf or anything, you just say the word. Why, when I think of how much you did for Abigail in her last years, it just breaks my heart that you're suffering so now. You were always at Brambleberry House helping with her taxes or paying bills for her or whatever she needed. You're a darling girl and I wouldn't hesitate a minute to tell that Lincoln City jury that very thing."

"Thank you, Mrs. Wardle," Anna answered. "While, again, I appreciate your offer, I don't think it will come to that. I'm not the one on trial, Grayson Fletcher is."

"I know that, honey, but from what I've read in the papers, it sounds like it's mostly his word against yours. I'm just saying I'm happy to step up if you need it."

"You're a dear, Mrs. Wardle. Thank you. I'll be sure to let the prosecutor know."

They chatted for a moment longer, about books and gardening and the best time to plant rhododendron bushes. Just as he was thinking again about trying to escape the store without being identified, he heard Anna say goodbye to the other woman. Out of the corner of his eye, he saw Betsy heading to the checkout counter that was at the end of his aisle.

He turned blindly to head in the other direction and suddenly ran smack into another cart.

"Oh!" exclaimed Anna Galvez.

"Sorry," he mumbled, keeping his head down and hoping she was too distracted to notice him.

No such luck. She immediately saw through the sunglasses. "Lieutenant Maxwell! Hello!"

"Oh. Hi. I didn't see you there," he lied. "This is a surprise. I thought you were going to be out of town today."

Her warm smile chilled at the edges. "My, uh, obligation was postponed for the rest of the afternoon. So instead I'm buying refreshments for one of the teen book clubs that meets after school at By-the-Wind. They're discussing a vampire romance so I'm serving tomato juice and red velvet cake. A weird combination, I know, but they have teenage stomachs so I figured they could handle it."

"Don't forget the deviled eggs."

She laughed. "What a great idea! I wish I'd thought of it in time to make some last night."

When she smiled, she looked soft and approachable and so desirable he forgot all about keeping a low profile. All he wanted to do was kiss her right there next to the organic soup cans.

He jerked his gaze away. "I guess I'd better let you get back to the shopping then. Your vampirettes await."

"Right."

He paused. "Listen, after I'm done here, I was thinking about taking a quick hike this afternoon. I know you said your dog could hang out with me but since you're here, maybe I'd better check that it's still okay with you."

"Absolutely. He'll be in dog heaven to have somebody else pay attention to him."

"Thanks. I'll bring him home about six or so."

"Take your time. I probably won't be done at the store until then anyway."

She smiled again, and it was much more warm and open than the other smiles she'd given him. He could swear it went straight to his gut.

"In truth," she went on, "this will take a big weight off my shoulders. I worry about Conan when I have to work long hours. Sometimes I take him into By-the-Wind with me since he loves being around people, but that's not always the easiest thing with a big dog like Conan. You're very sweet to think of including him."

Sweet? She thought he was *sweet?* He was a lieutenant with the U.S. Army who had been shot down by enemy fire. The last thing he felt was sweet.

"I just wanted a little company. That's all."

He didn't realize his words came out a growl until he saw that soft, terrifying smile of hers fade.

"Of course. And I'm sure he'll enjoy it very much. Have fun, then. I believe there were several area trail guides among the travel information I left in your apartment. If you don't find what you're looking for, we have several others in the store."

"I just figured I would take the Neah-Kah-Nie Mountain trail."

She stared at him in surprise. "You sound like you're familiar with the area. I don't know why, but for some reason, I assumed you hadn't been to Cannon Beach before."

He cursed the slip of his tongue. He was going to have to watch himself or he would be blurting out some of the other hikes he'd gone on with Aunt Abigail over the years.

"It's been a while," he answered truthfully enough. "I'm sure everything has changed since I was here last. A good trail guide will still come in handy, I'm sure. I'll be sure to grab it back at the house before I leave."

"If you get lost, just let Conan lead the way out for you. He'll head for food every time."

"I'll keep that in mind."

He smiled, hoping she wouldn't focus too much on his past experience in Cannon Beach. "Have fun with your reading group."

"I'll do that. Enjoy your hike."

With a last little finger wave, she pushed her cart toward the checkout. He watched her go, wondering how she could manage to look so very delicious in a conservative gray skirt and plain white blouse.

This was a stupid idea, he echoed his thought of earlier, for a multitude of reasons. Not the least of which was the disturbing realization that each time he was with her, he found himself more drawn to her.

How was he supposed to accomplish his mission here to check out the situation at Brambleberry House when all his self-protective instincts were shouting at him to keep as much distance as possible between him and Anna Galvez?

THEY WERE LATE.

Anna sat at her home office computer, pretending to work with her spreadsheet program while she kept one eye out the window that overlooked the still-empty driveway.

Worry was a hard, tangled knot in her gut. It was nearly seven-thirty and she had watched the sun set over the Pacific an hour earlier. They should have been home long before now.

Without Conan, the house seemed to echo with silence. She had always thought that an odd turn of phrase but she could swear even the sound of her breathing sounded oddly magnified as she sat alone in her office gazing out the window and fretting.

She worried for her dog, yes. But she also worried about a certain wounded soldier with sad, distant eyes.

They were fine, she told herself. He had assured her he could handle Conan even at his most rambunctious. He was a helicopter pilot, used to situations where he had to be calm under pressure and he was no doubt more than capable of coping with any difficulty.

Still, a hundred different scenarios raced through her brain, each one more grim than the last.

Anything could have happened out there. Neah-Kah-Nie Mountain had stunning views of the coastline but the steep switchbacks on the trail could be treacherous, especially this time of year when the ground was soaked.

She pushed the worry away and focused on her computer again. After only a few moments, though, her thoughts drifted back to Harry Maxwell.

How odd that it had never occurred to her that he might have visited Cannon Beach before. Is that why he seemed so familiar? Had he come into By-the-Wind at some point?

But if he had, wouldn't he have mentioned it at breakfast when she had talked about buying the store from Abigail?

It bothered her that she couldn't quite place how he seemed so familiar. She usually had a great memory for faces. But thousands of customers walked through By-the-Wind in a given year. There was no logical reason she would remember one man, no matter how compelling.

And he was compelling. She couldn't deny her attraction for him, though she knew it was completely ridiculous.

He was her tenant. That's all she could allow him to be at this complicated time in her life—not that he had offered any kind of indication he was interested in anything else.

Breakfast had been a crazy impulse and she could see now how foolish. It created this false sense of intimacy, as if an hour or so together made them friends somehow, when in reality he had only been at Brambleberry House a day.

No more breakfasts. No more chance encounters on the beach, no more bumping into him at the supermarket. When he and Conan returned safely from their hike—as she assured herself they would—she would politely thank him for taking her dog along with him, then for the rest of his time at Brambleberry House, she intended to do her absolute best to pretend the upstairs apartment was still empty.

It was a worthy goal and sometime later, when her pulse ratcheted up a notch at the sight of headlights pulling into the driveway, she told herself her reaction was only one of relief and maybe a little annoyance that he had left her to worry so long.

She forgot all about keeping her distance, though, when she saw him in the pale moonlight as he gingerly climbed out of his SUV then leaned on Conan as he limped his way toward the house.

CHAPTER SIX

SHE BURST THROUGH her apartment into the foyer just as he opened the front door, Conan plodding just ahead of him.

Max looked up with surprise at her urgent entrance, then she saw something that looked very much like resignation flash in his expression before her attention was caught by his bedraggled condition. Mud covered his Levi's and he had a long, ugly scrape on his cheek.

"Oh, my word! Are you all right? What happened?"

He let out a long breath and she thought for a moment he would choose not to answer her.

"I'm fine. Nothing to worry about."

"Nothing to worry about?" she exclaimed. "Are you crazy? You look like you fell off a cliff."

He raised an eyebrow but said nothing and she could swear her heart stuttered to a stop.

"That's not really what happened. Surely you didn't fall off a cliff, did you?"

"Not much of one."

"Not much of one! What kind of answer is that? Either you fell off a cliff or you didn't."

"I slid on a some loose rocks and fell. It was only about twenty feet, though."

Only twenty feet. She tried to imagine falling

twenty feet and then calmly talking about it as if she had merely stumbled over a curb. It was too big a stretch for her and her mind couldn't quite get past it.

"I'm so sorry! Did you hurt your arm when you fell?"

He shrugged. "I might have jostled it a little when I was trying to catch a handhold but I managed to stay off it for the most part and land on my left side."

"Please, just tell me Conan didn't trip you or something to make you fall."

He gave a rough laugh and she realized with some shock this was the first time she had heard him laugh. Smile, yes. Laugh, not until just this moment, when he was battered and bleeding and looking like something one of Conan's feline nemeses would drag in.

He reached down to scratch the dog's ears. "Not at all. He was off the leash about five meters ahead of me at the time I slipped. You should be very proud of him, actually. He's a real hero."

"Conan? My Conan?"

"If not for him, I probably would have slipped farther down the scree and gone off the cliff," he answered. "I don't know how he did it, as steep as that thing was, but he made it down the hill where I had fallen and practically dragged me back up, through the mud and the rocks and everything. With my stupid arm and shoulder, I'm not sure I could have climbed back up on my own."

She shuddered at the picture he painted, which sounded far worse than anything she had been conjuring up in her imagination before they arrived home.

Twenty feet! It was a wonder he didn't have a couple dozen broken bones!

"I'm so glad you're both okay!"

"I shouldn't be," he admitted. "It was luck, pure and simple. I should never have gone across that rock field. I could tell it wasn't stable but I went anyway. I don't blame you if you don't trust me to take your dog again. But I have to tell you, if not for Conan, I'm not sure I would be here right now. The dog is amazing."

Conan grinned at both of them with no trace of humility. She shook her head, fighting the urge to wrap her arms around her brave, wonderful dog and hold on tight.

"It was lucky you took him, then. And of course you can take him again. Anytime. Maybe he's your guardian angel."

Conan barked as if he agreed completely with that sentiment.

"Or at least helping him out," Max said with a rueful smile.

"You're so certain your guardian angel is a man?"

He made a face. "I haven't really given it much thought. Most women I know would have knocked me to the ground before I could take a step across dangerous terrain in the first place. A preemptive strike, you know?"

"Sounds like you know some interesting women, Lieutenant Maxwell."

"I had an…older relative who taught me most women are interesting if a man is wise enough to allow them room to be."

She blinked. Now there was something Abigail

might have said. She wouldn't have expected the philosophy to be echoed by a completely, thoroughly masculine man like Harry Maxwell but she was beginning to think there was more to the helicopter pilot than she'd begun to guess at.

"We could stand out here in the hall having this interesting discussion but why don't you come inside instead and let me help you clean up and put some medicine and bandages on those cuts on your face?"

As she might have predicted, he looked less than thrilled at the prospect. He even limped for the stairs and she felt terrible she had kept him standing even for these few moments.

"Thanks, but that's not necessary. I can handle it."

She raised an eyebrow. "One-handed?"

He paused on the bottom stair with a frustrated sigh. "There is that."

"Come on, Max. I'm happy to do it."

"I don't want to put you to any trouble."

"I had three rough-and-tumble older brothers and always seemed the permanently designated medic. I think I spent half my childhood bandaging some scrape or other. I'm not squeamish at the sight of blood and I have a fairly steady hand with a bottle of antiseptic. You could do worse, Lieutenant Maxwell."

He studied her for a moment, then sighed again and she knew she had won when he stepped gingerly down from the bottom stairs.

"I'm sorry you have to do this. First your dog and now you. The inhabitants of Brambleberry House are determined to look out for me, aren't you?"

Somebody has to do it, she almost said, but wisely

held her tongue while Conan barked his own answer as Max followed her into her living room.

ANNA GALVEZ INTRIGUED him more every time he saw her.

Earlier in the grocery store she had worn that slim gray skirt and white blouse with her hair tucked away and had looked as neat and tidy as a row of newly sharpened pencils.

Tonight, as she led the way into her apartment he was entranced by her unrestrained hair as it shivered and gleamed under the overhead lights in a luscious cloud that reached past her shoulders.

She had on the same white blouse from earlier—or at least he thought it was the same one. But she had traded the skirt for a pair of jeans and she was barefoot except for a flirty pair of turquoise flip-flop slippers.

As she led him inside Abigail's apartment, he caught sight of just a hint of pale coral toenail polish peeking through and he found the contrast of that with her slim brown feet enormously sexy.

If he were wise, he would turn right around and race up the stairs as fast as he could go with his now gimpy foot from the ankle he was certain he twisted in the fall.

The hard reality was he wouldn't be going anywhere fast. He hesitated to take off his hiking boot for fear the whole ankle would balloon to the size of a basketball the moment he did. It had ached like crazy the whole way down the mountain and he had a feeling he'd only made it home because his SUV was an automatic and his right leg was fine to work the gas pedal and the brake.

Like it or not, he was stuck in this apartment with Anna for the time being. He could probably do a credible job of washing the worst of the dirt and tiny pieces of mountain from his face but he had a couple of scrapes on his left arm that would be impossible for him to reach very well while the right was still in the damn sling.

It was Anna or the clinic in town and after all the time he'd spent being poked and prodded by medical types over the last six months, Anna was definitely the lesser of two evils.

"Sit down," she ordered in a drill-sergeant sort of voice.

He gave her a mocking salute but was grateful enough to take the weight off his ankle and the throbbing pain. He tried his level best not to wince as he eased onto her couch, feeling a hundred years old, like some kind of damn invalid in a nursing home.

She watched him out of those careful, miss-nothing eyes and he saw her mouth firm into a tight line. He suspected he wasn't fooling her for a moment.

"I just have to gather up a few first-aid supplies and I'll be right back," she said.

"I'm not going anywhere," he answered, which was the absolute truth.

Conan had disappeared into the kitchen—probably to find his Dog Chow, Max figured. If he'd been thinking straight, he should have stopped off and picked up the juiciest, meatiest steak he could find for the hero of the hour.

He leaned back against the sofa cushions and closed his eyes, ready for a little of the calm and peace he had always found in these rooms.

An elusive effort, he discovered, especially since the scent of Anna seemed to surround him here, sweet and sultry at the same time.

He allowed himself the tiny indulgence of savoring that delectable combination for only a moment before she bustled back with her arms loaded down by bandages and antiseptic.

"I don't need all that. Do I really look that terrible?"

She gave him a sidelong look and for just a moment, he sensed something in her gaze that stunned him to the core, a thin thread of attraction that seemed to tug and curl between them.

She was the first one to look away, busying herself with the first-aid supplies. "You want the truth, you look like you just tangled with a mountain lion."

He ordered his pulse to settle down and reminded himself of all the dozens of reasons there could be nothing between them. "Nope," he answered, trying for a light tone. "Just the mountain."

She smiled a little, then reached for the iodine. "Let's take care of the cut on your face first and then I'll check out your arm."

"I can do the face. I just need a mirror for that. I, uh, would appreciate a little help with the arm, though."

For a moment, she looked as if she wanted to argue and he wasn't sure if he was relieved or disappointed when she finally reached for his arm.

Her fingers were deliciously warm on his skin. Sensation rippled from his fingertips to his shoulder and to his vast chagrin, his heartbeat accelerated with the same thick jolt of adrenaline that hit him just as his bird lifted into the air.

Anna was some seriously potent medicine. One touch and he completely forgot about all his other aches and pains.

She gripped his arm firmly with one hand while she used her other hand to dab antiseptic on the scrapes along his forearm. He welcomed the cold, bracing sting of the medicine to counterbalance her heat.

His sudden hunger was a normal response to a lovely woman, he knew. It had been just too long and she was just too pretty for him to sit here without any reaction to her soft curves and silky skin.

"Tell me if I'm hurting you," she said after a moment.

Oh, you have no idea. Max choked down the words.

"Don't worry about it," he muttered instead.

"I mean it. You don't have to be some kind of tough-guy, stoic soldier. If this stings or I'm not careful enough, just tell me to stop."

"I'll be fine," he said gruffly, though it was a bald-faced lie. He couldn't tell her just how badly he wanted to close his eyes and lean into the gentleness of her touch.

What the hell was wrong with him? He had been fussed and fretted over by soft, pretty nurses for the last six months and none of them had ever sparked this kind of reaction in him.

He tried to tell himself it was just a delayed reaction to the adrenaline buzz of his fall—a sort of spit-in-the-face-of-death response. But he wasn't quite buying it.

Her sweep of hair brushed his skin as she bent over his arm and he wondered if she could see the goose bumps rising there.

She didn't appear to notice as she reached for a tube of antibiotic cream and slathered it on with the same slow, careful movements she seemed to do everything.

"You have a choice," she said after a moment.

"Do I?" he murmured.

"I can leave it like this or I can put bandages on the scrapes to protect them for a few days. It's up to you. I would recommend the bandage to keep things clean but it's your decision."

He wanted to tell her to stop but after he had spent several extra weeks in the hospital from a bad infection, he knew he couldn't afford to take any chances.

"Go ahead and wrap it. I might as well look like something out of a horror movie."

She smiled. "Wise choice, Lieutenant."

She pulled out gauze from her kit and wound it carefully around his arm. "If you need me to rewrap this anytime," she said as she worked, "I've got plenty."

"Right."

He figured he'd rather gnaw off his arm than endure this again.

He caught a flicker of movement in the room. Grateful for any distraction, he shifted his gaze and found Conan watching him with what looked like a definite smirk in his eyes, as if he knew exactly how tough this was for Max.

He gave the dog a stern look. *Thanks for the backup.*

When she finished his arm, she stepped back. "Are

you sure you don't want me to take care of your face while you're here and all the stuff is out?"

"No. Thanks anyway."

Just the thought of her touching his face with those soft, competent fingers sent shivers rippling through him.

"Anywhere else on you I need to take care of?"

Though his mind instantly flashed a number of inappropriate thoughts, he clamped down on all of them.

"Nope. I'm good. Thanks for the patch job. I appreciate it."

He rose and took only one step toward the door when her voice stopped him.

"You were limping when you came in and you still seem hesitant to put weight on your left foot. What's that all about?"

He turned back warily. "Nothing. I twisted my ankle a little when I fell but it's really fine. Just a little tender."

"You twisted your ankle and then you hiked back down to the trailhead and drove all the way here? Why didn't you say something? We need to put some ice on it."

He had to be the world's clumsiest idiot and right now he just needed to put a little space between himself and the enticing Anna Galvez before he did something he couldn't take back.

"It's really not a big deal. I can take care of it upstairs. You've done enough already."

More than enough. Or at least more than I can handle!

"Oh, stop it! How can you possibly take care of it

when you can't use your shoulder?" she pointed out with implacable logic. "I'm willing to bet your foot is swollen enough that you won't be able to even take off your boot by yourself, even if you didn't have your shoulder to contend with as well."

He knew she was right but he wasn't willing to concede defeat, damn it. He'd figure out a way, even if he had to slice the boot off with a hacksaw.

With his eye firmly on his objective—escape—he took another few steps for the door. "You can stop worrying about me anytime now. I can take care of myself."

"I'm sure you can. But you don't always have to," she answered.

He had no response to that so he took a few more steps, thinking if he could only make it to the door, he was home free. She couldn't physically restrain him, not even in his current pitiful condition.

But Abigail's blasted dog had other plans. Before he could take another step, Conan magically appeared in front of him and planted his haunches between Max and the doorway, looking as if he had absolutely no intention of letting him leave the apartment.

He faced the dog down. "Move," he ordered.

Conan simply made a sound low in his throat, not quite a growl but a definite challenge.

"You might as well come back," Anna said, and he heard a thread of barely suppressed laughter in her voice. "Between the two of us, we're here to make sure you take care of that ankle."

He gave Anna a dark look. "Are you really prepared for the consequences of kidnapping an officer in the United States Army, ma'am?"

She laughed out loud at that. "You don't scare me, Lieutenant."

I should, he thought. *I damn well should.*

Once again, he felt foolish for being so churlish when she was only trying to help. He could spend an hour trying to wrestle the boot one-handed or he could let her help him and be done in five minutes.

He sighed. "I would appreciate it if you would help me take off the boot. I can handle the rest from there. I've got ice upstairs."

"Of course. Come back and sit down."

He ignored Conan's look of triumph as he slowly returned to his spot on the sofa. Instead, he cursed his stupid arm and shoulder all over again.

If not for the crash and his subsequent injury, none of this would be happening. He would still be carrying out his duty, he would be flying, he would be in control of his world instead of here in Oregon wondering what the hell he was going to do with the rest of his life.

She knelt on the floor and worked the laces of his hiking boot. Her delicious scent swirled around him again and he told himself the fact that his mouth was watering had more to do with missing dinner than anything else.

Conan seemed inordinately interested in the proceedings. The dog plopped down beside Anna, watching the whole thing out of curious eyes.

The dog was spooky. Max couldn't think of another word for it. Though he felt slightly crazy for even contemplating the idea, he was quite certain Conan understood him perfectly well.

Throughout the day he had carried on a running

commentary with him and Conan barked at all the proper places.

He was trying to distract himself, thinking about the dog. It wasn't quite working. He still couldn't seem to avoid noticing the curve of Anna's jawline or the little frown of concentration on her forehead as she tried to ease his tight hiking boot over his swollen ankle.

He jerked his gaze away and his attention was suddenly caught by an open doorway and the contents lined up on shelves inside.

"You kept…" His voice trailed off and he realized he couldn't just blurt out his surprise that she had kept his aunt's extensive doll collection without revealing that he knew about the collection in the first place.

"Yes?"

He couldn't seem to hang on to any thought at all when she gazed at him out of those big dark eyes.

"Sorry. I, um, was just thinking that it, uh, looks like you've kept the original woodwork in the house."

"Actually, not in this room. There was some old water damage and rot issues in here and the trim was beyond saving. I was able to find a decent oak pattern that was a close imitation, though not exact."

"You wouldn't know it's not original to the house."

"I have an excellent carpenter."

"You must have to keep him on retainer with a house of this size."

She made a face, tugging a little harder on the stubborn boot. "Just about. It helps that he only lives a few houses down. And he's marrying Julia Blair, the woman who lives on the second floor."

As she spoke, she finally managed to tug the boot off his ankle.

Before he could jerk his foot away, she rolled the sock down and then gasped. "Oh, Max. That looks horrible! Are you sure it's not broken?"

His entire ankle was swollen to the size of a small cantaloupe and it was already turning a lovely array of colors. He felt like a graceless idiot all over again.

"It's only a little sprain. I just need to wrap it and everything will be fine. Thanks again for your help."

He was determined this time he would make it out of the apartment as he picked up his boot and leaned forward to rise to his feet.

"Max—" she started to argue, and he decided he just couldn't take another word.

Driven by the slow, steady hunger of the last half hour and his own frustration at himself, he bent his head and captured her mouth with his, knowing just a moment's satisfaction that at least he had discovered an effective way of shutting her up.

Okay, it was just about the craziest thing he had ever done in a lifetime of crazy stunts but he couldn't regret it. Not when her mouth was soft and slightly open with surprise and when she tasted like cinnamon and sugar.

Before this moment, he would have thought a kiss where only two sets of lips connected would lack the fire and excitement of a deep, full-body embrace, when he could feel a woman's soft curves against him, the silky smoothness of her skin, each pulse of her heart.

But standing in Anna Galvez's living room with every muscle in his body aching like a son of a bitch, simply touching her mouth with his was the most intense kiss he had ever experienced.

He felt the electrifying heat of it singe through him like a lightning strike, as if he stood atop Neah-Kah-Nie Mountain with his arms outstretched in the middle of a thunderstorm, daring the elements.

Hunger surged through him, a vast, aching need, and he couldn't seem to think straight around it.

This wild heat made no sense to him and contradicted every ounce of common sense he possessed.

If she wasn't a con artist, she was at least an opportunist. She struck him as tight and contained. Buttoned-down, even. Very much not the sort of woman to engage in a wild, fiery romance with a wounded soldier who would be leaving in a few weeks' time.

Despite what logic was telling him, he couldn't ignore her reaction to his kiss. Instead of jerking away— or even slapping his face—she made a breathy kind of sound and leaned in closer.

That tiny gesture was all it took to send his control out the window and he pulled her closer, suddenly desperate for more.

CHAPTER SEVEN

SOME TINY, LOGICAL corner of her brain that could still function knew this was completely insane.

What was she thinking to be here kissing Harry Maxwell—she barely knew him, he was her tenant, and right now the man couldn't even stand upright, for heaven's sake!

Usually she tried to listen to that common-sense corner of her mind but right now she found it impossible to focus on anything but the heat of him and his strong, commanding mouth on hers.

As he pulled her closer, she wrapped her arms around his waist. This was a little like she imagined it would feel to stand in the midst of the battering force of a hurricane, holding tight to the hard, immovable strength of a centuries-old lighthouse. His body was all heat and hard muscles and she wanted to lean into him and not let go.

She closed her eyes and savored the taste of him, heady and male, and the thrum of her blood as his mouth explored hers.

The house faded around her and she was lost to everything but the moment. Right now she wasn't a struggling businesswoman or an out-of-her-league homeowner. She wasn't a failure or the victim of fraud or an unwilling dupe.

She was only Anna and at this frozen moment in time she felt beautiful and feminine and *wanted*.

She didn't know how long they kissed, wrapped together in her living room with the sounds of their mingled breathing and the creaks and sighs of the old house settling around them.

She would have been quite willing to stand there forever. But that still-functioning corner of her mind was aware of him shifting his weight slightly and then of his sudden discordant intake of breath.

Awareness washed over her like the bitter cold of a January sneaker wave and she froze, blinking out of what felt like a particularly delicious dream into harsh reality.

What was wrong with her? He was a stranger, for heaven's sake! She'd known him for all of twenty-four hours and here she was entangled in his arms.

She knew nothing about this man other than that he could be kind to her dog and he disliked being fussed over.

This absolutely was not like her. She always tried to be so careful with men, taking her time to get to know them, to give careful thought to a man's positive and negative attributes before even considering a date with him.

And wasn't that course of action working out just great for her? a snide little voice sneered in her mind.

She pushed it away. She barely knew the man. Not only that, but he was injured! He could barely stand up and here she was throwing herself at him. She couldn't even bring herself to meet his gaze, mortified at her instant, feverishly inexplicable reaction to a simple kiss.

Why had he kissed her, though? That was the real question. One moment she had been urging him to take it easy with his sprained ankle—okay, nagging him—and the next moment his mouth had been stealing her breath, and whatever good sense she possessed along with it.

This sort of thing did *not* happen to her.

Still, she found some consolation that he looked as baffled and thunderstruck as she was.

In fact, the only one in the room who didn't look like the house had just imploded around them all was Conan, who sat watching the two of them with an expression that bordered on smug delight, oddly enough.

Max was the first one to break the awkward silence.

"Well, your nursing methods might be a little unorthodox, but I suddenly feel a hell of a lot better."

Her flush deepened. "I'm so sorry. I don't know what… I shouldn't have…"

He held up a hand. "Stop. I was trying to make a stupid joke. I completely started it, Anna. I kissed you. You have nothing to apologize about."

She tried to remember the steps in the circle breathing Sage was always trying to make her practice but her mind was too scrambled to focus on the calming method. She also still couldn't quite force herself to meet his gaze.

"I was way out of line," he added. "I don't know quite what to say, other than you can be sure it won't happen again."

"It won't?" Now why did that make her feel so blasted depressed?

"I don't make it a habit of accosting people who are only trying to help me."

"You didn't accost me," she mumbled. "It was just a kiss."

Just a kiss that still seemed to sing through her body, moments later. A kiss she could still taste on her lips and feel in her racing pulse.

"Right," he said after a moment. "Uh, I'd better get out of your way and let you get back to…whatever you were doing before we showed up."

She fiercely wanted him gone so she could try to regain a little badly needed equilibrium. At the same time, she couldn't help worrying about his injuries.

"Are you sure you'll be able to make it up the stairs?"

"Unless Conan stands in my way again."

"He won't," she promised. If she had to, she would lock the dog in her bedroom to keep him from causing any more trouble.

He paused at her door. "Good night, then. And thank you again for all your help."

A shadow of something hot and intense still lingered in the hazel depths of his eyes.

She told herself she shouldn't be flattered by it. But her ego had taken a beating the last few months with the trial and Gray Fletcher's perfidy. She felt stupid and incompetent and ugly in the knowledge that Gray had only pursued her so arduously to distract her from his shady dealings at her company—and that she had been idiot enough to fall for it.

Harry Maxwell didn't work for her, he didn't want

anything from her. He seemed as discomfited by the heat they generated as she was.

At the same time, the fact that this gorgeous man was at least interested enough in her to kiss her out of the blue with such heat and passion was a soothing balm to her scraped psyche.

He grabbed his boot and headed into the foyer. Though she knew his ankle had to be killing him, he barely limped as he headed up the stairs.

Abigail would have followed him right upstairs with cold compresses and ibuprofen for his ankle, no matter what the stubborn man might have to say about it.

But Anna wasn't Abigail. She never could be. Yes, she might invite the man over to breakfast to make him feel more welcome in Cannon Beach and she might fill his room with guidebooks and put a little first-aid ointment on his scrapes.

But Abigail had possessed unfailing instincts about people. She didn't make the kinds of mistakes Anna did, putting her trust in the completely wrong people who invariably ended up hurting her....

Though she knew he wouldn't appreciate her concern, she waited until she heard the door close up on the third floor before returning to her living room.

She closed the door and sagged into Abigail's favorite chair, ignoring Conan's interested look as she pressed a hand to her mouth.

What just happened here? She had no idea a simple kiss could be so devastatingly intense.

She had certainly kissed men before. She'd been engaged, for heaven's sake. She had enjoyed those kisses and even the few times she and her fiancé had gone further than kisses.

But she had always thought something was a little wrong with her in that department. While she enjoyed the closeness, she had never experienced the raw, heart-pounding desire, the wild churn in her stomach, that other women talked about.

Until tonight.

Just another reason why her reaction to a wounded soldier was both unreasonable and dangerous. She wanted to throw every caution to the wind and just enjoy the moment with him.

How on earth was she going to make it through the next few months with him living just upstairs?

Julia and the twins would be back in a week. Their presence would at least provide a buffer between her and Max.

Whether she wanted it or not.

SHE DIDN'T SEE Max Saturday morning before she left for the store. His SUV was gone and the lights were off on the third floor, she saw with some relief as she backed her van out through a misting rain that clung to her windshield and shimmered on the boughs of the Sitka spruce around Brambleberry House.

He must have left while she was in the shower, since his vehicle had been parked in the driveway next to hers when she returned with Conan from their morning walk on the beach earlier.

She spent a moment as she drove to By-the-Wind wondering where he might have gone for the day. Maybe the Portland Saturday Market? That was one of her favorite outings when she had the time and she was almost certain this was the opening weekend of the season. But would Lieutenant Maxwell really enjoy wandering through stalls of produce and flowers and local handicrafts? She couldn't quite imagine it.

Whatever he had chosen to do with his Saturday was none of her business, she reminded herself. She only hoped he didn't overdo.

She had fretted half the night that he wouldn't be able to get up and down the stairs with his ankle, that he would be trapped up on the third floor with no way of calling for help.

It was ridiculous, she knew. The man was a trained army helicopter pilot who had survived a crash, for heaven's sake, and she had no idea what else during his service in the Middle East. A twisted ankle was probably nothing to someone who had spent several months in the hospital recovering from his injuries.

Her worry was obviously all for nothing. With no help whatsoever from her or Conan, he had managed to get down the stairs, obviously, and even behind the wheel of his vehicle.

Since he was apparently mobile, she needed to stop worrying about the man, especially since she had a million other things within her control she could be stressing over.

She barely had time to even think about Max throughout the morning. Helen Lansing, her wonderful assistant manager who led the weekly preschool story hour on Saturday mornings—complete with elaborate puppets and endless energy—called in tears, with a terrible migraine.

"Don't worry about it," Anna told her as she mentally reshuffled her day. "Just go lie down in a quiet, dark room until you feel better. Michael and I can handle story hour."

The rain—or probably their parents' cabin fever—brought a larger than average crowd to the story hour. It might have been not quite as slick and polished as Helen's shows usually were but the children still seemed to enjoy it—and as a business owner, she certainly enjoyed the sales generated by their parents as they waited for their little ones.

By the time the last child left just before lunch, she was ready for a little quiet.

"I'll be in the office for a few moments working on invoices," she told Michael and Kae, her two clerks. "Yell if you need help."

She had just settled into her desk chair when her office phone rang. She didn't recognize the number and she answered rather impatiently.

"Sorry. Is this a bad time?"

Her mood instantly lifted at the voice on the other end of the line. "Sage! No, of course it's not a bad time. It's never a bad time when you call. How are you? How are Eben and Chloe?"

There was an odd delay on the line, as if the signal had to travel a long distance, though the reception was clear enough.

"Wonderful. Guess where I'm calling from?"

Eben owned a chain of hotels around the world and he and Sage frequently traveled between them, taking his daughter, Chloe.

Last month Sage had called her from Denmark and the month before had been Japan.

"Um, New York City?" she guessed.

"A little farther south. We're in Patagonia!"

"Really? I didn't know Spencer Hotels had a location down there."

"We don't. But Eben's considering it. He wants to capitalize on the high-end ecotourism trend so we're scouting locations. Chloe is having a blast. Just yesterday we went horseback riding through scenery so incredible, you can't imagine. You should have seen her up on that horse, just like she's been riding her whole life."

Sage's love for her stepdaughter warmed Anna's heart. When she and Sage inherited Brambleberry House, she used to be so envious of Sage for her vivid, outgoing personality.

Sage was much like Abigail in that every time she walked into a room, she walked out of it again with several new friends.

Anna never realized until they had become close friends how Sage's exuberance masked a deep loneliness.

That was gone now. Sage and Eben—and Chloe—were genuinely happy together.

"Sounds like you're having a wonderful time."

"We are. And how are things there? What's going on with the trial? I tried to call a few times last week to check in and got your voice mail."

"I know. I got your message. I'm sorry I haven't called you back. I've just been busy…"

Her voice trailed off and she sighed, unable to lie

to her friend. "Okay, truth. I purposely didn't call you back."

"Ouch. Screening my calls now?"

"Of course not. You know I love you. I just... I didn't really want to talk about the trial," she finally admitted.

"That bad?"

The sympathy in Sage's voice traveled all the way across the phone line from Patagonia and tears stung behind her eyes.

"Not at all, if you enjoy public humiliation."

"Oh, honey. I'm so sorry. I should have been there. I've been thinking all week that I should have just ignored you when you said you didn't want either Julia or me to come with you. You're always so blasted independent but sometimes you need to have a friend in your corner. I should have been there."

"Completely not necessary. We're on the homestretch now. The defense should wrap up Monday, with closing arguments Tuesday, and a verdict sometime after that."

"I'm coming home," she said after that short delay. "I should be there with you, at least for the verdict."

"You absolutely are not!"

"You're my friend. I can't let you go through this on your own, Anna."

"I can handle it."

She would rather have her tongue chopped into little pieces than admit to Sage how very much she longed for her friends to lean on right now.

"You handle everything. I know. And usually you

do a marvelous job at it. But you shouldn't have to bear this burden by yourself."

"If you cut short your dream trip to Patagonia with your family on my account, I will never forgive you, Sage Benedetto-Spencer. I mean it. You and Eben have already done more than enough."

"I should be there."

"You should be exactly where you are, horseback riding through incredible scenery with your husband and daughter."

Sage was silent for a moment and Anna thought perhaps the tenuous connection had been severed. "And you have to deal with a new tenant in the middle of all this, too. He's arriving any day now, isn't he?"

She rolled a pencil between her fingers. "Actually, he showed up a few days ago."

"And…?" Sage prompted.

"And what?" she said, stalling.

"What's he like?"

She had a wild, visceral image of his mouth on hers, of those strong muscles surrounding her, of his skin, warm and hard beneath her exploring fingertips.

How should she answer that? He was gorgeous and stubborn and infuriating and his kiss was magic.

"I don't really know. He's only been there a few days. So far everything has been…fine."

It was a vast understatement and she could only be grateful Sage was thousands of miles away and not watching her out of those knowing eyes of hers that missed nothing.

"Any sign of Abigail since your wounded soldier showed up or is she giving him a wide berth?"

"No ghostly manifestations, no. Everything has been quiet on the paranormal front."

"What about Conan? Does he like him?"

"Well, he did try to attack him last night in my apartment, but other than that, they get along fine."

"Excuse me? He attacked him? Our fierce and mighty watchdog Conan, who would probably lick an intruder to death?"

She sighed, wishing she'd kept her big mouth shut. Sage was far too perceptive and Anna had a sudden suspicion she would read far more into the situation.

"HeandConanwenthikingyesterdayonNeah-Kah-Nie Mountain and Lieutenant Maxwell fell and was scraped up a bit. He's already got an injury from a helicopter crash so it was hard for him to tend his wounds by himself but he's the, uh, prickly, independent type. He wasn't thrilled about me having to bandage his cuts. But Conan and I can both be persuasive."

"Okay, now things are getting interesting. Forget some stupid old trial. Now I want to know everything about the new tenant. Tell me more."

"There's nothing to tell, Sage. I promise."

Other than that she had kissed him and made of fool of herself over him and then spent the night wrapped in feverish dreams that left her achy and restless.

"What does he look like?"

Anna closed her eyes and was chagrined when his image appeared, hazel eyes and dark hair and too-serious mouth.

"He looks like he's been in a hospital too long and is hungry for fresh air and sunlight. Conan adores him and is already extremely protective of him. That's what last night was about. Conan didn't want him to go up the stairs until I'd taken a look at his swollen ankle."

"And did you? Get a good look, I mean?"

Better than she should have. "Sage, drop it. There's nothing between me and Lieutenant Maxwell. I'm not interested in a relationship right now. I can't afford to be. When would I have the time, for heaven's sake, even if I had the energy? Besides, I obviously can't be trusted to pick out a decent man for myself since my judgment is so abysmal."

"That's why you need to let Abigail and Conan do it for you. Look how well things turned out for Julia and for me?"

Anna laughed, feeling immeasurably better about life, as she always did after talking to Sage. "So what you're saying is that a fictitious octogenarian spirit and a mixed-breed mutt have better taste in men than I do. Okay. Good to know. If I ever decide to date again—highly doubtful at this point in my life—I'll bring every man home to Brambleberry House before the second date."

They talked a few moments longer, then she heard Chloe calling Sage's name. "You'd better go. Thanks for calling, Sage. I promise, I'll call you as soon as I know anything about the verdict."

"Are you sure you don't want me there?"

"Absolutely positive. When you and Eben and Chloe come back to Cannon Beach at Easter, we'll have an all-nighter and we can read the court transcripts together."

"Ooh, can we do parts? I've got the perfect voice for that weasel Grayson Fletcher."

She pitched her voice high and nasal, not at all like Gray's smooth baritone, but it still made Anna laugh. "Deal. I'll see you then."

She hung up the phone a few moments later, her heart much lighter as she focused on all the wonderful ways her life had changed in the last year.

Yes, she'd had a rough few months and the trial was excruciatingly humiliating.

But she had many more blessings than hardships. She considered Sage the very best gift Abigail had bequeathed to her after her death. Better than the house or the garden or all the antique furniture in the world.

The two of them had always had a cool relationship while Abigail was alive, perhaps afflicted by a little subtle rivalry. Both of them had loved Abigail and perhaps had wanted her affection for themselves.

Being forced to live together in Brambleberry House had brought them closer and they had found much common ground in their shared grief for their friend. She now considered Sage and Julia Blair her richest blessings, the two best friends she'd ever known.

She had a beautiful home on the coast, she had close friends who loved and supported her, she had two businesses she was working to rebuild.

The last thing she needed was a wounded soldier to complicate things and leave her aching for all she didn't have.

CHAPTER EIGHT

FEW THINGS COULD send his blood pumping like a heavy storm roiling in off the ocean.

Max walked along the wide sandy beach with Conan on his leash, watching the churn of black-edged clouds way out on the far horizon. Even from here, he could see the froth of the sea, a writhing mass of deep, angry green.

It wouldn't be here for some time yet but the air had that expectant quality to it, as if everything along the coast was just waiting. Already the wind had picked up and the gulls seemed frantic as they soared and dived through the sky, driven by an urgency to fill their stomachs and head for shelter somewhere.

At moments like this, Max sometimes wondered if he should have picked a career in the coast guard.

He could have flown helicopters there, swift, agile little Sikorsky Jayhawks, flying daredevil rescues on the ocean while waves buffeted the belly of his bird.

He had always loved the ocean, especially *this* ocean—its moods and its piques and the sheer magnificence of it.

Conan sniffed at a clump of seaweed and Max paused to let him take his time at it. Though he didn't want to admit it, he was grateful for the chance to rest for a moment.

Considering his body felt as if it had been smashed against the rocks at the headland, he figured he was doing pretty well. A run had been out of the question, with his ankle still on the swollen side, but a walk had helped loosen everything up and he felt much better.

The ocean always seemed to calm him. He used to love to race down from the house the moment Abigail returned to Brambleberry House from picking him up at the airport in Portland. She would follow after him, laughing as he would shuck off his shoes and socks for that first frigid dip of his toes in the water.

Max couldn't explain it, but some part of him was connected to this part of the planet, by some invisible tie binding him to this particular meshing of land and sea and sky.

He had traveled extensively around the world during his youth as his mother moved from social scene to social scene—in the days before Meredith sent him to military school. He had served tours of duty in far-flung spots from Latin America to Germany to the gulf and had seen many gorgeous places in every corner of the planet.

But no place else ever filled him with this deep sense of homecoming as he found here on the Oregon coast.

He didn't quite understand it, especially since he had spent much longer stretches of time in other locations. When people in social or professional situations asked him where he was from, as Anna had done at breakfast the other day, he always gave some vague answer about moving around a lot when he was kid.

But in his heart, when he thought about home, he thought of Brambleberry House and Cannon Beach.

He sighed. Ridiculous. It wasn't his. Abigail had decided two strangers deserved the place more and at this point he didn't think he could do a damn thing about it.

If his military career was indeed over, he was going to have to consider his options. Maybe he would just buy a fishing boat and a little house near Yachats or Newport and spend his days out on the water.

It wasn't a bad scenario. So why couldn't he drum up a little more enthusiasm for it, or for any of the other possibilities he'd been trying to come up with since doctors first dared suggest he might not ever regain full use of his arm?

He flexed his shoulder as he watched the gulls struggle against the increasing wind. They ought to just give up now, he thought, before the wind made it impossible for them to fly. But they kept at it. Indeed, they seemed to revel in the challenge.

He sighed as his ankle throbbed from being in one place too long. He felt weaker than a damn seagull in that headwind right now.

"Come on, Conan. We'd better head back."

The dog made a definite face at him but gave one last sniff in the sand and followed as Max led the way back up the beach toward Brambleberry House.

The storm clouds were edging closer and he figured they had maybe an hour before the real fun started.

Good. Maybe a hard thunder-bumper would drive this restlessness out of him.

He was grateful for his fleece jacket now as the temperature already seemed to have dropped a dozen degrees or more, just in the time since they set off.

The moment he opened the beach access gate at Brambleberry House, Conan bounded inside, barking like crazy as if he had been gone for months.

Max managed to control him enough to get the leash off and the dog jumped around with excitement.

"You like storms, too, don't you? I bet they remind you of Aunt Abigail, right?"

The dog barked in that spooky way he had of acting as if he understood every word, then he took off around a corner of the house.

As Max followed more slowly, branches twisted and danced in the swell of wind, a few scraping the windows on the upper stories of the house.

He planned to start a fire in the fireplace, grab the thriller he had been trying to focus on and settle in for the evening with a good book and the storm.

Yeah, it probably would sound tame to the guys in his unit but right now he could imagine few things more enjoyable.

A quick image of kissing Anna Galvez while the storm raged around them flashed through his mind but he quickly suppressed it. Their kiss had been a one-time-only event and he needed to remember that.

"Conan? Where'd you go, bud?" he called.

He rounded the corner of the house after the dog, then stopped dead. His heart seemed to stutter in his chest at the sight of Anna atop a precarious-looking wooden ladder, a hammer in her hand as she stretched to fix something he couldn't see from this angle.

The first thought to register in his distinctly male brain was how sexy she looked with a leather tool belt low on her hips and her shirt riding up a little as she raised her arms.

The movement bared just the tiniest inch of skin above her waistband, a smooth brown expanse that just begged for his touch.

The second, more powerful emotion was sheer terror as he noted just how far she was reaching above the ladder—and how precarious she looked up there fifteen feet in the air.

"Have you lost your ever-loving mind?"

She jerked around at his words and to his dismay, the ladder moved with her, coming away at least an inch or more from the porch where it was propped.

At the last moment, she grabbed hold of the soffit to stabilize herself and the ladder, and Max cursed his sudden temper. If she fell because he had impulsively yelled at her, he would never forgive himself.

"I don't believe I have," she answered coolly. "My ever-loving mind seems fairly intact to me just now."

"You might want to double-check that, ma'am. That wind is picking up velocity with each passing second. It won't take much for one good gust to knock that ladder straight out from under you, then where will you be?"

"No doubt lying bleeding and unconscious at your feet," she answered.

He was not going about this in the correct way, he realized. He had no right to come in here and start issuing orders like she was the greenest of recruits.

He had no right to do anything here. He ought to just let her break her fool neck—but the thought of her, as she had so glibly put it, lying bleeding and unconscious at his feet filled him with an odd, hollow feeling in his gut that he might have called panic under other circumstances.

"Come on down, Anna," he cajoled. "It's really too windy for you to be safe up there."

"I will. But not quite yet."

He wasn't getting her down from there short of toppling the ladder himself, he realized. And with a bad ankle and only one usable arm right now—and that one questionable after the scrapes and bruises of the day before—he couldn't even offer to take her place.

"Can I at least hold the ladder for you?"

"Would you?" she asked, peering down at him with delight. "I'm afraid I'm not really fond of heights."

She was afraid of heights? He stared at her and finally noticed the slight sheen of sweat on her upper lip and the very slightest of trembles in her knees.

A weird softness twisted through his chest as he thought of the courage it must be taking her to stand there on that ladder, fighting down her fears.

"And so to cure your phobia, you decided to stand fifteen feet above the ground atop a rickety wooden ladder in the face of a spring storm. Makes perfect sense to me."

She made a face, though she continued hammering away. "Ha ha. Not quite."

"Well, what's so important it can't wait until after the storm?"

"Shingles. Loose ones." She didn't pause a moment in her hammering. "We need a new roof. The last time we had a big storm, the wind curled underneath some loose singles on the other side of the house and ended up lifting off about twenty square feet of roof. The other day I noticed some loose shingles on this side so I just want to make sure we don't see the same thing happen."

"Couldn't you find somebody else to do that for you?"

She raised an eyebrow. "Any suggestions, Lieutenant Maxwell?"

"You could have asked me."

She finally stopped hammering long enough to look down at him, her gaze one of astonishment as she looked first at his arm in the blasted sling, then at his ankle.

He waited for some caustic comment about his current physical limitations. Instead, her lovely features softened as if he'd handed her an armload of wildflowers.

"I...thank you," she said, her voice slightly breathless. "That's very kind but I'm sort of in the groove now. I think I can handle it. I would appreciate your help holding the ladder while I check a couple of shingles on the porch on the east side of the house."

He wanted to order her off the ladder and back inside the house before she broke her blasted neck but he knew he had no right to do anything of the sort.

The best he could do was make sure she stayed as safe as possible.

He hated his shoulder all over again. Was he going to have to spend the rest of his life watching others do things he ought to be able to handle?

"I'll help you on one condition. When the wind hits

twenty knots, you'll have to stop, whether you finish or not."

She didn't balk at the restriction as she climbed down from the ladder. "I suppose you're going to tell me now you have some kind of built-in anemometer to know what the wind speed is at all times."

He shrugged. "I've been a helicopter pilot for fifteen years and in that time I've learned a thing or two about gauging the weather. I've also learned not to mess around with Mother Nature."

"That's a lesson you learn early when you live on the coast," she answered.

She lowered the ladder and he grabbed the front end with his left hand and followed her around the corner of the house. The house's sturdy bulk sheltered them a little from the wind here but it was still cold, the air heavy and wet.

"I thought you said you kept a handyman on retainer," he said as together they propped the ladder against one corner of the porch.

She smiled. "No, you're the one who said I should. I do have a regular carpenter and he would fix all this in a second if he were around but he's been doing some work for my friend Sage's husband on one of Eben's hotels in Montana."

"Your friend's married to a hotel owner?"

He pretended ignorance while his stomach jumped as she ascended the ladder again.

"Yes. Eben Spencer owns Spencer Hotels. His company recently purchased a property here in town and that's how he met Sage."

"She's the other one who inherited Brambleberry House along with you, right?"

She nodded. "She's wonderful. You should meet her in a few weeks. She and Eben bought a house down the coast a mile or so and they come back as often as they can but they travel around quite a bit. She called me this afternoon from Patagonia, of all places!"

She started hammering again and from his vantage point, he had an entirely too clear view of that enticing expanse of skin bared at her waist when she lifted her arms. He forced himself to look away, focusing instead on the Sitka spruce dancing wildly in the wind along the road.

"Does she help you with the maintenance on the house?"

"As much as she can when she's here. And Julia helps, too. The two of us painted my living room right after Christmas."

"She's the one who lives on the second floor, right? The one with the twins."

"Right. You're going to love them. Simon will probably talk your leg off about what it's like to fly a helicopter and how you hurt your shoulder and if you carry a gun. Maddie won't have to even say a word to steal your heart in an instant. She's a doll."

His heart was a little harder to steal than that. Sometimes he wondered if he had one. And if he did, he wasn't sure a little girl would be the one to steal it.

He'd never had much to do with kids. He couldn't say he disliked them, they just always seemed like they inhabited this baffling alien world he knew little about.

"How old are the twins?" he asked.

"They turned eight a month ago. And Sage's step-daughter, Chloe, is nine. When the three of them are together, there's never a dull moment. It's so wonderful."

She loved children, he realized. Before he'd gotten to know her a little these last few days, that probably would have surprised him. At first glance, she had seemed brusque and cool, not at all the sort to be patient with endless questions or sticky fingers.

But then, Anna Gálvez was proving to be full of contradictions.

Just now, for instance, the crisp, buttoned-down businesswoman he had taken her for that first night looked earthy and sexy, her cheeks flushed by the cold and the exertion and her hair blown into tangles by the wind.

He wasn't interested, he reminded himself. Hadn't he spent all day reminding himself why kissing her had been a huge mistake he couldn't afford to repeat?

"There. That should do it," she said a moment later.

"Good. Now come down. That wind has picked up again."

"Gladly," she answered.

He held the ladder steady while she descended.

"Thank you," she said, her voice a little shaky until her feet were on solid ground again. "I'll admit, it helped to know you were down there giving me stability."

"No problem," he answered.

She smiled at him, her features bright and lovely and he suddenly could think of nothing but the softness of her mouth beneath his and of her seductive heat surrounding him.

They stood only a few feet apart and even though the wind lashed wildly around them and the first few drops of rain began to sting his skin, Max couldn't seem to move. He saw awareness leap into the depths of her eyes and knew instinctively she was remembering their kiss as well.

He could kiss her again. Just lean forward a little and all that heat and softness would be in his arms again...

She was the first one to break the spell between them. She drew in a deep breath and gripped the ladder and started to lower it from the porch roof while he stood gazing at her like an idiot.

"Thanks again for your help," she said, and he wondered if he imagined the tiniest hint of a quaver in her voice. "I should have done this last week. I knew a storm was on the way but I'm afraid the time slipped away from me. With an old place like Brambleberry House, there are a hundred must-do items for every one I check off."

She was talking much more than she usually did and seemed determined to avoid his gaze. She obviously didn't want a repeat of their kiss any more than he did.

Or at least any more than he *should*.

"Where does the ladder go?"

"In the garage. But I can return it."

He ignored her, just hefted it with his good arm and carried it around the house to the detached garage where Abigail had always parked her big old Oldsmobile. Conan and Anna both followed behind him.

Walking inside was like entering a time capsule of his aunt's life. It looked the same as he remembered from four years ago, with all the things Abigail had loved. Her potting table and tools, an open box of unpainted china doll faces, the tandem bicycle she had purchased several years ago.

He paused for a moment, looking around the cluttered garage and he was vaguely aware of Conan coming to stand beside him and nudging his head under Max's hand.

"It's a mess, I know. I need to clean this out as soon as I find the time. It's on my to-do list, I swear."

He said nothing, just fought down the renewed sense of loss.

"Listen," she said after a moment, "I was planning to make some pasta for dinner. I always make way too much and then feel like I have to eat it all week long, even after I'm completely sick of it. Would you like some?"

He was being sucked into Anna's life, inexorably drawn into her web. Seeing Abigail's things here only reminded him of his mission here and how he wasn't any closer to the truth than he'd been when he arrived.

"No," he said. "I'd better not."

His words sounded harsh and abrupt hanging out there alone but he didn't know how else to answer.

Her warm smile slipped away. "Another time, then."

They headed out of the garage and he was aware of Conan glaring at him.

The sky had darkened just in the few moments they had been inside the garage and it now hung heavy and gray. The scattered drops had become a light drizzle and he could see distant lightning out over the ocean.

"I should warn you we sometimes lose power in the

middle of a big storm. You can find emergency candles and matches in the top drawer in the kitchen to the left of the oven."

"Thanks." They walked together up the front steps and he held the door for her to walk into the entryway.

He headed up the stairs, trying not to favor his stiff ankle, but his efforts were in vain.

"Your ankle! I completely forgot about it! I'm an idiot to make you stand out there for hours just to hold my ladder. I'm so sorry!"

"It wasn't hours and you're not an idiot. I'm fine. The ankle doesn't even hurt anymore."

It wasn't quite the truth but he wasn't about to tell her that.

He didn't want her sympathy.

He wanted something else entirely from Anna Galvez, something he damn well knew he had no business craving.

Upstairs in his apartment, Max started a fire in the grate while his TV dinner heated up in the microwave.

The wind rattled the windowpanes and sent the branches of the oak tree scraping against the glass and he tried to ignore the delicious scents wafting up from downstairs.

He could have used Conan's company. After spending the entire day with the dog, he felt oddly bereft without him.

But he supposed right now Conan was nestled on his rug in Anna's warm kitchen, having scraps of pasta and maybe a little of that yeasty bread he could smell baking.

When the microwave dinged to signal his own paltry dinner was ready, he grabbed a beer and settled into the easy chair in the living room with the remote and his dinner.

Outside, lightning flashed across the darkening sky and he told himself he should feel warm and cozy in here. But the apartment seemed silent, empty.

Just as he was about to turn on the evening news, the rocking guitar riff of "Barracuda" suddenly echoed through his apartment.

Not tonight, Mom, he thought, reaching for his cell phone and turning it off. He wasn't at all in the mood to listen to her vitriol. She would probably call all night but that didn't mean he had to listen.

Instead, he turned on the TV and divided his attention between the March Madness basketball games and the rising storm outside, doing his best to shake thoughts of the woman downstairs from his head.

He dozed off sometime in the fourth quarter of what had become a blowout.

He dreamed of dark hair and tawny skin, of deep brown eyes and a soft, delicious mouth. Of a woman in a stern blue business suit unbuttoning her jacket with agonizing slowness to reveal lush, voluptuous curves...

Max woke up with a crick in his neck to find the fire had guttered down to only a few glowing red embers. Just as she predicted, the storm must have knocked out power. The television screen was dark and the light he'd left on in the kitchen was out.

He hurried to the window and saw darkness up and down the coast. The outage was widespread, then.

From his vantage point, he suddenly saw a flashlight beam cutting across the yard below.

His instincts hummed and he peered through the sleeting rain and the wildly thrashing tree limbs to see two shapes—one human, one canine—heading across the lawn from the house to the detached garage.

What the hell was she doing out there? She'd be lucky if a tree limb didn't blow over on her.

He peered through the darkness and in her flashlight beam he saw the garage door flapping in the wind. They must not have latched it quite properly when they had returned the ladder to the garage.

Lightning lit up the yard again and he watched her wrestle the door closed then head for the house again.

He made his way carefully to his door and opened it, waiting to make sure she returned inside safely. Only silence met him from downstairs and he frowned.

What was taking her so long to come back inside?

After another moment or two, he sighed. Like it or not, he was going to have to find out.

CHAPTER NINE

SHE LOVED THESE wild coastal storms.

Anna scrambled madly back for the shelter of the porch, laughing with delight as the rain stung her cheeks and the churning wind tossed her hair around.

She wanted to lift her hands high into the air and spin around wildly in a circle in some primitive pagan dance.

She supposed most people would find that an odd reaction in a woman as careful and restrained as she tried to be in most other areas of her life. But something about the passion and intensity of a good storm sent the blood surging through her veins, made her hum with energy and excitement.

Abigail had been the same way, she remembered. Her friend used to love to sit out on the wraparound porch facing the sea, a blanket wrapped around her as she watched the storm ride across the Pacific.

Since moving to Brambleberry House nearly a year ago, Anna tried to follow the tradition as often as she could. Sort of her own way of paying tribute to Abigail and the contributions she had made to the world.

Conan shook the rain from his coat after their little foray to the garage and she laughed, grateful she hadn't removed her Gore-Tex parka yet. "Cut it out," she exclaimed. "You can do that on that side of the porch."

The dog made that snickering sound of his, then settled into the driest corner of the deep porch, closest to the house where the rain couldn't reach him.

Conan was used to these storm vigils. She would have thought the lightning and thunder would bother him but he seemed to relish them as much as she did.

Her heart still pumped from the wild run to the garage as she grabbed one of the extra blankets she had brought outside and used a corner of it to dry her face and hair from the rain.

Lightning flashed outside their protected haven and she shivered a little as she grabbed another quilt and wrapped it around her shoulders, then headed for the porch swing that had been purposely angled into a corner to shelter its occupants as much as possible from the elements.

She had barely settled in with a sigh and rattle of the swing's chains when thunder rumbled through the night.

Before it had finished, Conan was on his feet, barking with excitement.

"Settle down, bud. It's only the storm," she assured him.

"And me."

She gasped at the male voice cutting through the night and quickly aimed her flashlight in the direction of it. The long roll of thunder must have muffled Max's approach. He stood several feet away, looking darkly handsome in the distant flashes of lightning.

Her heart, already racing, began to pump even

faster. This had nothing to do with the storm and everything to do with Lieutenant Maxwell.

"Is everything okay out here?" he asked, coming closer. "I saw from my window when you went out to the garage to close the door. When I didn't hear you come back inside, I was worried you might have fallen out here or something."

He was worried about her? A tiny little bubble of warmth formed in her chest but she fought down the reaction. He didn't mean anything by it. It was just simple concern of one person to another. He would have been just as conscientious if Conan had been out here in the storm.

More so, maybe. He loved her dog, while she was just the annoying landlady who wouldn't leave him alone, always inviting him to dinner and making him help her nail down loose shingles.

"I'm fine," she finally answered, unable to keep the lingering coolness from her voice after his abrupt refusal to share pasta with her earlier. "Sorry I worried you. I was just settling in to watch the storm. It's kind of a Brambleberry House tradition."

"I remember," he answered.

She gave him a quizzical look, wondering what he meant by that, though of course he couldn't see her expression in the dark.

"You remember what?" she asked.

An odd silence met her question, then he spoke quickly. "I meant, I remember doing the same thing when I visited the coast several years ago. A coastal storm is a compelling thing, isn't it?"

He felt the same tug and pull with the elements as

she did? She wouldn't have expected it from the distant, contained soldier.

"It is. You're welcome to join us."

In a quick flash of lightning, she saw hesitation flicker over those lean features—the same hesitation she had seen earlier when he had refused her invitation to dinner.

Never mind, she almost said, feeling stupid and presumptuous for even thinking he might want to sit out on a cold porch swing in the middle of a rainstorm.

But after a moment, he nodded. "Thanks. I was watching the storm from upstairs but it's not quite the same as being out here in the thick of things, is it?"

"I imagine that's a good metaphor for the life of an army helicopter pilot."

"It could very well be."

"There's room here on the swing. Or you could bring one of the rockers over from the other side of the porch, but I'm afraid they're a little damp. This is the safest corner if you want to stay out of the rain."

"Says the voice of experience, obviously."

After another odd, tense little moment of hesitation, he sat down on the swing, which swayed slightly with his weight.

The air temperature instantly increased a dozen degrees and she could smell him, spicy and male.

Lightning ripped through the night again and her blood seemed to sing with it—or maybe it was the intimacy of sitting out here with Max, broken only by the two of them wrapped in a warm cocoon of darkness while the storm raged around them.

They settled into a not uncomfortable silence, just

the rain and the thunder and the occasional creak and rattle of the swing's chains.

"Are you warm enough?" she asked. "I only brought two blankets out and one is wet but I've got plenty more inside."

"I should be okay."

"Here. This one should be big enough for both of us." She pulled the blanket from around her shoulders and with a flick of her wrists, sent it billowing over both of them.

Stupid move, she realized instantly. Stupid and naive. It was one thing to sit out here with him, enjoying the storm. It was something else indeed to share a blanket while they did it. Though they weren't even touching underneath it except the occasional brush of their shoulders as they moved, it all still seemed far too intimate.

He made no move to push the blanket off, though, and she couldn't think of a way to yank it away without looking even more foolish than she already must.

"I imagine you've seen some crazy weather from the front seat of a helicopter," she said in an effort to wrench her mind from that blasted kiss the day before.

"A bit," he answered. "Sandstorms in the gulf can come up out of nowhere and you have to either play it through or set down in the middle of zero visibility."

"Scary."

"It can be. But nothing gets your heart thumping more than trying to extract a wounded soldier in poor weather conditions in the midst of possible enemy machine-gun fire."

"You love it, don't you?"

He shifted on the swing, accompanied by the rattle of creaky chains. "What?"

"Flying. What you do."

"Why do you say that?"

She shrugged. "I don't know. Your voice just sounds...different when you talk about it. More alive."

"I do love it." He paused for a long moment as the storm howled around them. "I did, anyway."

"What do you mean?"

This time, he paused so long she wasn't sure he would answer her. She had a feeling he wouldn't have if not for this illusive sense of intimacy between them, together in the darkness.

When he spoke, his voice was taut, as hard as Haystack Rock. "The damage to my shoulder is...extensive. Between the burns and the broken bones, I've lost about seventy percent range of motion and doctors can't tell me whether I'll ever get it back. Worse than that, the infection damaged some of the nerves leading to my hand. At this point, I don't have the fine or gross motor control I need to pass the fitness test to remain a helicopter pilot in the army."

"I'm so sorry." The words sounded ridiculously lame and she wished for some other way she could comfort him.

"I'm damn lucky. I know that."

He spoke quietly, so softly she almost didn't hear him over the next rumble of thunder. "The flight medic and my copilot didn't walk away from the crash."

"Oh, Max," she murmured.

He drew in a ragged breath and then another and she couldn't help it. She reached a hand out and squeezed his fingers. He didn't seem in a hurry to release her hand and they sat together in the darkness, their fingers linked.

"What were their names?" she asked, somehow sensing the words were trapped inside him and only needed the right prompting to break free.

"Chief Warrant Officer Anthony Riani and Specialist Marybeth Shroeder. Both just kids. Marybeth had only been in country for a couple of months and Tony's wife was pregnant with their second kid. They both took the brunt of the missile hit on that side of the Black Hawk and probably died before we even went into the free fall."

She couldn't imagine what he must have seen, what he had survived. She only knew she wanted to hold him close, touched beyond measure that he would share this with her, something she instinctively sensed he didn't divulge easily.

"The crew chief and I were able to get the wounded soldier we were transporting out before the thing exploded. We kept him stable until another Black Hawk was able to evacuate us."

"Was he okay? The soldier?"

"Oh. Yeah. He was a Humvee gunner hit by an improvised explosive device. He lost a leg but he's doing fine, home with his family in Arkansas now."

"That's good."

"Yeah. We were both at Walter Reed together for a while. He's a good man."

He finally let go of her fingers and though she knew it was silly, she suddenly felt several degrees cooler.

"I can't complain, can I?" he said. "I've still got

all my pieces and even with partial function, I should eventually be able to do almost anything I want. Except fly a helicopter in the United States Army, I guess. It's looking like I'll probably have to ride a desk from now on or leave the military."

"A tough choice. What will you do?"

He sighed. "Beats me. You have any ideas? Flying helicopters is the only thing I've ever wanted to do. I never wanted to be some hotshot fighter jet pilot or anything fancy like that. Just birds. I'm not sure I can be content to sit things out on the sidelines."

"What about being a civilian pilot?"

He made a derogatory sound. "Doing traffic reports from the air or flying executives into the city who think they're too busy and important for a limousine? I don't think so."

"You could do civilian medevacs."

"I've thought about it. But to tell you the truth, I don't know that I'm capable of flying anything at this point, civilian or military. Or if I ever will be. We're in wait-and-see mode, according to the docs, which genuinely stinks when you're not a very patient person."

The storm seemed to be passing over, she thought. The lightning flashes were slowing in frequency and even the rain seemed to be easing. She didn't want this moment to end, though. She was intensely curious about this man who had survived things she couldn't even imagine.

"I'm sure you'll figure it out, Max. My friend Abigail used to say a bend in the road is not the end, unless you fail to make the turn. You just need to figure out which direction to turn. But you will."

"I'm glad one of us has a little faith."

She smiled. "You can borrow mine when you need it. Or Abigail's. She carried enough faith and goodness for all of us and I'm sure some still lingers here at Brambleberry House."

He was again silent for a long time. Then, to her shock, he reached for her hand again and held on to it as the storm continued to simmer around them. They sat for a long time like that in the darkness, while Conan snored in the corner and the storm gradually slowed its fury.

Anna's thoughts were scattered but she was aware of overriding things. She was more attracted to him than any man in her entire life. To his strength and his courage and even to his sadness.

He had been through hell and though he hadn't directly said it, she sensed he suffered great guilt over the deaths of his crew members and she wanted to ease his pain.

She was also, oddly, aware of the scent of freesia drifting over the earthy smell of wet leaves and the salty tang of the sea.

If she were Sage or Julia, she might think Abigail was making her opinion known that Harry Maxwell was a good man and she approved.

She couldn't believe Abigail was here in spirit. Abigail had been such a wonderful person that Anna couldn't believe she was anywhere but in heaven, probably doing her best to liven up things there.

But at times, even she had to admit Abigail seemed closer than at others. The smell of freesia, for instance, at just the moment she needed it. She tried to convince herself Abigail had loved the scent so much it had merely soaked into the walls of the house. But that didn't explain why it would be out here in the middle of a March rainstorm—or why she thought she caught the glitter of colorful jewels out of the corner of her gaze.

She shivered a little, refusing to give in to the urge to turn her head. Max, sitting too close beside her to miss the movement, misinterpreted it. "You're freezing. We should probably head in."

"I'm not. It's just…" She paused, feeling silly for even bringing this up but suddenly compelled to share some of Sage and Julia's theory with him. "I should probably confess something here. Something I should have told you before you rented the apartment."

He released her hand abruptly. "You're married."

She laughed, though it sounded breathless even to her. "No. Heavens, no. Not even close. Why would you even think that?"

"Not even close? Didn't you say you were engaged once?"

"Yes, years ago. I'm not close to being married right now."

"What happened to the engagement?"

She opened her mouth to tell him it was none of his business, then she closed it again. He had shared far more with her than just the painful end to an engagement that should never have happened in the first place.

"He decided he wanted a different kind of woman. Someone softer. Not so calculating. His words. At least that's what he wrote in the note he sent with his sister on the morning of what was supposed to be our wedding day."

She knew it was ridiculous but the memory still stung, even though it seemed another lifetime ago.

"Ouch."

His single, abrupt word shocked a laugh out of her. "It's been years. I rarely even think about it anymore."

"Did you love him?"

"I wouldn't have been a few hours away from marrying him if I didn't, would I?"

"Seems to me a hard, calculating woman like you wouldn't need to love a man in order to marry him. My mother never did and she's been married five times since my father died."

Now that revealed a wealth of information about his life, she thought. All of it heartbreaking.

"I'm not hard or calculating! I loved Craig. With every ounce of my twenty-four-year-old heart, I loved him. That first year afterward, I was quite certain I would literally die from the pain of the rejection. I couldn't wait to move away from my friends and family in Utah and flee to a place where no one knew me or my humiliating past."

"What's humiliating about it? Seems to me you had a lucky escape. The guy sounds like a jackass. Tell me the truth. Can you imagine now what your life would have been like if you had married him?"

She stared, stunned that he could hit right to the heart of things with the precision of a sharpshooter. "You are so right," she exclaimed. "I would have been completely miserable. I was just too young and stupid to realize it at the time."

It was a marvelously liberating discovery. She supposed she had known it, somewhere deep inside, but for so long she had held on to her mortification and the shame of being jilted on her wedding day. Somehow in the process, she had lost all perspective.

That day had seemed such a defining moment in her life, only because she had allowed it be, she realized.

She had become fearful about trusting anyone and had learned to erect careful defenses to keep people safely on the perimeter of her life. She had focused on her career, on first making By-the-Wind successful as Abigail's manager, then on building the company after she purchased it from her and then adding the second store to further cement her business plan.

Though she didn't think she had completely become what Craig called her—hard, calculating, driven—she had certainly convinced herself her strengths lay in business, not in personal relationships.

Maybe she was wrong about that.

"So if you're not married, what's your big secret?"

She blinked at Max, too busy with her epiphany to follow the trail of conversation. "Sorry. What?"

"You said you had some dark confession to make that you should have told me before I rented the apartment."

"I never said dark. Did I say dark?"

"I don't remember. I'm sure it was."

"No. It's not. It's just…well, rather silly."

"I could use more silly in my life right now."

She smiled and nudged his shoulder with hers. "All right. What's your opinion on the paranormal?"

"I'm not sure I know how to answer that. Are we talking alien visitations or bloodsucking vampires?"

"Neither. I'm talking about ghosts. Or I guess ghost,

singular. As in the ghost that some residents of Brambleberry House believe shares the house with us. My friend Abigail."

"You're saying you think Abigail still walks the halls of Brambleberry House."

"I didn't say *I* believed it. But Sage and Julia do. They won't listen to reason. They're absolutely convinced she's still here and that Conan is her familiar, I guess you could say. She works through him to weave her Machiavellian plans. Though I don't really know if one should use that word when all her plans seem to be more on the benevolent side."

The rain had slowed and a corner of the moon peeked out from behind some of the clouds, lending enough light to the scene that she could clearly see his astonished expression.

He stared at her for an endless moment, until she was quite certain he must believe her barking mad, then his head rocked back on his neck and he began to laugh, his shoulders shaking so much the swing rocked crazily on its chains and Conan padded over to investigate.

She had never seen Max so lighthearted. He looked years younger, his features relaxed and almost happy. She could only gaze at him, entranced by this side of him.

The entire evening, she had been trying to ignore how attracted she was to him. But right now, while laughter rippled out of him and his eyes were bright with humor, the attraction blossomed to a hot, urgent hunger.

She had to touch him. Just for a moment, she told

herself, then she would go back inside the house and do
her best to rebuild her defenses against this man who
had survived horrors she couldn't imagine but who
could still find humor at the idea of a ghost and her dog.

Her heart clicked just like the rain on the shingles
she had just fixed as she drew in a sharp breath, then
leaned forward and brushed her mouth against his.

CHAPTER TEN

HER MOUTH WAS warm and soft and tasted like cinnamon candy.

For all of maybe three seconds, he couldn't seem to move past the shock of it, completely frozen by the unexpectedness of the kiss and by the instant heat that crashed against him like those waves against the headland.

He forgot all about his amusement at the idea of his aunt Abigail using a big, gangly dog to work her schemes from the afterlife. He forgot the rain and the wind and the vow he had made to himself not to kiss her again.

He forgot everything but the sheer wonder of Anna in his arms again, of those soft curves beside him, of her scent, sweet and feminine, that had been slowly driving him insane all evening long as she sat beside him, tugging at him until his senses were filled with nothing but her.

Her arms twisted around his neck and he deepened the kiss, breathing deeply of that enticing, womanly scent and pulling her closer until she was nearly on his lap.

For the first time since he had sat down on the porch swing next to her, he was grateful for the blanket around them. Now it was no longer a curse, lending an intimacy he didn't want. Instead, the blanket had become a warm, close shelter from the cold air outside, drawing them closer.

Nothing else existed here but the two of them and the wild need glittering between them.

Kissing her again had a sense of inevitability to it, as if all day he had been waiting for only this. Suspended in a state of hungry anticipation to once again feel her hands in his hair, her soft curves pressed against him, the rapid beat of his heart.

Since the first time he kissed her, his body had been aching to have her in his arms again. That's why he had punished his ankle with a long walk on the shore, why he had spent the morning at the gym he'd found in Seaside working on his physical therapy exercises, why he had done his best to stay away from Brambleberry House all day.

Now that he had rediscovered the wonder of a woman's touch—*this* woman's touch—he couldn't manage to think about anything else. And even when he wasn't consciously thinking about it, his subconscious had been busy remembering.

This was better than anything he might have dreamed. She was warm and responsive, her mouth eager against his.

It was an intense and erotic kiss, just the two of them alone in the night in this warm shelter while the storm battered the coast around them, and he wanted it to go on forever.

Still, he had a vague awareness even as their bodies heated that the storm was calming—or at least moving farther inland, leaving them behind. The lightning strikes became more infrequent, the rolling thunder more distant.

He didn't care. Nothing else mattered but having her in his arms, slaking this raging thirst for her.

She moved a little, her soft curves brushing against his sling, but she quickly drew back.

"Sorry," she exclaimed.

"You don't have to be careful. I'm sorry my arm is in the way."

"It's not. I'm just afraid of hurting you."

"Let me worry about that."

"Are you? Worried about it, I mean?"

"What red-blooded male in his right mind would worry about a stupid thing like a cast on his arm right now?" he murmured against her mouth.

Her low laugh sent chills rippling down his spine.

"Do that again," he said.

In the darkness, she blinked at him. "Do…what?"

"Laugh like that. I would have to say, Ms. Galvez, that was just about the sexiest sound I've ever heard."

"You're crazy," she said, though she gave a self-conscious laugh when she said it and he thought he just might be content to sit there all night letting his imagination travel all sorts of wicked roads inspired by the sound.

"I must be. That's what six months in an army hospital will get you."

"I'm so sorry you had to go through that," she whispered. "I wish I could make everything okay."

To his shock, she planted a barely there kiss on the corner of his mouth then one on the other side. It was a stunningly sweet gesture and he felt something hard and tight that had been inside him for a long time suddenly break loose.

Had anyone ever shown such gentle compassion to him? He sure as hell couldn't remember it. To his dismay, tears burned behind his eyelids and he wanted to lean into her and just lose himself in her touch.

A fragile tenderness wrapped around them like Aunt Abigail's morning glory vines. He pulled her more firmly on his lap, solving the quandary of his cast by lifting the whole thing out of the way and resting his arm against her back as she nestled against his chest.

They kissed and touched for a long time, until he was aching with need, until she was shivering.

"Are you cold?"

Her laugh was rough. "Not even close."

Still, even as she said the words, she let out a long breath and he sensed her withdrawal, though she didn't physically pull out of his arms.

"This is crazy, Max. What are we doing here? This isn't... I don't do this kind of thing. I...we barely know each other."

He was having a hard time making his addled brain think at all but the still-functioning corner of his mind knew she was absolutely right. He had only been here a few days and in that time, he had been anything but honest with her.

But he didn't agree when she said she barely knew him. Right now, he felt as if she knew him better than anyone else alive. He had told her things he hadn't been able to share with the shrinks at Walter Reed.

"I don't know what this thing is between us but I'm fiercely attracted to you."

She let out a shaky breath and pulled out of his arms with a breathless little laugh. "Okay. Good to know."

"But then, you probably figured that out already."

"I believe I did, Lieutenant. And, uh, right back at you. So what do we do about it?"

He had a number of suggestions, none of which he was willing to share with her.

Before he could answer at all, the porch was suddenly flooded with lights as the electricity flashed back on.

Her eyes looked wide and shocked and she slid away from him on the porch swing as Conan gave a resigned-sounding sigh.

"Is that some kind of message?" Max asked with a rueful laugh. "Maybe the ghost of Brambleberry House is subtly telling us it's time to go inside."

"Ha. Doubtful. If I bought in to Sage and Julia's theory, Abigail's ghost would more likely be the one who cut the power in the first place," she muttered.

"You didn't tell me they had a theory about the ghost. I just figured she maybe wanted to hang around and make sure you treated her house the way she wanted."

He couldn't quite imagine Abigail as a malicious poltergeist. Not that she didn't love a little mischief and mayhem, but she wouldn't have caused it at any inconvenience or expense to someone else.

Though he might have expected things to be awkward with the heat and passion that still sparkled between them, he felt surprisingly comfortable with Anna.

He enjoyed her company, he realized. Whether they were talking or kissing or sitting quietly, he found being with her soothing, as if she settled some restless spirit inside him in a way nothing else ever had.

"Abigail was always a bit of a romantic," Anna answered. "She would have enjoyed setting the scene like this. The rain, the storm. All of it."

While he was trying to picture his aunt working behind the scenes as some great manipulator, Conan ambled off the porch steps and out in the misting rain.

"You don't really think some…ghost had anything to do with what just happened, do you?"

"I'm afraid my feet are planted too firmly on the ground for me to buy in to the whole thing like Sage and Julia do. And besides, while I firmly believe Abigail could have done anything she set her mind to, cutting off power along the entire coast so the two of us could…" Her voice trailed off and he was intrigued to see color soak those high, elegant cheekbones. "Could make out is probably a little beyond her capabilities."

Just as she finished speaking, the porch lights flickered off for maybe two seconds before they flashed back on again.

When they did, her eyes were bright with laughter.

"I wish you could see your face right now," she exclaimed.

He scanned the porch warily. "I'm just trying to figure out if some octogenarian ghost is going to come walking through the walls of the house any minute now with a bottle of wine and a dozen roses."

She laughed. "I don't believe you have anything to worry about. I've never seen her and I don't expect to."

Her smile faded and her dark eyes looked suddenly wistful, edged with sadness. "I wish Abigail *would* walk through that wall, though. I wish you could have known her. I think you would have loved her. She was…amazing. That's the only word for it. Amazing. She drew everyone to her in that way that very few people in the world have. The kind of person who just makes people around her feel happy and important, whether they're billionaire hotel owners or struggling college students."

"She must have been a good friend."

"More than that. I can't explain it, really. I just think you would have loved her. And I *know* she would have adored you."

"Me? Why do you say that?"

"She was always a sucker for a man in uniform. She was engaged to marry a man who died in Korea. He was her one true love and she never really got over him."

He stared. "I never…" Knew that, he almost said, but caught himself just in time. "How do you know that?"

"She told me about him once and then she never wanted to talk about him again," Anna answered. "She said he was the other half of her heart and the best person she'd ever known and she had mourned his loss every single day of her life."

Why had Abigail never told him anything about a lost love? He supposed it might not be the thing one confided in a young boy. What bothered him more was that he had never once thought to ask. He had always assumed she loved her independent life, loved being able to come and go as she pleased without having to answer to anyone else.

He found it terribly sad to think about her living in this big house all these years, mourning a love taken from her too soon.

"I would think a heartbreak like that would have given her an aversion to military men."

Anna shook her head, her eyes soft. "It didn't. I know she had a nephew in the military. I don't even know what branch but she was always so proud of him."

"Oh?"

"Her Jamie. I never met him. He didn't visit her much but she was still crazy about him. Abigail was like that. She loved wholeheartedly, no matter what."

Her words were a harsh condemnation, and the hell of it was, he couldn't even defend himself. He might not have visited Abigail as often as he would have liked, but it wasn't as if he had abandoned her.

They had stayed in touch over the years, he just hadn't been as conscientious about it while he was deployed.

"She sounds like a real character," he said, his voice gruff.

She flashed him a searching look and opened her mouth but before she could speak, Conan bounded back up the porch steps and shook out his wet coat on both of them.

Max managed to pull the blanket up barely in time to protect their faces.

"Conan!" she exclaimed. "Cut that out!"

The dog made that snickering sound he seemed to have perfected, then sauntered back to the corner.

"If you're looking for a signal to go inside, I believe that's a little more concrete than some ghostly manifestation."

"You're probably right," he said, reluctance in his voice.

"You're welcome to stay out here longer. I can leave the lantern and the blankets."

"I'd rather have you."

The words slipped out and hovered between them. "Sorry. I shouldn't have said that. Forget it."

She blinked. "No, I—I…"

She looked so adorably befuddled in the glow from the porch light—and just so damn beautiful with that thick, glossy dark hair and that luscious mouth—that he couldn't help himself.

One more kiss. That's all, he promised himself as he pulled her closer.

She sighed his name and leaned into him. She was small and curvy and delicious and he couldn't seem to get enough.

He touched the warm, enticing skin above the waistband of her jeans. She gave a little shuddering breath and he felt her stomach muscles contract sharply. Her mouth tangled with his and she made a tiny sound of arousal that shot straight to his gut.

He feathered his fingers along her skin, then danced across it until he met an enticing scrap of lace. He curved his thumb over her and felt her nipple harden. She arched into him and a white haze of hunger gnawed at him, until all he could think about was touching her, tasting her.

She gasped his name.

"I need to stop or I'm afraid I won't be able to."

"To what?"

He gave a raw laugh and kissed her mouth one last time then leaned his forehead against hers, feeling as breathless as if he were a new recruit forced to do a hundred push-ups in front of the entire unit.

He wanted to take things further. God knew, he wanted to. But he knew it would be a huge mistake.

"To stop. I don't want to but I'm afraid what seems like a brilliant idea right now out here will take on an entirely different perspective in the cold light of morning."

After a long moment, she sighed. "You're probably right."

She rose from the porch swing first and though it was one of the toughest things he had ever asked of himself, he helped her gather the blankets and carry them inside the foyer.

"Good night, Anna," he said at her apartment door. "I enjoyed the storm."

"Which one?" she asked with a surprisingly impish smile.

He shook his head but decided he would be wise not to answer.

His last sight as he headed up the stairs to his apartment was of Conan sitting by Anna's doorway looking up at him, and he could swear the dog was shaking his head in disgust.

His TV had switched back on when the power returned and some Portland TV weatherman was rambling on about the storm that was just beginning to sweep through town.

He turned off the noise then went to the windows, watching the moonlight as it peeked between clouds to dance across the water.

What the hell was he going to do now?

Anna Galvez was no more a scam artist than his aunt Abigail.

He didn't know about Sage Benedetto but since he had come to trust Abigail's judgment about Anna, he figured he should probably trust it with Sage as well.

Anna had loved his aunt. He had heard the vast, unfeigned affection in her voice when she had talked about her, when she had told him how she wished he could have known Abigail.

She loved Abigail and missed her deeply, he realized. Maybe even as much as he did.

He would have to tell her the truth—that he was Abigail's nephew and had concealed his identity so he could basically spy on her.

After the heated embrace they had just shared, how was he supposed to come clean and tell her he had been lying to her for days?

It sounded so ugly and sordid just hanging out there like that, but he knew he was going to have to figure out a way.

As was often the case after a wild coastal storm, the morning dawned bright and cloudless and gorgeous.

Anna awoke in her bed in an odd, expectant mood. She rarely slept with the curtains pulled, so that she could look out at the sea first thing in the morning. Today, the waves were pale pink frothed with white.

Conan must have slept in. He was usually in here first thing in the morning, begging for his run, but she supposed the late-night stormwatching had tired him out.

She wished she could say the same. She had tossed and turned half the night, her body restless and aching.

She sighed and rolled over onto her back. She was *still* restless and achy and she was very much afraid Harry Maxwell had ruined stormwatching for her for the rest of her days. How could she ever sit out on the porch watching the waves whip across the sky without remembering the heat and magic of his arms?

Blast him, anyway.

She sighed. No. It wasn't his fault. She had known she was tempting fate when she kissed him but she hadn't been able to control herself.

She wanted a wild, passionate fling with Harry Maxwell.

She drew in a shaky breath. How was that for a little blunt truth first thing in the morning?

She was fiercely attracted to the man. More attracted than she had ever been in her life. She wanted him, even though she knew he would be leaving soon. Maybe *because* she knew he would be leaving soon.

For once in her life, she didn't want to fret or rehash the past. She wanted to live in the heady urgency of the moment.

She blew out a breath. Even if she ever dared tell them—which she wouldn't—Sage and Julia would never believe she was lying here in her bed contemplating such a thing with a man she had only known for a matter of days.

How, exactly, did one go about embarking on a fling? She had absolutely no idea.

She supposed she could take the direct route and go upstairs dressed in a flimsy negligee. But first she would have to actually go out and *buy* a flimsy negligee. And then, of course, she would have to somehow find the courage to put it on, forget about actually having the guts to walk upstairs in it.

She sighed. Okay, she didn't know exactly how she could work the logistics of the thing.

"But I *will* figure it out," she said aloud.

Conan suddenly barked from the doorway and she felt foolish for talking to herself, even if her only witness was her dog, who didn't seem to mind at all when she held long conversations with herself through him.

"Thanks for the extra half hour," she said to the dog.

He grinned as if to say *you're welcome,* then headed to the door to stand as an impatient sentinel, as was his morning ritual. She knew from long experience that he would stay there until she surrendered to the inevitable and got dressed to walk him down the beach.

This morning she didn't make him wait long. She hurried into jeans and a sweatshirt then pulled her hair back into a ponytail and grabbed her parka against the still-cold March mornings.

Conan danced on the end of his leash as she opened the door to Brambleberry House, then even he seemed to stop in consternation.

The yard was a mess. The storm must have wreaked more havoc than she'd realized from her spot on the seaward side of the house. The lawn was covered with storm debris—loose shingles and twigs and several larger branches that must have fallen in the night since she was certain she would have heard them crack even from the other side of the house.

Okay, she was going to have to put her tentative seduction plans for Harry Maxwell on the back burner. First thing after walking Conan, she was going to have to deal with this mess.

CHAPTER ELEVEN

SHE CUT CONAN'S walk short, taking him north only as far as Haystack Rock before turning back to head down toward home and all the work waiting for her there.

At least it was an off-season Sunday, when her schedule was more flexible. As a small-business owner, she always felt as if she had one more thing she should be doing. But one of the most important things Abigail had taught her was to be protective of her time off.

You've got to allow yourself to be more than just the store, Abigail had warned her in the early days after she purchased By-the-Wind. *Don't put all the eggs of yourself into the basket of work or you're only going to end up a scrambled mess.*

It wasn't always possible to take time off during the busier summer season, but during the slower spring and winter months she tried to keep Sundays to herself to recharge for the week ahead.

Of course, cleaning up storm debris wasn't exactly relaxing and invigorating, but it was better than sitting in her office with a day full of paperwork.

Her mind was busy with all that she had to do as she walked up the sand dunes toward the house. She let Conan off his leash as soon as she closed the gate behind her and he immediately raced around the corner of the house. She followed him, curious at his urgency, and was stunned to find Max wearing a work glove on his uninjured hand and pushing a wheelbarrow already piled high with fallen limbs.

Her heart picked up a pace at the sight of him greeting Conan with an affectionate pat and she thought how gorgeous he looked in the warm glow of morning, lean and lithe and masculine.

"Hey, you don't have to do that," she called. "You're a renter, not the hired help."

He looked up from Conan. "Do you have a chain saw?" he asked, ignoring her admonition. "Some of these limbs are a little too big to cart off very easily."

"Abigail had a chain saw. It's in the garage. I'm not sure when it was used last, though, so it's probably pretty dull."

She hesitated, trying to couch her words in a way to cause the least assault to his pride. "Um, I hate to bring this up but don't you think your shoulder might make running a chain saw a little tough?"

He looked down at the sling with frustration flickering in his eyes, as if he had forgotten his injury.

"Actually, she also had a wood chipper," she added quickly. "I was planning to just chip most of this to use as mulch in the garden in a few weeks' time. The machine is pretty complicated, though, and it's a two-person job. To tell you the truth, I could use some help."

"Of course," he answered promptly.

She smiled, lost for just a moment in the memory of all they had shared on the porch swing the night before.

She might have stood staring at him all morning if

Conan hadn't nudged her, as if to remind her she had work to do.

"Let me just find my gloves and then we can get to work."

"No problem. There's plenty out here to keep me busy."

She hurried inside the house and headed for the hall tree, where she kept her extra gardening gloves and the muck boots she wore when she worked out in the garden.

The man had no right to look so gorgeous first thing in the morning when she could see in the hall mirror that she looked bedraggled and windblown from walking along the seashore.

The idea of a casual fling had seemed so enticing this morning when she had been lying in bed. When she was confronted with six feet of sexy male in a denim workshirt and leather gloves, she wondered what on earth she had been thinking.

She had a very strong feeling that a casual fling with a man like Lieutenant Maxwell would turn out to be anything but casual.

Not that a fling with him seemed likely anytime in the near future. He had seemed like a polite stranger this morning, in vivid contrast to the heat between them the night before.

She sighed. It was a nice fantasy while it lasted and certainly helped take her mind off Grayson Fletcher and the misery of the trial, which would be resuming all too soon.

When she returned to the yard, she couldn't see Max anywhere. But since Conan was sprawled out at the entrance to the garage, she had a fairly solid idea where to find him.

Inside, she found him trying to extricate the chipper, which was wedged tightly behind an old mattress frame and a pile of two-by-fours Will had brought over to use on various repairs around the house.

The chipper had wheels for rolling across the lawn but it was still bulky and unwieldy. She stepped forward to give him a hand clearing a path. "I know, this garage is a mess. With every project we do on the house, we seem to be collecting more and more stuff and now we're running out of places to put it all."

"You'll have to build a garage annex for it all."

She smiled. "Right. A garage for the garage. Sage would love the idea. To tell you the truth, I don't know what else to do. I hate to throw anything away. I'm so afraid we'll toss an old lamp or something and then find out it was Abigail's favorite or some priceless antique that had been in her family for generations."

"You can't keep the house like a museum for her."

"I know. She wouldn't want that and what little family she had doesn't seem to care much about maintaining their heritage. But I still worry. My parents brought very little with them from Mexico when they came across the border. Their families were both poor and didn't have much for them to bring but sometimes I wish I had more old things that told the story of my ancestors and what their lives might have been like."

An odd expression crossed his features and he opened his mouth to answer but before he could, she pulled the last obstacle out of the way so they could pull out the chipper.

"Here we go. That should give us a clear path."

They pulled the chipper out of the chaotic garage and into the sunshine while Conan watched them curiously.

"Any idea how to work this thing?" Max asked.

She smiled. "A year ago, my answer to that question would have been a resounding no, but I've had to learn a few things since I've been at Brambleberry House. This home ownership thing is not for the weak or timid, I'll tell you that much. I've become an expert at removing wallpaper, puttying walls, even wielding a toilet snake. This chipper business is easy compared to that."

For the next two hours, they worked together cleaning up the yard while Conan lazed in whatever dappled bit of sunbeam he could find. It was a gorgeous, sunny early spring day, the kind she always considered a gift from above here in Oregon.

When the fallen branches were cleared and the beautiful wood chips from them stored at the side of the garage for a few more weeks until she had time to prepare the flower beds, Max helped her gather up the loose shingles and replace the gutter that had blown down.

"Anything else we can do?" he asked when they finished and were sitting together on the porch steps taking a breather.

"I don't think so. Not right now, anyway. It's an endless job, this home maintenance thing."

"But not a bad way to spend a beautiful morning."

She smiled, enjoying his company immensely. Even with only one good hand, he worked far harder than most men she knew. He carried heavy limbs under one arm and though he quickly figured out he couldn't push the wheelbarrow with one hand without toppling it over, he ended up dragging out Abigail's old garden wagon and pulling the limbs and wood chips in that.

"I used to hate gardening when I was a kid," she told him. "My parents always had a huge vegetable garden. We would grow peppers and green beans and sweet corn and of course we kids always had to do the weeding. I vowed I was going to live in a condominium the rest of my life where I wouldn't have to get out at the crack of dawn to pick beans."

"But here you are." He gestured to the house.

"Here I am. And you know something weird? Taking care of the garden and yard has become my favorite part of living here. I can't wait until the flowers start coming out in a few weeks. You will be astonished at Abigail's garden. It's a magic place."

He made a noncommittal sound, as if he wasn't quite convinced, and she smiled. "I guess you don't have much opportunity for gardening, living in base housing as you said you've done."

"Not in the army, no," he said in what she had come to think of as his cautious voice. "Various places I've stayed, I've had the chance to do a little but not much."

"You can do all you want at Brambleberry House while you're here. All hands are welcome in Abigail's garden, experienced or not."

"I'll keep that in mind."

Conan brought over a sturdy twig they must have missed and dropped it at his feet. Max obliged him by picking it up and tossing left-handed for the dog to scamper after.

It was a lovely moment and Anna found she didn't

want it to end. "Do you feel like a drive?" she asked suddenly.

"With a specific destination involved or just for the ride?"

"A little of both. I need to head down to Lincoln City to drop off some items that were delivered by mistake to the store up here. I'd love some company. I'll even take you to lunch at my favorite restaurant at Neskowin Beach on the way down. My way of paying you back for your help today."

"You don't owe me anything for that. I didn't do much."

She could have argued with him but she decided she wasn't in the mood to debate. "The offer's still open."

He shifted on the step and looked up at the blue sky for a long moment and then turned back at her with a rather wary smile. "It *is* a gorgeous day for a drive."

She returned his smile, then laughed when Conan gave two sharp barks, whether from anticipation or just plain excitement, she couldn't guess. "Wonderful. Can you give me about half an hour to clean up?"

"Only half an hour?"

She grinned at him as she climbed to her feet. "Lieutenant, I grew up with three brothers in a little house with only one bathroom. A girl learns to work her magic fast under those circumstances."

She was rewarded with a genuine smile, one that warmed her clear to her toes. She hurried through her shower and dressed quickly. And though she would have liked to spend some time blow-drying her hair and fixing it into something long and luxurious and irresistible, she had to be satisfied with pulling it into a simple style, held away from her face with a yellow bandeau that matched her light sweater.

She did take time to apply a light coat of makeup, though even that was more than she usually bothered with.

"It's not a date," she assured Conan, who sat watching her with curious eyes as she applied eyeliner and mascara.

This is not a date and I am not breathless, she told herself when the doorbell rang a few moments later.

She answered the door and knew that last one was a blatant lie. She felt as if she were standing on the bluffs above Heceta Head with the wind hitting her from every side.

He wore Levi's and a brushed-cotton shirt in a color that matched the dark spruce outside. Hunger and anticipation curled through her insides.

"Do you need more time?" he asked.

"Not at all. I only have to grab my purse. Oh, and Conan's leash. Are you okay with him coming along? He pouts if I leave him alone too long."

"I expected it."

That was one of the things she appreciated most about him—his wholehearted acceptance of her dog.

Conan raced ahead as they headed out to her minivan and waited until she opened the door. His customary spot was in the passenger seat but he seemed content to sprawl out in the cargo area this trip, along with the boxes she had carefully strapped down the day before.

She backed with caution out of the driveway and waited until they were on the road heading south before she spoke. "I know you've been at least as far south as Neah-Kah-Nie Mountain. Have you gone farther down the coast?"

"Not this trip," he answered. "It's been several years."

"I've been driving to Lincoln City two or three times a week for nine months and I still never get tired of it."

"Is that how long you've had the store there?"

She nodded, then fell silent, remembering her starry dreams of last summer, when she had first opened the second store. She had wanted so desperately for the store to succeed and had imagined opening a third and maybe even a fourth store someday, until everywhere on the coast, people would think of By-the-Wind when they thought of books and unique gift items.

Now her dreams were in tatters and most days when she drove this road, she arrived with tight shoulder muscles and her stomach in knots.

"Did I say something wrong?" Max asked, and she realized she had been silent for a good mile or more.

"No. It's not you. It's just…"

She hesitated to tell him, though the trial was certainly common knowledge.

No doubt he would hear about it sooner or later and it was probably better that she give him the information herself.

Her hands tightened on the steering wheel. "My professional life is a mess," she admitted. "Once in a while I'm able to forget about it for an hour or so at a time but then it all comes creeping back."

She was almost afraid to look at him to gauge his

reaction but she finally dared a quick look and found his expression unreadable. "Want to talk about it?"

"I don't want to ruin your enjoyment of the spectacular coastal scenery with such a long, boring, sordid story."

"Can a story be boring and sordid at the same time?"

The tongue-in-cheek question surprised a laugh from her when she least expected to find much of anything amusing. "Good point."

And a good reminder that she shouldn't take herself so seriously. She hadn't lost any team members to enemy fire. She hadn't been shot down over hostile territory or suffered severe burns or spent months in the hospital.

This was a tough hurdle and professionally and personally humiliating for her but it wasn't the end of the world.

She didn't know where to start and she didn't want to look like an idiot to him. But he had been brutally honest with her the night before and she suddenly found she wanted to share this with Max.

"I trusted the wrong person," she finally said. "I guess the story all starts with that."

COULD THE WOMAN make him feel any more guilty, however unwittingly?

As Max listened to Anna's story of fraud and betrayal by the former store manager of her Lincoln City store, shame coalesced in his gut.

She talked about how she had been lied to for months, how she had ignored warning signs and hadn't trusted her gut.

How was Max going to tell her he had lied about his identity?

He had a strong suspicion her past experience with this charlatan wasn't going to make her the forgiving sort when he came clean.

"So here we are six months later," she finally said. "Everything is such a disaster. My business is in shambles, I've got suppliers coming out of the woodwork with invoices I thought had been paid months ago and worse, at least two dozen of my customers had their credit and debit cards used fraudulently. It's been a months-long nightmare and I have no idea when I'll ever be able to wake up."

Max remembered his speculation when he read the sketchy information online about the trial that maybe she had been involved in the fraud, a partner who was letting her manager take the fall while she reaped the benefits.

The thought of that now was laughable and he was sorry he had even entertained the idea. She sounded sick about the trial, about the fraud, especially about her customers who had suffered.

"You said this Fletcher jerk has been charged?"

"Oh, yes. That's part of the joy of this whole thing, out there in the public eye for everyone to see what an idiot I've been."

"It's not your fault the guy was a scumbag thief."

"No. But it is my fault I hired the scumbag thief to mind my store and gave him access to the personal information of all my customers and vendors who trusted me to protect that. It's my fault I didn't supervise things as closely as I should have, which allowed him more room and freedom to stick his fingers in as many pies as he could find."

"That's a lot of weight for you to bear."

"My name is the one on the business license. It's my responsibility."

"When will the trial wrap up?"

"This week, I think. Closing arguments start tomorrow and I'm hoping for a quick verdict soon after that. I'll just be so glad when it's over."

"That bad?"

She shrugged and tried to downplay it but he saw the truth in her eyes. "Every day when I walk in the courtroom, I feel like they ought to hand me a dunce cap and a sign to hang around my neck—World's Biggest Idiot."

"You've sat through the entire trial?"

"Every minute of it. Grayson Fletcher stole from me, he stole from customers, he stole from my vendors. He took my reputation and I want to make sure he pays for it."

He had seen seasoned war veterans who didn't have the kind of grit she possessed in order to walk into that courtroom each day. He was astonished at the soft tenderness seeping through him, at his fierce desire to take her hand and assure her everything would be okay.

He couldn't do it. Not with his own deception lying between them.

"Anna, I need to tell you something," he said.

"What?" For just an instant, she shifted her gaze from the road, her eyes wary and watchful.

"I haven't been…" Honest, he started to say, but before the words were out, Conan suddenly interrupted him with a terrible retching sound like he had a tennis ball lodged in his throat.

Until this moment, the dog had been lying peacefully in the cargo area of the minivan but now he poked his head between the driver and passenger seats, retching and gagging dramatically.

"Conan!" she exclaimed. "What's going on, bud? You okay?"

The dog continued making those horrible noises and Anna swerved off the road to the wide shoulder, turned off the van and hurried to the side to open the sliding door.

Conan clambered out and walked back and forth a few times on his leash. He gagged once or twice more, then seemed to take care of whatever had been bothering him.

A moment later, with what seemed like remarkable nonchalance, he headed to a clump of grass and lifted his leg, then wandered back to the two of them, planted his haunches in the grass and looked at them expectantly.

Anna watched him, a frown on her lovely features. "Weird. What was that all about?"

"Carsick, maybe?" Max suggested.

"Conan's never carsick," she answered. "I swear, he has the constitution of a horse."

"Maybe he just needed a little fresh air and a convenient fern."

"So why the theatrics? Maybe he just needed attention. Behave yourself," she ordered the dog as she let him back into the back of the vehicle.

Conan grinned at both of them and Max could have

sworn the dog winked at him, though of course he knew that was crazy.

"We're almost to Neskowin and my favorite place," Anna said as she returned to the driver's seat. "Are you ready for lunch?"

He still needed to tell her he was Abigail's nephew. But somehow the time didn't seem right now.

"Sure," he answered. "I'm starving."

"Trust me, you're going to love this place. Wait until you try the chili shrimp."

HE COULDN'T REMEMBER the last time he had permitted himself to genuinely relax and have fun.

In the military, he had been completely focused on his career, on becoming the best Black Hawk pilot in his entire division. And then the last six months had been devoted to healing—first the burns and the fractures, then the infection, then the nerve damage.

All that seemed a world away from this gorgeous stretch of coastline and Anna.

While they savored fresh clam chowder and crab legs at a charming restaurant with a spectacular view, they watched the waves roll in and gulls wheel overhead as they laughed and talked.

She told him about growing up with three older brothers in Utah and the trouble they would get in. She told him about her father dying in an industrial accident and her mother's death a few years later from cancer.

She talked about her brother the biologist who lived in Costa Rica with his wife and their twin toddler girls, who knew more Spanish than they did English and could swim like little guppies. About her brother Daniel, a sheriff back home in Utah and his wife, Lauren, who was the only physician for miles around their small town and about her brother Marc, whose wife had just left him to raise their two little boys on his own.

He would have been content just to listen to her talk about her family with her hands gesturing wildly and her face more animated than he had seen it. But she seemed to expect some conversation in return.

Since he didn't think she'd be interested in the stepsiblings he had barely known even when his mother had been married to their respective fathers, he told her instead about his real family. About his army unit and learning to fly his bird, about night sorties when it was pitch-black beneath him as they flew over villages with no electricity and he felt like he was flying over some lunar landscape, about the strength and courage of the people he had met there.

After lunch, they took a short walk with Conan along the quiet, cold beach before continuing the short trip to Lincoln City.

Though he had been careful not to touch her all day, he was aware of the heat simmering between them. He would have to be dead to miss it—the kick of his heartbeat when she smiled, the tightening of his insides when she laughed and ran after Conan on the beach, the burning ache he fought down all day to kiss her once again.

She was the most beautiful woman he had ever known but he couldn't find any words to tell her so that didn't sound corny and artificial. As they reached the busy outskirts of Lincoln City, he watched, fascinated, as his lighthearted companion seemed to become more focused and reserved with each passing mile.

By the time they drove into a small district of charming storefronts and upscale restaurants and pulled up in front of the cedar-and-brick facade that said By-the-Wind Two, she seemed a different person.

"You can wait here if you'd like," she said after she had turned off the engine.

"I'd like to see your store, if that's okay with you," he said. There was a much smaller likelihood of anyone recognizing him as Abigail's nephew in Lincoln City than if he'd gone into the original By-the-Wind, he figured. Beyond that, he really did want to see where she worked.

"Can I carry something for you?" he asked.

"I've got six boxes here. They're extremely fragile so we would probably be better off making a few trips rather than trying to haul everything in at once," she said.

He picked up a box with his good arm and followed her to a side entrance to the store, which she unlocked and propped open for them. They carried the boxes into what looked like a back storage room then they made two more trips each, the last one accompanied by Conan.

After they set down the last boxes, Anna led the way into the main section of the store.

He looked around with curiosity and found the shop comfortable and welcoming, very much in the same vein as Aunt Abigail's Cannon Beach store. Something jazzy and light played on a hidden stereo system and the wall sconce lighting in the bookstore area made all the books seem mysterious and enticing. Plump chairs invited patrons to stay and relax and apparently they did. Several were occupied and he had the feeling these were regular customers.

A long-haired gray cat was curled up atop a low coffee table in one corner. Conan hurried immediately over to the cat and Max braced himself for a confrontation but the two of them seemed to have an understanding.

The cat sniffed, gave him a bored look, then sauntered away just as a woman with a name badge that indicated she worked at the store caught sight of them and hurried over to greet Anna.

She looked thin and athletic, with long, salt-and-pepper hair pulled back in a ponytail and round wire-rim glasses that didn't conceal her glare.

"Excuse me, what are you doing here? Get out."

Anna tilted her head, much as the long-haired cat had done. "Last I checked, I still own the place."

The older woman all but shook her finger at her. "This is supposed to be your day off, missy. What do I have to do, hide your van keys so you take some time off?"

Anna laughed and hugged the other woman. "Don't nag. I know. I just brought the shipment of blown glass floats that was delivered to the other store. They're all in the back waiting to be stocked. You should see them, they're every bit as gorgeous as the few samples we received. I was afraid I wouldn't have time to drop them off before court tomorrow and I know they're already a week overdue."

"We would have gotten by without them for another day or two."

"I know, but it was a lovely day for a drive. Sue Poppleton, this is my new tenant, Lieutenant Harry Maxwell."

The woman gave him a friendly, curious smile, then turned back to Anna. "Since you're here, do you have five minutes to help me figure out what I'm doing wrong when I try to cancel a preorder in the system?"

"Of course. Max, do you mind just hanging out for a moment?"

"Not at all," he answered.

He headed for a nearby display of local travel books and was leafing through one on local history when he heard the front door chime. He didn't think much about it, until he realized the entire section of the store had gone deadly quiet.

CHAPTER TWELVE

"GET OUT," HE HEARD Anna say with a coldness in her voice Max had never heard before.

Conan growled suddenly—whether at her tone or at something else, Max had no idea but he now burned with curiosity.

Not knowing quite what to expect, he stepped away from the display so he could get a clear view of the door.

The man standing just inside the store didn't look threatening at all. He was one of those academic-looking types with smooth skin, artfully tumbled hair, intense eyes behind scholarly looking glasses. Exactly the sort one might expect to find sitting in a bookstore on a Sunday afternoon with a double espresso and the *New York Times* crossword puzzle.

So why the dramatic reaction? Conan was standing in front of Anna like he was all set to rip the man apart and even her employee looked ready to start chucking remaindered books at his head.

The guy seemed completely oblivious to their animosity, his gaze focused only on Anna.

"Come on, Anna. Cut me a break here. I was across the street at the coffee shop and saw your van pull up.

I left an excellent croissant half-eaten in hopes you might finally give me a chance to explain."

"I don't need to hear any explanations from you. I need you out of my store right now."

Her voice wobbled, just a little, but in that instant Max figured it out. This must be the bastard who had screwed her over.

He took a step forward, thinking he could probably knock the guy out cold with one solid left hook, but he paused. Maybe it would be better to see how things played out.

Besides, she looked as if she had plenty of help.

"Call off your mutt, will you?"

The dog Max had never seen do anything but enthusiastically lick anyone who so much as looked at him still stood in a protective stance in front of Anna, low growls rumbling out of him.

"I ought to let him rip your throat out after what you've done."

"Come on, baby. Don't be like this."

He raked a hand through his hair and gave Anna what Max figured he probably thought was some kind of melting look.

Anna appeared very much frozen solid. "Like what?" she asked quietly. "Like a woman who finally found her brain about six months too late and figured out what a *cabrón* you are."

Max didn't know much Spanish but he'd heard that particular term in the army enough to know it was not a particularly affectionate or flattering one.

Sue chortled, which seemed to infuriate the man even more. His face turned ruddy beneath his slick tan and he took a step forward, only to pause when Conan growled again.

His mouth hardened but he stopped. "How long did you have to practice that injured victim act you played so well in court when you testified?"

"Act?" Anna's voice rose in disbelief.

"Come on. You knew what was up the whole time. You just preferred to look the other way."

Anna drew in a shaky breath and even from here, Max could see the fury in her eyes. "Get out. That is your last warning before I call the police. I'm sure the judge will just love to find out you've been in here harassing me."

"Careful, babe. *Harassment* is an ugly word. You don't want to be throwing it around casually. Of course, sometimes it's a perfectly appropriate word. The exact one, really. Like when a business owner coerces an employee to sleep with her."

Her features paled and she looked vaguely queasy. "I never slept with you, thank the Lord."

"She didn't coerce you into anything and you know it, you disgusting piece of vermin," Sue snapped, and Fletcher blinked at her as if he'd forgotten she was there.

"Every single employee of By-the-Wind could testify about how you were the one constantly putting out the vibe, hitting on her every time she turned around," she went on. "Sending her flowers, writing poems on the employee bulletin board, taking credit for everybody else's ideas just so you could convince her you were Mr. Wonderful."

Anna drew in a deep breath, not looking at all

thrilled by the other woman's defense of her. Instead, her color flared even higher. "Uh, Sue, maybe you should start unpacking those floats I brought so you can make sure none of them shattered in transit."

The other woman looked reluctant to leave but something in Anna's gaze must have convinced her to go. With one last glare at Grayson Fletcher, she headed for the stockroom.

As soon as she was out of earshot, Anna turned back to the man. "You are way out of line."

He shrugged. "Maybe. But if, say, I spoke to the local newspaper reporter covering the case, I could probably spin things exactly my way. You wouldn't look like the sainted victim then, would you?"

Anna opened her mouth to retort, but he cut her off before she could. "Of course, I could always keep my mouth shut, under the right circumstances."

"What circumstances?"

He shrugged. "If I *am* convicted on these bogus charges, maybe, just maybe, you could see your way clear to testifying on my behalf in the sentencing hearing."

She narrowed her gaze. "That sounds suspiciously like blackmail."

"Another ugly word. That's not it at all. I would just think in the interest of making things right, you would want to tell the judge you've had second thoughts and have had time to look at things a little differently," he said calmly.

She gazed at him for a long time. Just before Max was ready to step forward and kick the guy out of the store, she spoke in a quiet, determined voice.

"Go to hell, Grayson. Of course, I can comfort myself with the thought that by this time next week that's exactly where you're going to find yourself—the hell that passes for the Oregon State Penitentiary in Salem."

The other man's face turned a mottled red, until any trace of anything that might have been handsome turned ugly and mean. He took another step forward, not even stopping when Conan barked sharply.

"You should have left things alone." His low, intense voice dripped with rancor. "I would have paid everything back eventually. I was working on a plan. I tried to tell you that, but you were too damn uppity to listen. Well, you'll listen to me now. I have enough dirt on you that I can ruin you. You harassed me, you assaulted me, you threatened to fire me if I didn't sleep with you. That's the story I'm going to be feeding the pretty little local reporter. And then you framed me to hide your own crimes. When my civil suit is done, you're going to be lucky if I leave you with so much as a comic book. I'll take this store and your other one and that damn house you love so much. Then where will you be? A stone-cold bitch left with nothing."

She seemed to freeze, to shrink inside herself. Max, however, did not. He stepped away from the shelves and faced the other man down.

"Okay, time's up, bastard."

Anna lifted shocked eyes to his, as if she'd forgotten his presence. Max had dealt with enough of Fletcher's type in the military that he wasn't at all surprised to see his bullying bluster fade when confronted with direct challenge.

"Says who?" he asked warily.

"Between me and the dog, I think it's safe to say we can both make it clear you've outstayed your welcome."

Fletcher looked between Conan and Max, as if trying to figure out which of them posed the bigger threat, then he gave a hard laugh, regaining a little of his aplomb. "What are you going to do? Club me with your cast?"

Max gave the same grim, dangerous smile he used on recalcitrant trainees. "Try me."

The four of them stood in that tableau for several long seconds until Conan barked sharply, as if to add his two cents to the conversation. Fletcher stared at them again then gave Anna one last look of sheer loathing before he turned and stalked out of the store.

She wanted to die.

To walk down to the beach and dig the biggest, deepest hole she could manage and just bury herself inside it like a geoduck clam.

Bad enough that she had been caught unawares by Grayson and had stood there like an idiot letting him rant on and on with his damning—but completely ridiculous—allegations.

How much worse was it that Max had been a party to her disgrace?

Not exactly the best way to seduce a man, to show him unmistakable evidence what an idiot she was. When she remembered how she had actually thought she was coming to care for that piece of dirt, she just about thought she would be sick.

"Well, that was the single most humiliating ten minutes of my life."

Max moved closer and she alternated between wanting to bury her face in her hands so she didn't have to look at him and wanting to curl against that hard chest of his.

"You have no reason to feel humiliated. I'm the one who should feel humiliated. I didn't even get one good swing with my cast."

His disgruntled tone surprised a shaky laugh out of her. "I'm sure you can still chase him down at the bakery with his half-eaten croissant," she said. "Or send Conan over to bring him back."

"That kind of instant problem solving must be why you're the boss."

She laughed again, then realized her knees were wobbling. "Excuse me, I need to sit down."

She plopped down on the nearest couch, still fighting the greasy nausea in her belly, the sheer mortification that she had once been stupid and gullible enough to be attracted to a slimy worm like Grayson Fletcher.

"I told you my life was a mess."

"You've still got By-the-Wind."

"For now."

"Any chance he can make good on those threats?"

She sighed and pressed a hand to her stomach. Sexual harassment. How low could the man stoop?

"He can try, but there's absolutely no evidence backing him up. I refused to even date him for months. I didn't want any appearance of impropriety. The other employees can all confirm that. But he was so damn persistent and I was…flattered. That's what it comes down to. I only dated him for a month, but I swear I never slept with him."

Oh, why couldn't she keep her mouth shut? Did she really need to share that particular detail with Max?

"Then don't worry about it. I know his type. He's all bluff and bluster up front but the minute you confront him, he runs away like the rat he is."

"I'm just sorry you were tangled up in the middle."

"Funny, I was just thinking how glad I am that I was here to back you up."

She stared at him for a long moment, at the solid strength of his features, the integrity that seemed so much a part of him. The contrast between a sleazy, dishonest slimebag like Grayson Fletcher and this honorable soldier who had sacrificed so much for his country and still bore the scars for it was overwhelming.

"Thank you," she whispered.

With a full heart, she leaned across the space between them to kiss him softly. Compared to their heat and passion of the night before, this was just a tiny kiss of gratitude, just a slight brush of her lips against his, but it rocked her clear to her toes.

She was crazy about this man. She was aware she had only known him a few days but she was in serious danger of falling head over heels.

She eased away from him, feeling shaky and off balance.

"You're welcome," he murmured, and she wondered if she imagined that raspy note in his voice.

"What did I miss?"

At the sound of her employee's voice, Anna tried to collect her scattered wits. She took a deep breath and found Sue had come out of the stockroom carrying two of the colorful glass floats.

"Not much. He's gone."

"Good riddance. I don't care what you say, I'm calling the cops the next time he has the nerve to come in here."

"Sounds like a plan," Anna said. "Did I answer what you needed to know on canceling an order?"

"Yes. And now you need to get out of here and enjoy the rest of your day off." Sue had on that bossy mother-hen voice that Anna was helpless to fight. "Go have some fun. You deserve it."

She rubbed her hands on her slacks and turned back to Max as a customer came up to Sue and asked her for help locating an item.

"You're welcome to look around more if you'd like."

"I think I'm done here," he answered.

"Are you ready to go home, then?"

A strange light flickered in his eyes and she wondered at it, until she remembered his transitory life. The concept of home probably wasn't one he was used to considering.

"Good idea," he said after a moment, and his words were punctuated by Conan barking his approval.

DUSK WAS WASHING across the shore as they reached the outskirts of Cannon Beach and the setting sun cast long shadows across the road and saturated everything with color.

Brambleberry House on its hill looked graceful, welcoming, with its gables and gingerbread trim and the wide porch on all sides.

"I love coming home this time of day," she said as she pulled into the driveway. "I know it's silly but I always feel like the house has been waiting here all day just for me."

"It's not silly."

"Abigail used to say a house only comes alive when it's filled with people who love it." She smiled, remembering. "She used to have this quote on the wall. 'Every house where love abides and friendship is a guest, is surely home, and home, sweet home, for there the heart can rest.'"

He was quiet for a long time, gazing as she was at the house gleaming in the fading sunlight. "You do love it, don't you?" he asked, finally breaking the silence.

"With my whole heart. Rusty pipes, loose shingles, flaking paint and all."

"She knew what she was doing when she left it to you, didn't she?"

It seemed an odd question but she nodded. "I hope so. Sometimes I'm overwhelmed with the endless responsibility of it, especially when the rest of my life seems so chaotic right now. I have no idea why she left things as she did and bequeathed Brambleberry House to Sage and to me out of the blue, but I love it here. I can't imagine ever leaving."

He let out a breath, his eyes looking suddenly serious in the twilight. "Anna—"

Whatever he intended to say was lost when Conan began barking urgently from the cargo area of the van, as if he had expended every last ounce of patience.

She laughed. "Sorry. That sounds dire. I'd better take him down the beach a little to work out the kinks from the car ride. You interested?"

She thought she saw frustration flicker across his features but it was quickly gone.

"Sure. I've got kinks of my own to work out."

Conan leaped out of the van as soon as she hooked on his leash and practically dragged her behind him in his eagerness to mark every single clump of sea grass on the beach trail.

Just before they reached the wide stretch of beach, Max reached for her hand to help her around a rock and he didn't let go. They walked hand in hand with Conan ahead of them and warmth fluttered through her despite the cool spring wind.

She didn't want to the day to end. Even with the humiliation of the encounter with Gray Fletcher, it had been wonderful, the most enjoyable day she'd spent in longer than she could remember.

Conan obviously didn't share her sentiments, however. The dog could usually run for miles along the beach at any time of the day or night. But though he had been so insistent earlier, as soon as he had taken care of his pressing need, now he didn't seem nearly as enthusiastic to be walking. One moment he planted his haunches stubbornly in the sand, the next he tried to tug her back the direction they had come.

The third time he tried the trick, she gave a tug on the leash. "You don't know what you want, do you?"

"As a matter of fact, I do."

She looked over at Max and found him watching her in the fading sunlight, a glittery look in his hazel eyes that made her catch her breath.

"I was talking to Conan," she murmured. "He's

being stubborn about the walk. I think he's ready to
go back."

"Not yet," Max said quietly.

Before she could ask him why not, he pulled her
against him as the sun slid farther down the horizon.

All the heat and wonder they had shared the night
before during the storm came rushing back like the tide
and she couldn't seem to get enough of him.

She tried to be careful of his sling and his arm but
he lifted the sling out of the way so he could pull her
against his chest.

He kissed her for long moments, until they were
both breathing hard and the sun was only a pale rim
on the horizon.

"If we keep this up, we're going to be stuck down
here in the dark and won't be able to find our way
back."

"Conan will lead the way," she murmured against
his mouth. "He hasn't had dinner yet."

He laughed roughly and kissed her again. She
wrapped her arms around his waist, a slow heat churning through her. She couldn't seem to get close enough
to him, to absorb his hard strength and the safe harbor
she felt here.

She didn't know how long they stood there accompanied by the murmur of the sea, a salty breeze eddy-
ing around them. She would have been quite content
to stay all night if Conan hadn't finally barked with
thinly veiled impatience.

The moon had started to rise above the coastal
range, a thin sliver of light, but all was dark and mysterious around them.

"I guess we should probably head back."

She couldn't see his features but she was quite sure she sensed the same reluctance that was coursing through her.

Somehow she wasn't surprised when he pulled a flashlight from his keychain in the pocket of his leather bomber. He was a soldier, no doubt prepared for anything.

"I don't have night-vision goggles with me so this will have to do," Max said. He reached for her hand and they walked back up the beach toward Brambleberry House, whose lights gleamed a welcome in the darkness.

Her insides jumped wildly with nerves and anticipation. She didn't want this to end but how could she possibly scramble for the courage to tell him she wanted more?

They said little as they made their way back home. Even in his silence, though, she sensed he was withdrawing from her, trying to put distance between them again.

Her instinct was confirmed when they reached the house. She unlocked her apartment and opened the door for Conan to bound inside to find his food. She and Max stood in the foyer and she didn't miss the tight set of his features.

Desperate to regain the fleeting closeness, she drew in a shaky breath and lifted her mouth to his again.

After a moment's hesitation, he returned the kiss with an almost fierce hunger, until her thoughts whirled and her body strained against him.

After a long moment, he wrenched his mouth away. "Anna, I need to tell you something."

Whatever it was, she didn't want to hear it. Somehow she knew instinctively it was something she wouldn't like and right now she couldn't bear for anything to ruin the magic of this moment.

"Just kiss me, Max. Please."

He groaned softly but after a moment's hesitation he obliged, tangling his mouth with hers again and again until nothing else mattered but the two of them and the fragile emotions fluttering in her chest.

"I have been trying to figure out all day how to seduce you," she admitted softly.

His laugh was rough and strummed down her nerve endings. "I think it's safe to say you don't have to do anything but exist. That's more seduction than I can handle right now."

She smiled with the heady joy rushing through her. He made her feel delicate and beautiful, powerful in a way she had never known before.

"Come inside," she said, her voice soft.

He froze and she knew she didn't mistake the indecision on his features. "Anna, are you sure?"

"Please," she murmured.

With a ragged sigh, he yanked her against him and an exultant joy surged through her.

This was right. She was crazy about him, she thought. Head-over-heels crazy about this man.

She knew he wasn't going to be here forever, that he wanted to return to active duty as soon as possible and she would be alone again.

But for now, this moment, he was hers and she

wasn't going to waste this precious chance fate had handed her.

A soft, silken spell wove around them as they kissed their way inside her bedroom.

The rest of her house was tasteful and subdued, all whites on wood tones. Her bedroom was different. It was soft and feminine, with lavenders and greens and yellows.

How was it possible that Max could seem so overwhelmingly masculine amid all the girly stuff, the flounces and frills? she wondered. He had never seemed so dangerously, enticingly male.

She led the way to her bed, with its filmy white hangings and mounds of pillows. Max looked at the bed for a moment then back at her and his expression was raw with desire.

"I should probably warn you I haven't done this in a while. I've been redshirted for a while with my injury and before that I was in a country where there wasn't a hell of a lot of opportunity for extracurricular activities."

She couldn't seem to think with these nerves skating through her. "Good to know. I haven't, either. My engagement ended five years ago and I haven't been with anyone else."

His eyes darkened, until the pupils nearly obscured the green-gray of the irises.

"I don't know if I can take things slowly. At least not the first time."

She smiled. "Good."

He gave a rough laugh and kissed her again, then lowered her to the bed. "As much as I want nothing more than to take hours undressing you and exploring every inch of that glorious skin, I'm a little clumsy with buttons right now. With this damn cast, I can barely work my own."

"I've got two hands," she answered. Her fingers trembled a little as she slowly worked the buttons of her shirt and pulled her arms free. At least she had worn one of her favorite bra-and-panty sets, a lacy creation in the palest peach.

He swallowed hard. "I definitely don't think I can take things slowly."

He pressed his mouth to her bared shoulder, then trailed kisses along the skin just above the scalloped edge of her bra. She shivered, arching against him as he slid a hand along the bared skin at her waist then up until he touched her intimately through the lace.

She wanted more. She wanted to feel his skin on hers. He must have shared her hunger because he pulled the sling off, revealing the cast underneath that ran from his wrist to just above his elbow and began working the buttons of his shirt.

"Let me help," she said.

He leaned back to give her more access and she helped him out of his shirt and then went to work on the snaps on his Levi's.

"I can take it from here," he told her.

In moments, they were both naked and he was everything she might have dreamed, all hard muscles and lean strength.

Then she caught her first view of the full extent of his injuries and her heart turned over in her chest.

For some reason, she had thought the damage was

contained to his arm and shoulder. But rough, red-looking burns spread out from his collarbone to his pectoral muscles on the right side, crisscrossed by scars that were still blinding white against his skin.

"Oh, Max," she breathed.

Regret slid across his features. "I should have kept my shirt on. I'm so used to it by now I forget how ugly it is."

"No. No, you shouldn't have. I am so sorry you had to go through that."

She pressed her mouth just above the raw-looking skin at the spot where his shoulder met his neck, then again in the hollow above his collarbone.

"Does it hurt?"

He looked as if he wanted to deny it but he finally shrugged. "Sometimes. Right now, no. Right now, all I can think about is the incredibly sexy woman in my arms. Come up here and kiss me."

"Absolutely, Lieutenant," she said with a smile and settled in his arms.

They kissed and touched for a long time, exploring all the planes and hollows and secret places while those tensile emotions twisted through her, wrapping her closer to him.

He said he couldn't take things slowly but it seemed to her their teasing and touching lasted for hours. At last, when she wasn't sure she could endure another moment, he braced above her on his left forearm and he entered her.

She gasped his name and tightened her arms around him, hunger soaring inside her like bright, colorful kites on the wild air currents of the beach.

Had she ever known this sense of wonder, the feeling of completion, that scattered pieces of herself had only right this moment fallen into place?

She was floating higher and higher, her heart as light as air as he moved inside her, slowly at first and then faster, his mouth hard and urgent on hers with a possessive stamp that thrilled her to the core.

She held tight to him, her body rising to meet his, and then he pushed slightly harder and she gasped suddenly as she broke free of gravity and went soaring into the air.

He groaned her name, then with one last powerful surge he joined her.

Oh, heaven. This was heaven. She held him tightly as a delicious lassitude slid over her.

CHAPTER THIRTEEN

ABIGAIL WOULD HAVE APPROVED.

Anna lay next to Max, her arm across him, feeling his chest rise and fall with each slow, steady breath as he slept. Pale moonlight filtered in through her open window and played across his features, and she thought how vulnerable he looked in sleep, years younger than the hard-eyed soldier he appeared at times.

Abigail would have loved him. She didn't quite know why she was so certain but somehow she knew her friend would have been quick to include him in the loose circle of friends that Sage had called her lost sheep—people who were lonely or tired or grieving or who just needed to know someone else believed in them.

Max would have been drawn into that circle, whether he wanted it or not. Abigail would have taken him in, would have filled him with good food to ease all the hollows from those months in the hospital. If he ended up leaving the army, Abigail would have been right there helping him figure out his place in the world.

He made a soft sound in his sleep and her arm tightened around him. She rested her cheek against his smooth, hard chest, astonished at the sense of peace she found here in his arms, the tenderness that seemed to wind through her with silken ties.

She was in love with him.

The truth shimmered through her, bright and stunning, and she drew in a sharp breath, astonished and suddenly terrified.

Love. That wasn't in the plan. She was supposed to be having a casual fling, nothing more. The man had made no secret of his plans to leave as soon as he could. This whole situation seemed destined for disaster.

He wasn't the stick-around type. He couldn't have made that more plain. He had told her himself that he considered his base in Iraq more of a home than anywhere else he had lived. She remembered how sad that had seemed when he told her. It was even more tragic now that she had come to know him better, since she had seen a certain yearning in his eyes when he looked at Brambleberry House.

He needs a home. A place to belong. That's what he's always needed.

The words whispered into her mind and she frowned. Why on earth would such a thought even enter her mind, let alone with such firm assurance? It made absolutely no sense, but she couldn't shake the unswerving conviction that Harry Maxwell needed Brambleberry House, maybe more even than she did.

She couldn't make him stay. She knew that with the same conviction. She might want him to, with sudden, fierce desperation, but she couldn't hold him here.

When his shoulder healed, he would return to his unit, to his helicopter, and would go wherever he was needed, no matter how dangerous.

Even if his arm didn't heal as well as he hoped, she couldn't see him sticking around. Brambleberry House was a temporary stop on his life's journey and there was nothing she could do to change that.

She sighed, just a tiny breath of air, but it was enough to awaken him. Watching him come back to consciousness was a fascinating experience. No doubt it was the soldier in him but he didn't ease into wakefulness, he just instantly blinked his eyes open.

Her brothers always told her she did the same thing—one minute, she could be in deep REM sleep, the next she was wide-awake and ready to rock and roll.

They used to tease her that she slept with the proverbial one eye open, as if she was afraid one of them would sneak into her room during the night and steal her dolls. Not that she ever had many, but could she help it if she liked to protect what little she had from pesky older brothers?

"Hi," Max murmured, a sexy rasp to his voice, and Anna forgot all about brothers and dolls and sleeping.

"Hi yourself." She smiled, determined to savor every single moment she had with him. Why waste time wishing he could be a different sort of man, the kind who might be happy rattling around an old house like this for the rest of his life?

"Have I been asleep long?"

She shook her head. "A half hour, maybe."

"Sorry. I didn't mean to doze off on you."

"I didn't mind. It was…nice." A major understatement, but she wasn't about to risk scaring him off by revealing just how much she had treasured a quiet moment to savor being in his arms.

He gazed down at her, an oddly tender expression in his hazel eyes that stole her breath and left her stomach doing cartwheels again.

"It has been. Everything. I never expected this, Anna. You have to know that."

She smiled, her heart full and light. "I didn't, either. But a gift can be all the more rare and precious when it's unexpected."

"Is that more of Abigail's wisdom?"

"No. Just mine."

With surprising dexterity, he tugged her with his left arm so she was lying across his chest, then he twisted his hand in her hair so he could angle her mouth to meet his kiss. "You are a wise woman, Anna Galvez."

She smiled. "I don't know about that. But I'm learning."

They kissed and touched and explored for a long time there in the dark, quiet intimacy of her room. At last he pulled her atop him, letting her set the pace.

Their first union had been all heat and fire. This was slower, sweet and sexy and tender all at the same time.

I love you.

She almost blurted the words just before she found release again, but she caught them in her throat before she could do something so foolish.

He wasn't ready to hear them yet—and she wasn't sure she was ready to say them.

IT TOOK A long time for his heartbeat to slow back to anything resembling a normal pace. He lay in the dark watching the moonlight dance across the room and listening to Anna breathe beside him.

The soft tenderness seeping through his insides scared the hell out of him.

This wasn't supposed to happen. He wasn't supposed to care so much. But somehow this woman, with her tough shell that he had discovered hid a fragile, vulnerable core, had become fiercely important to him.

She soothed him. He didn't know how she did it but these last few days with her had been filled with a quiet peace he only now realized had been missing since his helicopter crashed.

He had been so damn restless since he was injured. But with Anna, the future didn't seem like a scary place anymore. She made him think he could handle whatever came along.

Except telling her the truth.

He let out a long, slow breath, guilt pinching away at the tranquility of the moment. He had to tell her Abigail was his aunt. The very fact that he was lying in her bed having this conversation with himself while she was naked and warm in his arms was evidence that he had allowed the deception to go on far too long.

But how, exactly, was he supposed to tell her that now? She would be furious and hurt, especially after they had shared this.

He stared up at the ceiling, trying to figure out his options. He ached at the idea of hurting her but he couldn't see any way out of it. Maybe it would be best all the way around if he just left town before this could go on any further.

She would be hurt and baffled if he suddenly disappeared. But what would hurt her more—wondering why he left or discovering he had deceived her, that he had slept with her under false pretenses?

What he had done was unconscionable. He could fool himself that his intentions had been honorable, that he had only wanted to make sure Abigail had been competent in her last wishes when she left the house to Anna and Sage Benedetto. He had been compelled to do something, if only to assuage his own guilt over his negligence these last few years.

Then he had come to Brambleberry House and Anna had made Abigail's French toast for him and bandaged his wounds and kissed him senseless and everything had become so damn tangled.

He hated the idea of leaving her. It seemed the height of cowardice, especially after what they had shared tonight. But what would cause the least harm to her?

"Will you come with me next week when the verdict is read?"

Her voice in the darkness startled him and he shifted his gaze from the ceiling to see her watching him out of those huge dark eyes.

"I thought you were asleep," he said.

"No. I was just thinking."

"About the trial?"

"Sorry. Everything comes back to that right now. I'll be so glad when it's over."

He kissed her forehead, pulling her into a more comfortable position. "It's been rougher on you than you let on, hasn't it?"

She didn't answer but he thought her arms tightened around him. "I've been okay. I have. I just… I think I could use someone else in my corner during the verdict. Would you come?"

Like his aunt, Anna was a strong, independent woman. He had a feeling asking for anything was difficult for her. The fact she had asked him to stand by her touched him deeply.

He could stay a few more days. He owed her that, and perhaps giving her the support she needed at this critical time would be a small way to atone for his deception.

"Yeah. Sure. I'll come with you," he answered. "And if he's found not guilty, we've always got clubbing him senseless with my cast to fall back on as Plan B."

She laughed and kissed him. He pulled her close, pushing away the chiding voice of his conscience for now.

A few more days of this sweet, seductive peace. That's all he wanted. Surely that wasn't too much to ask.

"ARE YOU READY for this?" Max asked her three days later as they sat on a park bench outside her store in Lincoln City enjoying the afternoon sunshine, the first since Sunday.

She made a face, her stomach fluttering with nerves. "Do I have a choice?"

"You always have a choice. You could just forget the whole thing and catch the next fishing boat out of town. Or I could make a phone call, get us a helicopter in here to fly us down the coast to an excellent crab shack I've heard about in Bandon."

"You're not helping."

He gave her an unrepentant grin and she couldn't help thinking how much lighter he had seemed these last few days. The occasional shadow still showed up in his gaze but he laughed more and seemed far more comfortable with the world.

The time they'd spent together since Sunday night had seemed magical. She never would have expected it, but the last two days of the trial passed with amazing swiftness. Even listening to the defense's closing arguments, where she had been painted as everything from an incompetent manager to a corrupt manipulator, hadn't stung as much as it might have a few days earlier.

Now she saw it for what it was—Grayson's desperate ploy to escape justice.

Between the trial and trying to stay on top of administrative duties at both stores, her days had been as packed and chaotic as always.

But the nights.

They had been sheer heaven.

When she returned to Brambleberry House Monday night, Max and Conan had been waiting for her with what he called his specialty—take-out Chinese. After dinner, Max started a fire in her fireplace and read a thriller with Conan at his feet while Anna did payroll and caught up on paperwork.

Eventually she gave up trying to concentrate with all this heat jumping through her insides. She had joined him on the couch and Max had tossed her reading glasses aside and kissed her while rain clicked against the window and Conan snored softly beside them.

Later—much later—she had fallen asleep holding his hand.

Tuesday had been largely a repeat, except he had grilled steaks for her out in the rain while she held an umbrella over his head and laughed at the picture he made in one of Abigail's frilly flowered aprons.

That was the moment she knew with certainty that what she felt for him wasn't some passing infatuation, that she was hopelessly in love with him—with this wounded soldier with the slow smile and the secrets in his eyes.

She had no idea what she was going to do about it—except for now, she was going to live in the moment and enjoy every second she had with him.

Her cell phone rang suddenly and she jumped and stared at it.

"Are you going to get that?" Max asked.

"I'm working up to it."

She knew it must be the prosecutor, calling to tell her the verdict was in and about to be read.

The jury had been deliberating for four hours and Max had been with her for two of those hours. She had called him as soon as the jury had started deliberations and he had rushed down to Lincoln City immediately, even after she told him it might be hours—or possibly days—before the jurors reached a verdict.

She was immeasurably touched that he had kept his promise to come with her when the verdict was read—and she was grateful now as she answered her phone with fingers that trembled.

"Hello?" she said.

"They're back," the prosecutor said. "Can you be here in fifteen minutes?"

"Yes. I'll be right there."

She hung up the phone and sat, feeling numb and shaky at the same time.

Max reached for her hand. "Come on. I'll drive your car. We can come back for mine."

He kept his hand linked with hers as they walked into the courthouse. "What will you do if he's exonerated?" he asked, the question she had been dreading.

A few days ago, she was quite certain that possibility would have devastated her. But she had learned she had a great deal in common with Abigail's favorite sea creatures. Like the by-the-wind sailors her store was named for, she would float where fate took her and manage to adapt. Even on that fishing boat Max joked about.

"I'll survive," she said. "What else can I do?"

He squeezed her fingers and didn't let go as they walked into the courtroom and sat down.

So much of her life the last several months had been tied up with this trial but in the end, the verdict was almost anticlimactic. When the jury foreman read that jurors had found Grayson Fletcher guilty on all counts of fraud, Anna let out a tiny sob of relief and Max immediately wrapped her in his arms and kissed her.

Max stayed by her side as she hugged the prosecutor, who had worked so tirelessly for conviction, and as she received encouraging words from several others in the community who had come to hear the verdict.

She finally allowed herself to glance at Grayson and found him looking pale and stunned, as if he couldn't quite believe it was real. A tiny measure of pity flickered through her, even though she knew he deserved the consequences for what he had done.

Still, she wasn't going to hold a grudge the rest of her life, she decided. Life was just too short for her to be bitter and angry at being duped.

"We need to celebrate," Max said after they left the courtroom. "I'm taking you to dinner tonight. Where would you like to go?"

"The Sea Urchin," she said promptly, without taking even a moment to think about her answer. "Sage's husband owns it and since it's a Spencer Hotels property, of course it's fabulous. The food there is unbelievable. The best on the coast."

"I love a woman who knows what she wants."

If only he truly meant his words, she thought, then pushed the thought away. She was deliriously happy right now and she wasn't going to spoil it by worrying about the future.

SHE HAD A hard-and-fast rule never to use her cell phone while she was driving except in an absolute emergency, especially on the sometimes curvy coastal road, but she was severely tempted as she drove her van home from Lincoln City to phone everyone in her address book to give them the happy news.

She restrained herself, focusing instead on following Max's SUV, since they had both driven down separately, and trying to contain the happiness bubbling through her.

Still, even before she had a chance to greet Conan, her cell phone rang the moment she walked in the door at Brambleberry House. She grinned when she saw Sage's name and number on the caller ID.

"All right, that's just spooky. How did you know the verdict was in?" she asked, without even saying hello.

Sage shrieked. "It is? I had no idea! Sue called me from the store hours ago when the jury went out for deliberation. I was just checking the status of things since I haven't heard from you. Tell me!"

Anna took a deep breath, thinking again how her life had changed since she inherited this house. A year ago, she would have had no one to share this excitement with except her employees. Now she had dear friends who loved her. She was truly a lucky woman.

"Guilty. Guilty, guilty, guilty!"

"Yes!" She heard Sage shouting the news to Eben and even over the phone, Anna could hear her husband's delighted exclamation.

"Oh, that's wonderful news. I hope they throw the book at the little pissant."

"This, from the world's biggest bleeding heart?" she teased.

"I care about things that deserve my time and energy," Sage said primly. "Grayson Fletcher does not."

"True enough," Anna replied.

"Oh, I'm so happy. I'm only sorry I wasn't there. With Julia gone, too, you're not going to have anyone to celebrate with!"

"Am, too," she answered. "For your information, I'm going to the Sea Urchin for dinner with Max."

There was a long, pregnant silence on the other end of the phone. "Max? Upstairs Max?"

Anna smiled, wondering how he would react to that particular nickname. "That's right."

"All right. What other secrets have you been keeping from me, you sly thing?"

Anna grimaced. She probably shouldn't have let that slip. But now that she had, she knew she wouldn't be able to fool Sage for long. "Nothing. Well, not much, anyway. It's just that Upstairs Max has been spending most of his time downstairs the last few days," she finally confessed.

That long pause greeted her again. "So does Conan like him?"

"Adores him. He treats him like his long-lost best friend."

"And have you smelled any freesia lately?"

Anna made a face. "Cut it out. Abigail's not matchmaking in this situation. She must be taking a break."

"Or maybe he's not the one for you."

Her heart gave a sharp little tug. "Of course he's not," she answered promptly. "He's only here a short time and then he's leaving again. I know that perfectly well."

"Are you sure?"

She wasn't certain of anything, other than that she was fiercely in love with Harry Maxwell. But she wasn't about to reveal that little tidbit of information to Sage.

"You know I'm going to insist on a full report from Julia as soon as she gets back. And the minute we get back to the States, I'm coming up there, even if I have to use up all my carbon offsets for the year."

"Sage, honey, stop worrying about me, okay? You

don't have to come up here to babysit me. Max is a wonderful man and I know you'll love him. But I also know this is only temporary. I'm fine with that."

After she hung up the phone some time later, those words continued to echo through her mind. Had she ever lied to Sage before? She couldn't remember. This one was a doozy, though. She wasn't fine. No matter how cool and sophisticated she tried to be about things, she knew she would be devastated when he left.

And he would leave. She knew that, somewhere deep inside of her, with a certainty she couldn't explain. Her time with him was limited. Even now, he could be preparing to leave.

Fight for him. He needs you.

The words whispered through her mind, so strong and compelling that she looked around the room to find a source.

He needs you.

The smell of freesia floated across the room and Conan looked up from his rug, thumped his tail on the floor, then went back to sleep.

Anna shivered, her heart pounding, then she quickly caught herself before her imagination went crazy. That's what happened when she talked to Sage. She lost every ounce of common sense and started believing in ghosts.

Not that it was bad advice. If she loved Max, shouldn't she be willing to fight for the man?

Starting tonight, she decided, and went to her closet for her favorite dress, a shimmery sheath in pale green that made her dark skin and hair look exotic and sultry.

She might not have a matchmaking ghost on her side, but she could take control of her own fate.

Max wouldn't know what hit him.

CHAPTER FOURTEEN

MAX RANG THE doorbell to Anna's apartment, aware of the sense of foreboding in his gut.

He was going to tell her tonight after dinner. No more excuses. He had put things off far too long and the time had come to confess everything. Maybe she would be so happy at the guilty verdict that she would be in a forgiving sort of mood.

Or maybe she would evict him and throw all his belongings out of her house.

He hoped not. He hoped she would find it in her to understand his motives. But either way, he owed her the truth.

Conan barked behind the door and a moment later, it swung open, revealing a vision in pale green.

From the first time he saw her, Max had considered Anna Galvez beautiful, with those huge brown eyes and her glossy dark hair and classically lovely features.

But right now she was truly breathtaking.

She had piled her hair up in a loose, feminine style, with curls dripping everywhere. She wore a sexy dream of a dress with a low back that showed off fine-boned shoulders and all that luscious skin of hers. She also wore more jewelry than he'd seen on her—a diamond

choker and matching bracelet and slim, dangly ear-
rings that glittered in the foyer light.

She looked lush and sensual and he wanted to stand
in the foyer of Brambleberry House all night just looking at her.

"Wow," he murmured. "You look incredible. I know
that sounds completely lame but I can't think of another word for it."

"Incredible is good." She smiled. "Come in. I'm
just about ready."

He wanted to devour her but he was afraid of mess-
ing up perfection so he stood inside the doorway while
she picked up a filmy scarf from a side table and
wrapped it around her shoulders, then grabbed one of
those tiny little evening bags women managed to cram
huge amounts of paraphernalia into.

Conan padded over to her wearing one of his pathetic take-me-with-you looks. The dog brushed
against her and Max held his breath. Meredith—hell,
most women he knew—would have gone ballistic to
have dog hairs on one of her fancy party dresses but
Anna simply laughed and scratched the dog's chin.

"I'm sorry, bud, but you know you can't go with
us to the Sea Urchin. You wouldn't want to. You'd be
bored senseless, I promise. But we'll be back later and
we'll play then."

The dog heaved a massive sigh and headed for his
favorite rug, but in that instant, that tiny interaction,
Max felt as if the entire house had just collapsed on
top of him.

Emotions washed through him, thick and raw and
terrifying, and for an instant of panic, he wanted to

turn on his heels and walk out of Brambleberry House and just keep on going.

He was in love with Anna Galvez. Not because she was achingly beautiful or because she made his heart race and the blood pool in his gut.

But because she was strong and courageous and smart and she made him believe in himself again.

He was in love with her. How the hell had that happened?

One minute, his life had been going along just fine. Okay, maybe not perfect. His shoulder problems were proving to be a major pain and he had no idea if he would still be in the army in a few weeks. But he had been dealing with the setbacks in his own way.

And then this woman, with her stubborn independence and her brilliant smile and her ambitious dreams, had knocked him on his butt. She talked to her dog and she knew her way around a wood chipper and she filled his soul with a peace he never realized had been missing.

"Max? Is everything okay?"

How long had he been staring at her? Too long, obviously. He drew in a ragged breath and realized she was watching him with concern while Conan seemed to be grinning at him.

"Yeah. Yeah. Fine. You just dazzle me."

He could tell she thought he was talking about her appearance and he decided not to correct the misconception.

"Thank you." She smiled. "The jewelry is Abigail's. She never went anywhere, even to the grocery store, without glittery stuff dripping from every available surface. She used to tell me, 'My dear girl, a woman my age has to use every available means at her disposal to distract the eye from all these wrinkles.'"

He could hear Abigail saying exactly that and he suddenly missed his aunt desperately.

"You don't need any jewels," he said. "You're stunning enough without them. The most beautiful woman I've ever known."

Her mouth parted slightly as her eyes softened. "Oh, Max," she whispered. "I do believe that's the sweetest thing anyone has ever said to me."

"It's the truth," he said gruffly.

She smiled with stunning sweetness and stepped forward to press her mouth against his.

His heart seemed to flop around in his chest like a rockfish on the line and he could barely breathe around the tenderness inside him. He kissed her, almost desperate with the need to touch her, taste her, burn every moment of this in his mind.

The magic he always found with her began to coil and twine around them and he closed his eyes as she wrapped her arms around his neck, holding him as if she couldn't bear to let go.

He was wondering just how long it might take for her to fix herself up again if he messed up all this perfection when Conan suddenly barked urgently and raced to the door.

A moment later, he heard the front door to the house open and children's laughter echo through the house.

Anna pulled away from him with a startled gasp, then her face lit up with joy. If she was breathtaking before, right now with her eyes bright and a wide smile lighting her features, she was simply staggering.

"They're back!" she exclaimed.

He couldn't seem to make his brain work. "Who?"

"Julia and the twins! Oh, this just makes this entire day perfect. Come on, you've got to meet them."

She looked a little windblown from the passion of their kiss but she linked her hand with his and opened the door. Conan rushed out first, just about tripping over his feet in his rush to greet two dark-haired children who were starting up the stairs, their arms loaded with backpacks.

"Conan!" both children shouted, dropping their bundles and hurrying back down the stairs.

The dog barked and jumped around them, licking first one and then the other while the boy and girl giggled and hugged him.

"Hey, I need a little of that love."

"Anna Banana!"

The little boy jumped up from hugging the dog and launched himself at Anna. She gave him a tight hug then turned to gather the less rambunctious girl to her as well.

"How are you, my darlings? I know you've only been gone a week, but I swear you've grown a foot in that time! What have you been eating, Maddie? Ice cream for breakfast, lunch and dinner?"

The girl giggled and shook her head. "Nope. Only for breakfast and lunch. We had pizza and cheeseburgers the rest of the time."

"You've been living large in Montana, haven't you?"

"We had tons of fun, Anna! You should have come

with us! We went on a horseback ride and we went sledding and skiing and then we went to Boise and visited Grandma and Grandpa for three whole days," the boy exclaimed.

The girl—Maddie—dimpled at her. "You look su-perpretty, Anna. Are you going to a ball?"

Anna smiled and hugged her again. "No, sweet-heart. Just to dinner at Chloe's dad's hotel."

"Ooh, will you bring me a fortune cookie?" the boy asked. "I love their fortune cookies."

"I'll see what I can do," Anna promised, just as a slim blonde woman tromped through the door carry-ing a suitcase in each arm. She dropped them as soon as she walked into the foyer and saw Anna greeting the children, and Max watched while the two women embraced.

"I just heard. Sage just called me. Oh, Anna, I'm so happy about the guilty verdict. Will is, too."

"Yeah," Maddie said with a grin. "You should have heard him yelling in the car. My ears still hurt!"

Anna laughed and looked behind them. "Where is Will?"

"He's getting the rest of our luggage off the roof rack. He should be here in a moment."

The woman glanced over Anna's shoulder at Max and though she gave him a friendly smile, he thought he saw a kind of protective wariness there. It made him wonder what Anna might have told her friends about him.

"Hi," she said. "You must be Harry Maxwell."

The false name scraped against his conscience like

metal on metal. He didn't know what to say, loath to perpetuate the lie any more than he already had.

Anna saved him from having to come up with a response. "I'm sorry," she exclaimed with a distracted laugh. "I was so happy to see you all again, I forgot my manners. Max, this is Julia Blair and her children Maddie and Simon. Julia, this is Lieutenant Harry Maxwell."

He nodded hello, then reached forward to shake Julia's outstretched hand.

"We're interrupting something, aren't we?" she said. "You both look wonderful and you're obviously on your way out."

"We're heading to the Sea Urchin to celebrate the verdict," Anna said.

"We can do it another time," Max offered. "I'm sure you two probably want to catch up."

"No, go on. Keep your plans," Julia said. "We can catch up later tonight over tea when the kids are in bed."

Max said nothing, though he thought with fleeting regret of the last two nights when he had slept with her in his arms.

"I was going to shut Conan in my apartment while we're at dinner but you're certainly welcome to take him upstairs with you. I'm sure he'll be so much help while you're trying to unpack."

"Thanks," the other woman said dryly.

"Let me help you with your luggage," Max said.

Julia gave a surprised glance at his omni-present sling. "You don't have to do that."

"You'd better let him," Anna said with a laugh. "The man doesn't take no for an answer."

"Doesn't he?" Julia murmured.

Max felt his face heat and decided he would be wise to beat a hasty retreat. He picked up one of the suitcases and carried it up and set it on the landing outside the second-floor apartment. He was just heading back down for the second suitcase, when he heard a male voice from the foyer below.

"We were only gone eight days. Why, again, did we need all these suitcases?"

Max froze on the stairway, his heart stuttering. He knew the owner of that voice.

And worse, the man knew him.

"Wow, ANNA. You look fabulous!"

Anna beamed at Will Garrett, who lived three houses down. Will was not only a gifted carpenter who had done most of the renovation work on Brambleberry House but, more importantly, he was a dear friend.

"I would say the same for you if I could see you behind all the suitcases," she said with a laugh.

"Here. How's that?" He set down the luggage and pulled her into a close hug. She hugged him back, her heart lifting at the smile he gave her. Every time she saw Will, she marveled at the changes in him these last six months since he and Julia had fallen in love again.

Before Julia and her twins came to Brambleberry House, Will had been a far different man. He had been lost in grief for his wife and daughter who had been killed in a car accident three years ago.

Anna had grieved with him for Robin and Cara. She

and Sage—and Abigail, before her death—had worried for him as he pulled away from their close circle of friends, drawing inside himself in the midst of his terrible pain.

They had all rejoiced when Julia moved in upstairs and they learned she had been his first love, when they were just teenagers.

The two of them had rediscovered that love and together, Julia and her twins had helped Will begin to heal.

"I heard the good news about that idiot Fletcher," Will said, too low for the children to overhear. "I couldn't be happier that he's finally getting what's coming to him. Maybe now you can put the whole thing behind you and move forward."

She thought of the progress she had made, how she had brooded far too long about everything. Her perspective had changed these last few days, she realized, thanks in large part to Max.

She *was* ready to move forward, to refocus her efforts on saving both stores. Through hard work, she had built something good and worthwhile. She couldn't just give up all that because of a setback like Gray Fletcher.

She looked up and saw Max standing motionless on the stairs. She smiled up at him, awash in gratitude for these last few days and the confidence he had helped her find again.

"I need to introduce you to our new tenant. Will, this is—"

He followed her gaze and suddenly his eyes lit up. "Max! What are you doing here?"

Max walked slowly down the stairs and Anna

frowned when Will gave him that shoulder tap thing men did that seemed the equivalent to the hug of greeting she and Julia had shared.

"Why didn't anybody tell me you were living upstairs? This is wonderful news. Abigail would have been thrilled that you've finally come home."

Anna stared between the two men. Will looked delighted, while Max's expression had reverted to that stony, stoic look he had worn so often when he first arrived at the house.

Her pulse seemed unnaturally loud in her ears as she tried to make sense of this new turn of events. "I don't understand," she finally said. "You two know each other?"

"Know each other? Of course!" Will exclaimed. "We hung out all the time, whenever he would visit his aunt. A couple weeks every summer."

"His...aunt?"

Will gave her an odd look. "Abigail! This is her nephew. The long-lost soldier, Max Harrison."

Anna drew in a sharp breath, her solar plexus contracting as if someone had socked her in the gut. She stared at Max, who swallowed hard but didn't say anything.

"That's impossible," she exclaimed. "Abigail's nephew's name was Jamie. Not Harry or Max. *Her Jamie.* That's what she always called him."

"My full name is Maxwell James Harrison. Abigail was the only one who called me Jamie."

She was going to hyperventilate for the first time in her life. She could feel the breath being slowly squeezed from her lungs. "Max Harrison—Harry Maxwell. I'm such an idiot. Why didn't I figure it out?"

"I can explain if you'll let me."

Lies. Everything they shared was lies. She had kissed him, held him, slept with him, for heaven's sake. And it had all been a lie.

She pressed a hand to her stomach, to the nausea curling there. First Grayson and now Max. Did she wear some invisible sign on her forehead that said Gullible Fool Here?

All her joy in the day, the triumph of the guilty verdict, the fledgling hope that she could now regain her life seemed to crumble away like leaves underfoot.

Julia, with her usual perception, must have sensed some of what was racing through Anna's head. She quickly stepped in to take control of the situation.

"Will, kids, let's get these suitcases out of the entryway and upstairs to the apartment. Come on."

The children grumbled but they grabbed their backpacks and trudged up the stairs, Conan racing ahead of them in his excitement at having them all back.

In moments, the chaos and bustle of their homecoming was reduced to a tense and ugly silence as she gazed at the man she thought she had fallen in love with.

Most people call me Max. She remembered his words, which very well might have been the only honest thing he had said to her since he moved in.

She moved numbly back into her apartment, only vaguely aware that he had followed her inside.

A hundred thoughts raced through her head but she could only focus on one.

"You lied to me."

"Yes," he answered. Just that, nothing else.

"What am I missing here?" she asked. "Why would you possibly feel like you had to lie about your relationship with Abigail and use a false name?"

He rubbed a hand at the base of his neck. "It was a stupid idea. Monumentally stupid. All I can say is that it seemed like a good idea at the time."

"That tells me nothing! Who wakes up in the morning and says, 'gosh, I think I'll create a false identity today, just for kicks'?"

"It wasn't like that."

"Then explain it to me!"

Her hands were shaking, she realized. This felt worse than the slick, greasy feeling in her stomach when her accountant had discovered the first hint of wrongdoing at the store. She was very much afraid she was going to be sick and she did her best to fight down the nausea.

"I was stationed in Fallujah when Abigail died. I didn't even know she died until several months later."

"Wrong!" she exclaimed. "Sage notified Abigail's family. I know she did! Not that it did any good. Not a single family member bothered to come to her funeral."

"Sage notified my mother. Not the same thing at all. I told you my relationship with my mother is difficult at best and she never liked Abigail. The only reason she let me come here all those summers was because she thought Abigail was loaded and would eventually leave everything to me. Meredith didn't think to mention to me that Abigail had even died until two months after the fact, and then only in passing."

"How can I believe anything you tell me?"

He closed his eyes. "It's true. I loved Abigail. I doubt I could have swung leave to attend a great-aunt's funeral but I would have moved heaven and earth to try."

"So how do we get from here to there?"

He sighed. "My mother is between husbands, which means that, as usual, she's short on cash. She suddenly remembered Abigail had this house that was supposed to be worth a fortune and she seemed to think it should have come to me, as Abigail's only living relative. And of course, to her by default if something happened to me in the Middle East. Imagine her dismay when she found out Abigail had left Brambleberry House to someone else. Two strangers."

The nausea roiled in her stomach, mostly that he could speak of his own mother regarding his possible demise with such callousness. "This was about money?"

"I don't give a damn about the money!" he said, with unmistakable vehemence. "My mother might but I don't. This was about making sure Abigail knew what she was doing when she left the house and its contents to two complete strangers."

"Strangers to you, maybe, but not to Abigail!" Anna's temper flared with fierce suddenness. "She was our friend. Sage and I both loved her dearly and she loved us. Obviously more than she loved some nephew who never even bothered to visit her."

He drew in a sharp breath. "It was a little tough to find time for social calls when I was in the middle of a damn war zone!"

She had hurt him, she realized. She wanted to take

back her words but how could she, when her insides were being ripped apart by pain?

She loved him and he had lied to her, just like every other man she'd ever been stupid enough to trust.

She could feel hot tears burning behind her eyes and she was very much afraid she was going to break down in front of him, something she absolutely could not allow. She blinked them back, focusing on the anger.

"Let me get this straight. You came here because you thought I was some kind of scam artist? That Sage and I had schemed and manipulated our way into Abigail's life so she would leave us the legacy that should have been yours."

He compressed his mouth into a tight line. "Something like that."

"And where did sleeping with me fit into that?"

CHAPTER FIFTEEN

HER WORDS HOVERED between them, a harsh condemnation of his actions these last few days. In her eyes, he could see her withdrawal, the hurt and fury he fully deserved.

Why had he ever been stupid enough to think coming to Cannon Beach was a good idea? He thought of the events he had set into motion by that one crazy decision. He hated most of all knowing he had hurt her.

"Everything between us has been a lie," she said, her voice harsh.

"Not true." He stepped forward, knowing only that he needed some contact with her, but she took a swift step back and he fought hard to conceal the pain knifing through him.

"I never expected any of this to happen. I only intended to spend a few weeks running recon here, getting the lay of the land. I just wanted to check things out, make sure everything was aboveboard. I felt like I owed it to Abigail because…"

Because I loved her and I never had a chance to say goodbye.

"Well, my reasons don't really matter. I swear, I tried to keep my distance but you made it impossible."

"What did I do?"

"You invited me to breakfast," he said simply.

You fixed up my scrapes and bruises, you listened with compassion when I rambled on about my scars, you kissed me and lifted me out of myself.

You made me fall in love with you.

The words clogged in his throat. He wanted desperately to say them but he knew she wouldn't welcome them. He had lost any right to offer her his love.

"I figured out a long time ago that you genuinely cared about Abigail and there was nothing underhanded in you and Sage Benedetto inheriting Brambleberry House."

"Well, that's certainly reassuring to know. Was that before or after you slept with me?"

"Anna—"

"So tell me, Max. As soon as you figured out I wasn't some con artist, why didn't you tell me who you were?"

He raked a hand through his hair. "I wanted to, a hundred times. I tried, but something always stopped me. The dog. The storm. I don't know. It just never seemed like the right time."

He sighed, wishing she would give him even the tiniest of signals that she believed any of this. "And then after we made love, I felt like we were so entangled, I didn't know how to tell you without hurting you."

Her laugh was bitter and scorched his heart. "Far easier to go on letting stupid, oblivious Anna believe the fantasy."

"You're not stupid. Or oblivious. I deceived you. Though I might have thought I had good intentions, that I owed something to Abigail's memory, it was completely wrong of me to let things go as far as they did."

She said nothing and he scanned her features, looking for any softening but he saw nothing there but pain and anger. "I never meant to hurt you," he said.

She stood in a protective stance with her shoulders stiff, and her arms wrapped tightly around her stomach, and he didn't know how to reach her.

"Isn't it funny how people always say that after the fact?" she said, her voice a low condemnation. "If you truly never meant to hurt me, you should have told me you were Abigail's nephew after you kissed me for the first time."

He had no defense against the bitter truth of her words. She was absolutely right.

He had no defense at all. He was wrong and he had known it all along.

"I'm sorry," he murmured, hating the inadequacy of the words but unable to come up with anything better. He should leave, he thought. Just go before he made things worse for her.

He headed to the door but before he opened it, he turned back and was struck again by how beautiful she was. Beautiful and strong and forever out of his reach now.

"Aunt Abigail knew exactly what she was doing when she left Brambleberry House to you," he said, his voice low. "She would have hated to see me sell this house she loved so much and she must have known that with my career in the army, I wouldn't have been able to give it the love and care you have. You belong here, in a way I never could."

He closed the door softly behind him and headed slowly up the stairs, every bone in his body suddenly aching to match the pain in his heart.

That last he had said to her was a blatant lie, just one more to add to the hundreds he had told.

She belonged here, that much was truth. But he couldn't tell her that these last few days, he had begun to think perhaps he could also find a place here in this house that had always been his childhood refuge.

The words to the poem she had quoted echoed through his memory. *Every house where love abides and friendship is a guest, is surely home, and home, sweet home, for there the heart can rest.*

His heart had come to rest here, with Anna. She had soothed his restless soul in ways he still didn't quite understand. He had come here hurting and guilty over the helicopter crash and the deaths of his team members, wondering what he could have done differently to prevent the crash.

He had been frustrated about his shoulder, worried about the future, grieving for his team and for Abigail.

But when he was with Anna, he found peace and comfort. She had helped him find faith again, faith in himself and faith in the future.

The thought of walking away from her, from this place, filled him with a deep, aching sorrow. But what choice did he have?

He couldn't stay here. He had made that impossible. He had been stupid and selfish and he had ruined everything.

"How is it humanly possible for one woman to be such a colossal idiot when it comes to men?"

Two hours after Max walked out of her apartment, Anna sat in Julia's kitchen. The children were in bed, exhausted from their journey, and Will had returned to his own home down the beach, the house where he and Julia would live after their marriage in June.

"That is a question we may never answer in our lifetimes." Sage's voice sounded tinny and hollow over the speakerphone.

"Sage!" Julia exclaimed, a frown on her lovely features.

"Kidding. I'm kidding, sweetheart. You know I'm kidding, Anna. You're not an idiot. You're the smartest woman I've ever met."

"So why do I keep falling for complete jerks?"

Conan whined from his spot on the kitchen rug and gave her a reproving look similar to the one Julia had given the absent Sage.

"Are you sure he's a complete jerk?" Julia's voice was quiet. "He is Abigail's nephew, after all, so he can't be all bad. I've been wracking my memory and I think I might have met him a time or two when we stayed here during the summers when I was a girl. He always seemed very polite. Quiet, even."

"I'm afraid I never met him so I can't really offer an opinion either way," Sage said on the phone. "He came to stay several years ago before he shipped out to the gulf but I was on a field survey down the coast the whole time. I do know Abigail always spoke about him in glowing terms, but I figured she was a little biased."

Anna remembered the solid assurance she had experienced several times that Abigail would have approved of Max and her growing relationship with him. It hadn't been anything she could put her finger on, just a feeling in her heart.

Fight for him. He needs you.

She suddenly remembered those thoughts drifting through her mind earlier in the evening when she had been preparing for the celebration that hadn't happened.

She was almost certain that had been a figment of her imagination. But was it possible Abigail had been trying to give her some kind of message?

She hated this. She couldn't trust him and she certainly couldn't seem to trust herself.

"He lied to me, just like Gray and just like my fiancé. With my history, how can I get past that?" she asked out loud as she set her spoon back in the bowl of uneaten ice cream.

She hadn't had much of an appetite for it in the first place but now the cherry chocolate chunk tasted terrible with this bitterness in her mouth.

"Maybe you can't," Sage said.

Julia said nothing, though an expression of doubt flickered over her features.

"You don't agree?" Anna asked.

The schoolteacher shrugged. "Do I think he should have told you he was Abigail's nephew? Of course. Deceiving you was wrong. But maybe he just found himself in a deep hole and he didn't know how to climb out without digging in deeper."

"And maybe he should have just buried himself in the hole when he got down far enough," Sage said.

Though Anna knew Sage was only trying to offer her support, she suddenly found she wanted to defend him, which was a completely ridiculous reaction, one she quickly squashed.

"I've been lied to so many times. I don't know if I forgive that."

"You're the only one who can decide that, honey," Julia said, squeezing her fingers. "But whatever you do, you know we're behind you, right?"

"Ditto from the Patagonia faction," Sage said over the phone.

Though she was quite certain it was watery and weak, Anna managed a smile. "Thank you. Thank you both. As tough as this is, I'm grateful I have you both."

"And Conan and Abigail," Sage declared. "Don't forget them."

The dog slapped his tail on the floor at the sound of his name but didn't bother getting up.

"How can I?" she said. She and Julia were saying goodbye and preparing to hang up when Sage suddenly gasped into the phone.

"The letter! We've got a letter for Abigail's nephew, remember?"

"That's right," Anna exclaimed. "I completely forgot it!"

"What letter?" Julia asked.

"From Abigail," Anna explained. "She left it as part of her estate papers for her great-nephew. Her Jamie."

"It was another of those weird conditions of her will," Sage added. "He could only receive it if and when he arrived in person to Brambleberry House. I was all in favor of mailing it to him in care of the army but Abigail's attorney stipulated her wishes were quite clear. We weren't even supposed to tell him about it until he showed up here."

"Why was she so certain he would come back to Brambleberry House after her death? Especially since she had gone to such pains to leave the house to you two, leaving him with no reason to return at all?" Julia asked with a puzzled frown.

"I don't know. I wondered that myself," Anna admitted.

She remembered how sad she had thought it that Abigail seemed so desperate for her nephew, who hadn't visited her much when she was alive, to come here, even after her death.

"She was right though," Sage said. "Just like she always was. He came back, just as she seemed to know he would."

Anna shivered at the undeniable truth of the words.

"You have to give it to him," Sage continued. "Do you know where it is?"

"In the safe in my office," she answered promptly. "I kept it there with all the other estate documents."

"I'd give anything to know what's in that letter. What do you think Abigail had to say to him?" Sage asked.

Anna wondered the same thing after she and Julia had said goodbye to Sage and she had returned downstairs to her own apartment and retrieved the letter from her safe.

She sat looking at the envelope for a long time, at Abigail's familiar elegant handwriting and those two words. *My Jamie.*

For the first time, she allowed herself to look at this from Max's perspective. He said he had loved his aunt and she knew she had hurt him tonight when she said Abigail must not have loved him enough to leave the house to him.

It had been a cruel thing to say, especially since she knew from the way Abigail talked about her nephew that she had adored him.

What would Anna have done if a beloved elderly relative had left a valuable legacy to two strangers? She probably would have been suspicious as well. Of course, she would have wanted to find out the circumstances. But would she have lied about her identity to investigate?

She couldn't answer that. She only knew that some of her anger seemed to be subsiding, drawing away from her like low tide.

She gazed at the letter. *My Jamie.* She was going to have to give it to him, but she knew she couldn't go knocking on his apartment door. She wasn't ready to face him again. Not yet. Maybe in the morning, she would be more in control of her emotions.

Still, some instinct told her she needed to deliver this tonight, whether she faced him or not. Praying she wouldn't encounter him wandering around in the dark, she moved quietly up the stairs and slipped the letter through the narrow crack under the door.

There you go, Abigail, she thought, and was almost certain she felt a brush of air against her cheek.

The task done, she stood for a long moment on the landing outside his apartment, her emotions a tangled mess and her heart a heavy weight in her chest.

MAX BACKED HIS SUV out of the Brambleberry House driveway just as the sun crested the coast range. His duffel and single suitcase were in the backseat and the letter that had been slipped under his apartment door was on the seat beside him.

He knew the letter was from Abigail. Who else? Even if he hadn't recognized her distinctive curlicue handwriting, he would have known from only the name on the outside.

My Jamie.

He had stared at that envelope, his heart aching with loss and regret. It even smelled like her, some soft, flowery scent that made him think of tight hugs and kisses on the cheek and summer evening spent in the garden with her.

Finally he had stuck it in the pocket of his jacket and walked down the stairs of Brambleberry House for the last time.

He knew of only one place he wanted to be when he read her final words to him. It seemed fitting and right that he drive to the cemetery to pay his last respects before he left Cannon Beach. He had been putting it off, this final evidence that Abigail was really gone, but he knew he couldn't avoid the inevitable any longer.

He found the cemetery and drove through the massive iron gates under winter-bare branches. Only when he was inside looking at the rows of gravestones, surrounded by tendrils of misty morning fog, did he realize he had no idea where to find his aunt's plot amid the graves.

At random, he picked a lane and parked his SUV halfway down it then started walking. He had only gone twenty feet before he saw it, a tasteful headstone in pale amber marble under a small statue of an angel, with her name.

Abigail Elizabeth Dandridge

Someone had angled an intricate wrought-iron bench there to look over the grave and the ocean beyond it. Anna? he wondered. Somehow it wouldn't have surprised him. It seemed the sort of gesture she would make, practical and softhearted at the same time.

He sat at the bench for a long time, until the damp grass began to seep through his boots and the wrought-iron pressed into the back of his thighs. He wasn't quite sure why he was so apprehensive to read Abigail's final words to him.

Maybe because of that—because it seemed so very final. Silly as it seemed, he hated that this was the last time anyone would call him the nickname only she had used.

Finally he opened the envelope. A tiny key fell out, along with several pieces of cream vellum. He frowned and pocketed the key then unfolded the letter, his insides twisting.

My dear Jamie,
I suppose since you're reading this, it means you have come home to Brambleberry House at last. I say home, my dear, because this is where you have always belonged. During the rough years of your childhood, while you were off at military school, even when you were off serving your

country with honor and courage, this was your home. You have always had a home here and I hope with all my heart that you have known that.

By now you must be thinking I'm a crazy old bat. I'm not so sure you would be wrong. I want you to know I'm a crazy old bat who has loved you dearly. You have been my joy every day of your life.

So why didn't I leave you the house? I'm sure you're asking. If you're not, you should be. I nearly did, you know. Since the day you were born, I planned that you would inherit Brambleberry House when I left this earth. Then a few years ago, something happened to change my mind.

I began to want something more for you than just a house. You see, houses get dry rot or are bent and broken by the wind or can even crumble into the ocean.

Love, though. Love endures.

I knew love when I was a girl, a love that stayed with me my entire life. Even though the man I loved died young, I have carried the memory of him inside me all these years. It has sustained me and lifted me throughout my life's journey.

I wanted the same for you, my Jamie. For you to know the connection of two hearts linked as one. So I began to scheme and to plot. You needed a special woman, someone smart and courageous, with a strong, loving heart.

*I knew from the moment I met Anna, she was
perfect for you.*

He stopped and stared at the gravestone as a chill
rippled down his spine. Impossible. How could Abigail
have known from beyond the grave that he would find
Anna, that he would fall in love with her, that he would
feel as if his heart were being ripped out of him at the
idea of walking away from her? With numb disbelief,
he turned his attention back to the letter.

*I wanted you to meet her, Jamie. To see for
yourself how wonderful she is. I thought if I left
you the house outright, you would quickly sell it
and return to the army, leaving all you could have
found here behind without a backward glance.*

*Anna and Sage would watch over my house
with loving care, I knew. And I also knew that
if I left the house to them, eventually you would
come home to find out why. I thought perhaps
when you did, you would find something far
more valuable here than bricks and drywall and
a leaky roof.*

*It was a gamble—a huge one. I only wish I
could be there to see if it paid out. Of course,
there was always a chance you might fall for
Sage, but I had other plans for her, plans that
didn't include you.*

*I can't even contemplate the eventuality that
you might not fall for Anna. You are too smart
for that—or at least you'd better be!*

Please know that my dearest wish is that you
will find joy, my darling Jamie.

All my love, forever,

Abigail.

P.S. In case you're wondering, the key is to a
safe-deposit box at First National Bank of Oregon where you will find record of my investment
portfolio. The proceeds are all to go to you, as
the legal documentation in the safe deposit will
attest and my attorney can confirm. I've played
the market well over the years and I believe you'll
find the value of my portfolio far exceeds the
worth of an old rambling house on the seashore.
I pray you will put my money to good use somewhere, even if I'm wrong about you and Anna
being perfect for each other.

He stared at the letter for a long, long time, there in
the cemetery with only the wind sighing in the trees
and a pair of robins singing and flitting from branch
to branch as they prepared their spring nest.

All these years, he had no idea his great-aunt was a
sly, manipulative rascal.

He ought to be angry at her for luring him here. She
had set him up, had played him every step of the way.

Instead, he laughed out loud, then couldn't seem to
stop. He laughed so hard the robins fluttered into the
sky, chattering angrily at him for disturbing their work.

"Oh, Abigail," he said out loud. "You are one in a
million."

How could he be angry, when her actions had been

motivated only by love for him? And when she was absolutely right?

Anna was a smart, courageous woman with a strong, loving heart. And she was perfect for him.

He couldn't just walk away from her, from the chance to see if he could find what Abigail wanted so much for them both.

He was gone.

Anna sat on the porch swing where Max had held her so tenderly the night of the storm and gazed out at the sleeping garden, at the rose bushes with their naked thorns and the dry husks of daylily leaves she hadn't cut down in the fall and the bare dirt that waited in a state of anticipation for what was to come.

He was gone and she was quite certain he wouldn't be back. His SUV was gone when she awoke and when she had let Conan out, she had found the key to his apartment hanging on her doorknob, along with a simple note.

I'm so sorry, he had written, without even signing his name.

The morning was cold, with wisps of fog coming off the sea to curl through the trees and around the garden. She shivered from it. She really should go inside and get ready for work but she couldn't seem to move from the porch swing.

Conan, his eyes deep with concern, padded to her and placed his head in her lap.

Just that tiny gesture of comfort sent the first tear trickling down her cheek, then another and another until she buried her face in her hands and wept.

She gave into the storm of emotions for only a few moments before she straightened and drew in a shaky breath, swiping at the tears on her cheeks. Of course he was gone. What did she expect? She had made it quite clear to him the night before that she couldn't forgive him for lying to her. Did she expect him to stick around hoping she would change her mind?

Would she have?

It was a question she didn't know the answer to. This morning, her anger had faded, leaving only an echo of hurt that he had maintained the deception even after they made love.

Julia's words kept running through her head.

Maybe he just found himself in a deep hole and he didn't know how to climb out without digging in deeper.

Yes, he had lied about his identity. But she couldn't quite believe everything else was a lie. He had stood up to Grayson for her that day in the store, he had come with her to the verdict, had held her hand when she was afraid, had kissed her with stunning tenderness. What was truth and what was a lie?

She loved him. That, at least, was undeniably true.

She let out one last sob, her hands buried in Conan's fur, then she straightened her spine. He was gone and she could do nothing about it. In the meantime, she had two businesses to run and a house to take care of. And now she needed to find a new tenant for her third-floor apartment so she could pay for a new roof.

Conan suddenly jerked away from her and went to the edge of the porch, barking wildly. She turned to see what had captured his attention and her heart stuttered in her chest.

Max walked toward her through the morning mist, looking lean and masculine and dangerous in his leather bomber jacket with his arm in the sling.

The breath caught in her throat as he walked toward her and stopped a half-dozen feet away.

"I made you cry."

"No, you didn't. I never cry."

He raised an eyebrow and she lifted her chin defiantly. "It's just cold out here and my allergies must be starting up. It's early spring and the grass pollen count is probably sky-high."

Now who was lying? she thought, clamping her teeth together before she could ramble on more and make things worse.

"Is that right?" he murmured, though he didn't look as if he believed her for an instant.

"I thought you left," she said after a moment.

He shrugged. "I came back."

"You left your key and vacated the apartment."

Where did this cool, composed voice of hers come from? she wondered. What she really wanted to do instead of standing out here having such a civil conversation was to leap into his arms and hold on tight.

He shrugged, leaning a hip against the carved porch support post. "I changed my mind. I don't want to leave."

"Too bad. You can't walk out on a lease agreement and then waltz back in just because you feel like it."

Amusement sparked in his hazel eyes. Amusement and something else, something that had her pulse racing. "Are you going to take me to court, Anna? Because I have to tell you, that would look pretty bad for you. I would hate to pull out the pity card but I just don't see how you could avoid the ugly headlines. 'Vindictive landlady kicks out injured war veteran.'"

She bristled. "Vindictive? *Vindictive?*"

"Okay, bad choice of words. How about, 'Justifiably angry landlady.'"

"Better."

"No, wait. I've got the perfect headline." He slid away from the post and stepped closer and her pulse kicked up a dozen notches at the intent look in his eyes.

"How about 'Idiotic injured soldier falls hard for lovely landlady.'"

"Because only an idiot would be stupid enough to fall for her, right?"

He laughed roughly. "You're not going to make this easy on me, are you?"

She shrugged instead of answering, mostly because she didn't quite trust her voice.

Just kiss me already.

"All right, this is my last attempt here. How about 'Ex-helicopter pilot loses heart to successful local business owner, declares he can't live without her.'"

Conan barked suddenly with delight and Anna could only stare at Max, her heart pounding so loudly she was quite certain he must be able to hear it. She didn't know quite how to adjust to the quicksilver shift from despair to this bright, vibrant joy bursting through her.

"I like it," she whispered. "No, I love it."

He grinned suddenly and she thought again how much he had changed in the short time he'd been at Brambleberry House.

"It's a keeper then," he said, then he finally stepped forward and kissed her with fierce tenderness.

Tears welled up in her eyes again, this time tears of joy, and she returned his kiss with all the emotion in her heart.

"Can you forgive me, Anna? I made a mistake. I should never have tried to deceive you and I certainly shouldn't have played it out so long. I never expected to fall in love with you. That wasn't in the plan—or at least not in *my* plan."

"Whose plan was it?"

"I've got something to show you. Something I'm quite sure you're not going to believe."

He eased onto the porch swing and pulled her onto his lap as if he couldn't bear to let her go. She was going to be late for work, Anna thought, but right now she didn't give a darn. She didn't want to be anywhere else in the world but right here, in the arms of the man she loved.

"I'm assuming you're the one who slipped the letter from Aunt Abigail under my door."

She nodded. "She was quite strict in her instructions that you not receive it until you returned to Brambleberry House in person. Sage and I didn't understand it but the attorney said that was nonnegotiable."

"That's because she was manipulating us all," he answered. "Here. See for yourself."

He handed her the letter and she scanned the words with growing astonishment. By the time she was done, a single tear dripped down the side of her nose.

"The wretch," she exclaimed, then she laughed out loud. "How could she possibly know?"

"What? That you're perfect for me?"

Her gaze flashed to his and she saw blazing emotion there that sent heat and that wild flutter of joy coursing through her. "Am I?" she whispered, afraid to believe it.

"You are everything I never knew I needed, Anna. I love you. With everything inside me, I love you. Abigail got that part exactly right."

She wanted to cry again. To laugh and cry and hold him close.

Thank you, Abigail. For this wonderful gift, thank you from the bottom of my heart.

"Oh, Max. I love you. I think I fell in love with you that first morning on the beach when you were so kind to Conan."

He kissed her, his mouth tender and his eyes filled with emotion. "I'm not the poetry type of guy, Anna. But I can tell you that my heart definitely found a home here, and not because of the house. Because of you."

This time her tears slipped through and she wrapped her arms around him, holding tight.

Just before he kissed her, Anna could swear she heard a sigh of satisfied delight. She opened her eyes and was quite certain that over his shoulder she caught the glitter of an ethereal kind of shadow drifting through the garden, past the edge of the yard and on toward the beach.

She blinked again and then it was gone.

She must have been mistaken, she thought, except Conan stood at the edge of the porch, looking in the same direction, his ears cocked.

The dog bounded down the steps and into the garden. He barked once, still looking out to sea.

After a long moment, he barked again, then gave that silly canine grin of his and returned to the porch to curl up at their feet.

EPILOGUE

IT WAS EASY to believe in happy endings at a moment like this.

Max sat in the gardens of Brambleberry House on a lovely June day. The wild riot of colorful flowers gleamed in the late-afternoon sunlight and the air was scented with their perfume—roses and daylilies and the sweet, seductive smell of lavender that melded with the brisk, salty undertone of the sea.

Julia Blair was a beautiful bride. Her eyes were bright with happiness as she stood beside Will Garrett under an arbor covered in Abigail's favorite yellow roses while they exchanged vows.

The two of them were deeply in love and everyone at the wedding could see it. Max was glad for Will. He had been given a small glimpse from Abigail's letters over the years of how dark and desolate his friend's life had been after the deaths of his wife and daughter. These last three months, Anna had shared a little more of Will's grieving process with Max and he couldn't imagine that kind of pain.

From what he could tell, Julia was the ideal woman to help Will move forward. Max had come to know her well after three months of living upstairs from her. She was sweet and compassionate, with a deep reservoir of love inside her that she showered on Will and her children.

"May I have the rings, please?" the pastor performing the ceremony asked. Then he had to repeat his request since Simon, the ring bearer and best man, was busy making faces at Chloe Spencer.

"Simon, pay attention," his twin sister hissed loudly. To emphasize her point, she poked him hard with the basket full of the flower petals she had strewn along the garden path before the ceremony.

"Sorry," Simon muttered, then held the pillow holding the rings out to Will, who was doing his best to fight a smile.

"Thanks, bud," Will said, reaching for the rings with one hand while he squeezed the boy's shoulder with the other in a man-to-man kind of gesture.

As Will and Julia exchanged rings, Max heard a small sniffle beside him and turned his head to find Anna's brown eyes shimmering with tears she tried hard to contain.

He curled his fingers more tightly around hers, and as she leaned her cheek against his shoulder for just a moment, he was astounded all over again at how very much his world had changed in just a few short months.

She had become everything to him.

His love.

When the clergyman pronounced them man and wife and they kissed to seal their union, he watched as the tears Anna had been fighting broke free and started to trickle down her cheek.

He pulled a handkerchief from the pocket of his dress uniform, and she dabbed at her eyes. For a woman who claimed she never cried, she had become remarkably proficient at it.

She had cried a month earlier when Sage Benedetto-Spencer told them she and Eben were expecting a baby, due exactly on Abigail's birthday in November.

She'd cried the day the accountant at her Lincoln City store told her they were safely in the black after several record months of sales.

And she had cried buckets for him when, after his latest trip to Walter Reed a month ago, he had come to the inevitable conclusion that he couldn't keep trying to pretend everything would be all right with his shoulder; when he had finally accepted he would never be able to fly a helicopter again.

Max could have left the army completely at that point on a medical discharge, but he had opted instead only to leave active duty. Serving part-time in the army reserves based out of Portland would be a different challenge for him, but he knew he still had much to offer.

The ceremony ended and the newly married couple was immediately surrounded by well-wishers—Conan at the front of the pack. Though he had waited with amazing patience through the service, sitting next to Sage in the front row, the dog apparently had decided he needed to be in the middle of the action.

Conan looked only slightly disgruntled at the bow tie he had been forced to wear. Maybe he knew he'd gotten a lucky reprieve—Julia's twins had pleaded for a full tuxedo for him but Anna had talked them out of it, much to Conan's relief, Max was quite certain.

"What a gorgeous day for a party." Sage Benedetto-

Spencer approached them with her husband. "The garden looks spectacular. I've never seen the colors so rich."

"Your husband's landscape crew from the Sea Urchin did most of the work," Anna said.

"Not true," Eben piped in, wrapping his arms around his wife. "I have it on good authority that you and Max had already done most of the hard work by the time they got here."

Max considered the long evenings and weekends they had spent preparing the yard for the ceremony as a gift—to himself, most of all. Here in Abigail's lush gardens as they'd pruned and planted, he and Anna had talked and laughed and kissed and enjoyed every moment of being together.

He loved watching her, elbow-deep in dirt, Abigail's floppy hat on as she lifted her face to the evening sunshine.

Okay, he loved watching her do anything. Whether it was flying kites with the twins on the beach or throwing a stick for Conan in the yard or sitting at her office desk, her brow wrinkled with concentration as she reconciled her accounts.

He was just plain crazy about her.

They spoke for a few more moments with Eben and Sage before Anna excused herself to make certain the caterers were ready to start bringing out the appetizers for the reception.

When she still hadn't returned a half hour later, Max went searching for her.

He found her alone in the kitchen of her apartment, which had been set up as food central, setting bacon-wrapped shrimp on etched silver platters. Typical Anna, he thought with a grin. Sure, the caterer Julia and Will had hired was probably more than capable of handling all these little details, but she must be busy somewhere else and Anna must have stepped in to help. She loved being involved in the action. If there was work to be done, his Anna didn't hesitate.

She was humming to herself, and he listened to her for a moment, admiring the brisk efficiency of her movements, then he slid in behind her with as much stealth as he could manage. She wore her hair up and he couldn't resist leaning forward and brushing a kiss along the elegant arch of her bared neck, just on the spot he had learned, these last few months, was most sensitive.

A delicate shiver shook her frame and her hands paused in their work. "I don't know who you are, but don't stop," she purred in a low, throaty voice.

He laughed and turned her to face him. She raised her eyebrows in a look of mock surprise as she slid into his arms. "Oh. Max. Hi."

He kissed her properly this time, astonished all over again at the little bump in his pulse, at the love that swelled inside him whenever he had her in his arms.

"It's been a beautiful day, hasn't it?" she said, soft joy in her eyes for her friends' happiness.

"Beautiful," he agreed, without a trace of the cynicism he had expected.

His own mother had been married six times, the most recent just a few weeks ago to some man she'd met on a three-week Mediterranean cruise. With his childhood and the examples he had seen, he had always considered the idea of happy endings like Julia and Will's—and Sage and Eben's, for that matter—just another fairy tale. But this time with her had changed everything.

"Anna, I want this," he said suddenly.

"The shrimp? I know, they're divine, aren't they? I think I could eat the whole platter myself."

"Not the shrimp. I want the whole thing. The wedding, the flowers. The crazy-spooky dog with the bow tie. I want all of it."

She blinked rapidly, and he saw color soak her cheeks. "Oh," she said slowly.

He wasn't going about this the right way at all. He had a feeling if Abigail happened to be watching she would be laughing her head off just about now at how inept he was.

"I'm sorry I don't have all the flowery words. I only know that I love you with everything inside me. I want forever, Anna." He paused, his heartbeat sounding unnaturally loud in his ears. "Will you marry me?"

She gazed at him for a long, drawn-out moment. Through the open window behind her, he was vaguely aware of the band starting up, playing something soft and slow and romantic.

"Oh, Max," she said. She sniffled once, then again, then she threw herself back into his arms.

"Yes. Yes, yes, yes," she laughed, punctuating each word with a kiss.

"A smart businesswoman like you had better think this through before you answer so definitely. I'm not much of a bargain, I'm afraid. Are you really sure you'll be happy married to a weekend warrior and high-school physics teacher who's greener at his new job than a kid on his first day of basic training?"

"I don't need to think anything through. I love you, Max. I want the whole thing, too." She kissed him again. "And besides, you're going to be a wonderful teacher."

Of all the careers out there, he never would have picked teaching for himself, but now it seemed absolutely right. He had always enjoyed giving training to new recruits and had been damn good at it. But high-school students? That was an entirely different matter.

Anna had been the one who'd pointed out to him how important the teachers at the military school Meredith sent him to had been in shaping his life and the man he had become. They'd been far more instrumental than his own mother.

Once the idea had been planted, it stuck. Since he already had a physics degree, now he only had to finish obtaining a teaching certificate. This time next year, he would be preparing lesson plans.

It wasn't the path he had expected, but that particular route had been blown apart by a rocket-fired grenade in Iraq. Somehow this one suddenly seemed exactly the right one for him.

He couldn't help remembering what Abigail used to say—*A bend in the road is only the end if you refuse to make the turn.* He was making the turn, and though he couldn't see it all clearly, he had a feeling the path ahead contained more joy than he could even imagine.

He rested his chin on Anna's hair. Already that joy seemed to seep through him, washing away all the pain. He couldn't wait to follow that road, to spend the rest of his life with efficient Anna—with her plans and her ambitions and her brilliant mind.

Suddenly, above the delectable smells of the wedding food, he was quite certain he smelled the sweet, summery scent of freesias.

"Do you think she's here today?" Anna asked him.

He tightened his arms around her, thinking of his aunt who had loved them all so much. "Absolutely," he murmured. "She wouldn't miss it. Just as I'm sure she'll be here for our wedding and for the birth of our children and for every step of our journey together."

Anna laughed softly. "We'd better hold on tight, then. If Abigail has her way, I think we're in for a wild ride. A wild, wonderful, perfect ride."

* * * * *

SUDDENLY A FATHER

Michelle Major

For Lauren. You are amazing in so many ways—
mother, teacher and friend.
I'm lucky and grateful to have you as my sister.

CHAPTER ONE

MILLIE SPENCER TOOK a deep breath, wiped a few stray potato chip crumbs from her sundress and knocked on the door a second time.

As she waited, her eyes scanned the front porch of the large shake-shingle house, empty save for an intricate spiderweb inhabiting one corner. The wraparound porch practically begged for a wooden swing, where a person could sit on a late-summer afternoon sipping a glass of lemonade and watching the world go by. As a girl, Millie had longed for a place like that, but in the tiny condo she'd shared with her mother there'd been no room for any space of her own.

Still no one answered, so she rapped her knuckles against the door once more. This house sat at the edge of town in Crimson, Colorado, but only a few minutes from her sister's renovated Victorian near Crimson's center.

She was here as a favor to her sister—half sister—Olivia. Or was Olivia doing the favor for Millie? Millie'd shown up on Olivia's doorstop a few days ago, beaten down both emotionally and financially. To her relief, Olivia and her husband, Logan Travers, hadn't asked many questions, just welcomed Millie into their home. Up until today, Millie had spent most

of her time curled on the couch watching bad reality
TV and overdosing on junk food.

Now she was here, sent to help Logan's recently injured brother and his daughter. Except it appeared they
weren't home. Which was weird, since Logan had said
his brother, Jake, couldn't drive yet. It was a beautiful
late-August day, so maybe the two had walked to the
park Millie'd seen a few blocks over.

She was ready to leave when the door opened a
crack. She could see a sliver of a man's face through
the opening. "We don't want any," he said, peering
down at her.

"Any what?" She leaned forward, trying to get a
glimpse beyond him into the house. Curiosity almost
always got the best of her.

"Cookies or popcorn or whatever you're selling,"
he answered quickly, glancing behind him before the
eye she could see, a startlingly blue eye, tracked back
to her again. It was the same blue as Logan's, so this
must be the brother. "Do you have a parent with you?"

Her mouth dropped open and she pulled herself up
to her full height, all five foot two. And a half. When
she wore heels. "I'm not…" she began, but the man
muttered a curse and disappeared into the house.

He hadn't shut the door when he'd turned away. She
could still only see through the couple-inch slat, and
without a second thought, she extended her foot and
nudged the door open wider. She stretched forward
but didn't step into the house. "Hello?" she called and
her voice echoed.

The entry was devoid of furniture. Olivia had told
her Logan's brother had recently returned to Crimson,

so maybe he had furnishings for his home on order. She hoped his purchases included a porch swing.

A sound reached her from the back of the house. Another curse and a child crying. She bit down on her lip and grabbed her cell phone from her purse, intending to call Olivia and Logan for backup. But the crying got louder, followed by a strangled shout of "no," and Millie charged forward, unable to stop herself.

She came up short as she entered the back half of the house. Rays of sunshine streamed through the windows, lighting the open family room as well as the kitchen beyond. Her gaze caught on the family room. Unlike the front of the house, the room looked furnished, although it was hard to tell because dolls, stuffed animals and an excess of pink plastic covered every square inch. It looked as if a toy store had thrown up all over the place. Did Jake Travers really have only one child? There was enough stuff here to keep a whole army of kids busy. She forced her eyes away from the girlie mess to the kitchen.

Two tall bar stools were tucked under the island, which was littered with cereal boxes and various milk and juice cartons. A mix of what looked like chocolate milk and grape juice spilled over the counter onto one of the stools and the tile floor, soaking a pile of soggy Cheerios from an overturned bowl.

Jake stood in the middle of the kitchen with his back to her. She noticed immediately that he was tall and broad, wearing a gray athletic T-shirt, basketball shorts that came almost to his knees and an orthopedic boot on his right leg that covered him from midcalf to foot.

He also sported a purple tutu around his waist. Despite the chaos of the situation, she almost smiled at that. No wonder he hadn't wanted to open the door for her.

In front of him, a little girl was crying and jumping up, grasping for a stuffed animal he held out to the side. It might have been a rabbit and was dripping more juice on the floor. The child had no hope of reaching it. Millie guessed he was well over six foot. When Olivia had sent her here to help Logan's poor, injured brother, Millie had pictured a debilitated invalid, not the hulking man before her.

She almost backed out of the room and fled, but at that moment the young girl's eyes met hers. They were the same shade of blue as her father's, so big they almost looked out of place on her heart-shaped face. Her hair was several shades darker than her father's, hung past her shoulders, and although she had the enviable natural highlights that children got, it looked as if it could benefit from a good brushing. She wore a pale pink leotard and matching tutu, the very essence of a tiny ballerina. Other than the juice stains down the front of it. Millie felt an immediate connection to her.

The child fell silent except for a tiny hiccup. Her eyes widened as she pointed at Millie. "It's a real life fairy."

JAKE TRAVERS BREATHED a sigh of relief before turning to see what his daughter, Brooke, was pointing at. He hardly cared if a real life fairy was standing in his house. It had stopped Brooke's crying and already the pounding in his head was starting to subside.

But it wasn't a fairy staring at him from the far side

of the family room. The girl he'd tried to chase away
minutes earlier held up a tentative hand and waved at
him. Not a girl, he realized now. She was a woman, a
tiny sprite of a woman, but the morning light silhou-
etting her body revealed the soft curves underneath
her flowery flowing dress.

"I'm Millie," she said, nodding, as if willing him to
understand her. "Millie Spencer. Olivia's sister? She
and Logan sent me over." She tucked a strand of chin-
length, caramel-colored hair behind one ear, the bracelets at her wrist tinkling as she moved.

Brooke let out an enraptured gasp. "Look, Daddy,
she sparkles."

He narrowed his eyes as he set the dripping stuffed
bunny onto the counter. Millie Spencer indeed appeared to be shimmering in the light.

She looked down at her bare arms and laughed, a
sound just as bubbly and bright as the noise from her
bracelets. "It's my lotion, sweetie," she said, taking a
step forward. "I must have grabbed the one that glitters."

He watched his daughter's face light up. "I want
glitters," she answered, her tone dreamy.

"You said Logan sent you?" Jake crossed his arms
over his chest, careful of the splint that cradled his
right hand. Glitter was the last thing he needed in this
already chaotic house.

Millie scrunched up her pert nose. "I was under the
impression Logan talked to you about me. That you
need help because of..." She waved her hand up and
down in front of him. More tinkling from the bracelets.

His back stiffened. Jake hated his injuries, how

they'd changed his life and how out of control he felt these days. He vaguely remembered Logan calling last night to suggest babysitting help for Brooke and someone who could drive Jake to his physical-therapy and doctors' appointments. But Jake had been in the middle of burning a frozen pizza and had only half listened to his brother's well-meaning offer.

Jake didn't need help. At least he didn't *want* to need help. Especially not from someone who looked as if her best friend was Tinker Bell.

"We're all good here."

She glanced around the room before her gaze zeroed in on his waist. "Are you sure about that?"

"We were having dance lessons," he mumbled as he pulled the crinkly tutu Brooke had insisted he wear down off his hips. He flicked it to the side and gave Millie a curt nod. He could handle this on his own. That was how he'd gotten by most of his life. He wasn't about to change now.

"I want glitters." Brooke tugged at the hem of his T-shirt.

He placed his uninjured hand on his daughter's head, smoothing back her long hair. His fingers caught on something that felt suspiciously like a wad of gum. Damn. He smiled and made his voice soft. "No glitter today, Brooke. Do you want to watch a show?"

Her mouth pinched into a stubborn line. "Glitters," she repeated then ducked away from his touch. "And Bunny." She grabbed the stuffed animal off the counter before he could stop her.

She squeezed the bunny to her chest. Jake couldn't stifle his groan as a trickle of purple liquid soaked her pink blouse. The last bit of command he had over his life seemed to seep away at the same time.

He turned back to Millie, but she'd disappeared.

Oh, no, he thought to himself. Not now when he was willing to admit defeat.

Lifting Brooke and Bunny against his chest with his good arm, he tried to ignore that his shirt was already soaking through. "Let's go find our fairy," he told his daughter and was rewarded with a wide grin.

MILLIE DIDN'T STOP when Jake Travers called her name. She concentrated on the warm sun and cool mountain breeze instead of her tumbling emotions. Even as a favor to Olivia, Millie had no intention of sticking around where she wasn't wanted. She made the mistake of turning around halfway through the yard when the little girl cried out.

Jake was struggling down the porch steps, his daughter clutched to his side as he balanced most of his weight on the nonbooted foot. "Are you really going to make me chase after you like this?" he asked as she met his gaze.

"I thought things were *all good*," she said as she retraced her steps toward the house.

He stood at the edge of the grass. "I'm used to taking care of myself. Needing help is a bit of a foreign concept."

"Everyone needs help from time to time."

He pursed his mouth into a thin line. "Not me."

Jake was clearly disconcerted by his current circumstances, and Millie felt a twinge of sympathy for him. She could spout platitudes about everyone needing help, but she'd been fending for herself long enough to understand his reluctance to rely on another person.

Before she could answer, Brooke squirmed in her father's arms and he reached out to steady her. Millie saw him wince as the girl's elbow jabbed into his splinted wrist. He lowered Brooke slowly to the ground and she clung to his leg. Millie noticed that liquid from the sopping wet stuffed animal had not only drenched his shirt, which now clung to a set of enviably hard abs, but a trail of wetness also leaked into the black orthopedic boot that covered his leg.

He didn't seem to notice, just stared at his daughter as if he wasn't sure how he'd ended up with a small child wrapped around him.

Millie cleared her throat and he looked up. "Sorry. I haven't been a dad for very long. It's still sometimes amazing that she's really mine."

"How old are you, Brooke?" Millie asked, squatting down to the girl's level.

Brooke, suddenly shy, kept her gaze on her bunny but held up four fingers.

Millie glanced at Jake, her eyebrows raised.

"What did Logan and Olivia tell you about me?" he asked.

"Not much," she admitted. "That you're a surgeon who travels around the world. You were injured during an earthquake on an island near Haiti and need help with your daughter while you recover."

One side of his mouth curved. "That's an abbreviated version."

"So I gathered," Millie answered. She held out a

hand to Brooke. "Sweetie, can I help you give Bunny a bath? She's dripping all over your daddy's leg."

"Bunny's a boy," Brooke and her father said at the same time.

Millie smiled. "He's not going to smell very good if that juice dries on him. How about we wash him off, then you can watch while he goes in the dryer?"

Brooke released the death hold she had on Jake's leg the tiniest bit. "He wants a bubble bath."

"Of course he does." Millie straightened and took a step forward, wiggling her fingers. "Can you show me the bathroom? We'll take good care of him."

With a tentative nod, Brooke took Millie's hand. This brought her only a few inches from Jake, who smelled like a strangely intriguing mix of grape juice and laundry detergent. "I'd like to understand the whole story," she said quietly.

He nodded, his deep blue eyes intent on hers. "I'll get changed then explain it." He lowered his voice and added, "I'd rather not discuss the details in front of Brooke."

The little girl tugged her toward the house. "Bunny wants to smell good."

Millie started to follow but paused as Jake pressed his uninjured hand to her bare arm. She almost flinched but caught herself, focusing on the warmth of his fingers.

His hand lifted immediately. "I just wanted to say thank you."

"I haven't done anything yet."

He leaned in to whisper in her ear, "My daughter

hasn't cried for the past fifteen minutes. You have no idea what an accomplishment that is."

Although she knew it meant nothing, Millie was surprised to feel a tiny kernel of happiness unfurl in her chest along with a shimmer of awareness for Jake Travers. Best to ignore the awareness and focus on the happiness. It had been so long since she'd accomplished anything of value in her life. She'd learned to appreciate even the smallest victory.

"It's going to be okay, Jake," she said, hoping beyond all reason that she could make it true for both of them.

CHAPTER TWO

IT TOOK JAKE longer than he wanted to get cleaned up, which was one more thing to add to his current list of frustrations. As a surgeon with Miles of Medicine, an international medical humanitarian organization, he was used to moving quickly. He'd made efficiency a priority in his life—in movement, time and, most important, relationships. He lived simply, able to pack up with an hour's notice based on where he was most needed.

The place he was most needed right now was in Brooke's life, but it galled him how inept and incapable he felt. He hadn't even bothered with a proper shower because the hassle of maneuvering himself in and out with his ankle and arm wasn't worth the trouble. Without the boot or splint, he couldn't put weight on his right leg or use his right arm. Instead he'd done his best to wash off the sticky juice residue in the master bath before dressing in his current uniform of a T-shirt and baggy shorts, the only clothes he could change into quickly despite his injuries.

The door to the guest bathroom was closed as he came down the hall. He was grateful his sister-in-law had found him a rental property with two bathrooms in the main part of the house so that Brooke could have her own space. He couldn't make out the words over the sound of running water but could hear her sweet voice rising and falling as she spoke to Millie Spencer.

Unwilling to deal with the reality of how much he needed help quite yet, he started the monumental task of cleaning the kitchen. He'd wiped down most of the counters and covered the floor with almost half a roll of paper towels before Millie followed Brooke into the room.

His daughter cradled Bunny in her arms in a fluffy towel. "Daddy, sniff." She held out the stuffed animal to him. "He smells so good."

He breathed deeply but all he got was a big whiff of wet fake fur. "That's nice," he told Brooke.

Millie grinned at him over Brooke's head. "Laundry room?"

"To your left just past the table."

She carried a small plastic stool in her hands. "Let's get Bunny dry, Brooke. You can watch him spin while your daddy and I talk."

To Jake's surprise, Brooke nodded. Since he'd brought his daughter to Crimson, the only time she would let him out of her sight was when she slept. Maybe Millie Spencer was some sort of kid whisperer. Jake sure as hell needed one.

"So you're Olivia's sister?" he asked as Millie walked back into the room a few minutes later.

When she nodded, he added, "You two don't look alike."

"She's actually my half sister. We have the same dad."

"Did you grow up together?"

Her shoulders stiffened even as she gave him a gentle smile. "I'm guessing we only have a few minutes before your daughter gets bored watching the dryer. Is this really how you want to use that time?" She crouched down and began cleaning the paper towels from the floor.

"You don't have to do that. It's my mess."

She didn't stop to look at him. "Tell me about you and Brooke."

When her chin-length hair fell into her face, she didn't bother to push it away. He wanted to reach out himself, to see if the caramel-colored strands were as soft as they looked. The skin on her arms looked just as smooth, although he noticed how toned they were as she wiped up the spill.

"I first learned that I had a daughter two months ago." He continued straightening the kitchen as her attention remained on the floor. Somehow the fact that both of them kept busy made it easier to tell the story. "Brooke's mother was a doctor I knew from my travels, another aid worker. We were only together a few times when our paths crossed in the field. Then Stacy disappeared." His fingers gripped the cup he'd just picked up so hard the plastic began to bend. He released his hold and loaded the cup into the dishwasher. "She found me where I was working near Haiti a couple of months ago to tell me I had a four-year-old daughter back in Atlanta who was asking about her father. Stacy wanted to give me a chance to be a part of Brooke's life."

"That must have been a real shock." Millie stood and threw the wad of paper towels into the garbage.

Jake thought about her observation as he watched her wet a dish towel and begin wiping down the tile floor around the spill. "You *really* don't have to do that."

"It will be sticky otherwise," she answered. "Keep talking, Jake."

He hated this part of the story and the guilt and helplessness that went with it. Jake had spent most of his childhood feeling helpless to stop the damage his father caused in their family, and when he'd finally broken free, guilt over the siblings he'd left behind had become his replacement companion.

He'd never expected to return to Colorado, but it was the only real home he'd ever known. The fact that both of his brothers had settled in Crimson and seemed happy with their lives was part of why he'd brought Brooke to his hometown. For a few brief moments when he'd first arrived, he'd hoped this place would have some special effect on him. But he'd only felt overcome by memories and more trapped than when he'd been injured.

His family understood enough of what had happened that they didn't ask questions he couldn't answer. "I was shocked, to say the least. I'd never planned on having kids. My work is my life. Being a dad wasn't part of the master plan. But I didn't have time to think about what I wanted. Stacy and I argued and she left the hospital late at night. We'd been down there just a few days because of an earthquake and I'd been running on too much coffee and too little sleep. I didn't even get a chance to process what she'd told me, but I followed her to the hotel. Once we got inside, there was an aftershock almost as big as the original. The roof of the hotel caved in, and she was killed."

Millie straightened once more, shock evident on her face. "Brooke's mother died?"

He gave a curt nod. "She should have never come down there like that. Things were too unstable."

"It was a big risk."

He looked past her, his guilt weighing so heavily that he finally had to explain in detail how he'd destroyed so many lives. "Stacy had called and emailed me over the course of several months. I thought she wanted to get together again and was avoiding her. I left her no choice but to track me down. In the end, I couldn't help her because I was pinned under the rubble of the building. I held her hand in those last moments, but that's all." He gingerly crossed his arms over his chest. "Her parents were taking care of Brooke, but Stacy made me promise to look after her. She left custody to me, a man who didn't even know his own daughter." He shook his head, still unable to believe the events that had brought him here. "I had surgery on my wrist and ankle and then went to find Brooke."

"The grandparents were willing to let her go?"

"For now." He clenched his uninjured fist. "Brooke didn't hesitate, which was the craziest part. Stacy had talked about me, had told Brooke she was going to find her father. My picture was in a frame on Brooke's nightstand. I walked into their house in Atlanta, and she reached for me as if I'd been her dad forever. Like she'd been waiting for me."

"Kids can be pretty amazing," Millie whispered.

"I don't know the first thing about being a dad, but I owe it to that little girl and her mother to try. Stacy's parents still want to raise Brooke. I'm not sure what's going to happen—there's some nerve damage to my hand and it's questionable whether I'll be able to go back to my old job."

"But you won't leave Brooke?"

He heard the unspoken accusation in her tone and almost welcomed it. Everyone he knew had been tip-toeing around his future since he'd come back to the States. "I want what's best for her. You saw me today. It's highly unlikely that I'm it."

"You're her father." Color flushed bright in Millie's cheeks. "You can't desert her now that she depends on you."

He shrugged. "I'm in way over my head here."

"I can help," she answered immediately.

Jake could feel that tension radiated through her, an edginess at odds with her pixie haircut, hippie-girl sundress and shimmering skin. "Why do you want to help?" he asked, taking a step toward her. "What's your story, Millie Spencer?"

A sliver of panic flashed in her eyes before she regulated her gaze. "I've worked at both elementary and preschools, but I'm between jobs. I'm almost finished with a degree in early childhood education and am taking a break from classes, which is why I came to visit Olivia. We didn't grow up together, so we're just getting to know each other. She invited me to Crimson while I have some free time. Getting to know someone and mooching off them for several months are two different things. I need a job while I'm here, and I'm great with kids."

"Do you have references?"

"Of course. Although I just saved the beloved Bunny and cleaned your kitchen floor. I'd say that's a pretty good reference for myself."

He held up his hands, his right arm difficult to hold out straight. "Like I said, being a dad is new to me. I want to make sure I do the right thing for Brooke."

She nodded, as if she approved of his answer. "I have a list of references in my car. I'll get it before I leave. Is Brooke in preschool?"

He rubbed his hand across his face then pointed to a pile of papers stacked on a nearby desk. "Registration is on the to-do list. I can't believe how wiped out I am by the time she goes to bed."

"I can help," Millie repeated.

"I can't drive yet and have regular physical-therapy and doctor appointments."

"That's fine, too." Her posture relaxed. "Olivia offered me the apartment above her garage. She and Logan live pretty close, so I can be here whenever you need."

He shook his head. "There's a guest suite off the family room toward the back of the house. You can stay there."

Her eyes widened. "That's not…"

"Look at me." He shifted on his bad leg. "I can't drive. Hell, I can barely bend down to pick something off the floor. If anything happens to Brooke, I want to make sure you're close."

He didn't mention the blistering relief he already felt at not being solely in charge of keeping his daughter alive. Jake had managed through a lot of high-stakes situations, but nothing had scared him like the responsibility of fatherhood. He hadn't realized how much it weighed on him until the possibility of Millie presented itself.

She continued to frown.

"I'm harmless," he said, flashing his most convincing smile.

Millie's eyes rolled in response. "Hardly."

"I'm desperate," he said softly.

Her smile was gentle and genuine. "That I believe. Are you sure this is a good idea?"

"Nothing about my life is good at the moment but…" His voice trailed off as Brooke walked back into the kitchen.

"The dryer dinged," she said, bouncing up and down on her toes. "Is Bunny ready?"

"Nothing?" Millie asked.

"One good thing," he amended. "She's the only bright spot I have. I'm going to make things right for her." He looked at his daughter. "What would you think about Millie becoming your nanny and helping with things around the house?"

"She's Mary Poppins," Brooke yelled happily. Her eyes widened as she turned to Millie. "Will you bring the glitters?"

"Of course." Millie smiled then glanced at Jake, her expression wry. "I'm not quite Mary Poppins, but we've got a deal."

"ARE YOU KIDDING ME?" Millie yelled as she burst through the back door of her sister's house thirty minutes later. "Next time you should mention that you're sending me into pure chaos before I get there."

Olivia Travers stood on the far side of the island in the oversize kitchen. She shrugged her shoulders and tried, but failed, to hide the small smile that curved the corner of her mouth. "Would you have gone if I'd explained the whole story to you?"

"Gone where?" the woman sitting on one of the bar stools asked.

Millie recognized Olivia's friend Natalie Holt from the last time she'd been in Crimson. A tiny pang of jealousy stabbed at her heart for the life Olivia had made in this quaint Colorado mountain town. Millie had never been great at cultivating friendships.

"To Jake's." Olivia drummed her nails in a nervous rhythm on the granite counter. "What happened?"

Natalie swiveled in her chair. "Yes, what happened? Jake was always my favorite of the Travers brothers. Tall, blond and wicked smart."

"Well, now he's tall, blond and a hot mess," Millie answered, omitting the part about how terrified he seemed of failing his daughter.

"Emphasis on *hot*, I imagine." Natalie nabbed a chocolate chip cookie from the plate on the counter. "Want one?" she asked Millie.

"Did Logan make them?" Millie asked, inching forward, temporarily distracted by her unwavering devotion to all things chocolate.

Olivia nodded and pushed the plate toward Millie. "I'm sorry, Mill. But he needs help. I knew you'd be able to get through to him. Logan and Josh are worried."

"Then why is he alone with his daughter?" Millie couldn't help the recrimination in her voice. "What kind of family leaves someone in his condition to fend for himself?"

"What condition?" Natalie made a face. "I didn't even know Jake was in town. Why am I always the last to know everything?"

"Sorry," Olivia answered. "Jake wanted some privacy until he got settled."

"Whatever." Natalie reached out to pat Millie's arm. "You're new around here, Millie, so let me explain how hard it is to stay mad at Saint Olivia. She's just too damn sweet."

"Tell me about it," Millie muttered, scooting forward to take a cookie. Logan was a phenomenal baker, even if she questioned his skills as a brother.

"Have a seat," Natalie said, patting the chair next to her. "I don't have to pick up my son for another hour and I'm guessing whatever's happening with Jake is way more interesting than any bad reality TV that's on at the moment." She looked between Olivia and Millie. "Who wants to spill it? You know I'm not going to tell anyone."

Olivia sighed. "Jake was injured while on a medical mission near Haiti, an aftershock from a big earthquake. At the same time, he discovered he had a four-year-old daughter." Natalie's mouth dropped open, but Olivia continued, "The girl's mother died when a hotel roof collapsed but had granted him custody. So he's brought Brooke to Crimson while he recovers. She's adorable and totally dependent on him. He's working with an orthopedic surgeon he knows at the hospital between here and Aspen. It's a renowned sports medicine center and I guess he has some friends there. At this point, they're not sure if he has permanent nerve damage in his right hand or what exactly the injuries mean for his surgical career."

"I can't believe you didn't tell me any of that," Millie said.

"I thought it would be better if Jake explained the situation," Olivia said quietly. "And I wanted you to meet Brooke before you said no to working for him."

"Because I'm a sucker for kids." Millie broke the cookie in half and popped the whole thing in her mouth, chewing furiously. "I'm a total sucker."

"I don't think that at all," Olivia answered. "But you love working with children. You have a gift."

"You can't say that," Millie said stubbornly. "You barely know me. I could mess up that girl."

Olivia blew out a frustrated sigh. "I don't understand what happened at your internship last spring, but I know it's a shame you're giving up on your dreams."

"I'm not giving up," Millie argued. "I took a semester off school. Big deal."

"Hold on, ladies." Natalie held one hand out toward each of them. "Not that this demonstration of sibling dysfunction isn't fascinating, but let's get back to Jake." She pointed at Olivia. "From what little I know about him, I'm guessing he won't let anyone in the family help out. He always was a loner."

"He's only letting us assist with the bare essentials,"

Olivia agreed. "Sara's away at a movie premiere for a few days."

"Is it weird hanging out with a Hollywood star?" Millie couldn't help the question. She was oddly fascinated by the life her half sister had created for herself in Crimson. Olivia's friend Sara Wellens had been a popular child actor years ago and had recently had a resurgence in her career. She was also married to Jake's younger brother Josh, and together they ran a guest ranch outside of town.

Olivia smiled. "She's just Sara when she's in Crimson. You'll like her, Millie. She's got some of your spunk."

Millie couldn't imagine having anything in common with an A-list actress, but she didn't argue.

"Before she left," Olivia continued, "the two of us went over with groceries and meals for the freezer. We wanted to take Brooke out for the day, but she wouldn't leave Jake's side. Logan and Josh have been taking turns stopping by, but it's the same for them."

"Poor baby," Natalie murmured. "This has to be hard for her." She turned to Millie. "But Brooke liked *you*?"

Millie nodded. "Kids trust me. I think it's because I'm small. My mom is the same way—we put people at ease." She pushed her hair away from her face with one shoulder and took another cookie. "We're nonthreatening."

"Right," Olivia said with a harsh laugh. "Your mother was a threat to my family for decades. Joyce may be small, but she packs quite the emotional punch."

Millie didn't know how to respond to that. She and Olivia shared a father, a US Senator who'd remained married to Olivia's mother up until his death a few years ago. Married, but not faithful. Millie's mother, Joyce, had been Robert Palmer's mistress for almost thirty years. She'd built her life around being available to him whenever he needed her, never asking anything in return—no financial support, no pleas to leave his wife. Joyce was the perfect other woman, making the time Robert spent with them fun and easy—a break from the pressures of real life.

But it hadn't been a break for Millie. She'd needed more. She'd wanted a father who would come to school functions and swim-team meets. Hell, she would have been happy being able to tell her friends she *had* a father. But her mother had insisted they keep silent about Robert for the sake of his reputation and career. It had always been about him.

So, yes, she and her mom both had a gift for making people feel comfortable. Comfortable walking all over them. Millie didn't know how to do relationships any other way. That was why she gravitated toward children. Kids didn't keep secrets or have ulterior motives. And that was what had drawn her to Crimson, Colorado, and the half sister she hardly knew. Olivia had been kind to her, even though she had every reason to hate Millie. They were joined by a family history that had damaged them both.

"I'm not my mother." She hated that her chin trembled as she said the words.

"Thank heavens for that. But Jake is part of my family now." Olivia's voice was solemn. "Logan hardly sleeps at night for how bothered he is that Jake insists on doing everything himself. I asked you to do this because I trust you, Millie. Maybe I see something in you that you can't see in yourself right now, but it's there. I hope spending time in Crimson will enable you to discover it again." She smiled. "This place is special that way."

Emotion welled in Millie's chest. If Olivia believed she could help Jake Travers and his daughter, she wanted to prove her sister right. No one had ever put much stock in Millie. She'd been taught from a young age that the way to get ahead was to not make demands—to be amiable and fun and nothing more.

But Jake and Brooke needed more if they were going to make it as a family unit.

"You might be pushing it talking about Crimson being special," Natalie added, her expression doubtful. "My experience begs to differ."

Millie was certain Olivia's friend was trying to lighten the mood, for which Millie was grateful. "You're a Crimson native, right?"

"Born and raised." Natalie gave an exaggerated flip of her dark hair. "And only a little ashamed to admit it."

"You're still here," Olivia pointed out. "It's a wonderful place."

Natalie shrugged. "It has its good points. The Travers brothers are three of them." She turned to Millie. "So are you going to stay and help Jake, whether he wants it or not?"

This was it. Her chance to make a run for it. Millie knew Olivia would smooth things over with Jake as best she could. This entire situation had *train wreck* written all over it. She'd promised herself that she was going to start looking out for number one, but the instinct for self-preservation just wasn't in Millie's DNA.

She bit down on her lip until it hurt then nodded. "Although it's probably another on my long list of bad decisions, I'm going to stay."

CHAPTER THREE

As soon as he heard Brooke's happy squeal, Jake knew Millie was back.

It had been almost two hours since she'd left to get her things from Olivia and Logan's, and the possibility that she wouldn't return had occurred to him only a couple thousand times.

He wouldn't have blamed her.

She might need a job, but his messed-up life was too complicated for most people to handle. Yes, his brothers and their wives had offered support more times than Jake could count since he'd returned to Crimson. But he was the oldest and the brother who'd never needed anything.

How could he admit to them that he was so weak?

All of their offers only brought back the flood of guilt about how he'd deserted their family years ago. He'd gotten a college scholarship that had enabled him to leave Crimson and their alcoholic father and never look back. Which he hadn't, even when his younger siblings needed him. Even when Logan's twin, Beth, had died in a tragic car accident. Even years later for their mother's funeral. Jake had used school, then his residency and his work to avoid the past.

He'd only returned because he had nowhere else to

go. But he'd do all he could not to let himself depend on his brothers. He didn't deserve their kindness.

Still, they'd given it to him. Millie was proof of that. Jake would have gotten around to finding a nanny for Brooke, although even that had been difficult because he was too afraid of seeing pity in a stranger's eyes when they heard his story. Jake didn't want anyone's pity.

He lifted himself off the sofa, where he and Brooke had been watching some show about an oversize red dog in between her frequent trips to the window to watch for "Fairy Poppins," as she'd named Millie.

Millie had made it to the front door, a large roller suitcase at her feet and a duffel bag slung over her shoulder.

She met his gaze and blew out a breath. "You thought I was going to ditch you guys."

"I'm glad you're here," he answered, not bothering to deny his doubts. Years of being a surgeon had taught him to keep his emotions off his face, and it was disconcerting that she could read him so easily. "Let me take your bag."

"I can manage." Her eyes tracked to his right side for a moment.

"I'm not a total invalid, Millie." He reached out, plucked the bag from her shoulder and turned into the house.

He was pretty sure he heard her mutter, "Invalid, no. Idiot, maybe," but chose to ignore it.

"Want to see your room?" Brooke scooted past him, tugging Millie behind her.

He caught the faint scent of chocolate chip cookie, and his mind went immediately to his youngest brother. Logan had been baking since he was a kid. In fact, Jake and Brooke had made their way quickly through a batch of Logan's oatmeal scotchies just last week.

"Me and Daddy cleaned it," Brooke continued.

"Impressive," Millie called over her shoulder.

"You haven't seen it yet," he answered and took the handle of her wheeled suitcase in his uninjured hand. He was glad Millie and Brooke had already disappeared toward the back of the house, since his progress was slow and not so steady as he balanced her luggage on his good side.

Eventually he made it to the back half of the house, where there was a bedroom, a bathroom and small sitting area. Sara had found this house for him to rent. He was grateful for her forethought in making sure it contained enough space for live-in help. Clearly she hadn't underestimated his postsurgical needs the way he had.

A bead of sweat trickled between his shoulder blades, another reminder of his weakness. Brooke popped out of the bedroom, beckoning him with a large swipe of her arm. "In here, Daddy."

Daddy.

She used the word so freely, although he'd done nothing to earn it. Of course, he knew how little that meant in the grand scheme of things. If the name *father* was given based on merit, Jake's dad would have had the title stripped from him decades before he'd died.

He poked his head in the room but didn't enter. Something about stepping into Millie Spencer's temporary bedroom felt as if it might mean more than he wanted it to.

"Does everything seem okay?" he asked, looking all around except where Millie was perched at the edge of the bed.

She stood quickly, her attention focused on brushing the quilt smooth. Apparently he wasn't the only one affected by the unexpected intimacy of the moment.

"Perfect." Her voice squeaked just a little, making him smile. She glanced at her watch. "Do you have plans for dinner?"

"Pizza," Brooke yelled. "Can Fairy Poppins eat with us, Daddy?"

He saw Millie stifle a laugh. "You can call me Millie, Brooke."

"Millie Poppins?"

"Just Millie."

"What do you like on your pizza, Ms. Poppins?" he asked when Brooke's face fell.

"Don't you start now." Millie made a face. "And I'm fine with anything."

"Bacon and pepperoni," Brooke shouted.

"Inside voice," Millie told her.

Brooke crossed her arms over her chest. He hadn't known his daughter long, but already he could see a temper tantrum brewing. "She gets excited about pizza," he explained to Millie.

"Inside voice," she repeated, and suddenly he realized that Fairy Poppins had more backbone than he'd expected.

"We have pizza *a lot*," Brooke told Millie. Jake no-

ticed that her decibel level had lowered a few notches.
One point, Millie Spencer.

"Tomorrow we'll go to the grocery store." Millie
ruffled Brooke's hair then turned to Jake. "Do you
have peanut butter?"

"Um…yes."

Brooke shook her head. "Pizza and peanut butter
don't go."

"It's for the gum in your hair," Millie told her.
"We'll work on that after dinner."

"Mommy didn't let me have gum." Brooke stuck
her fingers in her mouth, sucking hard.

"I bet you miss her very much," Millie said softly,
bending to Brooke's level.

Brooke went totally still, but swiped the hand that
wasn't occupied across her eyes.

Jake cleared his throat. "Millie's going to unpack
now, Brooke. Would you help me order the pizza?"

She didn't move. Although it had happened only a
couple of times since he'd picked her up from Stacy's
parents, it scared the pants off Jake when she got like
this. He knew what it was like to be paralyzed with
emotion. "If you come with me, we'll get cinnamon
sticks for dessert."

The promise of sugar broke the spell. She nodded
and wiped her fingers on the front of her purple cotton dress. Without a word, she lifted her still-glisten-
ing hand to him. He swallowed and took it, once again
dumbfounded that she trusted him so completely.

Millie stared at him, her hands clutched to her chest.

"We have a lot to talk about," he told her.

"Yes," she whispered, her lips barely moving.

"Pizza first," Brooke yelled, then repeated in a lower tone, "Pizza first."

"Pizza first," he agreed and led his daughter out of the room.

WHILE JAKE TUCKED Brooke in for bed later that night, Millie found a bottle of wine pushed to the back of the refrigerator and poured a tall glass. She wasn't a big drinker by nature but definitely needed some liquid fortification before talking to Jake Travers alone.

She took out a second glass as he came into the kitchen.

"I hope you don't mind that I helped myself," she said, turning to him.

"Knock yourself out," he answered.

If only it were that easy.

"Would you like a glass?"

He shook his head. "I take one pain pill a day when Brooke goes to bed. It doesn't mix well with alcohol."

"How much pain are you in?"

"It's not that bad," he said, not meeting her eyes. "It gets worse when I'm on my feet a lot or don't take time to rest."

"Which you don't, being a full-time father."

Stretching the splinted arm out in front of him, Jake curled his fingers a few times. "I have an appointment with the doctor tomorrow morning then physical therapy. I've had to cancel my last two appointments because Brooke wouldn't stay with anyone and I didn't want to take her with me."

"She's really bonded to you."

He looked at her now. The intensity in his gaze al-

SUDDENLY A FATHER

most knocked her over. "It blows me away. I have no idea what I'm doing, and she doesn't care one bit."

"You're trying," Millie answered. "That counts for a lot."

His eyes narrowed, studying her. Millie realized she was doing exactly what her mother had always done. Smoothing things over, trying to make the man in front of her feel better even though she barely understood his situation. One of Millie's biggest weaknesses, inherited directly from her mother, was her habit of caring too quickly. She led with her emotions, and her first inclination was always to view people through rose-colored glasses.

For all she knew, Brooke would be better off with her grandparents. But Millie understood what it was like to have a father who only dropped in occasionally, always bearing toys or some other bribe for affection. Gifts couldn't make up for the long absences, to a little girl feeling alone and deserted by someone she wanted so desperately to love her.

Brooke had already lost one parent. Millie had to help Jake see that he could be a father, that an imperfect parent who was a solid part of his daughter's life was better than a fly-by-night dad.

She picked up the pad of paper and pen she'd found in one of the drawers and stepped forward to the kitchen table. "Let's make a list of what needs to be done, the schedule for you and Brooke, and where I fit into everything."

His blue eyes darkened and Millie suddenly had a clear picture of where she'd like to fit—pressed up against Jake's lean frame. He was more than a foot taller than she, so she could imagine how safe she'd feel tucked along his side. She didn't want to have this awareness of him—it felt new and unsettling, especially in the quiet of the evening. When Brooke was around, she was the focus of both their attention. Now Millie couldn't help but notice every detail about Jake, from the fullness of his mouth to the broad stretch of his shoulders underneath his faded T-shirt.

She also saw the tiny lines of exhaustion bracketing the edges of his eyes. That evidence of his fatigue brought her back to the present. She wasn't here because of her undeniable attraction to him as a man. Of course she had a reaction to him. Like Natalie said, all three of the Travers brothers were drop-dead gorgeous. Millie knew Olivia's husband, Logan, and had met the middle brother, Josh, on her first visit to Crimson. But there was something about Jake that drew her to him in a way she'd never experienced before.

More than anything that reaffirmed her commitment to keeping their relationship strictly professional.

"Money," she blurted.

He paused before lowering himself into the chair across from her. "Cutting right to the chase? I like it. We haven't discussed your salary."

"We should… I know you'll pay me…and I want to help you… I probably should have asked yesterday but…"

"One thousand."

"One thousand what?"

"Dollars. The majority of my rehabilitation will take place in the first month and a half, according to the doctors. By then, I'll know if the nerve damage has healed enough for me to do surgery again. Brooke's grandparents are coming out in two weeks, but I still want you full-time through the duration of my stay in Crimson."

"One thousand dollars for six weeks of work?" Millie hadn't made much working in preschools over the past couple of years, but her ability to live on a tight budget only went so far.

One side of his mouth quirked. "I'll pay you one thousand dollars a week for six weeks. You're staying at the house, so it's like you're on twenty-four-hour call. You'll have no rent, and I'll buy all the groceries."

She felt her eyes widen. "I can't accept so much money."

"I don't think that's the right response," he said with a laugh. "And I can't cook. I buy the groceries, but you're in charge of meals." He patted his flat stomach. "I can't handle another night of take-out pizza."

"You're a terrible negotiator," Millie said. "No one starts with their best offer."

His smile widened. "How do you know that's my best offer?"

"Are you some sort of secret billionaire who can throw money around like it's nothing?"

"I have plenty of savings and a great disability policy." He leaned forward, the tips of his fingers brushing the back of her hand. "I believe you get what you pay for, and you're worth what I'm offering."

He was touching one tiny patch of her skin, but she felt the reverberation of it through her entire body. Before tonight, no one had ever thought she was worth much. She'd taken jobs in preschools and day-care centers because she liked being around kids. It had taken her years to believe she might actually have some talent for teaching. But when she'd tried to make a career of that, she'd made a mess of her college internship.

Millie knew she needed this job as much as Jake needed her. Not for the money, but because her self-confidence had been torn to shreds. She wanted to prove that she could make a difference.

For someone.

For this man.

"You won't regret it," she said softly, tapping her pen against the pad of paper. "Now let's start that list."

CHAPTER FOUR

JAKE JERKED AWAKE, pushing the covers aside as he scrambled from the bed. His heart raced as memories of the earth shaking while the hotel collapsed around him assaulted his mind. The intense pain that shot through his leg when he tried to put weight on his right foot brought him back to reality. He sank to the edge of the bed, bending forward with his hands on his knees, and took several breaths to clear his head.

Reliving those last moments of the aftershock had become a recurring nightmare. He and Stacy Smith, Millie's mother, had never been in love—theirs was a relationship born from close proximity and convenience. But he'd cared about her and still couldn't accept that he hadn't been able to save her. Now a little girl—his daughter—was motherless.

For the hundredth time, he wished it would have been him instead. Sure, his brothers would have mourned him, but there was no one who needed him the way Brooke needed her mother. His daughter had been sad but accepting of her loss, a fact that only made Jake want to change the past even more, as impossible as that was. He was trying his best to honor Stacy's request that he form a relationship with Brooke even though he continued to feel out of his element at every turn.

He glanced at the clock, then toward the window at the light peeking through the edge of the curtain. Normally his dreams woke him in the predawn hours and he'd lie awake with his guilt and panic until Brooke came in to start the morning. But if it was really close to eight, he'd slept over an hour longer than normal. Hoisting himself onto his feet, he grabbed a T-shirt from the dresser and made his way to the kitchen.

"Daddy!" Brooke called when she spotted him in the doorway that separated the back hall from the family room and kitchen. His heart twisted as she ran across the room, a plastic tiara askew on her head despite the fact that she still wore her polka-dot pajamas.

She grabbed his hand and tugged him through the family room, which was now shockingly clean compared to how it had looked the previous night.

"Me and Fairy Poppins cleaned," Brooke said as if she could read his mind.

"Millie," a voice called from behind the pantry door. "You know my name is Millie, Brookie-Cookie."

His daughter dissolved into a fit of giggles as Millie shut the pantry. This morning his new nanny looked less like a woodland sprite and more like a woodcutter's fantasy come to life. She wore faded cargo shorts and a soft flannel shirt over a cream-colored tank top. Her chin-length hair was pulled back from her face with a wide headband, showing her delicate features to full advantage. Although she was tiny, the cut of the shorts made her legs look long and trim, and

Jake had to shut his eyes to stop his gaze from roaming her body.

"We made pancakes," Brooke told him. "The real kind from homemade."

"Homemade pancakes?" He crouched down to her eye level. "They smell delicious, sweetie. Thank you for making breakfast."

"Thank Fairy—I mean Millie—too."

He straightened again and turned to Millie, who was pouring juice into three glasses. "I didn't even know we had the ingredients to make pancakes."

She nodded but didn't look at him. "The cupboards and refrigerator are well stocked. I was a little surprised, to tell you the truth."

"Olivia and Sara keep the groceries coming. I haven't even used half the stuff they've brought."

"That makes sense."

He watched her set the juice on the kitchen table. Up until this point, all he'd managed was bagels and cereal for breakfast. "Thank you, Millie."

"It's my job," she answered, and for some reason those three words annoyed the hell out of him. "Do you want coffee?"

"I'll get it." He moved toward the counter at the same time she turned from the table. She ran straight into him then stumbled. Despite the pain that shot through his leg, he reached out to steady her, keeping his fingers on her arms until she looked up at him. "Thank you for breakfast."

"You're welcome," she said, her voice breathless in a way that made him think she wasn't totally immune to him.

Strange how gratifying that felt.

"I'll pour the coffee." Reluctantly, he released his hold on her. "You ladies sit down and start."

He joined them a minute later as Millie was spooning fresh fruit onto each of the plates.

"Daddy, will you cut my pancakes?" Brooke asked, sliding her plate toward him.

"I can do it," Millie said, reaching over the table.

"I want Daddy to cut them."

"You bet." He didn't look at Millie as he picked up a knife in his right hand. It was awkward with the wrist brace. The truth was he hadn't cut a damn thing, even food, since before the accident. He forced his stiff fingers to grip the knife and slowly sliced the two pancakes, embarrassed that a trickle of sweat had curled down his back by the time he was finished. "How about syrup?" he asked when he'd finished, making his voice casual.

"Lots!" Brooke bounced up and down in her seat.

He poured the syrup, then set the plate down in front of his daughter.

"Yum," she said around the first mouthful.

"How often do you have physical therapy?"

He quickly put down the knife as he met Millie's gaze. Was it that obvious how much difficulty he was having?

"I'm scheduled for three days a week." He used his fork to carve off a bite of pancakes from his own stack. "I've missed a couple of sessions, though, so I've been doing the exercises at home."

"I don't like Daddy to leave me," Brooke announced matter-of-factly.

"Your daddy has to go to his appointments so he can get better. We'll have lots of fun together until he's done."

"Can I have my screen time then?"

He glanced at Millie. "What's screen time?"

"You know, the amount of time Brooke has each day to watch television or play games on the computer."

"Like PBS Kids," Brooke clarified for him. "You know, when I play 'Curious George.'"

"I thought that was educational." He stabbed a few more pancake pieces onto his fork. "Isn't educational a good thing?"

Millie gave him a gentle smile—a teacher smile, he thought with a spark of irritation. The kind that reminded him that he didn't know what he was doing as a parent.

"Educational television *is* good, but..."

"Not like the zombies," Brooke interrupted. She scrunched her face up at the memory.

Millie's eyes widened a fraction. "Zombies?"

Jake blew out a breath. "A commercial for some TV show came on while I was watching SportsCenter. It was graphic... I turned it off as soon as I realized."

"It gave me nightmares." Brooke licked a bit of syrup off the tip of one finger. "Like Daddy has when he thinks of Mommy."

He heard Millie suck in a breath but kept his eyes focused on the table, unable to form a coherent response to his daughter's observation.

"My dreams about Mommy are nice," she continued. "I have a good one about when she took me to the zoo and we saw a baby orangutan. I'm going to give Daddy some of my dreams at night. Then we can both sleep better."

Now he did look at his daughter, unable to keep his eyes off her. "Thank you, sweetheart. I want you to keep those good dreams for yourself." It was difficult to speak past the ball of emotion knotting at the base of his throat.

"I have plenty." Brooke smiled at him then turned her attention to her plate, using her fork to make designs in the leftover syrup.

He heard a tiny whimper and glanced over at Millie, who quickly wiped at the corners of her eyes with a napkin. "How about if we save your screen time for tonight, Brooke? Let's rent a movie to watch after dinner. We need to drop your daddy off at his appointment and then we'll go to the park. Maybe pack a picnic lunch?"

Brooke nodded. "I like mac 'n cheese for lunch."

"Got it." She stood and cleared most of the dishes from the table.

Jake followed her to the sink. "Is it any wonder," he whispered, "that I let her have as much 'screen time' as she wants? Without the TV or computer as a distraction, she'd be slaying me with her innocent comments all day long." He put down his plate and gripped the edge of the counter. "I'm in over my head here, Millie. It's not a sensation I'm used to, and I don't know how to handle it."

"You'll be fine. This is new for both of you. Brooke went through a huge loss. The most important thing is that you're here for her. She *needs* you, Jake."

He wasn't sure if he could handle being needed, if he had the strength to make it work. But that wasn't a conversation for right now. Brooke's unconditional love coupled with Millie's expectations of him doing the right thing crippled him almost as much as his injuries. His motto during emergency missions had always been Stay in the Moment. He could only deal with one thing at a time and right now that was getting caught up on his physical therapy. He was in no position to make any decisions about the future until he knew what his body would be able to handle.

"Thanks for breakfast," he told Millie before turning away.

Her hand on his bare arm stopped him. Her touch was cool and soft against his skin. "You'll be fine, Jake," she repeated. "We're going to make sure of it."

He gave a tense nod then walked to the kitchen table, reaching down to straighten Brooke's tiara. "Best pancakes ever."

Her smile was bright. "Millie's going to teach me how to make Frenchy toast tomorrow."

"I can't wait." He unstuck a strand of hair from her cheek. "I'm going to get cleaned up for my appointment. Wash your face and hands and we'll pick out an outfit for today."

She shook her head. "Millie will help me get dressed." She grinned. "She's a girl, Daddy, so she's better at clothes than you."

He'd wager Millie was better with everything relating to kids than he, but he didn't point out that fact.

"Sounds like a plan, Stan."

"Daddy." She giggled. "You know my name's not Stan."

He thumped the heel of his palm against his forehead. "I keep forgetting. It's a plan, *Brooke*."

"Silly Daddy. That's better."

One tiny thing was better. He only wished he could fix the rest of their problems so easily.

BY THE TIME she got the dishwasher loaded, the table wiped down and Brooke cleaned and dressed for the day, Millie had almost gotten her emotions under control.

Almost.

There was no doubt that Millie had gone through hell as a child, never able to claim her father publicly or even tell anyone she knew the man who'd helped create her. Her visits with Robert Palmer had been behind closed doors or incognito. She'd hated all the pretending she'd had to do. Hated that when her father was around, her mother insisted that Millie not trouble him. There had been no help with homework, no demands for more of his time or requests to attend a school performance. But she'd known him. He'd been a presence—albeit an occasional one—in her life.

Brooke had lost her mother, and at four, Millie knew the girl couldn't truly understand the permanence of the situation or what it meant for someone to be dead. It was trauma at a level Millie could hardly comprehend. Yet Brooke seemed to be handling it with a mix of cheerfulness and poignant honesty that touched Millie to her core.

She smiled as Brooke played with her hair while Millie strapped the girl into her car seat. It was a tight fit in the back of her VW Beetle, not a car she'd planned on using to haul around a child and her very tall father. She focused on the task at hand and tried to ignore the fact that her back end was on full display as she adjusted the child safety straps to make Brooke more comfortable.

Readjusting her headband, she turned then narrowed her eyes at the smug smile playing at the corner of Jake's mouth.

"I'm not thinking what you think I am," he said softly, his blue eyes appearing several shades darker than she remembered. "Promise."

"Toss me Bunny." She held out her hands, willing her body to stop responding to the wicked gleam in his eye.

Instead he took the few steps toward her until they stood toe to toe. He placed the stuffed animal in her arms then traced his finger from the corner of her jaw down her neck, straightening the collar of her flannel shirt in the process. "You're blushing."

"I'm just hot."

"You're *just* hot," he repeated.

"Not like that. You know what I mean. It was a lot of work maneuvering that car seat into the back of the Beetle."

He gave a small laugh. "Right now I'm wondering how I'm going to maneuver *myself* into your car."

"It's not that small. You'll fit fine." When he flashed a wide grin, she groaned but couldn't stop herself from smiling in response. Something about Jake put her at ease enough to enjoy the playful banter. "Get your mind out of the gutter, Dr. Travers." She turned and handed Brooke the stuffed animal then went around the car to slip in behind the wheel.

She tried not to watch as Jake attempted to fold himself into the passenger seat. "How tall are you, Millie?"

"Five feet, two and a half inches."

He gave her a look out of the corner of his eye.

"In half-inch heels," she amended. "You're what, six-three?"

"And a quarter." He adjusted the seat back then lifted his booted leg into the car and shut the door. "If an extra quarter inch matters to you."

"Daddy, you're smushing me," Brooke said, and Millie saw the girl kick her foot into the back of Jake's seat.

He moved the seat up again, his knees grazing the dash. "Is that better?"

"Uh-huh. Bunny needs room to spread out."

"Lucky Bunny," Jake mumbled.

Millie looked over, ready to continue their verbal sparring until she noticed the tight set of his mouth. Jake's head was resting back against the seat, his eyes closed.

She placed her hand on his arm. "Are you okay?"

He gave a small nod but didn't open his eyes. "Just not used to this much moving around so early in the day. Sad but true."

"It will get better." She realized she'd said a version of that phrase almost a dozen times in the past twenty-four hours. Speaking the words out loud, unfortunately, didn't make them reality.

She backed the car out of the driveway and followed Jake's directions to the hospital. When she'd visited Olivia before in Crimson, there had still been snow on the ground. Now the whole valley had come to life and the mountains rising up from the outskirts of town were a mix of the dark green of pine trees and the lighter shades of aspens. Even Brooke seemed awed by their surroundings, as she was quiet for most of the drive.

She pulled into the hospital's parking lot fifteen minutes later.

"You can drop me off at the main entrance," Jake said before she could ask the question.

"No!" Brooke suddenly shouted from the backseat. "Daddy, don't go. Don't go to the hospital."

Jake turned as best he could toward the back of the car. "We talked about this, Brooke. I have an appointment and then I'll be with you again. Millie's going to take care of you until then."

"No," Brooke said again. This time Millie could hear the tears in the young girl's voice. "You can't leave me."

Millie's heart ached at those words. Jake met her gaze. "What do I do?"

"Brookie-Cookie," Millie said over the girl's sniffling, "we'll walk your daddy into the hospital." She parked the car in a space as close to the front of the hospital as she could find. "You can see where they're going to do the physical therapy and the office where his doctor works. If you want, we can stay and wait for him."

"Okay." Brooke's voice was a tiny whimper.

Millie could see a muscle tick in Jake's jaw but ignored him as she unstrapped Brooke from her car seat and helped her out of the car. Brooke took her father's hand as they walked toward the sliding doors at the front of the building. She sang a song to Bunny as she skipped along, once again content since she wasn't being separated from her father.

Millie came to Jake's other side. "She's afraid of losing you if you're out of her sight for too long," she whispered.

"I could be here for a couple of hours." He glanced at her. "Do you really want to hang out here all morning?"

"I'm hoping that if she sees the office and maybe meets some people, that will make her feel better and we can leave." She shrugged. "If not, we'll stay." She made her smile bright. "You're paying me a lot of money to take care of your daughter. I'll make it work, Jake."

He led them to the elevators and, once they reached the third floor, down the hall to the rehabilitation and physical-therapy offices. He walked forward, Brooke still glued to his side, to check in at the reception desk.

"I have a nine-thirty appointment," he told the woman behind the counter.

Millie watched as the woman glanced up then did a double take. She could imagine Jake got that reaction quite a bit, although he didn't seem to notice. "Oh, my goodness," the woman gushed, "it's really you."

Jake's expression remained blank.

"Don't you remember me?" The woman smiled. "I'm Lauren Bell. We went to high school together. You missed the five-, ten-and fifteen-year reunions, Jake. And you were our valedictorian." She tsked softly. "Of course, I see your brothers around town but never hear anything about you. I know you became a doctor and you travel all around the world. It must be so exciting."

Jake glanced at Millie with a look that screamed for help. She shook her head.

"It's…um… Yes, I'm a surgeon." He held up his arm. "I was a surgeon."

"Well, we'll take good care of you." Her smile faltered as Brooke stood on her tiptoes to see over the counter. "I didn't know you had a child."

"Me neith—"

Millie coughed.

"This is my daughter, Brooke."

Brooke waved and lifted her stuffed animal in the air. "This is Bunny."

"And your wife?" Lauren asked with a curious glance toward Millie.

"I'm not married," Jake explained. "Millie is Brooke's nanny while we're in town."

The predatory gleam that flamed in Lauren Bell's eyes had Millie clenching her hands. "A bunch of us from the old group get together for happy hour at the Two Moon Saloon on Fridays after work. You should join us sometime. If the nanny does evenings."

"The old group," Jake repeated slowly. "Yeah, sure, I'll see what I can do."

Brooke tugged on his hand. "You won't leave me, right?"

Millie saw him close his eyes for a moment. When he opened them, he gave a sweet and sexy—damn him—smile to Lauren Bell. "Since we're friends, Lauren," he said, leaning forward as if he were sharing a secret, "do you think it would be okay if Brooke had a little tour of the offices before I got started? Maybe you could introduce us to some of the therapists and she could see what I'm going to be doing while I'm here." He winked. Millie suppressed a gag. "She's kind of nervous and I'm sure you know all the ins and outs of how things work around here."

Lauren stood and called over her shoulder, "Rhonda, watch the front desk for a few minutes." She turned back to Jake. "Does the nanny need to come with us?"

He shook his head without looking at Millie. "Just you, me and Brooke."

Millie was surprised Lauren didn't do a fist pump in the air.

"I'll take you back. Come through that door to the left of the waiting room and I'll meet you there."

Jake led Brooke past Millie. "Good start, right?"

She rolled her eyes. "For someone who has no charm, you really laid it on thick just now."

"Who said I had no charm?"

"Personal observation."

"I've got loads of charm, Fairy Poppins." He wiggled his eyebrows. "But only a lucky few are on the receiving end of it."

Millie coughed out a laugh. Without taking her eyes off Jake she said, "Your 'old friend' is dousing herself with body mist at the moment. Be careful how you wield that charm, Dr. Travers. It's quite a weapon."

He gave a mock shudder. "Let's go, Brooke, and whatever you do, don't let go of my hand."

She saw Brooke squeeze his fingers tighter. "Be

back soon, Millie," the girl said, clutching Bunny to
her chest.

Ten minutes later, the door to the waiting room
opened again. Millie tossed aside the magazine she'd
been pretending to read as Brooke skipped through
the door, followed by her father.

"Look, look," Brooke squealed, running forward
to Millie. "I got a stressy ball, and a pen and notepad with the phone number here on it." She thrust the
notepad forward. "So if we need to call Daddy when
he's here, we can."

"We don't need to stay?"

Brooke shook her head. "Daddy's going to text me
pictures to your phone so I can keep track of him. And
we'll get lunch ready because he's going to be really
hungry after his therapy stuff."

Millie stood as Jake walked up. She could see a
woman in a polo shirt and khaki pants waiting just inside the reception door for him. "Everything's good?"

He nodded. "Your idea worked." He ruffled
Brooke's hair. "Now that Bunny has seen everything
that happens at the office, he feels much better about
me being here." His gaze was warm on Millie, making
parts of her body tingle that had no business coming
to life for Jake Travers. "Thank you," he said softly.

Before she could reply, Brooke held up the stuffed
animal. "Give Bunny a kiss goodbye, Daddy."

Jake's mouth dropped open an inch. "How about
a high five?"

Her mouth set in a stubborn way that made Millie think of Jake. Already like father, like daughter.
"A kiss."

MICHELLE MAJOR 295

He bent forward and touched his lips to the animal's grungy fur.

"Me, too," Brooke said, angling her cheek toward him.

He glanced up at Millie, emotion clouding his eyes. She nodded, the tingling in her body rapidly progressing to a full-on tremble.

Jake kissed his daughter's cheek then the top of her head. Millie wasn't sure if the sigh she heard came from her or the therapist waiting for him. Jake straightened and she noticed a faint color across his cheeks. The doctor was actually blushing. Why was vulnerability so darned appealing when it came wrapped up in an alpha-male package?

He glanced at the clock on the wall then met her gaze, looking embarrassed and flustered. "I'm going to meet with one of the orthopedic surgeons on staff after this. Give me a few hours and I'll be ready to go."

"Remember the pictures, Daddy."

"I will, Brooke. You ladies have fun."

He walked away but looked over his shoulder before the waiting-room door closed behind him. "Thanks again, Millie. For everything this morning."

She lifted her hand, trying for a casual wave but feeling pretty sure she looked more like she was having an uncontrollable body spasm. "Just doing my job," she called out brightly.

His eyes clouded a bit at her words and she immediately regretted them. But before she could say anything else, he was gone.

CHAPTER FIVE

AFTER STRUGGLING TO get Brooke back into her car seat, Millie left a message for her sister. She needed to do something about her car situation if she was going to be driving Jake and Brooke all over Crimson.

While she waited to hear back, she and Brooke went to the grocery and then stopped at the bakery she'd seen on her way through town. The main street through downtown was bustling with people on this gorgeous late-summer day. She knew that tourism was big business in Crimson. Olivia had been married to the town's former mayor before she divorced him and met Jake's brother Logan. Now she managed the community center that offered programs for both locals and nonresidents. The popular gift shop attached to the center sold goods from local artists. Jake's other brother, Josh, owned and operated a guest ranch on the outskirts of town along with his Hollywood-actress wife, Sara.

The town was picture-postcard cute, and she could understand why tourists would find this town irresistible. Colorful Victorian buildings lined the street, and the majestic peaks of the Rocky Mountains served as a backdrop. Crimson embodied a kind of small-town charm and friendliness she guessed might be lacking in tonier mountain resorts.

"What's your favorite kind of muffin?" she asked Brooke as they made their way to the Life Is Sweet bakery.

"Blueberry," Brooke answered without hesitation.

"Yum. Mine, too." Millie tipped her sunglasses back on her head. "I bet they have blueberry."

"We need Frenchy toast bread," Brooke added, tossing her rabbit into the air.

"And bread for French toast," Millie agreed. Plus a giant vanilla latte, she thought to herself.

The moment she opened the door to the bakery, the smell of sugar, bread and roasting coffee filled the air. She took a deep breath and led Brooke toward the counter. The interior was adorable, with pale yellow walls and lights strung across the ceiling. The counter was made of wood planks, and the same warm trim was at the base on the walls and around the door frames.

A large chalkboard menu filled the back wall of the room and the glass display was filled with scrumptious-looking cakes, muffins, cookies and pastries. A cluster of tables sat to one side of the room, and a few customers were clearly enjoying their selections.

Brooke let out a rapturous sigh. "I love it here," she whispered.

Millie smiled. "Me, too, Cookie." She spotted Natalie Holt at a table near the front of the store and waved.

"Hey, girl." Natalie motioned Millie and Brooke to join her. She sat with another woman, who smiled as they approached. "How's the first day with the hot doc going?"

Millie made a face. "This is Jake's daughter, Brooke," she told Natalie.

"Oops." Natalie smiled, not looking embarrassed at all. "Nice to meet you, sweet pea."

Brooke grabbed hold of Millie's shirt but smiled at Natalie. "Millie calls me Cookie." Brooke held out her stuffed rabbit. "You can too if you want. This is Bunny. My mommy gave him to me for my birthday. She's dead now."

Natalie's smile turned gentle. She reached out a hand to gently pet the stuffed animal. "I bet having Bunny with you helps you remember your mommy."

Brooke nodded then looked up at Millie. "Can I have a blueberry muffin now?"

"You're in luck." Natalie pointed to the woman across from her, who was dabbing at her eyes. Millie understood the effect Brooke could have with her candid innocence. "This is Ms. Katie and she owns the bakery."

The woman, who looked young for a business owner, stood and held out her hand to Millie. "I'm Katie Garrity. It's nice to meet you. I'm also a friend of your sister's."

Millie took her hand. "Olivia's made a good life in Crimson," she said, trying not to sound jealous of her sister's perfect life filled with friends in a community she loved. Trying not to *feel* jealous.

"She's a wonderful part of our community." She bent down in front of Brooke. "Did I hear you say you'd like a blueberry muffin?"

"They're my favorite."

"I just happen to know that fresh blueberry muffins came out of the oven a little while ago. They should be cooled by now. Would you like to come to the kitchen? We'll wrap one up for you."

Brooke bounced on her toes. "Can I go, Millie?"

"As long as you listen to Ms. Katie when you're with her." Millie held out her hand. "How about if I hold Bunny until you get back?"

"He wants to go with me." Her big blue eyes met Millie's again. "You won't leave me, right?"

"I'll be right here."

"What would you like, Millie?"

"A vanilla latte if it's not too much trouble."

Katie's smile was as sweet as the scent of her pastries. "No trouble at all."

"Fairy Poppins likes blueberry muffins, too," Brooke announced.

Millie heard Natalie choke back a laugh. Katie's grin widened.

"You know that's not my name," Millie told Brooke.

"It's the name Daddy calls you."

"Daddy and I are going to have a talk later," Millie said, blowing out a breath.

Katie put a gentle hand on Brooke's back. "Let's see about those muffins."

They disappeared into the back of the bakery as Millie sank into the chair across from Natalie. "This is way more complicated than I expected."

"Second thoughts?" Natalie asked.

Millie shook her head. "No, but I wish I knew how to help more." She pointed to Natalie. "You handled

Brooke's comment about her mother better than I did the first time she made one to me."

"I work at a retirement home, sometimes in the Alzheimer's unit." Natalie shrugged. "I deal with a lot of honesty and a lot of death. Kids are different than seniors, but people need to talk about the ones they've lost. It doesn't help to pretend like everything's normal when it isn't."

"You're right. I know that. I took a college class on children and grief, but it's different when the situation is real."

"Where's Jake today?"

"He's at the hospital. He had a physical-therapy appointment and was meeting with a doctor after."

"From what Olivia and Sara have told me, it's a good sign that Brooke was willing to stay with you."

"I think so. There's just so much to do. Brooke needs a normal schedule. Jake needs time to process everything that's happened. She takes all of his attention when they're together."

"What about preschool?"

"I don't know if Jake will go for that. He's already paying me more than he should to be the nanny. I could certainly teach her whatever a preschool could."

"But you can't get her the socialization with children her own age. I'm sure she had activities before everything changed." Natalie pulled her purse off the empty chair next to her. "There's a fantastic preschool here in town, Crimson Community Preschool. Most of us just call it CCP. My son went there and loved every minute of it."

"Do you only have one child?"

Natalie nodded. "I'm raising Austin on my own, so one is plenty. He's eight now. It's been just the two of us for as long as he can remember."

"That must be difficult. A single mother raised me, so I have an idea of how much work it can be. Do you have family in town?"

Natalie shook her head. "My mom is here but busy with her own life. Austin and I are a good team. My friends support me, and the people I work with are great."

"Have you lived in Crimson your whole life? You never left, even for college or—"

"I never saw any reason to leave," Natalie said quickly, and Millie got the impression she didn't want to talk about her life in Crimson any further. That was fine. Millie knew all about keeping things to herself.

Natalie took out a pen and notepad from her purse and copied a number from her phone onto the paper. "Here's the preschool's number. Talk to Laura Wilkes, the director. Tell her you're a friend of mine."

Millie took the paper. "Thank you."

"You *do* have friends here," Natalie said as she stood. "Crimson is a great place, Millie. You should think about sticking around for good. It would make Olivia happy and I think you'd like it here."

"I don't..." Millie tapped her fingers against the table. She almost couldn't imagine being part of a community like Crimson. It was too good to be true. "I'll think about it."

Katie and Brooke reappeared from the kitchen just then. Katie balanced two plates in one hand and held a travel cup of coffee in the other. Brooke grasped a large brown paper bag under one arm.

"I've got to get back to work," Natalie called. "Thanks for the coffee break, Katie."

"Anytime," Katie said as she approached the table. "Drop Austin off whenever works best tonight. I'm excited to hang out with him."

"You're the best." With a wave to Brooke, Natalie headed out of the bakery.

Katie set the coffee cup and plates down on the table and took a seat near Millie. "Brooke told me you also needed bread for French toast. I gave you a loaf of brioche that will be perfect."

"Thanks," Millie said and took a long drink of coffee. "This is perfect."

Her phone beeped and she glanced down at it. "Your daddy sent you a picture, Brookie-Cookie." She held out the phone so Brooke could see the photo of Jake waving with his good hand while his other one was stretched out on a table as he squeezed a small ball. "He's doing exercises to make his hand stronger."

"I used to do exercises at tumbling class." Brooke put the bag on an empty chair, Bunny perched on top. "Ms. Katie has a mixer this big," she told Millie, arms outstretched. "And so much sugar for making things sweet."

"Like these muffins." Millie patted the seat next to her. "Climb up here and let's eat." She took her wallet from her purse and looked at Katie. "How much do I owe you for all of this?"

"It's on the house," Katie answered easily. "A 'welcome to Crimson' gift."

"You don't have to do that." Millie pulled out a twenty-dollar bill and tried to hand the money to Katie.

The other woman waved it away. "I want to. It's a nice thing you're doing, helping out Jake."

"He's paying me," Millie protested.

Katie smiled. "I know all the Travers brothers, although I was closest in age to Josh growing up. It's going to be hard for Jake being back in town like this. He was a bit of a loner growing up and so darn smart."

"He's got a lot to deal with, but he's doing okay." Millie found it odd that she felt the need to defend him to someone who probably understood a lot more about the situation than she did.

Katie leaned over to look at the photo on Millie's phone. "Talk about getting better with age," she said then gave a low whistle. "It's been years since I've seen Jake, but he never fails to impress. You know everyone in the family has been so worried about him. They've managed to keep what happened under wraps, but that can only last so long in a town this size."

"The woman working the front desk at the physical-therapy office recognized him. I guess they went to high school together. Her name was Lauren."

"Lauren Bell?" Katie scrunched up her nose. "She should have the details of his return posted on Facebook within hours."

"Isn't that a HIPAA violation?"

"Not those details. I mean about Jake—what he looks like now, details about his daughter—"

"The fact that a hot, single doctor has returned to town is big news, huh?"

"In certain circles."

One of the young guys working behind the counter called out to Katie and she stood. "I've got to get back to work," she told Millie. "After Labor Day things will slow down around here. Maybe we can get together for a hike?"

"A hike?"

Katie laughed. "You know, walking on a trail in the woods. Quite popular in Colorado."

"Right." Millie knew what a hike was; she just couldn't believe Katie Garrity was inviting her on one. Growing up, Millie and her mom had kept to themselves. Her mother thought it made things easier when Millie's father came around—they could be available at a moment's notice and there weren't questions from curious friends about Millie's dad or lack of one.

It was a habit that had stuck, the inability to form lasting friendships. It was part of what had kept Millie moving from place to place once she'd left home. But something about this quaint mountain town already lulled her into a strange sense of belonging. She wondered if it was time to explore that more.

"I grew up in the city," she told Katie. "I don't have a lot of experience with nature-ish stuff. But I'd like to hike with you."

"Then I'm guessing you've never fly-fished."

"I've never any kind of fished."

Katie's eyes took on an excited gleam. "Add that to your list, Millie. I'm going to make it my personal mission to turn you into a mountain girl."

"Me, too!" Brooke said, taking another big bite of muffin. "I can be a mountain-girl princess."

"We need more of those around here," Katie agreed. "I'll see you two soon, I hope."

Millie couldn't help her smile as Katie walked away. She was already half in love with the town of Crimson, Colorado.

JAKE WAS ALREADY counting the days until he could escape his hometown. There was a reason he hadn't returned to Crimson for so many years. He liked privacy, the unfamiliar and starting new adventures. Coming back to Crimson was like trying to fit into a pair of shoes he'd grown out of a long time ago. It felt uncomfortable and cramped.

Maybe his mood had more to do with the past couple of hours. According to both the physical therapist and the orthopedic surgeon he'd seen, his wrist was healing on schedule. But there was still a question as to whether he'd ever regain full range of motion in his fingers or if the intermittent numbness in his hand would stop. He'd received several messages from the director of the agency he worked for over the past week, wanting an update and to make plans for the future.

How could Jake make any decisions without knowing if the career he'd worked so hard for was finished?

He stepped out into the bright light of a beautiful Colorado day, unable to appreciate the bluebird sky or pine-scented breeze that greeted him. He scanned the parking lot for Millie's yellow Beetle, then saw her waving from the side of a Ford Explorer. As he got closer, Jake noticed the writing on the side of the

SUV that read Crimson Ranch, the name of the guest ranch his brother owned outside of town.

"Where'd you get this thing?" he asked, not bothering to hide the irritation in his voice.

Millie shrugged. "I saw it idling at the curb downtown with the keys in the ignition, so I took it."

"Smart aleck." He shook his head, but felt the ghost of a smile curl one side of his mouth. "This is one of Josh's vehicles."

"Glad you noticed," she said sweetly.

"Where's your car?"

"At the ranch." She tossed a set of keys in the air and caught them. "I made a trade."

"What use does Josh have for a VW Beetle?"

"He doesn't, but we need a car with more room."

"I don't need help from my brother. Your car was fine."

She patted the hood of the Explorer. "Well, I think a big rig kind of suits me."

He choked out a laugh at that. He heard a muffled shout from the back of the Explorer.

"As much fun as it is to argue about something so meaningless, you might want to greet your daughter. I didn't want her running through the parking lot, but she's beside herself with excitement to see you."

He took a deep breath, hoping to ease a little of the tension that had built around his shoulders. He stepped forward and opened the SUV's back door. "Hey there, Brooke." Thanks to the extra height of the Explorer, he was able to lean in and ruffle his daughter's hair without a problem.

"Daddy, you're back. You didn't die in the hospital."

Jake's mouth went dry. "I'm just fine, princess. My appointments were great and the doc says I'll be able to get rid of the boot and my wrist splint in a few weeks."

Brooke gave him a smile that almost cracked his heart in two. "I'm glad you didn't die, Daddy." Before he could answer, she continued, "Millie and I had so much fun. We went to the playground and the bakery with a ginormo mixer. I had a blueberry muffin and so did she, but I didn't finish mine, so she ate them both. We bought lots of healthy stuff at the grocery and some food you like, too. Then we made sandwiches and we're going to have a picnic with a blanket and lemonade. And I got a bug catcher at the grocery for grasshoppers and ladybugs and stuff."

"Sounds like your morning was more fun than mine."

"It was the best," she confirmed.

He knew he shouldn't care that the best morning his daughter had spent since they'd arrived in Crimson didn't involve him, but it was a difficult fact to ignore. "I'm ready for that picnic," he said and closed her door before climbing into the front passenger side.

"She missed you," Millie said softly as she shifted the car into Drive.

"While having the best day ever," he answered, aware that he sounded like a petulant schoolboy.

"I mean it, Jake. Brooke talked about you all morning long and she loved getting the photos you texted."

She pulled out onto the county road in front of the hospital, back toward town. He wanted to give her a phone book to sit on while she drove since she looked so small in the Explorer compared to how she'd fit in her tiny Beetle. Jake, on the other hand, relished the additional space to stretch out his leg.

"Did you see Josh when you picked this up?"

She shook her head. "Josh was taking a group out on an ATV tour. Sara was there with her friend April. We're going to dinner at the ranch tonight. Logan and Olivia are coming, too."

"No."

She glanced over at him, "Why? Are you too tired? We can go home now so you can rest."

"I'm not too tired." He scrubbed his hand across his face. "I'm used to going days without sleep, operating for hours at a time. One morning of physical therapy isn't going to wear me out." Which wasn't exactly true, but his pride wouldn't allow him to admit as much.

"Do you have other plans?" Her voice took on a vaguely suspicious tone. "Maybe with your *old friend* Lauren?"

"I don't want to have dinner with my brothers. It's as simple as that."

She shook her head. "That's not simple at all. They care about you, Jake. They want to know everything's okay."

"Everything's not okay, Millie." He squeezed shut his eyes. "I'm a shell of who I was before the accident. I don't want them fawning all over me, trying to make things better."

"They love you," she said gently. "They're your family. Why did you come back here if you don't want to see them?"

"I didn't know where else to go."

He saw her glance at him out of the corner of her

eye and turned his head toward the window. Colors flashed by—a mix of the deep greens of pine trees and lighter-colored aspens gave way to fields with knee-high grasses and open pastures with herds of cattle grazing. He'd loved spending time in the woods as a kid, always a little removed from his younger siblings. He'd been quiet and studious, making mischief in his own way but nowhere near the hell-raising Josh, Logan and Beth had been a part of in their youth.

Jake was almost eight years older than the twins. By the time they came along, he already had dreams of leaving the life he knew behind. Their father had been a mean drunk and their mother had stayed devoted to him even when things were the worst. On the surface, it would have appeared that Jake had nothing in common with his blue-collar father. Nothing except that Jake was the spitting image of Billy Travers. Billy had always told Jake that he was going to grow up to be just like him. He knew his dad must have meant it as a compliment, but it had scared the hell out of Jake. Billy took credit for Jake's talent in math and science, claiming that his future had been just as bright until Janet had gotten pregnant with Jake at seventeen.

Jake didn't believe it was true. His father had drunk away any promise of his future and that had nothing to do with Billy's family. But Jake had been terrified into believing it could go the other way, that he could grow up into the same kind of spiteful, bitter man his father was. So he'd left Crimson and never looked back, even when things had gotten worse in his family. Even when the twins reached high school and he'd heard about their wild streak. Even when it had become clear that his little sister was out of control.

By the time Jake had been ready to intervene, it was too late. Beth had been killed in a car accident caused by a drunk driver. Logan didn't want anything to do with him, and Josh had been consumed with his life on the rodeo circuit. Jake had been finishing his residency at the time, sleep deprived and stressed. So he hadn't even tried to pull his family back together.

He'd failed his brothers. Now when he'd finally returned, he couldn't stand to take their support, no matter how much he needed it. The sound of Brooke singing sweetly from the backseat penetrated his mind, pulling him back into the present.

All of this was for her, he reminded himself. It didn't matter how hard it was for him. Brooke was his only priority.

He rolled his head along the seat rest until he faced Millie. "I'll go to dinner tonight," he told her. "For Brooke's sake."

CHAPTER SIX

JAKE WAS AFRAID he might grind his teeth to dust before the night was over. He forced the smile to remain on his face as he sat at the table between Brooke and his sister-in-law Sara.

He knew Millie had thought a big family dinner would be a good distraction, but thanks to the way his brothers were fawning all over him, he couldn't focus on anything except his injuries.

It was a perfect summer evening. The temperature this high in the mountains was warm but comfortable. A refreshing breeze blew up from the river that edged the far side of the property. They were eating outside on the big back patio of the main house on Crimson Ranch. The view of the mountains was so incredible, Jake could see why families would choose this place for their vacations.

According to Josh, the most recent group of guests had left earlier in the afternoon and the next batch would arrive two days from now. It was only family on the ranch tonight.

Brooke put down the last bite of her hamburger, her eyes scanning the table and the ground around her chair. "I left Bunny inside."

Jake thought it was a good sign that his daughter had forgotten her stuffed animal, even for a few minutes.

"I'll get him for you." Jake pushed away from the table.

"No, let me," Josh offered quickly.

"I can do it," Logan said.

Josh scrambled to his feet at the same time as Logan.

Jake froze, watching his brothers.

Millie let out a disbelieving laugh. "How many tall, strapping men does it take to retrieve a stuffed rabbit?"

There was a moment of awkward silence at the table.

"I'm finished eating," Claire, Josh's daughter, finally said. Claire was almost fourteen and it had been adoration at first sight for Brooke. "Brooke, why don't we get Bunny and go up to my room? I'll paint your nails."

"Can I go, Daddy?" Brooke turned to Jake.

"Sure thing." He glanced at Claire. "Thank you."

"It's cool." Claire smiled. "I like having a little cousin."

A lot more than he liked having two younger brothers at the moment.

Olivia stood as the girls went into the house. "Logan made his famous brownies tonight."

"I've got ice cream that will go great with it," Sara said as she jumped up from her seat. "I'll go in with you."

He watched Olivia give a meaningful look to Millie. "Would you make coffee to go with dessert?"

He glanced at Josh and Logan, both of whom were

stacking plates and handing them to their wives. They must have planned time alone with him. Just what he needed, some sort of family intervention.

Millie got out of her chair slowly. "I'm pretty sure you don't need me to make the coffee," he heard her mumble under her breath.

He could tell she was torn between her reluctance to be shuffled off with the wives and not wanting to appear rude to their hosts.

As she followed Sara and Olivia into the house, Jake took a drink of his beer.

"Is alcohol allowed with your meds?" Josh looked concerned.

"It's one beer." Jake took a deliberately long pull from it.

"How about a glass of water?" Logan asked.

"You two…" Millie sounded frustrated as she stalked back to the table, still carrying empty dishes. "What's the problem? He's having a drink."

Josh's mouth thinned. "Jake doesn't drink."

"Never," Logan added.

"You mean in high school?" she asked. "So what? Not everyone did. He's an adult now. Legal age." She set the plates on the table and plopped down into her chair, clearly not willing to be brushed off so easily. "Give the mother-hen routine a rest, guys."

She looked fierce, her eyes gleaming as she stared down his brothers, both of whom were more than twice her size. His little Fairy Poppins had a backbone of steel, he realized. It felt good to have someone in his corner, sticking up for him—even if she didn't understand why Josh and Logan were so disturbed by him having a beer.

"Our father was an alcoholic," he said quietly, reaching out to lay his hand on the nape of her neck. It felt good to touch her, grounding in a way he needed right now. "He always said I was going to grow up to be just like him."

Millie's big eyes clashed with his. "But you're not..."

He shook his head. "I guess it was because I looked so much like him. Or because I was quiet in the same way he was. Who knows? But I took it that he meant he expected me to become a drunk like him. For that reason, I vowed never to touch alcohol."

Logan sat forward across the table. "He made us do some kind of weird blood-brothers handshake to solidify it."

Jake almost smiled at the bittersweet memory. "Damn, you and Beth were probably only seven years old at the time."

"All I remember is that Jake was thrilled at the prospect of all of us being cut so he could patch us up after." Josh looked at Millie. "He always wanted to be a doctor. Carried a first-aid kit around with him everywhere."

"That's because you guys and your idiot friends were always getting hurt."

"Blood brothers?" Millie's voice sounded a little faint.

Jake held out his palm to display the tiny crescent scar at its base. Logan and Josh did the same.

"Beth wouldn't do it," Logan said then chuckled.

"Oh, wait, I forgot. Millie has the same issue with blood that Beth did. I found her in Olivia's kitchen a few months ago almost passed out from the sight of a little blood."

Jake noticed that the color had washed out of her cheeks. "Are you okay?"

She swallowed then nodded. "I can handle talking about blood. Just like you can handle a couple of beers. Right?"

"I realized several years back that I'm not like our father." *In that respect,* Jake added silently.

"Then get off his back," she said to Josh and Logan, pointing a finger at each of them. "You can't expect him to abide by every vow he took when you were kids."

"We're worried." Josh crossed his arms over his chest.

"We want to help," Logan added. "The accident scared the hell out of us, Jake. This may not be a tight-knit family, but you're still our brother. Tell us what you need."

A miracle, he wanted to answer. Because the truth was he didn't know what the hell he needed. To rewind the past and keep Stacy from dying. To know he was going to be able to do surgery again once his hand and leg healed. To understand the first thing about being a father. "Just give me some time."

"You can stay, you know." Josh fiddled with his beer bottle as he spoke. "In Crimson. It's a good town to raise a kid. To make a home."

Home. The word echoed in the silence for several seconds. Jake realized that was what both of his brothers had done. They'd made a home in this town, despite all of the history and tangled memories that still surrounded Crimson from their childhood.

"I'm here for now," Jake answered. "That's all I can tell you. Don't push me for something more."

He rubbed his fingers against his forehead, where a dull pounding beat a steady rhythm against his skull.

Millie took a deep breath next to him. "Actually, the talk about blood did make my stomach kind of queasy." She turned to him. "Would you mind if we went back to the house now?"

Her eyes didn't give away anything, but he doubted that she wanted to leave because her stomach hurt. She knew he was at the end of his ability to keep up any semblance of being social. Hell, she understood him better than anyone else in the world at this moment. It made him feel weak that he couldn't even handle an entire evening with his family. But he couldn't deny the truth of it.

"I'll get Brooke," he said and pushed back from the table.

At CLOSE TO eleven that night, Millie threw off her covers and climbed out of bed, pausing in the doorway of her bedroom. She'd been in and out of bed at least a half dozen times since she'd tucked Brooke in when they returned home from dinner at the ranch.

Jake hadn't said much on the drive back to the house, and she wondered whether she'd overstepped the bounds by inserting herself into his conversation with Josh and Logan. She knew the brothers meant well, but it had also been obvious that being the cen-

ter of all that smothering attention wasn't helping Jake
in the least.

Brooke had wanted Jake to read her a story after
she'd said good-night to Millie. At first he'd protested,
saying Millie could do the job of putting Brooke to bed
better than he. But once he'd been in the room, propped
against the headboard with his daughter snuggled to
his side, she'd seen the tension ease out of his shoulders. Even though he couldn't see it, he needed his
young daughter as much as she needed him.

It had felt foolish to wait around for Jake to be finished. What was she going to say to him anyway, especially after telling his brothers to leave him alone?

She'd retreated to her room, but had left the light on
at first and the door open a crack—in case he'd wanted
to seek her out. He hadn't, of course. Such a guy.

She could still hear the muffled sounds of the television and hated how much she craved his company,
even after being there for only a short time. An idea
rooted in her brain about Jake's issues with Crimson
and his reluctance to make any sort of plan for the future. It was a flimsy excuse, perhaps, but as Millie
padded toward the family room she told herself that
this was a conversation they should have when Brooke
wasn't within earshot.

One soft table lamp and the glow from the television were the only things that lit the family room. A
loud crash sounded from the TV, making her jump.
An old Bruce Willis action movie was playing. Jake
was sitting on the couch, his booted foot propped up
on the coffee table.

She paused in the kitchen, the tile floor cool under

her feet. The window above the sink was open and a summer breeze blew in, making goose bumps rise on her arms. Doubts flooded her mind and almost had her turning around to retreat back to her bedroom. Nothing about being so close to Jake late at night in this darkened house was a good idea.

Before she could move, the sound clicked off from the TV.

"You can come all the way over," he said quietly. "I won't bite."

Silly that her heart was beating so frantically. She came around the corner of the couch, suddenly wishing her gauzy summer pajamas were made of heavier fabric. "How did you know I was standing there?"

"I've been waiting for you." Jake hit a button on the remote and his face was thrown into shadow.

Millie perched on the corner of the sofa nearest the table lamp, only a few feet from Jake but close to the only light source in the room. She wasn't ready to be in the dark with him.

Jake didn't look at her but picked up a glass from the sofa's armrest, swirling the clear liquid and ice before taking a long drink. "It's club soda, if you were wondering," he said after a moment.

"I wasn't."

Now he did turn to her, his gaze disbelieving. "Really? After everything you heard tonight, you aren't the least bit concerned that I'm going to turn into a drunken, pill-popping wreck thanks to the accident? That's how it really started with my dad. He'd been drinking forever, but he was off work for a while after he fell from a ladder on a job site and hurt his back. He did construction and odd jobs. But from that time, the work was more sporadic and the drinking more regular. I could be a real chip off the old block. That's what Jake and Logan think, the basis for all of their concern."

She shook her head. "I think you're using your father's issues as a convenient excuse to avoid facing what's happened to you. I think you like throwing your brothers off the scent of the real problem."

One of his brows rose. "Which is?"

"How scared you are of failing."

She saw his left hand ball into a fist. "Look at me, Millie. Don't you think I've already failed?"

"At what?"

After a moment he whispered, "I couldn't save Stacy."

Millie inched closer, propelled by frustration and temper. "You're not invincible, Jake. What happened to her was a tragic accident. But she chose to come to the island, even knowing how unstable things were. That decision was on her." When he started to speak, she held up a hand. "And no, I don't think you know much about failure. Trust me, I'm a bit of an expert. I bet you haven't failed at a single thing in your entire life. Because instead you run away when things get too hard. You take the easy way out."

"Easy way?" His eyes narrowed. "I put myself through college and medical school on my own. I am… I was a damn good surgeon. I go to places most people couldn't imagine. You think that's easy?"

She shrugged. "I didn't say you aren't willing to work hard. But I know you're smart." She lifted her hand to make air quotes. "Valedictorian of your class."

She was baiting him now, probably unfairly, but she had a feeling this might be the only way to break through his defenses. "I think you used your intelligence to break out of this town, and there's nothing wrong with that. But you sacrificed your relationships with your brothers in the process. As a girl who grew up without any siblings, I can tell you how much I wanted someone to truly understand what I had to go through as a kid."

"I get that." He dropped his head to the back of the couch, exposing the tanned skin of his neck and throat. Stubble shadowed his jaw, making him look both tired and a little more rugged than she was used to.

"You might be a brilliant surgeon," she continued, fighting to keep her voice steady, "but you chose a career path that almost guarantees you won't form long-term relationships with people. You said yourself that you go wherever you're needed, your bags are always packed. So it might be challenging and stressful, but you can manage it. Having a daughter is different. A potentially career-ending injury is different."

"You think I don't know that?"

"I think you aren't willing to face it. Because for the first time in your life the things that are on the line really matter. If you fail at this, the stakes are off-the-charts high. That's scary, I know. But not dealing with the fear isn't going to make it go away, Jake."

He moved his foot off the coffee table and leaned forward, elbows on his knees, his hands pressing either side of his head. "So now you're a kid whisperer *and* an armchair psychiatrist?"

"I'm actually sitting on the sofa."

He lowered one hand, turning to her, a ghost of a smile playing on his lips. "A comedian as well. Lucky me."

"Am I right?"

He drew in a breath then blew it out. "Even if you are, what am I going to do about it?"

"*We're* going to make a plan."

His smile widened. "I thought you weren't the planning type, Millie."

"The plan is for you." She fluttered her fingers in the air. "I'm a free spirit. That's how my mother raised me."

"Bull."

"Excuse me?" She shook her head. "Ask anyone who knows me. I don't like to be tied down…" She frowned as his mouth quirked. "But not because I'm running away. I like change and movement, being flexible."

He rolled his eyes.

"But this isn't about me." She pointed a finger at him. "It's about you. And Brooke. You have to commit to her, Jake."

"I brought her to Colorado."

"That's an extended trip, not a commitment."

JAKE STARED AT her for several long moments. Millie had hit the nail on the head with that comment. He'd brought his daughter to Crimson because he'd made a promise to a dying woman, not because he suddenly had fantastic parental instincts. In the back of Jake's mind, he still believed Brooke would be better off with her grandparents. He could visit when his schedule allowed, maybe plan a few trips around her school schedule once she got old enough.

He didn't truly think he had more to give than that.

"What do you expect me to do?"

"How long until your injuries heal?"

"They want me to do physical therapy for another four weeks. By then, the nerves should have healed enough to know whether there's permanent damage." He paused then added, "Enough impairment to end a career anyway."

"Your decision about being a full-time father to Brooke shouldn't be based on whether or not you can perform surgery. She isn't a second-string priority."

"You think I don't know that, Millie?"

Her voice softened. "You need to give being a parent a real shot. Commit to trying, to making it work. If not and you let someone else raise her, as wonderful as Brooke's grandparents might be, you'll always wonder if you could have done more."

"I have been giving this a real shot." He gestured to the row of toys Millie had organized earlier along the far wall of the family room. "I have twenty-gazillion pounds of pink plastic cluttering a rental house in a town I never expected to see again. Doesn't that count as a real try?"

"Halloween."

"What about Halloween?"

"I want you to promise you'll stay with Brooke until then. It gives you over two full months together. You need to stay, no matter what you hear about your injuries. Even if her grandparents arrive and try to convince you that she'd be better off with them."

He gave a harsh laugh. "It's like you know Stacy's parents already."

"I know that all of you have been through something tragic." She shifted closer and placed her fingers on his wrist. "I also know that the relationship you have with your daughter will affect her for the rest of her life."

He lost himself for a moment in her bright eyes. Once again, this tiny pixie of a woman made him want to try to be the kind of man he wasn't sure existed inside him. "No pressure."

"I know you're scared to fail her."

He stared at her fingers on his arm, her nails brightly colored against his skin. Slowly, he lifted her fingers, lining up his hand with hers, palm to palm. Her fingers barely came past his knuckles—that was how tiny her hand was in his. "Did your father fail you, Millie?" he asked.

He felt her hand stiffen against his, and he laced their fingers together before she could pull away. "My father is an example of the point I'm trying to make. You can't fail if you don't try." Her eyes clouded with sadness. "It will be so much worse for Brooke if she grows up believing she wasn't worth the effort. That I know for sure."

An ache sliced through him for the little girl Millie used to be, the one who never believed she was worthy of her father's attention. He might be afraid, but Jake would never give that burden to his daughter. He lifted his other hand and traced the line of her jaw with two fingers. His hand might go numb at regular intervals and he didn't know if he'd ever be able to perform another surgery, but at this moment the feel of Millie's soft skin under the tips of his fingers seemed like all he needed in the world.

Her eyes fell closed and it felt like an invitation. He leaned closer and brushed his mouth across hers, savoring her softness as her breath mingled with his. "So sweet," he murmured, moving his hand to the back of her neck to bring her nearer to him.

She wrapped her arms around his shoulders and gave the tiniest moan in the back of her throat. The sound brought parts of his body to full attention. Never had Jake been so affected by a woman. He was all for mutual pleasure, but the innate need thundering through his veins was something wholly new for him. It felt as though everything about Millie Spencer was made to entice him, from the way she smelled like springtime flowers to the softness of her skin.

She was an intoxicating mix of strength and vulnerability wrapped up in a package of feminine grace. "Your father was an idiot," he whispered against her mouth. "You're worth the effort, Millie. This is worth it all."

He'd meant the words as a compliment, but she suddenly jumped to her feet, tugging at the hem of her pajama top. "We can't do this," she said, a look of panic in her eyes. "You can't do this, Jake."

He stood and reached for her but she backed away. "It was a kiss, Millie. That's all. I don't think I was the only one who was enjoying it, either."

She shook her head, looking miserable. "I'm not that kind of woman."

"What kind of woman?" He felt his temper kick in. What the hell was she talking about?

"The kind that… You can't… We can't…" She squeezed her eyes shut. "I work for you, Jake. That's all."

"And you think I'm assuming this is a perk of paying you. That you have to watch my kid and then service me when she goes to bed. Is that what you think of me, Millie?"

"No. I didn't mean—"

"Forget it." He scrubbed his hand over his face. "The kiss never happened. It wasn't part of the bargain. I get it. No matter what happens with my recovery, I'm here until Halloween. I'm going all-in with Brooke although I still highly doubt I'm her best bet." *That I'm anyone's best bet,* he thought to himself. "But I'm going to try. If I fail, then at least I gave it a shot. That's what you want, right?"

She nodded, pulling on her lower lip with her teeth. She didn't look at him, though. One damned kiss and she couldn't even make eye contact.

"You got your way. Congratulations." He stepped around her. "I hope you know what you're doing."

CHAPTER SEVEN

MILLIE HAD NO IDEA what she was doing. She lay in bed the next morning replaying the events of the previous night over in her head. Jake had kissed her. She'd wanted him to; there was no doubt about it. The minute his mouth had touched hers, her whole body came to life. His claim that she'd "enjoyed" it was an understatement, to say the least. The kiss had tilted her world on its axis and she wasn't sure she could right it again.

But she had to try. She was going to deny her attraction to Jake Travers no matter what. Not only because she worked for him, but to prove she could deny it. Millie was determined not to be like her mother, who'd turned every interaction she had with men into something calculating. As much as her mom was always the fun, good-time girl, she also used her sexuality as a weapon to manipulate men. It had slowly chipped away at her self-worth in the process.

Millie would not be that person. She was going to stand on her own two feet, even when the ground beneath her was mucky and unstable.

With that thought spurring her on, she got dressed, then headed to the kitchen to get started on the French toast before Brooke woke up. To her surprise, Jake was already standing at the stove, his daughter setting plates and forks at the table.

"Good morning," she said as her feet touched the tile. "You two are up early."

"Daddy's making quesadillas," Brooke sang out. "He can cook, Millie. And not just delivery pizza."

"Quesadillas?" She glanced at Jake and willed the color to stop creeping up her cheeks.

"Breakfast quesadillas," he clarified. "Have a seat, ladies. They're almost ready."

She sat in the chair Brooke held out for her but wanted to escape back into her bedroom. As much as the quiet intimacy of last night had shaken her, watching Jake in all his domestic glory was just as unsettling. He wore another pair of loose athletic shorts and a faded University of Colorado T-shirt that stretched across the muscles of his back and shoulders. His hair was tousled from sleep and a shadow of stubble covered his jaw.

Why was it so damned appealing to watch a man in the kitchen? Or maybe she was just over her head with this particular man.

She took a quick sip of her juice as he came to the table, unable to make eye contact with him for fear he'd be able to read in her eyes the lie that she'd told him last night. Her brain might want to keep their relationship professional, but her body had ideas of its own.

He slid a few sections of quesadilla from the pan to her plate and she watched as he did the same for Brooke, unable to look away from the movement of his hands. Maybe she should have started the day with a cold shower.

There was a bowl with sliced fruit in the middle of the table, so she distracted herself by spooning some out for each of them.

"Coffee?" Jake asked, his voice tinged with humor.

She glanced up at him then and he raised his brows, as if he could read every inappropriate thought in her mind. "Thanks," she muttered as he filled her cup.

"The breakfast-dillas are yum-mo," Brooke said as she took another big bite. She reached out to pat Millie's arm. "We can make Frenchy toast tomorrow, right?"

Jake folded himself into the chair next to Brooke. "Did you say *French toes*?" He leaned closer to his daughter. "I can't eat French toes. What if the feet weren't washed first?" He mock shuddered and Brooke dissolved into a fit of giggles.

"Daddy, you're so silly." She licked at the cheese dripping from her quesadilla. "But you make good breakfast."

"I'm glad you like it," he answered then smiled at Millie. "What do you think?"

She could read the challenge in his gaze. "An A for effort," she admitted then took a small bite of one wedge. It was a perfect combination of egg and cheese with the tortilla grilled to a crispy golden brown. "It's actually pretty good. Where did you learn to make these?"

"I did a stint in a little village in southern Mexico called Chiapas. I learned to get creative with eggs and tortillas."

"I thought you didn't cook."

He shrugged. "My skills are limited, but I'm trying."

Suddenly his gaze wasn't teasing or challenging. It was hopeful and open and almost knocked Millie to the floor. She realized that when Jake Travers really tried at something, there was probably very little he couldn't accomplish. Like making her heart open to him.

"Mommy said breakfast was the most important meal of the day." Brooke set Bunny on the empty chair and spread a napkin in front of him. She broke off a small piece of quesadilla and laid it on the napkin along with a strawberry.

Jake's jaw went slack as he stared at his daughter.

Millie filled the silence. "You learned a lot of really smart stuff from your mommy."

Brooke nodded and took a sip of juice.

"What do you have planned for today after your therapy appointment?" Millie asked Jake.

He looked at her as if it was a trick question.

"I made a call to the preschool Natalie Holt recommended. Brooke is going to visit the classroom, and the director has time today after lunch to talk about enrollment. I was hoping you could be there, too. It's your decision, after all."

"My decision," he repeated.

"I don't want to go to school. My friends aren't there." Brooke crumpled the napkin and grabbed on to her stuffed rabbit, pulling him close to her chest. "I want to stay with Daddy."

Her big eyes filled with tears. Millie could feel Jake's resistance crumbling.

"How about we just give it a try?" she coaxed. "You

and your daddy can decide if it's right for you once you take a look and meet the teacher." Millie smiled. "After that we can visit Katie at Life Is Sweet for a homemade cookie."

The girl perked up at that. "Chocolate chip?"

"Of course," Millie promised.

"Okay. I'll try it." She scrunched up her nose. "But I probably won't want to stay." She hopped off her seat. "I'm finished. Can I have screen time now?"

"Sure," Jake answered immediately.

She skipped away toward the front of the house, where the office was located.

"Great attitude," Millie said when she was gone. "Wonder where she gets it?"

"How do you avoid the big meltdowns with her?" Jake shook his head. "I swear she was crying every other minute before you got here. I live in constant fear of those tears."

"Believe it or not, kids want a schedule and rules. It helps ground them." She waved her hand at the table. "Looks like having a plan has made a difference to you already."

"Two months. I'm giving it my all for two months. We'll see what happens after that."

"You sound like Brooke and her thoughts on pre-school. But I have great faith in both of you."

Jake gave a small laugh. "Which brings up a good point. I don't know anything about choosing a pre-school, Millie. You're the one with the teaching de-gree—"

"Not yet," she corrected. "Remember I'm on a break from school. Who knows if I'll even go back." She stood quickly, grabbing the plates from the table. What had possessed her to share that little tidbit with him?

Keeping her back to Jake, she rinsed the dishes in the sink.

"Afraid of failure?" came a voice in her ear a few moments later. She whirled around, still holding the nozzle of the kitchen sprayer.

"Whoa!" Jake jumped out of the line of fire with a laugh just as she let go of the sprayer. "Be careful where you point that thing."

"I'm not afraid of failure." Millie tried to keep her words steady, but couldn't help the slight catch in her voice. "And I'm *not* running away."

"I didn't say you were."

She turned back to the sink and flipped off the water.

"Hey." Jake placed a hand on her shoulder. She continued to focus her gaze on the stainless steel in front of her. "I was joking, Millie. I know this is about me." He paused then added, "I'm sorry for last night. I don't want to take advantage of you or make you uncomfortable."

She waved off his concern. "It's okay. It was probably my fault. I know I—"

Now he did spin her around. "You did nothing wrong," he said, bending so he could look into her eyes. His were so blue and honest she couldn't help but nod.

"You either. It was a moment. It happened. We got it out of our systems."

He brought his face within inches of hers. "Are you sure about that?"

She forced herself to nod and he stepped back, straightening. "Good to know." He turned and collected the rest of the dishes. When the kitchen was cleaned, Jake walked to his bedroom to change clothes for his appointment.

Millie drove him to the hospital, but this time, Brooke was okay letting him out at the doors by the main entrance.

He said goodbye and climbed out of the Explorer. Before shutting the door, he turned back to Millie. "For the record, I didn't get anything out of my system last night," he said. "Just so you know."

Millie sucked in a breath, but he disappeared before she could answer.

JAKE CRADLED HIS wrist in his good arm as he left the physical-therapy office two hours later. The exercises left him feeling both reinvigorated and exhausted, hopeful that he was making progress and frustrated that it wasn't faster or easier.

He took the elevator to the ground floor of the hospital and started toward the front entrance, where Millie and Brooke would pick him up. His name was called and he turned to the sound. A woman and a man, both in white lab coats, walked toward him.

"Lana?"

The tall brunette smiled at him. "I heard you were in town."

He shook his head. "What are you doing in Crimson?"

"Finishing up my fellowship," Lana Mayfield answered. "And getting lucky enough to cross paths with my favorite med-school study partner again." She turned to the man standing next to her. "Jake, I want to introduce you to Vincent Gile, the medical director at Rocky Mountain West."

The older man held out a hand. "It's a pleasure to meet you. You're a bit of a legend around here."

Jake shook Vincent's hand. "I don't understand..."

"The people of Crimson are extremely proud of their world-traveling Dr. Travers. You'd be surprised how many patients ask if I've met you." The man chuckled. "Like the medical community is one big social-media outlet. But I'm happy to finally put a face with your name and list of accomplishments."

"My list of..."

"Don't be modest, Jake." Lana shook her finger at him. "First in our class graduating from med school then on to your charity work all around the globe. You've got quite a reputation."

"We were all sorry to hear about your injuries," Vincent added. "I want you to know we'll take good care of you here at West. If there's anything you need, just let me know." He took a step closer. "I also hope you'll let me take you to lunch while you're in town. Crimson is a great place to live, as I'm sure you know. Now that you're back, I'd like to talk to you about a possible future here."

Jake felt his mouth drop open. "That's kind of you. But as I'm sure you're aware, I don't know the long-term effects of the accident yet. There's a chance..."

Vincent waved away Jake's concerns. "If you're interested, we'll find a place for you. A local doctor on staff, especially one as well respected in the community as you, is not something I'd pass on, I can tell you that."

The man's cell phone beeped. "I have a meeting. How about lunch next week?"

"Sure," Jake answered, stunned at Vincent Gile's interest in him.

"I look forward to it." The cell phone beeped again. "Gotta run." With a quick nod to Lana, Vincent turned and headed back toward the elevator. Jake and Lana watched him go.

When the metal doors closed, Jake let out a long breath. "Is he always like that?"

"Intense and direct?" Lana laughed. "Absolutely." Her expression turned serious. "He manages a great hospital for someplace so remote."

"Remote? I wouldn't call Crimson remote."

She smiled. "I did both medical school and my residency in Chicago. Remember? This place moves like molasses compared to what I'm used to."

"You don't like it here?"

"It's fine for now," she said with a shrug of her delicate shoulders. She reached forward and gave him a quick hug. "I like it better now that you're in town."

"Thanks." Jake didn't know how else to respond. He'd met Lana his second year of med school. He'd managed to graduate from college in three and a half years and applied directly to medical school from there. He'd been young and hungry to prove that he could handle the rigors of med school, but it had been a challenge. He'd received scholarships but still had to work part-time at a neighborhood diner to pay for books and expenses. That didn't leave much time for any type of a social life. Lana had been just as ambitious, only her motivation was to prove to her neurosurgeon father that she'd inherited his talent.

They'd become study partners and dated casually, mostly because neither had the time or energy to make a real relationship work. They'd ended up at the same hospital for residency, but lost touch when their careers had taken them on separate paths.

When he'd first met her, Lana had been the exact opposite of everything Jake had grown up with in Crimson. She was sophisticated, confident and coolly beautiful. The years hadn't changed that. Unlike most of the doctors he'd met in Crimson, who adopted a mountain-casual look even while on the clock, Lana wore an expensive and exquisitely tailored suit under her lab coat. Her hair was glossy, pulled back into a smooth ponytail at the nape of her neck.

For a moment an image of Millie's sprite-like tumble of hair came to his mind. Strange that he'd think of Millie while talking to Lana.

"I missed you after you moved on," she said now, bringing him back to reality.

"Yeah, sorry." He remembered that she'd texted him after graduation. "I was traveling so much, it was hard to keep up with friends."

She dipped her chin and smiled at him. "I get off at six. Let's have dinner and catch up. I want to hear all about your adventures." She placed a hand on his arm. "My fellowship is over at the end of September. I was thinking I might like to try something new. Maybe with Miles of Medicine. It would be fun to coordinate our schedules." She gave his arm a squeeze. "Like the old days."

The old days when all he had to worry about was ingesting enough caffeine to keep up with his round-the-clock shifts. A day with Brooke made overnights during his residency look like a cakewalk.

"I've got a lot going on right now and doubt I'll be decent company by the end of the day," he said, not mentioning that most of his fatigue came from the responsibility of parenthood. "Another time."

Her smile dropped a bit but she nodded. "Definitely. It's good to see you, Jake." She reached up on her tiptoes and gave him a kiss on his cheek. "You make this town suddenly seem much more interesting."

He took a step back. The gleam in her eye made him a little nervous. "See you around, Lana." He walked quickly out of the hospital, dropping his sunglasses over his eyes as he did.

He spotted the Explorer parked near the edge of the patient-drop-off area. As he got closer, he could hear music coming from the open windows. It wasn't a song he recognized, although the melody sounded vaguely familiar. Brooke's high-pitched, little-girl voice was belting out song lyrics. He stopped in his tracks as Millie joined her.

Millie's voice was just like her—bright and bubbly—and totally mesmerizing as she harmonized with the tune Brooke was singing.

He opened the car door and started to speak, but Millie held up one finger. "This is the big finale," she whispered on a quick breath before singing again.

A glance to the back of the car showed Brooke with

her eyes closed, a rapturous look on her face as she continued to sing, blissfully unaware of his return.

A man in scrubs wheeled an elderly woman past the car and they both turned to look at Millie, who waved cheerfully.

"Do you want to roll up the windows for this?" Jake asked.

She ignored him, her voice rising to join Brooke's at the end of the song.

Despite himself, Jake felt chills roll down his back. Her voice was like a caress as she sang about playing all day in the sun.

After a few moments, the song ended and Millie flipped off the volume on the radio control.

"That was awesome," she said, turning to give Brooke a high five. "You are the best Ariel I've ever heard."

"You sound just like a princess," Brooke answered, and Jake could see Millie's stock rise several notches in his daughter's estimation.

"*The Little Mermaid* was my favorite movie when I was a kid," she told Jake, easing into the parking lot. "I combed my hair with a fork for months after seeing it the first time." She was practically bouncing in her seat. "How was your appointment? Did it run late?"

He blinked several times to keep up with the various conversation threads. "I saw someone I knew from my residency. And why would you comb your hair with a fork?"

"Daddy doesn't watch princess movies," Brooke said from the backseat.

"Everyone watches princess movies. We'll rent one

tonight." Millie wiggled her eyebrows at Jake. "You'll love it."

"I can't wait." The funny part was Jake realized he meant it.

Millie and Brooke took turns telling him about their morning until they pulled in front of a small brick house on one of the side streets leading from downtown.

"This looks lovely," Millie murmured.

She was right. The brick on the house's exterior was painted a pale yellow with dark blue trim and shutters. Planter boxes hung under the windows, and the flowers each held were cheerful, as if they were giving a warm welcome to each person who walked up the path that led to the front door.

"I don't want to do this," Brooke said quietly from the backseat.

Me neither, Jake agreed silently as he watched a group of mothers trickle up the sidewalk, kids in tow.

"It's just a visit," Millie reminded Brooke. "You're brave like a princess, Brookie-Cookie." She gave Jake a meaningful look, as if he was supposed to add something more to the conversation.

He got out of the SUV and opened the back door. "I'll hold your hand the whole time," he offered without thinking, then felt like an idiot. Why would that matter?

To his surprise, Brooke nodded. "Okay, Daddy. As long as you don't leave me."

He smiled. "I'll be right here."

Taking her hand in his, Jake led Brooke toward the front door of the house, Millie at his side. "Tell me again why you can't just teach her what she needs to know," he whispered.

"This is about socialization and her development." She glanced around him to Brooke. "It's important for her to have time away from you."

"She does," he argued. "When I'm at the hospital."

Millie shook her head and gave him a gentle elbow to the ribs. "It's just a visit."

A woman who looked to be around fifty years old greeted them. Silver hair just grazed her shoulders. She wore an apron with the words Crimson Community Preschool in block lettering across the front. If Jake had to imagine what an ideal preschool teacher would look like, this woman was it. Her face was kind, her smile gentle as she held out her hand. "I'm Ms. Laura," she said, speaking directly to his daughter. "Are you Brooke?"

Brooke nodded and took a small step forward. "This is Bunny. He's scared, so he has to stay with me."

Ms. Laura patted the stuffed animal on the head. "It's nice to meet you, Bunny," she answered without missing a beat. She turned her gaze to Jake and Millie.

"Thanks so much for letting us come by today," Millie said quickly. "We spoke on the phone. I'm Millie Spencer, the nanny, and this is Brooke's father, Jake Travers."

"Laura Wilkes," the woman responded. "Welcome to all of you." She pointed to a doorway off the entry of the house. "Why don't you take a look around? School starts next week, so we do small group orientations to talk to the children about how their day will go. We have two new additions to the older class, so Brooke won't be the only one joining us."

"We're just visiting." Brooke spoke to Bunny, not making eye contact with the teacher.

"That's fine." Laura Wilkes bent down to Brooke's level. "If you and your daddy like it here, Brooke, I hope you'll come back. I think you'd enjoy our time together."

Jake felt his daughter's grip tighten on his hand even as she inched forward. "Let's go, Daddy."

He took several steps toward the main room of the preschool before he realized Millie wasn't following him. "Are you coming?" he asked, glancing over his shoulder at her.

She gave him a reassuring smile. "In a minute. You two go ahead." She turned back to Laura, and Jake allowed himself to be led into the room, certain that Millie was purposely hanging back so he and Brooke would do this on their own.

His throat went dry as he took in the colorful tables with blocks and building equipment. An art station was situated near the center of the room, complete with easels and paints. In the corner was a play kitchen, shelves of neatly stacked food near one side.

The four mothers in the room all turned as he and Brooke walked in. A couple of the kids looked over and he felt Brooke stiffen next to him. He was pretty sure he and his daughter shared the same instinct at this moment, which was to get the hell out of there. Instead, he plastered a smile on his face.

"Hi," he said, lifting his splinted arm in a wave.

"I'm Jake and this is my daughter, Brooke. We're new to Crimson and visiting the preschool today."

The women stared at him for a few moments, then descended like a litter of puppies on a new toy. Introductions were made as they drew him forward. Jake found that when Brooke's hand began to slip from his, he was the one holding on tight.

"It's okay, Daddy." She handed him Bunny. "I'm going to play in the kitchen." He watched her follow another girl to the far side of the room.

Just like that, he was left alone. He gave another halfhearted smile. "I'm sort of new to being a dad," he admitted. "Brooke's been living with her mother up until a few weeks ago." He didn't bother to mention all that went into that statement, and the women didn't seem to care.

They extolled the virtues of the preschool and Ms. Laura to the point Jake felt as if he'd entered some tiny kid-sized cult. As he watched Brooke interact with the other kids in the room, smiling and laughing, he realized it might be worth it.

One of the moms shared that she was also a single parent and invited him to coffee to discuss tips for making it work. Jake backed away so fast he almost tripped over a beanbag chair behind him. Thankfully, Laura Wilkes walked into the room at that moment.

Millie was nowhere in sight. He wondered where his nanny had disappeared to and why she'd left him alone with this horde of overfriendly mothers.

"Friends," Laura said to the children scattered around the room, "let's gather on the carpet." The kids scampered forward as if this Ms. Laura was the Pied

Piper. Talk about commanding a room. The preschool director, for all her sweetness, was definitely in charge.

He expected Brooke to find him, but she took a seat on the floor next to the girl she'd been playing with in the kitchen.

"It's funny," one of the mothers said quietly. "You spend so long wanting them to become more independent. Then it's hard when they do."

He nodded, unsure how else to answer. He hadn't spent *so long* wanting anything from Brooke, but somehow he understood exactly what the woman meant.

Laura explained the daily schedule for the school, the different types of learning environments, how the classroom changed and special events for the year, including a class musical to coincide with the Halloween party. He smiled at the look of utter rapture on his daughter's face as she listened intently to information about snack time, recess and different projects Ms. Laura had planned.

When the children and parents were released a half hour later, he wasn't surprised that Brooke came running up to him, quickly saying, "I'm going to do school here, Daddy."

"You like it that much?" A pang of disappointment shafted through him. He knew it was good that she felt comfortable at the school and he couldn't blame her. But even as he constantly felt unsure of himself as a father, Brooke's dependence on him was the only solid thing in his life right now.

"I love it," she assured him. "Bunny does, too." She

took the stuffed animal from him and gave its scruffy head a big kiss.

Millie ducked into the classroom as Laura was walking the rest of the families out. "Pretty cool, right?" She bent and Brooke came forward to give her a big hug. "I'm proud of you, Cookie. You did great here today."

He wished he'd thought to say that. He wished he could show affection so naturally, but that had never been a part of Jake's makeup.

"Where were you?" He waved his hand around the room, unable to stop his irritation from spilling out. "This is your area of expertise and you left me to fend off the moms by myself."

Millie chuckled in response. "Oh, no. Not the moms," she said in mock horror. "I was filling out paperwork."

Oh. So she hadn't quite deserted him.

Laura Wilkes walked back into the room. "What did you think, Brooke?"

"Good," she answered. "Do I get my own cubby?"

Laura nodded. "And a shelf for your art projects. You can take Bunny on a tour of the rest of the room and across the hall where we have snack time while I talk to your daddy and Millie."

"You have a very sweet daughter," Laura said after Brooke left the room.

"I can't take credit for that," Jake answered.

Laura's smile was gentle. "Millie explained the situation to me. We'll take good care of her while she's at the preschool. Do you have any questions for me?"

"I wouldn't know where to start." Jake looked at Millie. "Do I have any questions?"

She shook her head. "Laura has been here over fifteen years. She has a wonderful philosophy for the children and most of what they learn is through hands-on play."

Jake looked at her blankly.

"That's good," she assured him.

"We use parent volunteers in the classroom," Laura added. "You're welcome to sign up out in the entry. I'll need a lot of help for the fall musical. My teaching partner also moved suddenly due to a family emergency. I'm interviewing this week and would love to have someone in place before school starts. If that doesn't happen, I'll be relying on volunteers even more until I can fill the position."

Jake nudged Millie, who only said, "Thanks for letting us come in today, Laura. I think this will be just what Brooke needs. We'll plan on seeing you the Tuesday after Labor Day for the first day of school."

She took a step toward the door, but stopped when Jake placed a hand on her arm. "You should hire Millie," he told Laura and heard Millie hiss out a breath. "She's a teacher."

"Not certified," Millie said quickly, frowning at Jake. "I haven't finished my degree yet."

Laura's face brightened. "We don't need someone certified for the teaching-assistant position. If you're interested, I'd love to talk to you about it."

Millie hesitated. "I'm not sure that I'd have the time with what Jake and Brooke need."

"We'll make it work." Jake shrugged at the glare Millie shot him.

"Okay...well..."

"Think about it," Laura told Millie. "Give me a call if you want to know more about the job. I have two candidates right now, but I'm not sure either of them is a good fit."

Millie nodded, but her mouth was grim. Jake didn't understand. He thought she'd be thrilled to have an opportunity to teach again. Hadn't Olivia told him how much her sister enjoyed working with kids?

They said goodbye and walked to the car.

"Don't ever do that to me again," Millie said under her breath as Brooke climbed into her car seat.

"Do what?" Jake was genuinely confused. "Try to help you?"

"I'm not the one who needs help." She crossed her arms over her chest. "My life is fine. I manage fine. I'll decide what kind of work I do and don't want. If you're looking to get rid of me, just say it, Jake."

He held up his hands. "I'm not trying to get rid of you, Millie. What would make you think—"

She shook her head. "Forget it." She closed her eyes, took a breath and opened them again, a sunny smile spreading across her face. "This was a huge success. The preschool is perfect for Brooke. The moms are going to love you. Everything's just great." She leaned into the car. "Who wants to celebrate at the bakery?"

"Me," Brooke shouted, raising both hands above her head.

"Let's go, then." After strapping Brooke's car seat, she shut the door and moved toward the driver's side.

Jake caught her arm. "What just happened there?"

"Nothing," she answered. But the smile was forced and didn't meet her eyes. Then her gaze softened. "Nothing, Jake. Please let it go."

After a moment, he nodded. "Okay. Let's get a cookie."

She exhaled, obviously relieved.

He would let it go for now, he thought as he got into the Explorer. But not for good. As sunny and bright as Millie appeared, there were shadows in her, a darkness she tried—but couldn't quite manage—to hide. Jake planned to find out what put it there.

CHAPTER EIGHT

JAKE CLIMBED THE steps to his brother's house two days later, after Logan had picked him up from his latest visit to physical therapy.

"You're getting around better," Logan commented as he followed Jake up the stairs.

"Still worried you're going to have to break my fall when I lose my balance?"

"Not one bit."

Jake purposely fumbled then grinned as Logan scrambled to right him.

Jake straightened. "Liar."

Logan swore under his breath. "Next time, I'm going to let you go down."

Olivia opened the door as they came to the top. "He's all bark, no bite," she said as she held open the door, then followed him into the kitchen.

"Excuse me?" Logan put an arm around his wife's waist and pulled her close. "Have you already forgotten last night?"

"Get a room," Jake muttered in a good-natured tone. He was happy for his brother. Logan had taken the death of their sister the hardest. Jake had tried to reach out years after Beth's death when Logan had seemed to be spiraling out of control. He'd wanted—albeit belatedly—to help his youngest brother come to terms with his grief, as if Jake was such an expert on that. But Logan hadn't wanted the interference of an older brother who'd left him and the rest of the family behind years ago. Jake had always wondered if Logan would make it to the other side of his pain in one piece and was grateful he seemed so content with his life since he'd returned to Crimson.

"Can I get you something to drink?" Olivia asked, playfully pushing Logan away. "I spoke with Millie earlier. She was taking Brooke to the children's museum over in Aspen this afternoon since you had plans with Logan."

He could hear the question in her voice. Jake had asked Logan to pick him up from the hospital, but actually wanted time to talk to Olivia.

"I want to know what's going on with your sister," he said, deciding it was best to cut straight to the point.

Olivia's delicate features took on a look of both confusion and concern. "Is something wrong with Millie? Do you have a problem with her? Is she not taking care of Brooke?" Her tone turned indignant. "Because I can tell she loves that little girl already. I've seen them together. I met them at the park yesterday and—"

"Sweetie, let him finish his thought." Logan smoothed the hair away from her face in an unconscious gesture.

Jake shook his head. "I don't have a problem with Millie."

The tension sagged out of Olivia's shoulders. "Sorry. It's weird. Millie and I are only now getting to know each other, but I feel very protective of her. She's my baby sister, you know?"

Jake's eyes flicked to Logan. "Yes, I know."

"Have a seat, Jake." Logan pulled out one of the high stools from the kitchen island.

"I'm worried about her," Jake said as he lowered himself into it. "There are things she's not telling me. Nothing to do with Brooke. She's fabulous with Brooke—different than I could ever be. Yet it works for all of us."

"She's got a gift with children."

"Which is my point. We were at the local preschool a few days ago. The director needs someone to help a few hours a day. It would be perfect for Millie."

"Early childhood education is her major."

"Right. But she wasn't interested. In fact, when I mentioned her background she all but bit off my head." He leaned forward. "Do you know the details of why she left school?"

Olivia shook her head. "Something happened at her student teaching assignment. I just figured Millie got bored of the day-to-day routine. She talks a lot about wanting her freedom and not making big commitments. It has to do with how she was raised, I think. Her mother was the ultimate free spirit." She gave a wry smile. "It's what drew my dad to her."

"Millie isn't her mother." Jake felt his temper flare.

"I know," Olivia answered quickly.

"For all her claims of being so footloose, she loves order and a schedule—at least on her own terms. She's got Brooke on a regular sleeping routine, limits her screen time, counts the fruit and vegetable servings she has each day. Hell, she has all of the toys in the house put away in their own special places each night. She can be fun and spontaneous, but she's also the most organized person I've ever met."

He shook his head. "It doesn't make sense that she would leave school and nothing explains why she wouldn't want the experience that the preschool can give her."

He looked up to find both Logan and Olivia staring at him.

"You just strung more words together than I've heard you speak in the past decade," Logan said, scratching his jaw.

"You care about her," Olivia added.

"She's responsible for my daughter," Jake said, unwilling to address his feelings. "Of course I care."

They both continued to watch him. "Don't read more into this than what it is. Brooke's grandparents arrive next week. Millie thinks she's going to turn me into the perfect father, but that's not going to happen." He looked to Logan for confirmation. "With our background, I'm not cut out to be a parent to anyone."

"Josh thought the same thing," Logan answered, "but he's doing fine with Claire."

"That's different." Jake straightened. "Josh was nothing like Dad."

"You're not like him, either."

Jake wanted to believe that but wasn't convinced.

"Josh and I are driving up the mountain today to do some maintenance near the trailhead above the ranch. Want to come with us?"

Jake held up his hand. "I'm not much help on the trail these days."

"We'll find some way for you to be useful."

He thought about going back to the empty house before Millie and Brooke returned then nodded. It had been years since he'd spent any time with his brothers. Part of him was worried they'd have nothing to talk about, but a larger piece didn't care. He'd spent so much time alone in his life. Even when he was working out in the field, Jake had always remained a little apart from the group. Being with his daughter and Millie had made him realize he liked feeling as if he belonged. Maybe he could learn how to translate that into a relationship with his brothers.

"Sure. I'd like that."

He was surprised at how happy his agreement seemed to make Logan.

"Are you and Millie bringing Brooke to the Labor Day Festival this weekend?" Olivia asked. "I'll be working a booth for the community center, and Sara and Josh will bring guests from the ranch. We can all meet up if that works?"

"The Labor Day Festival like when we were kids?"

Logan nodded. "This is the thirty-fifth year. Remember, you used to walk us into town because Mom and Dad wouldn't go? Somehow you always came up with the money so we could get cotton candy, hot dogs and have enough left over for a few rides."

Jake remembered. He'd spend all summer each year collecting soda-pop cans and pilfering change from his father's dresser to have money to show his siblings a good time at the festival. It was the one weekend they all looked forward to each year, when they could forget the troubles at home and simply have a good time. Other than the people he'd encountered at the hospital and locals at the bakery, Jake had managed to avoid running into many people who knew him back then. It was exactly the way he wanted it to remain.

"Brooke would love it," Olivia said, breaking his reverie.

"I'm sure she will." He nodded. "I'll talk to Millie." He thought of his promise to go "all-in" on being a good parent. "Plan on seeing us there."

"DADDY, YOU NEED to wear the crown."

Millie smiled at the horrified expression that crossed Jake's face as Brooke climbed the back steps to the porch and placed the ring of dandelions on top of his head.

"You're the prince."

"Can I be the prince without wearing flowers in my hair?" He met Millie's gaze and grimaced.

She shook her head at the same time Brooke said, "You have to wear the crown."

Millie and Brooke had spent the past hour playing in the backyard, creating a kingdom of rock-and-log thrones, pretend soup and the flower crowns. It was the kind of play Millie had loved as a girl, when she'd spent most of her time in the small woods next to their condo during her father's visits. The condo wasn't large and her mother had always wanted privacy with her dad, leaving Millie to fend for herself outdoors. Neither of her parents had ever joined her on her imaginary adventures, so she'd been surprised when Jake had returned home from an afternoon spent with his brothers and come to sit on the patio steps, helping to stir mud-and-leaf stew for his daughter.

He adjusted the band of flowers. Somehow the whimsical crown didn't detract from his masculinity. In fact, the contrast somehow made him look even more appealing. As if he needed help in that area.

The doorbell sounded from inside the house.

"Pizza's here," Brooke announced.

"We didn't order pizza tonight," Millie told her. "Remember, we made lasagna after the museum today. It's in the oven."

"I'll see who it is," Jake said, standing but not removing the flowers from his hair. "Maybe I left something in Logan's car."

As he walked into the house, Millie lay back on the quilt she'd spread in the yard. She felt emotion uncurl in her stomach, a mix of happiness and hope she hadn't experienced in a long time. Being with Brooke gave her life a sort of gentle purpose she relished. It was odd to feel as if she belonged in this little girl's life. Her feelings for Jake were more complicated, but there was an underlying sense of rightness she couldn't deny. Even if it was only temporary, she planned to savor every moment she had in Crimson.

She closed her eyes as Brooke began to rain blades of grass down on her.

"It's a magic blanket," the girl told her. "When you fall asleep with this covering you, your dreams come true."

It had been so long since Millie had dared to dream, she didn't know how to respond. Instead, she enjoyed the warmth of the early-evening sun and the smell of fresh grass surrounding her. The tiny pieces of grass tickled her bare arms and legs, and she let herself relax in the moment.

After a few minutes Jake's voice broke her reverie. "Brooke, will you come up here?" His voice sounded different than it had a few minutes ago, tighter and more controlled. "I have a friend I'd like you to meet."

Millie sat up, blinking several times to shake the daydreams that had so quickly populated her brain. Dreams of love, a family and a place that would finally feel like home. As Brooke skipped over to the porch, Millie stood and dusted the grass off her denim shorts and the Life Is Sweet T-shirt Katie had given her when she and Brooke had made their now-daily stop to the bakery earlier.

Jake stood on the porch, a woman at his side whom Millie didn't recognize. She couldn't have been a Crimson native. Everything about her, from her silk blouse to her pencil skirt and leather pumps, screamed "big city." Even though she'd grown up in DC, Millie had never fit that mold thanks to her mother's unconventional influence.

She quickly pulled down the hem of her shirt and tucked her hair behind her ear, groaning as more grass blades fell to the blanket around her. Tucking the blanket under her arms in front of her like a shield, she slowly made her way to the edge of the porch.

"Lana," Jake said, his hand on the base of the woman's back, "this is Millie Spencer, Brooke's nanny."

The woman gave Millie a long look up and down. Up close, she was stunning—with high cheekbones and glossy hair that was arranged in a sleek knot at the back of her neck. Millie noticed that the dandelion crown drooped in Jake's injured hand and she quickly pulled the flowers out of her hair.

"How sweet," Lana said, but her patronizing tone made Millie feel anything but sweet. "You have a daughter *and* a nanny." She put her hand on Jake's arm and squeezed, leaning closer. "We definitely have a lot to catch up on, Jake."

Lana bent over Brooke as if she was examining her, the tight smile still in place. "How old are you, honey?"

"Four," Brooke answered, holding Bunny in the telltale death grip that Millie had come to know meant the girl was nervous. Jake didn't seem to notice.

"Lana and I did our residency together," Jake told Millie. "She's a brilliant doctor and is finishing a fellowship at the clinic here in Crimson."

"Brilliant," Millie repeated. "That's nice." She was all too aware of her disheveled appearance and bare feet in comparison to Lana, who looked as if she'd just stepped out of a fashion magazine or boardroom, not a county hospital in the mountains of Colorado. No one in the world had ever described Millie as brilliant. As her mother always told her, the Spencers had other ways of attracting attention besides their brains. Millie had always wanted to be one of the smart ones, wishing she'd inherited more than her father's brown eyes.

"Lana brought dinner," Jake said with a slightly apologetic wave in Millie's direction.

"We made lasagna," Brooke told him. "Remember? I cut the cheese." She laughed at the joke she and Millie had shared earlier. Millie smiled along with her but noticed Lana's brows furrow.

She thought she saw one corner of Jake's mouth curve, but it was so quick she might have imagined it. "The lasagna will hold until tomorrow. Right, Millie?"

Her face burned but she nodded. "Sure."

"I don't know if I have enough for everyone." Lana's mouth turned into a perfect pout. "I picked up Chinese." Millie watched as the woman's chin dipped. "Kung pao chicken used to be your favorite, Jake. Do you remember all those takeout nights after our shifts?"

Millie wanted to gag as Jake stuttered. "I…uh… guess."

"I thought it would just be the two of us, but of course I want to include your daughter." She slid Millie a pointed look.

She might not be "brilliant," but Millie could take a hint. "I'll wrap up the lasagna for another time. You three can have dinner. I ate a big lunch, so I'm not that hungry."

"You had a salad," Brooke pointed out.

"It was a *big* salad."

Lana clapped her hands together, clearly having expected to get her way. "Perfect."

"I bet there'd be enough. Are you sure, Millie?" Jake's voice was so kind it made her throat tight.

She gave a jerky nod. "I'm going to clean up out here. Brooke, wash your hands before eating, okay?"

"Yep." With a quick glance at Millie, the girl ran back into the yard and plucked up the final crown of flowers. She returned and handed it to Lana. "You can be the dinner princess," she said with a smile.

Lana held the flowers gingerly in her hands. "Thanks," she said as if Brooke had handed her a wiggling snake.

"Let's go, Cookie." Jake scooped up Brooke and Bunny in one arm. "We don't want the food to get cold."

And with that Millie was left alone in the backyard. She couldn't be mad, she told herself, despite the ball of emotion lodged in her chest. Lana was a friend of Jake's. She'd been a colleague, someone he shared things in common with and could relate to on a meaningful level. She looked perfect next to him, like a doctor's wife should look. That woman could say whatever she wanted about catching up, but Millie recognized the look of possessiveness in her eyes. She'd been part of Jake's past, and from the looks of it, she had every intention of becoming part of his future.

Millie was a temporary fix. She was the nanny. The hired help. She was a placeholder, like she'd always been in life. That had been enough for her mother, but never for Millie. Her wishes didn't seem to matter. When it was time to have fun, make messes and take a break from life, Millie was the type of person you wanted around. When it was time for things to get real, she was left behind.

Just like always.

THERE WERE TIMES Jake knew his life would be easier if he lived on a mountaintop in some remote part of the world where there weren't any women to be found for miles.

Tonight was one of those times.

He hadn't planned on Lana Mayfield showing up at the house with Chinese. Hell, he didn't even remember what he'd eaten most of his residency since the times he hadn't been at the hospital had passed in a blur. If she said he liked kung pao chicken, he wasn't going to argue. He hadn't understood that it might be a big deal to postpone the meal Millie and Brooke had made for another night.

Mistake number one.

He'd also assumed that when Millie had so quickly agreed that it would be best that she be left out of the dinner, it had meant she wanted time to herself. A night off. A break. He could certainly understand why she would want that.

Mistake number two.

Of course, he hadn't realized he'd made either of those mistakes until his sister-in-law Sara had called a few minutes ago.

Millie had remained in her room until they'd finished eating. Then she'd taken Brooke in to have a bath and get ready for bed. He'd gotten the distinct vibe Lana would have liked to stay longer, but he knew Brooke would want him to read her a bedtime story. Those quiet moments with his daughter had become the highlight of each day for him.

As he was heading back toward Brooke's bedroom after Lana left, he'd picked up Sara's call. She'd asked about the lasagna—apparently it had been a Crimson Ranch recipe—and when he'd explained the delay in eating it, he'd been greeted with a heavy silence on the other end of the line.

Not a good silence.

"I thought you were the smart brother," she said finally and proceeded to explain—in great detail—why his actions had been rude and probably hurtful to Millie. That hadn't been his intention and he wondered how he was going to fix it.

Only a short time ago, Jake had been able to fix any number of physical injuries and illness. Now he was at a loss.

He hoped Sara had been wrong in her assessment of the situation.

"Sorry if I messed up dinner plans," he said, blocking Millie's path out of Brooke's room.

"No big deal. I had some email to catch up on."

"So you enjoyed a little time to yourself?"

She leveled a look at him then flashed the brightest smile he'd ever seen. "It was peachy."

"You do so much with Brooke…" he said, trying another tactic.

"You pay me," she shot back immediately.

He took a breath. "Yes, but you don't have to be on call twenty-four hours. If you want a night off, I can handle things here."

"With Lana?" Her voice was icy cold.

Allowing Lana to stay for dinner was mistake number three, apparently.

"She's an old friend. Nothing more."

"You don't owe me an explanation." More frost.

He looked down at her, wanting to make this better but not having any idea how to accomplish that.

She still smelled like the outdoors, fresh and clean and too damned appealing. He liked her bubbly and happy, but he found he liked her irritated, too. That was a big problem. A blade of grass still clung to her hair, and he loosened it from the soft strand, his body going tight at her quick intake of breath.

"I'm going to take a shower," she said. He had an immediate image of water pouring over her skin.

Mistake number four.

He nodded and let her walk past then took a deep, head-clearing breath before moving toward his daughter.

Thirty minutes later, he eased the door to Brooke's room closed. He could hear Millie in the kitchen and resolved that he would not make more of a mess of this evening than he already had.

She had her back to him, standing in front of the open freezer door.

"Looking for leftovers?" he asked as he came to stand at the edge of the room.

Obviously—he hoped—she hadn't heard him come into the room. She spun around and hurled her spoon at his head. It twirled in the air then hit him directly between the eyes.

"Ouch." He rubbed at the spot on his forehead and bent forward to retrieve the spoon.

Millie rushed toward him, their heads almost colliding. She grabbed on to his shoulders, pressing the front of her body against him as she tried to drag him toward the center island. For a moment he didn't resist, so overwhelmed by the feel of her soft curves and the scent of ripe berries and chocolate—a combination of her shampoo and ice cream, he guessed.

She tugged on him, but he stopped moving. "What are you doing, Millie?"

She wrenched at him again, not quite knocking him off balance. "I thought you were going to faint."

"From being dinged in the head with a teaspoon?" He grinned at the thought. Millie looked completely serious.

"How many fingers am I holding up?"

"Two."

"Do you have a headache?"

His head wasn't the part of his body with the ache at the moment.

"I'm fine. It hardly hurt. I was just picking up the spoon." He held it up for her to see. "Sorry I startled you."

"I thought you were with Brooke."

"She fell asleep."

Jake couldn't help but notice she hadn't moved away from him. He tried to remain as still as possible to prolong his pleasure in this moment.

His gaze flicked to the refrigerator. "What were you doing in the freezer?"

She bit down on her lower lip and looked away before answering, "Having dinner."

"Ice cream?"

She nodded.

"Why didn't you eat with us?"

"There wasn't enough food."

"Bull. We would have made it work."

She tried to pull away but he held her fast. "I spent

enough of my life being the third wheel to my mom and dad. I wasn't going to be the fourth one tonight." Her voice held so much vulnerability and sadness, he almost couldn't stand it. "It's fine. Really. I work for you. We're not friends. We don't—"

"No." He cut her off, raising his hands to cup her face, forcing her to look him in the eye. "We *are* friends, Millie. Hell, you're one of the few I have in my life. I've never been great at making friends."

Her sweet lips pressed together. "Lana Mayfield and her trip-down-memory-lane Chinese would argue with that."

"Lana is great." He leaned in closer, just a breath away from her. "It was nice to see her. But she isn't…"

MILLIE WAITED FOR him to finish his sentence then got distracted looking into his blue eyes, which had gone several shades darker as he watched her.

"She isn't what?"

His mouth grazed hers ever so slightly, the light pressure making her ache for more.

"You," he whispered, the word humming against her skin. "She isn't you."

Millie sighed as he deepened the kiss, relishing the strength and warmth of him. The kiss was a revelation because as much power as she knew he possessed, he didn't wield it against her. He allowed her to lead, to explore him at her own pace. There was an intimate give and take as their tongues met and melded. Still he held back, reining in his need and stoking hers in a way she'd never before experienced.

It left her wanting more. She wound her arms

around the back of his neck. Her fingers laced through the soft hair that curled at his collar, urging him closer. He took her silent invitation, enveloping her in his embrace.

The moments turned into minutes as they stood wound around each other.

"You feel so good." He released her mouth to press kisses along her jaw and then down her neck, nipping at her skin then soothing those heated spots with his tongue. His fingers touched her back underneath her pajama top and her whole body ached from the pleasure of it.

"More," she whispered and let her own hands snake under his T-shirt to the hard muscle of his back and torso.

They were a tangle of arms and legs as he claimed her mouth again. She felt her knees tremble and he steadied her with his injured hand, the fabric of his splint scratching against her exposed skin.

She felt her control slipping. She was about to lose herself in the moment. She wanted to lose herself to this man.

The thought was scary enough to have her wrench away, pressing her palms to the kitchen counter to steady herself.

For a few minutes the only sound was the hum of the refrigerator and her heavy breaths as she tried to regain control of herself. She stole a glance at Jake out of the corner of her eye. He watched her from hooded eyes, his arms loose at his sides. Although he looked totally in control, she could see his chest rise and fall in an unsteady rhythm. At least she wasn't alone in how much the kiss had affected her.

"I can't do this," she said faintly. She picked at a corner of the tile countertop. "It isn't right."

"It sure as hell felt right." She thought she heard condemnation in his tone, but maybe that was her own voice ringing in her head.

"I work for you, Jake."

"We're friends, Millie."

"Not that kind of friends."

Her mother had been her father's secretary when they'd first met. From the stories Millie had always heard, he'd swept her off her feet and left her mother unable to resist him. Millie had always promised herself that she would never lose sight of who she was. She would never allow a man to make her forget what she wanted from life.

She'd always thought of her mother as weak. But in this moment she understood how her dad had been able to capture her mother's heart in one moment and take command of her life for the next two decades. Because all she wanted was to wrap herself around Jake Travers and never let go. No matter if she wasn't good enough or smart enough. She didn't care about consequences or commitment. She'd always fought to remain in control of her emotions and her actions, but every time that resolve slipped Millie found herself in trouble.

Now she was standing on the edge of a yawning cavern, and she knew if she didn't pull herself away she'd be lost.

She could lose herself in Jake.

Hugging her arms around her body, she straightened and looked at him.

"I'm not going there… We can't go there."

"What's wrong, Millie?" His gaze pinned her in place. "What happened to you to make you so scared?"

She took a breath. "I'm not scared. I called the preschool. I'm interviewing with Laura tomorrow. If things work out, I'll start the Tuesday after Labor Day, the same hours as Brooke so I'll still be able to take care of her."

"Okay, good. I think you'll be perfect for that." He shifted. "I meant what I said, Millie. You're not on call twenty-four hours here. If there are other things you want to do or you need time off—whether for a job or something else—we'll make that work."

"I'll take you up on that."

How else was she supposed to answer? *No, thanks. I don't have a life or friends or any hobbies. The only time I feel remotely content is when I'm with you and your daughter. That's how pathetic I am.*

No, she wouldn't admit any of that. Instead, she'd walk away.

As hard as it was. As much as it hurt. Because walking away had always been easier than staying and fighting for things she didn't believe she deserved.

"And that's all?" His voice pierced her thoughts.

"That's all," she agreed then turned and fled back to the safety of her bedroom.

CHAPTER NINE

MILLIE POPPED A CHIP into her mouth and took a long sip from her margarita.

"Nothing cures what's ailing you quite like tequila," Natalie said and poked her gently in the ribs.

"I wish it were that easy." Millie scooped more salsa onto a chip.

She'd met Natalie, Olivia and Katie at the local Mexican restaurant for a girls' dinner. Sara had flown to California for a night to attend some fancy Hollywood party, so she was the only one missing from the group of friends.

Friends.

Millie rolled the word over in her mind, liking the sound of it. Usually she dealt with issues privately, or she called her mother. Her mom wasn't much on listening, but she always had enough going on to distract Millie from her own problems.

When Olivia had called earlier, Millie hadn't meant to share everything, from Brooke's grandparents arriving early to Jake's none-too-subtle suggestion that she get a life of her own. But it had all come spilling out. To her surprise, Olivia had immediately suggested that a girls' night out was just what Millie needed.

Jake had seemed shocked that Millie was actually

leaving for the night. As shocked as Millie that the women she was getting to know in Crimson would make time for her.

But they were here, and Millie felt the comforting arms of new friendship wrap around her. She blinked against the tears that pricked at the backs of her eyes.

"Too spicy?" Katie asked from across the table, a knowing look in her green eyes.

"Something like that."

"So tell us all about Dr. Easy-On-The-Eyes and the trouble he's causing." Natalie nudged her again.

"No trouble," Millie said quickly. "I love being with Brooke, and Jake's very helpful in his own way."

"For a guy who doesn't know the first thing about being a father," Olivia suggested.

"Exactly."

"And when he kissed you…" Natalie prompted.

"It was…" Millie broke off, realizing that she hadn't mentioned their kiss to anyone, not even her sister. Mortified, she thumped the palm of her hand against her head. "It was nothing. It didn't happen. I'm a total idiot."

"There's no use denying anything with Natalie," Olivia told her. "She's like a mind reader." She shook a chip at Natalie. "Your time will come and we'll all be here to witness it."

"Oh, no," Natalie argued. "My time has come and gone. I want nothing to do with men. Been there, done that. Got the amazing kid to prove it. Back to you, Millie."

"It was really nothing. Less than…"

"A kiss from Jake Travers is less than nothing?"

The food was delivered to the table at that moment, allowing Millie to collect her thoughts before answering. "It was lovely, as you might imagine."

"Lovely," Katie repeated with a sigh.

Natalie snorted. Olivia smiled across the table.

"It meant nothing and we agreed it wouldn't... couldn't happen again. I work for him. His priority is Brooke."

"Doesn't stop either of you from being human," Natalie commented as she forked up a bite of taco salad.

"It stops me from acting on it." Millie picked up her fish taco.

"Logan and Josh want him to stay in Crimson, even after he's fully recovered." Olivia's gaze was kind. "You could stay here, too."

"It's a wonderful place," Millie agreed, "but I don't want to impose on your life any more than I already have."

"You're my sister, not an imposition."

"And Jake isn't..."

"You like him?" Olivia formed the words as a question, but Millie knew her feelings were obvious to each of these women.

"He's not for me." She wiped her fingers on her napkin. "There's a woman working at the hospital he knew from his residency. I think they dated or something. She brought dinner over the other night."

"Competition. Nice." Natalie tapped her fork on her plate. "What's she like, this harpy who's after your man?"

Millie nearly choked on her taco. "She's a doctor—

smart, beautiful and totally different from me. But he's not my man. She's not competition. It isn't—"

"Just know we've got your back if you ever need it," Natalie said.

The words brought another wave of emotion cresting in Millie's chest. No one ever had her back. "I'm not looking for a relationship."

Olivia tilted her head. "But if the right person comes along, it's a shame to ignore it."

"Olivia tried to ignore Logan," Natalie said. "We were witnesses."

"Whatever happens," Katie offered, "it's nice that Jake has you in his life right now. I never imagined him as a father, so having someone to help ease this transition has to be a big deal for him."

Easing the transition. That was exactly what she was doing. Nothing more. But as she laughed and talked with these women, Millie realized how much she wanted to have a life that included friends and a community like Crimson. It was difficult to miss something you'd never had. Now that she'd experienced this kind of support, how could she go back to her solitary life?

BROOKE'S GRANDPARENTS ARRIVED two days early. It shouldn't have surprised Jake. He was fairly certain they were trying to catch him unaware, probably hoping to find Brooke and him living in chaotic squalor filled with empty pizza boxes and dirty clothes.

That might have been the case if it hadn't been for Millie. He hadn't lied when he told Olivia that her sister was the most ruthlessly organized person he knew.

Millie's demeanor might be all rainbows and sunshine but she ran the house with the precision of a military sergeant.

Thanks to that, Janis and John Smith seemed shocked to find Brooke happily ensconced in a home-made Play-Doh project at the kitchen table.

Her hair was done up in one of the intricate braids that she begged Millie for each morning. Her ballet getup was clean, her face scrubbed after lunch, and she hummed along with the kids' channel playing from the speakers attached to the computer.

She took the arrival of her grandparents in typical stride. "Nana, Papa, do you want some pizza?" she asked, holding up her colorful creation.

Janis dabbed at her eyes. "Oh, sweetie, I've missed you so much. Come over here and give your nana a kiss."

Brooke dutifully got up from the table and dusted off her palms. She let Janis wrap her in a tight embrace then gave John a hug, as well.

The front door opened at that moment. He heard Millie's voice. "I brought cookies from Life Is Sweet."

Jake watched as she stopped in the middle of the family room.

"Brooke's grandparents are here," he told her as if that wasn't obvious.

"Fairy Poppins is home," Brooke told her grandparents. "She's my nanny. She's nice and she likes blueberry muffins the best."

"A nanny?" One of Janis's brows rose. "Is that really necessary?"

"I'm in the leg brace for at least another week, Janis.

I can't drive, and I have to get to my appointments. What would you propose as an alternative?"

"I thought you came to Crimson because your family is here. Can't they help you?"

He wasn't going to explain that he didn't want or deserve his brothers' help. "This works best."

She shook her head. "Stacy was a hands-on mother."

"Stacy traveled quite a lot for her work," Jake argued. "She told me as much."

"She had us," Janis countered.

"And a good day care so if—"

"Stop." Millie's voice interrupted their argument. "This isn't helping."

Jake's gaze moved to his daughter, who had inched her way over to the table to grab Bunny. He knew what that meant.

"The nanny's right," John said. He held out his hand. "I'm Brooke's grandfather, John Smith. I'd guess you don't always go by Fairy Poppins."

"Millie Spencer." Millie shook John's hand, giving him a sweet smile. "I'm so sorry for your loss, but I'm happy to meet you both. Brooke should be surrounded with all the people who love her."

"My point exactly." Janis sniffed. "Which is why we want her back in Atlanta, where she can be with family."

"She has family in Crimson, too." Jake knew he was being baited but couldn't seem to help his response.

"Where are they?" Janis hitched her chin as if making an important point. "Why is she being cared for by a s-t-r-a-n-g-e-r?" She spelled the final word.

Jake wanted to growl with frustration. "She's being cared for by me. Her father. The way Stacy wanted."

Millie stepped forward. "My sister is married to Jake's youngest brother, Logan," she said, gently leading Brooke back to the table. "I'm in town for a few months and I have experience working with children, so I offered to help Jake for a bit. His family *is* involved. I know he wants both of you to be involved, as well." She gave him a pointed look.

"That's true. I don't want to make things more difficult for Brooke." He took a breath then continued, "I'm glad you're here, Janis. We need to make an effort with each other. It's the only way this is going to work."

Janis didn't look convinced, but John took her arm. "Have a piece of your granddaughter's pizza, hon." Millie moved out a chair so Janis could sit next to Brooke.

"Can Nana have a cookie?"

"Of course," Millie answered. "Can I get either of you something to drink?"

"A glass of water, I suppose. I bake my cookies from scratch, but I'll try a bite of one if it makes you happy, sweetie."

"I bake cookies, Nana." Brooke spread her arms wide. "Katie—she owns the bakery—has a mixer this big that I can use. Millie makes her pancakes and Frenchy toast from scratch. Daddy can only do eggs."

Janis sniffed then began to roll tiny pieces of Play-Doh between her fingers. "Your mother spent hours as a girl making Play-Doh creations. Remember how many colors we have back at Nana and Papa's house?" She refused to make eye contact with Jake.

John tipped his head toward the front of the house and Jake followed the older man to the office. "This is difficult for Janis," John said once they were out of earshot.

"It's hard for all of us." Jake wasn't feeling particularly sympathetic at the moment.

"That little girl is all we have left of our daughter."

The anger went out of Jake like a deflated balloon. Of course these two people were hurting. By all accounts, Stacy's parents were wonderful people. They'd been devastated by their daughter's death. Then Jake had come in and taken their granddaughter from them. "I'm sorry, John. I don't want to hurt you and Janis." He ran a hand through his hair. "I'm doing my best to honor Stacy's wishes."

"When this all started, you agreed it would be best for Brooke to live with us in Georgia."

A dull ache settled in Jake's chest. "I want to get to know my daughter. Even if... When she comes to live with you, I will still be a part of her life."

The older man nodded slowly. "I'm glad to hear you say that, son. I wasn't sure you felt that way when we first met."

"It was a lot to digest." Jake didn't try to mask the bitterness in his voice.

"I loved my daughter." John's voice broke off and he cleared his throat then continued, "She was the best part of our lives. Janis and I still can't believe she's gone. But I never agreed with her keeping Brooke a secret from you. I know she had her reasons, but that doesn't make it right."

"She had her reasons," Jake repeated. Stacy had

practically spit them at him the night he'd found out about Brooke. Everything had centered on her belief that he was unable to commit, that he wouldn't make the changes she thought necessary to be a true father to his daughter. "Then why, John? Why did she find me like she did? Why did she ask me to take care of Brooke with her last breath? What changed? Why now?"

"I don't know. I wish I did. Janis and I were shocked when she left to go to you. She wouldn't talk about it, only told us it was best for Brooke. Her first priority was always Brooke. Ours is, too. You have to know that Janis only means well."

"But she doesn't believe that I do? What happens if I share custody with you? Is Janis going to let me be involved?"

"Will you want to be involved?" He pointed to Jake's arm. "If you're able to take up where you left off with your agency, how involved will you really be? I know you're doing your best here, Jake. Is that enough?"

He'd thought the same thing only weeks ago. His plan had been to come to Crimson, fulfill a mother's dying wish that he get to know his daughter, then move on from there. As cold as it sounded, getting to know Brooke had been one more thing to check off his list. One thing to fill the time while his body healed before he returned to regular life. No wonder Janis seemed so shocked at his attitude now.

Something had changed in him. His feelings for his daughter had changed him. And Millie. Her belief that he could become a decent father was a powerful influence on his intentions. He wanted to believe she was right.

"You can't believe it's best for Brooke to have her grandmother and her father at odds. Janis isn't going to listen to me, but you have to convince her that we need peace between us. For Brooke's sake."

John nodded. "I'll do my best."

"That's all any of us can do." Jake held out hope that his best would be good enough.

The Labor Day Festival was in full swing by the time Jake, Millie and Brooke caught up with Jake's brothers and their wives. They were seated at two tables set up off to the side of the main food-tent area. The sun had just ducked behind the mountain peak, leaving the evening light tinged in a soft shade of pink. Millie loved the energy of the event.

Residents laughed and talked, greeting each other by name under the glow of hanging lights while families in town for vacation appeared to soak up the gold rush–themed activities. Millie held the bag of gems and "fool's gold" Brooke had panned for earlier and tipped back the straw cowboy hat Jake had bought for both her and Brooke at one of the booths. A bluegrass trio played from the stage nearby, the music filling the air along with the scents of carnival food. An older couple danced together in front of the stage, and Millie wondered if she'd ever experienced a more perfect night.

"I love cotton candy," Brooke announced to the group, licking her fingers. The spun sugar seemed to be a four-year-old version of perfection.

"You polished that off in record time," Jake said as he dipped the corner of a napkin into his water cup. "But no more sweets or you'll end up with a tummy ache tonight." He gently wiped the napkin across Brooke's cheek, cleaning off a spot of dried cotton candy.

Millie's heart swelled at his unconscious movements and the way he smiled at his daughter as he worked.

"Except maybe a funnel cake," Brooke said, her tone serious. "Uncle Josh said I haven't lived until I tried a funnel cake. I want to live."

Jake threw a look to his brother who shrugged. "At least she gets her sweet tooth honestly," Josh offered. "It's a Travers tradition."

"Remember the year Beth was sick all the way home?" Logan laughed. "That girl loved candy like no other."

Brooke tugged on Jake's plaid shirt. "Who's Beth, Daddy?"

All eyes went to Jake. "She was my sister, sweetie. Your uncle Logan's twin. But she died when she was in high school. It was very sad for all of us."

Brooke gave him a knowing smile. "It's sad when someone dies. But maybe Aunt Beth is friends with Mommy in heaven."

Millie thought it was a testament to how far Jake had come in his relationship with Brooke that he didn't look shocked at her observation. "I bet they are good friends, Cookie," he answered.

Logan gave Olivia's shoulder a gentle squeeze, making Millie's heart melt a tiny bit. He took his wife's hand in his, kissed her knuckles and stood. "Let's go track down the funnel-cake booth, Brooke. I could use more dessert myself."

"We'll come, too," Josh said, wrapping his arm around Sara's waist. "Claire is here with a group of friends and I want to make sure she's okay."

"You mean you want to stare down any boy who comes within twenty feet of her," Sara said with a laugh.

"That, too," he agreed then turned to Jake and Millie. "We'll be back in a bit. Do you two need anything?"

Millie shook her head.

"I'll bring you some funnel cake," Brooke promised.

"Have fun, sweetie." Jake pointed a finger at his two brothers. "One funnel cake and that's the end of her sweets for the night."

"Spoken like a true parent." Logan swung Brooke onto his shoulders while she laughed, turning to wave to Jake and Millie as the group walked away.

"This has been a wonderful evening," Millie said when they were alone at the table. "Thanks for including me in it."

"The Labor Day celebration is a big deal in Crimson. Always has been." After a moment he reached across the table and laced his fingers with hers. "I'm glad you're here, Millie. I couldn't imagine doing any of this without you."

She didn't know how to respond without revealing how quickly her feelings for him had grown. They sat in a comfortable silence for several minutes, listening to the band and people watching. A group of kids, clearly siblings, walked by them, herded by an older brother who was trying to keep his young charges under control. She saw Jake's mouth harden into a thin line as they passed.

"You had a lot of responsibility for your brothers and sister," she said softly.

"Someone had to," he answered, not meeting her gaze. "I could have done better."

When he started to pull his hand away from hers, she tightened her grip.

"Josh and Logan love you," she told him. "They don't hold you responsible for the fact that you all had a crummy family life. You were just a kid, too."

"I was the oldest."

"But still a boy. You helped out the best you could. Children aren't supposed to raise each other." She gave a gentle tug on his hand and smiled, trying to lighten the mood. "I'm sure you read *Lord of the Flies* in school. You know leaving kids in charge doesn't work."

To her relief, he let out a small chuckle. "Well, we weren't quite stranded on a deserted island, but I appreciate your point."

He lifted their hands, turned them over and placed a soft kiss on the inside of her wrist. "You make me smile, Millie. Thank you." His touch left shivers across her skin. Millie felt herself leaning closer to him. He tucked a loose strand of hair behind her ear and trailed one finger along her jaw. "I want to kiss you again," he whispered.

Desire pooled low in her belly at his words. *Let's*

get on with it, her body practically screamed. But she shook her head. "Not here. Brooke and the others could come back at any moment."

Jake let out a breath. "Maybe not here," he agreed, "but just know that I want to kiss you." He flashed her a rakish grin. "A lot."

The way his voice went a little hoarse on those last words made her whole body tingle. She had half a mind to pull him out of the chair and hide behind one of the nearby booths for a chance to make out like teenagers. Before the thought had fully formed in her head, Brooke came running back to the table.

"I brought funnel cake," she squealed, thrusting a wax-paper package toward them.

Millie dropped Jake's hand and wiped a bit of powdered sugar from the girl's cheek. "I can't wait."

She glanced up at Jake, and he gave her a small wink. She realized her words could refer to more than just the carnival dessert and felt a blush creep into her cheeks.

She was way in over her head here and took a big bite of funnel cake, trying to tamp down her feelings as she swallowed the sweet, doughy dessert. Millie wasn't worried about getting a stomachache, but her heart was another matter.

CHAPTER TEN

JAKE WOKE IN the middle of the night later that week, drenched in sweat, his heart pounding. Another nightmare. He rubbed his hands over his eyes and sat up on the edge of the bed until he could get his breathing under control.

The doctor had given him sleeping pills, but he hated taking them, afraid he'd miss something if Brooke needed him. But all his attempts to grit his way through the nights were failing miserably.

The dreams didn't come every night, but when they did he was a prisoner to them, reliving the last few minutes of Stacy's life, the deafening roar of the building's foundation giving way and the mad tremble of the ground under his feet.

He heard a sound from outside his bedroom and noticed a faint light shining under the closed door. He'd woken Brooke once before yelling out in his sleep and hoped his daughter was still tucked away in her bed. The last thing he wanted to do was scare her. His leg protested at the speed with which he made it across the hall. But instead of Brooke asleep, he found Millie holding her close as the two slowly swayed around the room, Millie singing softly in her beautiful voice.

Her eyes widened slightly as he came into the room,

darting down then up his body before remaining glued to his face. Jake realized he was wearing only boxers and started to turn to put on a shirt.

Brooke lifted her head at that moment. "Daddy," she said, her voice still drowsy with sleep, "you had a baddy dream."

"I did, sweetie." He walked toward her when she reached for him. "I'm sorry I woke you."

"Millie was singing me back to sleep." He went to lift Brooke out of Millie's arms, but his daughter latched her arm around his neck and pulled him close. "She can sing for you, too."

Their three heads were close together now and it was almost impossible to keep from touching Millie as Brooke remained in her arms. He could feel Millie's warmth, smell the flowery scent of her shampoo. His nanny looked impossibly beautiful and sweet in the soft glow of Brooke's night-light.

She'd come home earlier, her eyes gleaming with happiness, from another dinner out with friends. She'd been almost buzzing with excitement, as if actually having fun with a group of girlfriends made her happy in a way she hadn't felt before. He liked her like that, he'd realized, and had told himself that he was going to put more fun back into both of their lives.

"Your daddy will put you to bed again," Millie said, extracting herself from the embrace. Jake saw her chest rise and fall and wondered if her heart was beating at the same annoyingly frantic pace as his.

"I need to go potty first." Brooke squirmed in his arms.

She headed toward the bathroom in the hall, leaving Jake and Millie alone in the room. The intimacy of the moment crashed through him. He shouldn't be aware of this woman the way he was. He shouldn't want her like he did but couldn't seem to stop himself.

"Doesn't right now prove this isn't going to work?" He ran his hands through his hair.

"What are you talking about?" Her voice sounded hoarse and she took a step back. She wore another pair of cotton pajama pants and a thin tank top.

"She woke up because of my nightmare."

Millie gave a gentle nod. "She wanted to go to you, but I wasn't sure if that was a good idea."

"Because I might lash out in my sleep?"

"I know you wouldn't hurt her."

"You don't know that. Hell, I don't know that. My daughter can't even sleep through the night because I wake her up with my yelling."

"Things take time to settle, Jake."

"What if they don't? What if I can't settle?" He broke off, hating the tremble in his voice. That was his biggest fear, that he couldn't do this. That he'd fail. He didn't want to fail Brooke, but for all the things he was getting right, did it really matter? What if he was truly like his father, unable to do the right thing when it counted?

Millie came forward now, her eyes intent on his. He expected her to walk past him, but she slid her arms around his neck. Her fingers threaded through his hair as she pulled his head down to hers. But she didn't kiss him. Her lips touched his ear, grazing the soft skin there.

"Breathe, Jake," she whispered. "Take a deep breath."

He did. His hands wound around her waist, pulling her against him, and he buried his face in her softness, taking in her scent. In and out until his breathing calmed.

Still she held him, nothing more. And he let her. It had been so long since he'd derived comfort from someone in this way, his knees went weak with it. He'd stood on his own, by himself, for as long as he could remember. But now this tiny pixie of a woman drove away his late-night demons with the light that radiated from her core. How did she know that this was exactly what he needed, when he didn't even realize it himself?

"I believe in you," she said softly after a moment. "I believe you can make this right."

His chest constricted at those words. He was used to proving himself. He'd made a career of working medical miracles in remote jungles and war-torn villages. But she gave him the gift of her faith without asking him to do a thing to earn it except stay. Try.

How could he deny her?

She broke away as Brooke returned to the room. His skin burned from where she'd been pressed against him and he felt the loss of her touch like a physical blow.

"Good night again, Brookie-Cookie." Millie bent and kissed the top of the girl's head. "Sweet dreams to you both."

As Brooke placed her hand in his, Millie left without another word.

THINGS WERE QUIET in the house the next morning when Millie got out of bed. She took an extra long shower to try to make herself feel normal, thanks to that 2:00 a.m. interlude, which had left her dizzy with emotions.

But as much as she wanted Jake Travers, he needed her to keep her focus. He would make a wonderful father if he could only get past his doubts. That was where she came in, not for anything else.

She tiptoed down the hall to Brooke's bedroom, since the girl got up at the same time each day. Today was the first morning of preschool and she didn't want Brooke to feel rushed. Millie's hand shot to her mouth to cover her sharp intake of breath at the scene in front of her.

Apparently, Jake had remained in his daughter's bedroom last night. He was asleep on one side of the bed, most of his body near the edge as Brooke lay with her feet pushed into his side, diagonal on the bed. The girl had all the covers tucked around her, leaving Jake ever so visible.

Millie took in the slivered scar on his shoulder along with his lean, rangy muscles. He shifted and she jumped back, not wanting to be caught staring at him this way.

She made her way back to the kitchen thinking that if he had stayed all night with Brooke, maybe some of her confidence in his parenting abilities had rubbed off on him. She used to love to sneak into bed with her mother and feel not so alone in the world. Her mom had encouraged it and they'd spent many Saturday mornings curled up in bed watching cartoons. But when her father visited, there had been a strict no-access policy to her mother's bedroom. It had never seemed fair to Millie that she be the one to be cast off so easily when it was her father who made her mother cry when he left.

By the time she'd toasted bagels and cut up fruit for breakfast, Jake and Brooke were sliding into chairs at the kitchen table.

"Morning, you two sleepyheads." She put plates down in front of each of them.

"Hi, Millie," Brooke said cheerfully. "After you left, Daddy tucked me in." She giggled. "Then he fell asleep in my bed. And then I took all the covers and pushed him off the side."

"Twice," Jake clarified. To her relief—and disappointment—Jake had put on a T-shirt so his impressive body was covered.

Brooke scrambled off her chair. "I forgot Bunny. He's still sleeping." She ran back toward her bedroom.

"Thank you for last night." Jake gave her a slow smile. "I know it's above and beyond what you signed up for with this job."

"No worries," she said quickly. She still had trouble making eye contact with him as her mind kept drifting back to the image of him on the edge of the bed, his features gentled in sleep. His hair was still bed tousled and his cheeks held a shadow of stubble that appealed to her way too much.

"I get the brace off my ankle today," he said, unaware of the effect he was having on her. "You won't have to cart me around anymore."

"I don't mind." She turned to the sink, trying to

get a grip on her rioting hormones before she made a fool of herself.

Apparently he took her short answers as anger over the previous night. "Millie, I'm sorry about last night. You made a huge difference to me and I—"

The end of his sentence was cut short when the doorbell rang.

"Nana and Papa are here," Brooke sang out as she barreled down the hall and around the corner, Bunny tucked under her arm.

"That can't be." Millie checked the clock on the oven. "It's barely eight o'clock. They were going to take her out for ice cream after preschool today but…"

Janis Smith bustled into the kitchen. "Hope you don't mind," she said as she took in Jake at the table with Millie standing before him. "We wanted to see Brooke off to her first day of school." Her lips pursed into a thin line. "It seems like you're getting a late start, Jake. Stacy was always an early bird and made sure Brooke was dressed and ready to go with time to spare."

"There's plenty of time," Millie said between her teeth.

She saw John Smith shoot Jake an apologetic look.

"Daddy's tired because I pushed him off the bed." Brooke grinned as she climbed back into her seat and took a bite of banana.

"Why weren't you sleeping in your own bed?" Janis's tone was light but laced with disapproval.

"Daddy was in *my* bed," Brooke told her.

Millie thought the woman would faint dead away. Before she could respond, Brooke continued, "He has bad dreams about Mommy dying and wakes up at night. But she's in heaven, so it's okay. And I helped him feel better. Even when I took all the covers." She spoke around a big bite of bagel.

No one said a word and Millie figured they were all as speechless as she was. Janis Smith had gone still as stone. Tears shimmered in the older woman's eyes.

"I'm going to get dressed," Brooke said as she finished the rest of her bagel. "Millie, will you braid my hair?"

"Of course, Cookie." She picked up Brooke's plate from the table. "Your nana can help you pick out an outfit. Then I'll come back to do your hair."

She placed a hand on Janis's arm. "Would you help her, please?"

The touch seemed to shake the woman out of her shock. "I'd love to. Let's go, Brooke."

"I'm sorry," Jake said to John as Janis and Brooke left the room. "I know it upsets Janis to talk about Stacy."

John shook his head, wiping at the corner of one eye. "This is hard on all of us, son. I left the camera in the car. I'll just go get it now."

When he was gone, Jake stood from the table. "I let their only daughter die."

"Jake," Millie whispered, "it wasn't your fault. You know that. They know that."

He only shook his head. "I'm going to shower. We're walking her to preschool, right?"

Millie nodded. "Unless you think it's too much on your leg."

"I can do it, Millie."

She forced a bright smile on her face. "I never doubted you."

CHAPTER ELEVEN

MILLIE MIGHT HAVE faith in him, but Jake had enough doubts swirling around his mind for both of them. He couldn't believe how hard it was to leave Brooke at the preschool.

Not for her, of course. His social-butterfly daughter had marched into the preschool as if it was her long-lost home. He felt a huge knot clamp down on his stomach. Janis was audibly sniffing next to him.

"It's sometimes more difficult for the parents," Laura Wilkes said from the doorway where she watched the children gather on the rug.

"And grandparents," Janis said with a loud snuffle. John had chosen to wait outside, smart man.

Millie, who was also starting her first day as a teacher's aide, was sitting in a rocking chair near one side of the brightly colored rug. She leaned forward to speak to one of the boys, gently patting his head as he gazed up at her and sidled closer. Jake could understand the boy's desire to get closer to Millie. Jake had the same reaction. Something about her very presence soothed him. Now he'd have the whole morning to himself, not a prospect he found appealing.

"Do I just leave them—I mean her—here?"

Laura smiled. "That's the idea. She'll be fine, Dr. Travers." She leaned closer. "They both will."

Another family came into the front hall of the preschool at that point, and Jake backed away, tugging Janis with him. He adjusted his sunglasses as they walked into the morning sun.

"She's a wonderful little girl," Janis said.

"Yes, she is."

"Just like her mother."

"Come along, Janis." John held out a hand. "We'll see her in a few hours." He looked at Jake. "Are you walking back to the house?"

"You two go on. My brother's working on a house a few blocks from here, so I'm going to head there. He's giving me a ride to the hospital this morning."

"We could do that," John offered even as Janis stiffened.

"It's fine. Thanks."

Jake stood in front of the preschool for several more minutes. A few parents walked in and out as he watched. All of the children going in seemed happy to be there, which was a good indication that Brooke would love it, as well. He knew his daughter was adaptable to almost any situation. Look at how quickly she'd bonded with him, after all. He heard the murmur of young voices and then laughter spilled out from the classroom.

He had no idea it would be so difficult to be away from Brooke like this. Now he had a better understanding of how she'd felt when he'd gone to his physical-therapy appointments. He felt something at his feet and looked down to see an enormous cat winding its way through his legs.

"You get left behind, too, sweetheart?" He bent and scratched the cat behind the ears, rewarded by the sound of loud purring. "I've got nothing to offer you. Go on, then." The cat patently ignored him, much like both Millie and Brooke when he argued for televised sports during their nightly allotment of screen time. She continued to nuzzle him, especially enjoying the edge of his orthopedic boot. He let the quiet purr and the softness of her fur relax him until he felt able to leave the front yard of the preschool building.

Walking along the quiet streets of Crimson made him think about growing up in this town and how much he'd wanted to escape. For years Jake couldn't separate emotions about his childhood from the way he felt about Crimson. They seemed tied inexorably together. Now he realized the town hadn't been responsible for his miserable family life. The fact that both of his brothers could be so happy here was proof of that.

He saw Crimson now for what it was—a picturesque small mountain town filled with good, decent people. Everyone he'd met at the hospital, especially those who had recognized his name, had been friendly and supportive. Most had actually seemed proud of his accomplishments, as if his success reflected well on the town as a whole. As if they'd expected him to succeed in life.

What a novel concept.

Logan was unloading cabinets from the back of his truck as Jake walked up.

"How was the first day?" his brother asked, peering at him from underneath a Broncos ball cap.

"She's like Beth was as a girl—fearless and totally confident." Until the words popped out of his mouth, Jake hadn't remembered that about his baby sister. But now he smiled at the memories of Beth running roughshod over all three of her brothers.

"In that case, you're in big trouble." Logan shook his head but laughed. Jake knew Logan had adored his twin sister.

"I'm sorry I didn't come back when you needed me. I should never have left you all with him. Then Josh took off with the rodeo tour, and you were even more alone."

"I don't blame you, Jake. Or Josh."

Jake thought back to Logan's anger after Beth's death. "You did back then."

"I blamed everyone back then." Logan handed him a toolbox. "Carry this to the house for me."

He hefted the oversize toolbox under his good arm.

"I blamed myself most of all," Logan told him as he pulled two large pieces of trim wood out of the back of the truck. "I learned that living in the past doesn't do much to help with the future."

"Your wife teach you that?"

"Among other things," Logan said with a wink.

Jake held the door open and Logan maneuvered through.

"I'm proud of you," Jake said, setting the toolbox on the counter.

Logan stilled. "What makes you say that?"

"It should have been said years ago. I wish we'd

had the sort of parents to tell you—to tell any of us—something positive. I know Mom tried with you but not hard enough. You had a rough go of it early on, Logan. You came through that and you've got a good life."

"I remember how he used to go after you," Logan said after a moment. "I could never figure it out. Josh and I were the wild ones, always making noise and trouble. But you took the brunt of his anger when he was drinking. I still don't understand why."

"He wanted to break me," Jake answered quietly. "He said I thought I was better than him. I got good grades and had a future. Maybe it was because he'd wasted his own chances, and the way we looked alike reminded him of that."

"It wasn't fair."

"He wasn't fair to anyone. But the three of us made it through. Every day I wish Beth had, too."

Logan watched him for several moments then nodded. "What time is your appointment today?"

"In about an hour."

"Great." Logan came over to the toolbox and pulled out a hammer. "You can help until then."

Jake held up his splint arm. "Are you sure that's a good idea?"

"I trust you, bro."

Jake took the hammer, his own heart pounding in his chest. "Let's get to work."

"ADMIT IT, YOU really do like driving a big car."

Millie patted the front hood of her yellow Beetle. Josh had it waiting out in front at the ranch for her, washed and ready to go.

She'd known Jake was getting his leg brace off today, which would make him able to drive, but it had still been a bit of a shock to see him behind the wheel. Somehow driving him around had given her a sense of being needed. She knew he still needed help, but somehow the balance of power had shifted in her mind.

He'd been waiting at the end of the school day, and Brooke had raced into his arms. Even Janis couldn't deny Brooke's unwavering affection for her father. The girl had been reluctant to leave for ice cream and a movie with her grandparents, and Jake hadn't seemed to want to let her go. But he'd given her a hug and gently persuaded her what fun the afternoon would be with Janis and John. She'd seen John silently mouth "thank you" to him as the trio walked away.

Millie was exhausted after her first day helping to teach the group of two dozen preschoolers. She was contracted to work only the first two hours of the day but had found she didn't want to leave when her shift was through. Tired as she might be, she figured she'd had almost as much fun as Brooke over the course of the morning. The kids were energetic and sometimes needy, but Millie loved interacting with them. Laura Wilkes was gentle in her teaching, treating each child as an individual—just the sort of teaching mentor Millie had always wanted.

It was so different from the university internship that had ended so badly. Millie had needed to stop several times that morning to get control over her wayward emotions. She'd believed she was at fault for how things had gone at her previous school, but working with Laura for just a day had done wonders for her battered confidence.

After Brooke and the Smiths had gone, she and Jake had driven to Crimson Ranch for her car. "I like looking down on people," she told him with a smile. "But Bugsy is my one true love."

"Bugsy? You named your car?"

"Of course." She bent and gave the front glass a small kiss. "This car has been across the country twice, with me through a half dozen moves, a couple of university transfers and countless dead-end jobs. Up until I got to Crimson, Bugsy was the best friend I ever had."

"You kissed your car," he said, his voice dazed. "I don't understand you one bit, Fairy Poppins."

"Don't you have one thing that's seen you through all your trials and tribulations?"

He shook his head. "Not one thing."

"You do now."

His eyes darkened and she quickly clarified, "Brooke. You have your daughter."

"For now," he agreed.

"Forever," she countered.

His gaze rose to look past her to the mountains. The hills were still covered in green, with just a few splashes of the yellow that would soon dot the hillside as the aspens turned color in the fall. She knew autumn came early at this altitude. Already the temperature dropped almost ten degrees each evening before warming again during the day.

"Want to go for a walk?"

His question surprised her. "Where to?"

"Down by the river." He pointed. "Josh, Sara and everyone on the ranch are busy with guests. Brooke and the Smiths won't be back from the movie for another hour."

"Your leg is up to it?"

He nodded. "I need to exercise it more now that the boot is off to regain my strength."

Watching Jake in his fitted T-shirt and cargo shorts, she couldn't imagine him becoming much stronger. His body was so different from hers and she had to admit she appreciated him physically.

She started walking, not liking the turn her thoughts were taking. He outpaced her easily with his long strides, but they fell into an easy rhythm, matching their steps as they made their way down the path that wound through the ranch's back property. She loved the smell of the wild grasses mixed with the pine trees that flanked the trail.

As they approached the river, the sound of gurgling water grew louder. She'd never been much of a mountain girl, but Millie was learning to love the wildness of the terrain surrounding Crimson. A rabbit darted out from a low bush near the river's edge.

"We used to hunt those as kids."

"You killed rabbits?"

He grinned at her. "I never tried very hard, but that's what you did to keep busy out where we lived. Josh was a better shot."

"Don't let Brooke hear you talk about killing bunnies. She'll be scarred for life."

"I'm pretty sure I've already accomplished that."

He picked up a flat rock and skipped it across a calm section of water.

"You saved her, Jake. She loves being with you, being a part of your life."

"I can't take the place of her mother."

"No one can," Millie agreed. "But Stacy isn't here. You have to stop regretting what you can't change."

"Good advice." Jake picked up another rock. "Ever skipped stones?"

"Across the Potomac? Uh…no."

He took her hand and closed her palm around the rock, warmed from the sun and his touch. "It's all in the wrist action."

"Where have I heard that before?"

He laughed and shook his head. "Try it."

She concentrated and flipped the rock, watching as it sailed through the air and landed with a plop into the water.

He handed her another one, this time coming to stand behind her. His fingers covered hers, showing her the motion. With his body pressed to her back, Millie had trouble concentrating but eventually tossed the stone toward the creek. It hit the water then bounced twice before disappearing into the river.

"I did it." She spun around and grabbed his arms, bouncing on her toes. "I skipped it."

"You're a natural."

She sank back to her heels but didn't move away from him. His hands slid down her arms, making her tingle with need.

He leaned down, his mouth inches from hers. "You told me not to kiss you again."

"That was smart of me," she whispered then licked her suddenly dry lips.

His eyes smoldered. "Are you feeling smart right now, Millie?"

She felt many things right now, but the most prominent was a deep, aching desire to touch and be touched by Jake Travers. Definitely not smart, but she didn't care one bit.

Slowly, she wound her hands around his neck, closing the few inches between them. "I was never known for my brains," she said and closed her mouth over his.

Only to have him pull away. "Don't say that." He pressed a gentle kiss to her forehead. "You're smart, fierce and way more capable than you give yourself credit for, Millie Spencer."

She gasped a little, amazed at how much his words meant to her. How much she needed to hear them. She didn't know how to respond, nor did she trust her voice. Instead she kissed him again.

This time he didn't move from her. This time he kissed her as if his life depended on it, gently sucking her bottom lip into his mouth then running his tongue across the seam of her lips. She opened for him and the kiss turned deeper, hotter. Millie kept her eyes closed, reveling in the feel of him holding her close. His strong hands massaged the knots in her back as he drove her wild with his mouth.

She couldn't remember ever being so wrecked by a kiss. Despite what she knew was right, she wanted more. She'd told him they couldn't do this, but she needed him so badly.

He straightened suddenly just as she heard the sound of a horse whinnying nearby.

"We shouldn't—" she began.

"Don't, Millie. I'm not going to apologize and you won't tell me that was a mistake. Nothing that feels so damn good could be a mistake." He scrubbed his hand over his face. "This doesn't change anything. I want you. You want me. That doesn't mean I don't respect you. I'm not sure who did you wrong, but don't blame yourself or me for some other man's mistakes."

He was right. She knew it. Jake wasn't her father or any of the other men who had tried to take advantage of her. It wasn't his fault, but she couldn't quite let go of the belief that it might be hers.

"We should get back. I want to start dinner before Brooke gets home. She'll be wiped out after her first day of preschool and the afternoon out with her grandparents."

He looked at her intently, as if he wanted to say more. Finally he nodded and turned back toward the ranch.

I want you. That doesn't mean I don't respect you.

The words echoed in her head as they made their way along the path. He might respect her now, but how long would that last once he knew the whole truth?

CHAPTER TWELVE

THE NEXT FEW WEEKS were the most normal that Jake could remember in his entire life. In fact, he was pretty sure he hadn't understood how much fun normal could be until he'd returned to Crimson.

With his leg unencumbered and his hand healing on schedule, he took the hospital's director, Vincent Gile, up on his suggestion that Jake help out in the free clinic at the hospital. Three times a week he volunteered during the morning hours—and sometimes late into the afternoon—seeing to indigent patients and those who needed but couldn't afford medical attention.

He'd been on the front lines of crisis medicine for so long, he'd forgotten how comforting it could be to simply help someone in need. It might not be as exciting or heart pumping as what he was used to, but the change suited Jake. Part of the reason he'd chosen to work with Miles of Medicine was because he didn't like staying in one place. The idea of establishing long-term relationships, especially with people who would depend on him, was bone-chillingly scary given how he'd failed his younger siblings for so many years.

Now it seemed like a challenge he was ready for, each patient a puzzle he looked forward to solving. Some of the cases were mundane but the gratitude he received from the clinic's patients made it well worth it. Crimson was a beautiful town, but not nearly as wealthy as nearby Aspen. Some people gave up a lot to live in the mountains. They worked hard but barely scraped by with the local cost of living. Jake was glad to help them and it was good to feel productive again. On the days he wasn't working, he spent the afternoons with Brooke and Millie or helping Logan on his kitchen renovation. He relished the normalcy of his own little slice of Americana in ways he hadn't believed possible.

His new appreciation of normal might explain why he was so pleased at the prospect of a couple of beers at the local bar after work. Or perhaps it was the woman fidgeting in the seat next to him. Jake pulled up to the curb and turned off the car.

"You didn't have to bring me with you," Millie said from her seat next to him.

"But I wanted to," he told her.

"I'm the nanny. What will your hospital friends think?" She tucked her hair behind her ear.

"That I've got more damn willpower than any guy imaginable to keep my hands off of you?"

Instead of making her laugh the way he'd intended, he saw the sides of her mouth pull down. "They'll think we're sleeping together," she muttered.

"Millie." He reached out and turned her face to his. "Why do you care what a bunch of people you don't know think about you?"

"Easy for you to say. You're 'the doctor,' the local hero come home. I'm nobody."

"Not to me." He sighed and rubbed his fingers along

the back of her neck, trying to release some of the tension there. "We're friends. This is an engagement party for one of the nurses at the clinic. No one is going to be paying attention to you and me. Relax. This is supposed to be your night off. Our night off."

Logan and Olivia had invited Brooke for a sleepover, and to Jake's surprise, his daughter had wanted to go. Her grandparents had been shocked since Brooke had been adamant about not spending the night at their rented condo. She was okay when Janis and John took her for ice cream or to the park, but that was as much time as she'd spend with them. Jake didn't understand it but figured it had more to do with her wanting to stick close to him. But she hadn't hesitated when his brother came to pick her up tonight. She'd bounced down the steps toward Logan's truck, thrilled at the prospect of spending an evening baking with her Uncle Logan.

Jake hadn't planned to attend the hospital get-together, but he'd quickly realized that being in the house alone with Millie all night was going to be too much temptation. They hadn't kissed again since that day at Crimson Ranch, but he found himself wanting her more every moment.

Even now, when she was filled with unwarranted nerves. Everyone he knew loved Millie, from his family to the parents and kids at the preschool. She was a ray of sunshine everywhere she went, especially in his dull life.

"The people from the hospital are nice, Millie. And they're hardly my friends. I've worked with them a couple of weeks." He leaned closer. "You're my friend. We're going to have fun tonight. I promise."

Slowly, she nodded. "Sorry. I don't know what's wrong with me."

"If you can tame a room full of rowdy preschoolers, hanging out with this bunch should be no problem."

They walked together the half block to the bar, Jake resisting the urge to take her hand in his. He wasn't lying when he told her she was his friend. Millie was probably the best friend he'd had in his life. He'd always lived alone, but now sharing the ups and downs of daily life with her, even in the short term, created a level of intimacy that went beyond his physical desire for her.

Sure, that was still there. Always there. At this point, wanting her seemed like the least of his worries. The way he depended on her as a part of his life was a lot scarier.

The bar, the Two Moon Saloon, was as crowded as he'd expect on a Friday night. It hadn't changed much since Jake had come to retrieve his father here on weekend nights when he was a kid. Wood paneling still lined the walls and there was a mix of booths and four-top tables to one side of the room with a small dance floor near the back. In a far corner there were two pool tables and he noticed several people from the hospital gathered in that area. The beer signs that hung on the walls had been updated with labels of local and nationally known microbrews. But the bar still held the same somewhat sweet smell that he remembered—a strange combination of alcohol and perfume. The scent had made him want to retch as a kid.

As the oldest, Jake had been the one his mother sent to collect his dad on nights when he was too drunk to make it home on his own. Jake would make the twenty-minute trek from their ramshackle house into town and eventually coax his father to follow him home. He'd always tried not to make eye contact with any of the other customers or bartenders; he didn't want to know who was on hand to witness his dad's sloppy end to any given night.

Now he was surprised to find the smell didn't cause a reaction in him. Maybe it was because Millie was so close that the scent of her shampoo wafted up to him, covering the smells that evoked so much shame from his past.

One of the nurses waved them over to a couple of tables in front of the bar that had been pushed together. He made introductions and noticed that Millie's nervousness seemed to settle as she spoke with a few of the women. He recognized Natalie Holt and remembered that she was part of Millie's new group of friends.

He took a beer with his good hand when it was handed to him but didn't do more than sip on it. He'd never be much of a social drinker thanks to the memories he had of his father.

He sat with a couple of the other docs from the hospital. Lana Mayfield scooted a chair next to his after a few minutes.

"So what's your plan?" she asked when the people around them started in on a heated debate about the Broncos' prospects for the upcoming football season.

"Enjoy the evening," he answered, purposely misinterpreting her question. "Toast the happy couple."

She shook her head. "Come on, Jake. Your ankle is healed, and from everything I've seen, there won't be permanent nerve damage in your hand. I want to know what's next for you." She slid her hand along his shoulder, leaning so close that her breast pressed up against his arm. He could smell the hint of alcohol on her breath. "I'd like to be a part of your future."

He flexed his fingers around the bottle of beer on the table in front of him. As much as he'd wanted his hand to get better, he was ignoring the signs that pointed to a full recovery. As long as he could use his injuries as an excuse, he didn't need to deal with the decisions he'd have to make.

"It's complicated, Lana." He caught Millie looking at him from where she stood nearby with Natalie, but her gaze snapped away. "I've got to think of my daughter and what's best for her."

She wrinkled her nose. "I thought the grandparents were willing to take her."

"We'd agreed to that, yes. But things can change."

"You haven't changed, Jake. I don't believe it. You were the most single-minded person I'd ever met. You knew you wanted to be a doctor, how you wanted to practice medicine, and you made it happen. You're not the kind of person who settles down. You need the pressure and excitement to really feel alive." She pressed closer to him. "We both need that. We're two of a kind, you and me."

He doubted that. He moved his chair back, extricating himself from her awkward embrace.

"Anybody want to dance?" Natalie suddenly stood next to their table, Millie held at her side by Natalie's hand clamped around her wrist. "The DJ's just getting started." Her eyebrows rose as she glanced between Jake and Lana, disapproval clear on her pretty face.

Millie kept her head turned toward the dance floor.

"I wasn't much of a dancer before the accident," Jake admitted. "I think I'll pass."

"Are you sure?" Natalie tilted her head toward Millie. "Might be worth giving it a try."

"We're in the middle of a private conversation here," Lana told them, her eyes narrowed on Millie. "Discussing important hospital business. Doctor business. Neither of you would understand."

He was about to argue when Natalie leaned forward. "It doesn't take a medical degree to understand that you've got a stick lodged—"

"Come on, Nat." Millie tugged at her friend. "Let's go dance."

Damn. He ground his teeth as they walked away. He knew Millie had silly hang-ups about being in the company of people who were better educated than she, not that it mattered one bit to most people in Crimson. He didn't think Lana had been purposely cruel, but she was a snob. Jake couldn't believe he hadn't noticed what an irritating trait that was before now.

Maybe he wasn't a great dancer, but if it meant an excuse to get close to Millie, he was willing to give it a shot. She looked beautiful tonight, wearing a pale patterned blouse and a short denim skirt with sandals that laced around her ankles. Her skin glowed from the shimmery lotion that Brooke liked her to wear.

He appreciated it for an entirely different reason and wanted the chance to touch Millie, to be close enough to have her scent invade his senses once again. He pushed back from the table before Lana's next comment stopped him.

"Looks like your nanny found a partner without you."

Millie and Natalie were dancing with a group of men—tourists, by the looks of their clothes. One of the guys—dark-haired, from what Jake could tell—took Millie's hand and twirled her as a popular country song rang out over the speakers. Jake took another drink of his beer and turned back to Lana, but his gaze kept straying to his lovely nanny on the dance floor.

After a few songs, Natalie, Millie and their entourage went to the bar for drinks. He saw the man lean into Millie and her laugh in response. She looked happy, fun and so full of life. This was where she was supposed to be, he realized, not stuck in the house with him and Brooke every night. This was the first time he'd seen her free-spirit side in action.

Soon the group around them had expanded. Jake realized that for all Millie's worry about fitting in, he was the one left on the outside. Too serious, too quiet. Just like he'd always been.

Lana never left his side, however, and after a while his head started to pound from her relentless hinting about their "possible future" together. Millie and the others had returned to the dance floor and he wasn't about to watch her enjoy herself in someone else's arms for a minute longer.

"I'm going to grab some air," he told Lana, standing.

"I'll go with you." Her smile was suggestive.

"That's okay. I'm not great company right now."

Before she could argue, he turned away. He wouldn't leave Millie here until he made sure Natalie would bring her home, but he needed to clear his head first. He hadn't seen how much Millie'd had to drink but was pretty certain the group had done at least a couple of shots.

He tried to keep his eyes focused on the exit, but his gaze slid to the dance floor once again. Through the crowd he caught sight of the dark-haired punk pulling Millie tight against his body. Jake was about to look away when he noticed the look of distaste on Millie's face. She shook her head and squirmed away but the guy held her tighter, bending to whisper something in her ear. She shook her head, the disapproval turning to fear in a split second.

Which was as long as it took Jake to change course, muscling his way through the other people on the dance floor. He pulled the man away by his shoulder, narrowly resisting the urge to punch the guy's smug face.

"What the—" the man sputtered as Jake put his arm around Millie, leading her away.

She looked up at him. Tears shimmered in her eyes. "You don't have to…"

"Let's go." Jake moved as quick as he could through the bar's customers toward the front door. He could tell Millie needed to get away.

The guy stepped in front of him, giving Jake a little shove. "Dude, she's with me. Find your own girl."

"Maybe you should take no for an answer, buddy.

She's not with you anymore." Jake tucked Millie to his side, away from the man's grasp. "Get the hell out of my way."

"She wanted it." The man tilted his head toward Millie. "Some of them like it a little rough, you know."

A tremble rolled through Millie and he heard her give a little sob. That a jerk like this could bring her to tears infuriated Jake. And when the man reached for her, Jake's temper snapped. Without thinking he reached up and slammed his fist into the guy's face.

A searing pain sliced through Jake's arm. By instinct, he'd thrown the punch with his right hand. His injured hand. He sucked in a breath, trying not to let the pain take him down.

The man staggered back a few steps then steadied himself. He would have come at Jake, who was at a definite disadvantage with Millie plastered against him and the throbbing of his splinted hand.

But the bouncer from the front door wrapped his meaty arms around the guy. "Go on, Dr. Travers," he said to Jake. Jake recognized him from the clinic—he'd brought his mother in to be treated for a stomach infection last week. "I'll take care of this joker."

Jake made it out of the bar and a few steps down the sidewalk before he let go of Millie and doubled over in pain. He muttered every curse word in his vocabulary then gently flexed his fingers. At least they weren't broken.

"Oh, no." Millie was back at his side in an instant. "You hit him with your bad hand. What were you thinking?"

Jake straightened, taking deep gulps of the cool

evening air. "I thought he was hurting you. That you were scared to pieces. I thought I was rescuing you."

"Who said I needed rescuing?" Her words were sharp but her tone gentle. She lifted his arm, cradling his hand in hers. She drew her fingers along his, raising them and kissing his knuckles that were already swelling. He felt a tear drop onto his finger and slip down the inside of his splint.

"Millie."

She shook her head, wiping the back of her sleeve across her face. "I'll drive home."

"You've been drinking."

"Fine." She kept her gaze averted from his but didn't let go of his hand. "You drive."

They walked to the car in silence, and the pain in his hand subsided to a dull ache.

He unlocked the car and opened the passenger-side door. Millie let go of his hand to climb into the Explorer.

"Millie, look at me. Please."

She turned, her emotions cut off from him.

"What happened back there?"

"You could have done permanent damage to your hand," she snapped. "It's not totally healed, Jake."

He shook his head. "On the dance floor. When that guy held on to you. Your reaction…"

"It was nothing. He freaked me out, that's all. I could have handled it." She bit down on her lip and Jake let it go because if there was one thing he didn't want, it was to make her cry again.

The ride home took only a few minutes. Millie looked out the window the entire time, her hands clasped tightly together in her lap. When he parked, she was out of the car like a shot, practically running up the front walk.

He trailed her into the house, expecting her to retreat to her bedroom, where she knew he wouldn't follow. Instead she went to the kitchen and, without flipping on a light, took one of Brooke's animal-shaped ice packs from the freezer. She returned to him, and he hissed as the cold touched his swollen skin.

"There was more to that than you being freaked out." He tipped up her chin. "You were scared, Millie. You should never be frightened of a man in that way."

He saw her swallow as she blinked several times. Damn. He hadn't wanted tears.

"It was my fault," she said after a moment, her voice just a whisper in the quiet house. "I led him on."

"You danced with him. I saw you. There was nothing more to it than that."

"I gave him ideas."

"Watching you floss your teeth would give a man ideas." That earned him a wisp of a smile. "It doesn't mean they get to act on them. You deserve to be cherished, Millie." He paused, unsure of how much to reveal. Then because the pain was clouding his mind, her scent was wreaking havoc on his senses and because the dark added some bit of protection, he added, "I would cherish you."

As she watched him, he saw in her eyes the same desire that coursed through him. But as much as he wanted to act on it, Jake held back. She was fragile at this moment, and he needed to be the kind of man who wouldn't take advantage of that.

So he began to move back, to leave her in peace as she'd once requested.

But when she rose up and brought her lips to his, all thoughts of leaving her alone vanished. He couldn't have pulled away from her at that moment if his life depended on it.

HE LET HER CHOOSE. After what had happened to her at the bar, Jake didn't press her for more than she could give. He said he would cherish her and she believed him.

For that and so many other reasons, she wanted him.

She hadn't meant to lead the guy on in the bar. She'd only wanted to dance, get lost in the moment and try to drown out the disappointment she felt that Jake was spending his time with Lana. But Millie knew that sometimes men took more than she offered, felt as if they were entitled to more than she was willing to give.

Not Jake. It was virtually impossible for him to want more from her because she was ready to give him everything. That thought made emotion unfurl inside her chest. She pressed closer to him, wanting to lose herself in his strength, only to jump back with a gasp at the ice pack she held between them.

He took it from her hand and tossed it aside. She lifted her chilled fingers to the pulse beating in his throat.

He shuddered then bent to kiss the center of her palm. "Millie," he said in a husky tone, "I want you. All of you. But only if it's what you want, too."

"Yes." The syllable came out on a whoosh of air.

He lowered his mouth to hers, taking control of the

kiss, deepening it then drawing back. He interlaced their fingers and led her through the darkened house down the hall to his bedroom.

Her eyes darted to Brooke's empty bedroom across the hall. Jake turned when she hesitated. "You can stop this at any time, Millie. Just walk away."

She didn't want the night to end, so she stepped forward, her hands splaying across his chest, and pushed him into his bedroom. His arms lowered to her waist and he lifted her as if she were no more than a child.

The feel of being in his arms, the safety and power of him, was all she'd imagined and more. Millie trusted him, perhaps not with her heart but definitely with her body.

He took the few steps to the bed and, stripping the quilt away, lowered her onto the sheets. Kneeling beside her, he undid first one sandal and then the next. He removed his splint then smoothed his palms up her bare legs to the backs of her knees, tickling the sensitive skin there.

She wiggled on the bed, unused to feeling so vulnerable in front of anyone. "I can handle this part."

"Let me," he said with a sexy smile, leaning forward to trail his mouth against her skin at the edge of her skirt.

Millie felt need and desire fan to life even brighter inside her. When he tugged the skirt down past her hips, she shut her eyes, unable to meet his gaze.

His fingers skirted the edge of her panties and she sent up a silent prayer of thanks that she'd at least put on decent underwear for the night. He began to work on the buttons of her shirt.

"Millie, open your eyes. Look at me." His voice was husky and low.

She took a breath and met his hot stare. "I'm not used to this kind of attention," she whispered, trying to make a joke, but her voice caught on the last word.

"You should be. You should be cared for and worshipped. You are smart, clever and beautiful both inside and out." He spread the shirt open and she shivered as air touched the heated skin of her belly. "You deserve so much more than you've allowed yourself to have, Millie."

"Hey, Pot, meet Kettle," she answered without thinking. Then she could have kicked herself. Here was a man trying to make proper love to her, and thanks to her thrumming nerves, she was joking. Talk about looking a gift horse…

Jake threw back his head and laughed. "Come here," he told her and she rose to kiss him as he pushed the shirt off her arms. She could feel him smiling against her mouth but soon the kiss turned hot and needy again.

His fingers worked the clasp at the back of her bra and she clamped the front of it to her chest. Even though the lights were out, moonlight streamed in from the window. Millie felt suddenly exposed in a way she hadn't expected.

"Do you want to close the blinds?"

Jake nipped at the underside of her jaw. "Nope."

She gave him a little push. "Well, I'm not going to be the only one without my clothes on here."

He sat up and shucked his shirt over his head.

Heat radiated off his body, all sculpted lines and

muscle. Two fading scars crisscrossed one shoulder, reminding her of what he'd been through. When she reached out to draw the tip of one finger down his chest, a tremble passed through him. Jake was holding himself back for her, and her heart opened to him because of it.

She moved forward, letting her bra drop as she molded her body to his. His touch turned possessive and hot and her body responded to him in the same way. His tongue traced the edge of her nipple before he took the peak into his mouth. Millie slid her fingers through his hair, urging him up to kiss her once more. They tangled together in the sheets, learning the nuances of each other. He continued to whisper sweet words to her, this Jake so different from the serious, sometimes emotionally distant man she'd first met.

He didn't leave any part of her unexplored, using his fingers then his mouth to bring her to the edge of desire. Millie wasn't totally inexperienced. She'd had a couple of boyfriends and understood sexual attraction. This was something totally different, so much more than she'd ever felt with a man.

Just as she thought she couldn't take any more of his teasing touch, he lifted away from her, taking a condom from the nightstand before he wrapped her in his arms again.

"Now?" he whispered and she marveled at his restraint.

Unable to speak, she nodded and opened to him completely.

She loved the feel of him around her and then inside her. Pressure built and she scraped her fingernails along the hard planes of his back, drawing a hoarse moan from him in response. As much as she wanted to hold back a part of herself, Millie didn't do things in half measures. When she gave herself over to him and to her own pleasure, she knew the highest peak of bliss and also the nagging sense she had lost herself to this man and it would likely end in heartbreak.

But that was a worry for another night.

Jake kept her cradled in his arms as she drifted to sleep then woke her hours later with soft, warm kisses along her spine. They made love again, lazily, taking their time with each other and the passion that banked between them.

When morning came, the dawning light had her questioning her sanity. She cursed her lack of willpower and the fact that she'd let her heart lead her down a path her head knew would be her downfall. She needed to collect herself, to gain some physical and emotional distance. She was an expert at compartmentalizing. If only she could figure out where to put last night, Millie thought she might have a chance at making it through the next several weeks.

She went to climb from the bed, but Jake pulled her back against him.

"Are we okay, Millie?"

"We're great, although we're going to be late for breakfast if I don't get in the shower." They were meeting Olivia, Logan and Brooke at Life Is Sweet later that morning.

"This doesn't have to change anything."

It changes everything.

"I know." She squirmed out of his embrace, feeling emotion knot in her chest. She didn't want to talk now, didn't trust herself to speak without revealing her feelings for him. She knew from her mother that showing her heart would give him the upper hand. If she kept her heart guarded, she could hold on to her power. She'd watched her mother give away her power over and over again, watched it seep out of her, leaving her a shell of a woman whose only purpose in life was to keep a man happy.

Millie couldn't let herself fall into the same trap. She was overreacting, but she couldn't help it. This was the exact reason she'd limited herself to only casual relationships. She was wired just like her mother, and it had always terrified her that with one misstep, she'd find herself down the same rabbit hole.

Taking the sheet with her, she grabbed her clothes from the floor and retreated to the other end of the house. She turned the water in the shower as hot as she could stand it, hoping the heat would burn away her fears and regret. One night, she admonished herself. It didn't have to mean anything. Jake had told her as much.

The shower door slid back, and she started as Jake climbed in with her, filling up the small space. She stepped away, her back practically pressed to the cold tile, and wrapped her arms around herself.

"What are you doing?"

He reached out, but instead of touching her, he adjusted the nozzle above his head so that water once again sprayed down on her, keeping her warm. As if his proximity wasn't enough.

"Does last night change things, Millie?"

She wiped at her face, blinking to see him clearly. "You said yourself it doesn't." She jerked her thumb toward the bathroom. "There isn't exactly room enough for two in here."

One side of his mouth curved. "There's plenty of room." He snagged her hand and placed it on his bare chest, over his heart. She focused on the steady beat of it as he spoke.

"I said it doesn't *have* to change anything. Not that I don't want it to." His heartbeat increased its pace. "This is new to me, Millie. Everything about this past month has been new to me. I don't know what the hell I'm doing, and I don't want to hurt you in the process. You get to decide. If this is more than one night, I'll be thrilled. If last night was an aberration, I'll respect that. You choose."

Once again, he was giving her the power. He meant it, she knew, but in putting the decision in her hands he was cracking the last of her defenses. She wanted so much more from this man than he probably knew how to give. She took a breath, ready to tell him that they couldn't go forward.

The look of vulnerability in his eyes stopped her. His heart beat like crazy beneath her fingers and she knew she wasn't alone in her fear. Their pasts and the emotional scars they'd both buried so deep bonded them. It was a link, maybe even a foundation. For the first time Millie thought she might have a chance of being on equal footing in a relationship. These were uncharted waters for both of them. Maybe together was the only way to make it through to calmer seas.

"I choose you," she said softly. "I choose us."

His eyes closed for a moment and she saw him take a shuddering breath. But when he opened them again, the vulnerability was gone, replaced by smoldering desire.

"Then let's see if we can't make this shower fit the both of us," he said and drew her to him once again.

CHAPTER THIRTEEN

JAKE FOUND HIMSELF distracted for the next several days as Millie's words echoed in his head.

I choose us.

When had he ever been anyone's choice? He'd always worked and fought for what he wanted, and all he'd ever focused on was work. Now he had so many other things to occupy his time.

His cell phone beeped again, another text coming through. Another text that he ignored. He'd been avoiding the director of the agency for the past week. A few of his coworkers had called, too. There was never any lack of projects and needs, and Jake had always been the doctor most willing to travel on a moment's notice to far-flung locations with minimal facilities. Substandard accommodations and difficult cases had been part of the appeal to him, a way to challenge himself while remaining emotionally uninvolved.

Now he couldn't believe he'd ever been satisfied living like that. His time with Millie and Brooke had made him long for more, allowed him to believe a normal family life might be attainable for someone like him.

He still got daily reminders that he was in over his head. Today's came at rehearsal for Brooke's preschool fall musical. The program was some sort of mountain-animal festival. Each of the kids was supposed to be a tree, flower or critter from around the area. It was hard for Jake to tell them apart. He saw a couple of kids with brown felt draped over their shoulders and small head-bands that had ears sticking out. Bears, he assumed.

"Aren't the costumes perfect?"

Jake turned to see one of the mothers standing next to him.

"Um…sure. Very creative."

She smiled. "I made most of them myself."

He'd gotten to know a few of the parents, but because Millie worked at the school he'd left most of the mommy socializing to her.

"Your nanny does a great job with the kids."

He nodded as Millie wiped the tears of a crying girl. Laura Wilkes had put Millie in charge of today's rehearsal. Brooke waved to him from where she stood near the far side of the makeshift stage. They'd cleared out the preschool room to use for the program. He waved to his daughter, who was dressed as a…

"She makes a very cute fox."

A fox. Right. That was what he was going to guess.

Millie came over to them. The girl who had been crying was holding her hands together in front of her costume's lower half.

"It's hard to remember to take a potty break when there's so much excitement," Millie said. "Can one of you help the kids run through the rest of the program while I help her change clothes?" She handed a note-book to Jake. "Here are the notes for the performance."

Before he could answer, she walked away toward

the bathroom. He looked to the other mom, holding out the notebook.

"Sorry." She shook her head. "I just stopped by to drop off my son's snack. I have to pick up his older sister at dance class." She patted Jake on the shoulder. "You'll be fine."

Just like that, Jake was left on his own with over a dozen preschoolers looking at him. His heart pounded as he took a step toward them. One of the boys stuck his finger up his nose and another girl's lip trembled.

"Daddy, why do you look so angry?" Brooke pulled on the front of her fox costume, which consisted of a red sweater and pointy ears. "You're scaring Helena. And Derek is eating his boogers, which is disgusting. And someone didn't flush today when they went number two. And—"

Jake held up a hand. "Okay, Cookie. Thanks for sharing all of that."

He pointed at the girl with the quivering lip. "You. Helena, right? No tears, got it?"

Helena nodded even as tears streaked down her cheeks.

"No tears!"

"Daddy, stop yelling." Brooke walked over to Helena. "Come and stand next to me. I'll protect you."

"Protect her from me?" Jake eyed his daughter. Panic bubbled up in him. Were fathers supposed to know how to deal with groups of kids? Wasn't that what moms were for? His daughter was stuck with him. While he was clueless.

She threw him a look. "Daddy, take care of the boogers."

He tried. Really, he tried. But it was as if the kid hadn't eaten in weeks and snot was on the dessert buffet.

Fifteen minutes later, Jake was drenched in sweat and his head pounded. The kids had abandoned pageant rehearsal and were running circles around him. Literally.

He tried grabbing for one of the boys, but the kid ducked away from his grasp. Then all of the children stilled. Jake turned around to the sound of singing. Millie walked back into the room, singing a song about children stopping their play so they could listen to her.

And they did.

Jake had tried yelling, pleading, bribes, whatever he could think of, but nothing had worked. All Millie did was sing a little ditty and they fell into line like a platoon of army cadets.

Amazing.

She was amazing.

"How's it going?"

"Perfect," he answered, wiping his brow.

She flashed a knowing smile. "Not always as easy as it looks."

"It never looked easy," he muttered.

She rounded up the kids then directed Jake to help them take off their costumes and hang them for safe-keeping.

Parents, mostly mothers, began trickling in to pick up their children. They seemed impressed that Jake was there helping. He felt like a total fraud as they discussed plans for the pageant, volunteer roles, snack charts and other things most mothers seemed to know intrinsically. He smiled and nodded, but was secretly relieved when he was left alone with Brooke and Millie.

Jake sank into one of the tiny chairs at the preschool table, his knees practically level with his chin. Millie bustled around the room, humming under her breath as Brooke scooped dried beans from a small plastic pool in the center of the room then spilled them out again. Dried beans as a toy—one more thing he would have never thought of.

After a moment, Millie came up behind him. Her legs pressed against his back as she bent to swiftly kiss his cheek while Brooke was occupied. They'd agreed to keep their relationship quiet since it was so new. He imagined his daughter would love the thought of Millie as a potential stepmother, but Jake wasn't ready to go down that road quite yet.

"That was awful," he said with a groan.

Millie ran her fingers through his hair. "You managed."

"Hardly. I made a girl cry and watched one of the boys attempt to eat his weight in snot."

"Derek," Millie answered without hesitation. "We're working on that."

"I totally panicked, Millie. Those kids looked to me. I was in charge. I couldn't handle it." He shook his head. "Janis would have known what to do."

"Jake…" Millie's tone was patient. "You're a dad, not a child-care expert. You did fine. The kids survived."

"No thanks to me."

"Why are you being so hard on yourself?" She lowered herself to the chair next to him, patting his arm, her gaze sympathetic. "You've got years to get good at this."

He suppressed a shudder. "That's just it. What if I never get good? What if I don't want to?" He felt her gaze on him but couldn't look at her. "I'm a doctor. I know how to sew up the human body, but the thought of making a costume for my daughter is terrifying."

"You buy them online," she countered.

"That's not the point and you know it. I want to be a part of Brooke's life. I love her and can't imagine life without her. But I still don't believe I'm her best bet for every day."

"You're her father."

"That's biology. Lord knows my father didn't add a damn thing except misery to my childhood. Yours wasn't much different. I might do more harm than good to her. That would kill me."

"You won't, Jake."

"You don't know that." He shook his head as he watched his daughter. "Janis and John are pressuring me about a custody agreement. The agency is pressuring me to commit to a timeline for returning to the field."

Millie stiffened. It was the first time he'd mentioned going back to his old job. "I thought you liked working at the hospital here."

"I do, but it's temporary."

"It doesn't have to be."

"I'm not cut out for this," he whispered. "As much as you want it to be."

"Me?" She stood. "This isn't about me. It's about the daughter who needs you in her life."

"I'd be in her life. Only not the way *you* want me to." He turned away, unwilling to see the disappointment he knew he'd find in her gaze. It was the same emotion he'd read on the faces of his brothers and sister when he left home, and he couldn't stand to fail someone he cared about again.

Millie heard the door to the preschool open as Jake's words trailed off. He was right to stop this argument, of course, for many reasons. But she didn't want it to end without convincing him that she was right. She couldn't let go of her determination to see him settled as a full-time father for Brooke.

But when she caught sight of the woman peeking her head around the door to the main room, Millie's heart took off at a frantic pace.

She whirled as Jake stood up behind her, his finger resting lightly on her back as if to give her support. She stepped away from his touch.

"Mrs. Bradley," she said, taking a hesitant step forward. "What are you doing in Crimson?"

"Hello, Millie." The woman adjusted her bun and gave the room an approving glance. "You didn't return my calls, so I contacted your sister. She told me I could find you here."

Millie's heart sank as she thought about how much detail Karen Bradley might have shared with Olivia. Jake cleared his throat behind her.

"Oh, right," Millie sputtered. "This is…" She

paused, as if she'd forgotten Jake's name. "Let me introduce you to—"

"I'm Jake Travers," he said, reaching out a hand.

"Karen Bradley, dean of the College of Education from the University of Las Clara."

"Mrs. Bradley was my course adviser when I was at school," Millie told him.

Jake nodded. "Millie works for me here in Crimson."

"Works for you?" Karen's brows furrowed. "I thought you worked at the preschool, Millie."

Before Millie could answer, Brooke ran forward. "Millie is a Fairy Poppins. That means she's my nanny." The little girl pushed her hair back from her face. "I'm Brooke. He's my daddy." She pointed to Jake. "My mommy died when she went to find him. She's in heaven now, but I wish she was still here with me."

Karen's gaze didn't waver from Brooke's. Karen Bradley was an expert on early childhood education, having spent her career teaching and writing books that were used in college classrooms around the country. Millie had always felt intimidated by her faculty adviser, but she trusted that Karen could handle Brooke's honesty about her mother's death. "That must have been very hard for you." She bent to Brooke's level as she spoke.

The girl nodded in response. Her fingers flexed as if she was holding Bunny to her side, but the stuffed animal was tucked away in one of the preschool cubbies. It had been a big step for Brooke to relinquish her hold on Bunny during preschool hours and now

Millie wanted the girl to have the comfort of the familiar lovey in her arms.

"It's good that your daddy is here for you."

"When I had my birthday party, I wished for a daddy. I told Mommy I would trade all my presents for having a daddy like my friends. He was my birthday wish, so Mommy went to get him for me." She spread her arms wide. "But there was a big earf-quake and she got dead."

Millie heard Jake suck in a breath and realized she was holding hers. None of them had understood exactly what had prompted Stacy Smith to seek out Jake when he'd known nothing about Brooke for years. She realized it was the girl's own request. Somehow it made Jake's presence in Brooke's life all the more poignant.

"You're a brave girl, Brooke."

Brooke looked to Millie. "Can I get Bunny out of his cubby?"

"Of course."

As the girl left the room, Millie dabbed at the corner of her eye. She couldn't make eye contact with Mrs. Bradley or Jake.

"I'm sorry for your loss," she heard Karen say to Jake.

"It's not... We weren't... It's a long story." He touched Millie's elbow. "Do you two need some privacy?"

"That would be—" Karen began at the same time Millie said, "Nope. All good here."

She dug deep and managed to produce a sunny smile. "Mrs. Bradley, are you on vacation?" She gave a laugh that sounded forced even to her own ears. "I'm happy you looked me up but I don't know—"

"It's about Daniel Blaine." Karen's eyes flicked to Jake. "Are you sure you don't want to speak about this alone?"

Millie was certain she didn't want to speak about Daniel Blaine at all. "I don't know what there's left to say. Two sides of the story and all that. I learned an important lesson so—"

"Two other women have come forward and made accusations about his inappropriate advances."

"Oh."

"Inappropriate advances," Jake repeated. "What is that about?" He turned to Millie. "Did some man hurt you, Millie?"

"No." She shook her head. "It wasn't like that. I didn't think…" She glanced at Karen Bradley. The woman studied her with a mix of understanding and sympathy. "I think Mrs. Bradley and I do need a few minutes. Jake, I'll lock up here and meet you back at the house." She kept her gaze trained on the floor.

"Are you sure? I can stay or call Olivia if you need support." He reached out for her but she shrugged away.

"I'm on her side," she heard Karen say.

She watched Jake begin to walk away but didn't hear his response through the roaring in her ears. After a few moments, she sank down into the child-sized chair once more. "Why did you come here to tell me this?"

Karen remained standing. "Several reasons. You

were put on academic probation because of the incident between you and Daniel."

"Because no one believed me," Millie said on a hiss of breath. Anger and humiliation washed over her as she thought of that time.

"I'm sorry." Karen lowered herself to the edge of the table. "I'm here to apologize and make things right with you." She paused then added, "We also need you to come back and make a formal statement. Testify, if necessary."

Millie lifted her head. "Come back?"

Karen nodded. "We need you, Millie."

IT WAS CLOSE to seven before Millie returned to Jake's house. After her conversation with Karen, she'd walked the streets of Crimson. In her short time here, she'd come to love this tiny town. She passed the older section, with houses in neat rows, and imagined settlers who had founded Crimson making their way over the mountains to begin a new life. They were people of great strength who had tamed these wild lands. She knew some had come for the chance of striking gold and making their fortune, but others came for a fresh start.

She understood why. The mountains could be grounding, inspiring and humbling all at the same time. She could imagine a place in this community, but her conversation with Karen Bradley had been a reminder that Crimson wasn't her home.

It had been so easy to leave the past behind, to ignore it in place of pretending that she was a clean slate. But that wasn't the case, and she couldn't move forward without dealing with everything that had come before.

Jake was just reading Brooke a story when Millie got to the house.

"Do you have time for a good-night song, Brookie-Cookie?" Millie asked from the girl's bedroom door.

"Millie!" Brooke held open her arms, and Millie came forward to give her a hug, breathing in the smell of her watermelon shampoo and clean soapy skin.

She loved this little girl, just as she loved Brooke's father.

The realization, while not new, came as a shock just the same. She couldn't make eye contact with Jake, who rose from the bed when she sat down.

"Night, sweetie," he said, bending forward to ruffle Brooke's hair. He placed a soft kiss on top of the girl's head. Millie remembered that first day at the house when Jake had seemed almost afraid to touch his daughter. He'd come so far. She wanted to beg him not to give up now.

With Brooke tucked into bed, Millie made her way back to the center of the house. Jake sat on the couch, the end-table light the only thing illuminating the large family room.

"Thanks for taking care of things," she said. "I didn't mean to leave you on your own for the whole night."

He pierced her with his gaze. "Come here, Millie."

"I'm pretty tired. Long day, you know."

"I know we need to talk about what that woman said to you."

Millie paused and tried to look casual. "It's fine. Misunderstanding. We got it all worked out."

"Does Olivia know?"

"Nothing happened," Millie answered, unable to keep the edge out of her voice.

"If you don't come and explain it to me, I'm going to call your sister."

"Is that a threat?"

"I don't care what you call it. I want to know what happened to you."

Millie knew he wasn't going to give up. As much as she didn't want to talk about this, it would be easier with Jake than Olivia. Her sister had a protective streak a mile long and Millie figured she'd never hear the end of it if Olivia got involved.

She sat gingerly on the edge of the couch, not trusting herself to be too close to Jake.

"I promise it's not a big deal. There was a little trouble with the principal at the elementary school where I interned. It's fine now."

"Did he hurt you?" Jake's voice was soft but laced with ice.

"No." She took a breath. "Not really. He was so helpful and supportive when I started. We were friends and he was like a mentor to me. We got close, but he misinterpreted how close I wanted to be."

"What did he do?"

She flicked her fingers. "He got a little handsy, you know."

"I don't know. Explain it."

Millie felt as if she was being interrogated and crossed her arms over her chest, not liking what the situation revealed about her and her weakness. "He tried to kiss me, made it clear that he wanted our relationship—if that's what you could call it—to go to the next level."

"A level that involved sex?"

Jake's bluntness made her wince. "He said that my reference letter was tied to how I performed in all aspects of the job."

"Sexual harassment."

"We'd gone out for drinks. I liked him—not like that but I thought I could trust him. He was married, with kids, and had a great reputation at the college. His school staff loved him. He said I'd given him mixed signals and I couldn't be trusted with dads. That I'd be a dangerous teacher because I made men want me. He told me no one would trust me with their children." Saying the words out loud made the humiliation burn hot and bright in her throat once again.

"You know that's crap, right?"

"I do now. But..." Her voice trailed off.

"But what?"

She made herself look him in the eye, despite her embarrassment. "But that's how my mom managed her life. Not that she wasn't faithful to my father. She was. But whether it was him or the mechanic or the landlord, she would bat her eyes and smooth talk the men in her life into helping her and taking care of whatever needed fixing. It was an art form for her and one of the few things she tried to teach me when I was growing up."

She took a breath. "She told me it's where my power came from, but I watched her give hers away every time she made herself into nothing more than an object for those men. I vowed never to live my life that way. Sometimes I think I have too much of her in me, that I can't help myself."

Shifting on the sofa, she ran her fingers along a seam on one of the cushions. "That's what Daniel Blaine told the people at the university. I was so embarrassed I didn't mention it to anyone. But he was afraid I would, so he beat me to it. He went to the academic board and my adviser—Karen Bradley—and said that I'd come on to him. Of course I denied it but the damage was already done."

"They believed him?"

"Most of them did. Karen had doubts, but there wasn't anything she could do."

"She could have stood up for you."

Millie shrugged. "She did her best. I was close to being expelled. She made sure I only got academic probation for a semester." Millie hated that her eyes filled with tears. "I'd put all of my money into school and it left me at loose ends. So I came here. Olivia had been so nice when we met, but she doesn't owe me anything. I don't want her involved in cleaning up my mess."

"She loves you, Millie. She's your sister."

"My mom loves me, too. That didn't mean she had my best interest at heart. I love being in Crimson. But Karen wants me to go back to California. Daniel accosted two other student teachers. It went pretty far with one of them." She shook her head. "If only they'd believed me, maybe this wouldn't have happened. If I was more reliable, if I looked like someone who wouldn't get into that kind of trouble." She gave a watery laugh. "Heck, if I looked like Olivia, the situation would have ended a different way."

"It isn't your fault." Jake stood then moved to sit next to her. He took her hands in his. She felt her fingers shaking, but somehow didn't mind Jake seeing her so vulnerable. "You can't blame yourself because some guy took advantage of you."

"If I hadn't—"

"Enough. You didn't do anything wrong."

She couldn't remember ever wanting to lean on someone the way she did Jake. It felt totally right when he pulled her into his lap. His hand came around her neck, slowly massaging the muscles there. With a sigh, she let her cheek drop to his shoulder. They stayed that way for several minutes, Jake's strong presence relaxing her.

"What happens next?" he asked quietly.

She thought about that for a while before speaking. "I go back."

"When?" She felt him tense beneath her. "For how long?"

"I won't leave you and Brooke in a lurch. Karen wants me to fly to California next week to make a formal statement. It will only take a day. I've already called Olivia and she can help out with Brooke while I'm away. I made a commitment and I'll honor that."

"That's not what I mean."

"I ran away, Jake." She burrowed into his shoulder. "I should have fought harder to have them believe me. I should have fought Daniel more. I want to be a teacher. I think I'd be good at it."

"You'll be an amazing teacher, Millie. Anyone can see that."

"Just like you're turning into a great father."

He gave a small laugh. "Nice change of topic. But this time it's about you."

"It's about us both." She drew in another breath and met his gaze. "We're in limbo together."

"It's a limbo, then?"

"You know what I mean. Each of us is trying to figure out what's next. You with Brooke, and me with another chance to finish my education."

"In California," he supplied.

"For a time, yes."

He didn't respond to that, only continued to look at her with a gaze that warmed her to her toes. She was wrapped in Jake's embrace, the silence of the house creating what felt like a cocoon for the two of them. At this moment, she didn't want to think about the future or what would happen—or not—between them. She only wanted to be here, now, with him.

She leaned forward and touched her tongue to the seam of his lips.

"Millie," he whispered. "You don't have to do this. You've been through a lot today."

"I want this." She nipped at the corner of his mouth. "I want you."

He slanted his mouth over hers, deepening the kiss. It told her that he felt the same and even more. Without words, he told her everything she needed to know.

His hands moved on her skin, and desire built in her.

"I want you in my bed. Beneath me, on top of me, any way you'll have me."

She knew those were only love words. He couldn't really mean them because what she wanted was his whole heart. She didn't believe Jake was ready for that.

She untangled from his embrace and stood. Disappointment flashed across his face until she reached out her hand to him. "Stay with me."

The request almost felt silly since they'd lived under the same roof for nearly a month now, but he laced his fingers with hers as if he might understand her unspoken desire. He followed her to her bedroom and they undressed each other slowly, discovering the intricacies of each other's bodies as they whispered words of need and want.

When they lay wrapped together a long time later, Millie felt Jake begin to drift to sleep then tense. "I should go back to my room," he said, kissing the tip of her nose.

"In the morning," she whispered, snuggling deeper into him.

When he remained rigid, she clasped her hands on either side of his head. "You can trust yourself with me."

His features gentled and he kissed her again. "How do you always know what I'm thinking?"

"I know you."

"The nightmares come when I'm deep in sleep, Millie. If I'm here with you and I strike out, I could hurt you."

"You won't hurt me, Jake." She traced the skin under his eyes. "When was the last time you had a decent night's sleep? I've seen your phone. You set the alarm to go off every hour in the night. That isn't restful."

He shrugged. "If I wake myself up at regular intervals, the dreams don't seem to come. That's what I always do, but I'm not sure I can manage it in your room. It's worth it not to disturb Brooke. I don't want her to be scared of me. I remember what that was like."

"Your father was a horrible man. That's not who you are."

He eased away from her. "It's still better this way."

"No." She drew him back against her. "Try it tonight, Jake. I'm a light sleeper. If you get agitated, I'll move away."

"You're so precious, Millie." He stared at her, as if trying to solve a puzzle, then took a short breath and relaxed onto his back, moving her so she lay sprawled across his chest. "You go to sleep. I'll stay here until you are."

She knew this was an argument she wouldn't win, so she agreed. But several minutes later, she felt his breathing turn regular and she knew he'd succumbed to exhaustion. Millie lay there several more minutes, savoring his warmth around her. Soon her own eyes drifted shut, and she didn't fight that, either.

CHAPTER FOURTEEN

JAKE WOKE IN the early morning more rested than he'd felt in months. He hadn't left Millie's bed, but no bad dreams had plagued him. He'd held her tight against him, his own personal security blanket. As she'd promised, her warm presence had kept the nightmares at bay.

He leaned forward to kiss her neck. She sighed and smiled, turning until she was facing him. Her eyes didn't open but she brought her arms around him, drawing him in for a passionate kiss then deep inside her, their lovemaking slow and sweet.

When he finally left her bed, he put more ice on his hand, then walked quietly back to his side of the house before Brooke woke. He felt normal, which was something new for him. It was something he could get used to.

He'd taken on an extra shift at the clinic today, so when Brooke wasn't looking he gave Millie a quick kiss then said goodbye to his daughter.

"Why do you have to leave, Daddy?" Brooke asked, turning those big blue eyes on him.

"I'm only going to work, Brookie-Cookie. I'll be back before you know it."

"You work too much," she complained. "Mommy did, too, and then she died."

"I'm not going to die," he answered after a startled moment. "You've been to the hospital. You know it's safe there."

Brooke stomped her foot. "I don't want you to go. What if you don't come back?"

He glanced to Millie for some relief, but she gave him a small shake of her head. He was on his own. Great.

He bent lower to look into his daughter's eyes. "Nothing is going to happen to me, Brooke."

"What if it does?"

"It won't."

"But what if—"

"Enough." He stood and drew in a breath. His daughter's sweet chin trembled as she watched him. He'd raised his voice, and suddenly he was transported back to his own childhood, to being afraid to ever speak, never knowing what kind of response he was going to get from his father, whose mercurial moods could change in an instant.

"I promise I'll be back," he said, gentling his tone. He wasn't used to having his schedule questioned. Normally he could go wherever he wanted whenever he wanted. No one bothered to care. Things were different now, he knew, but it was an adjustment. "You have preschool. I have work. It will be okay." He felt out of his element but he bent and picked up his daughter. "I love you, Brooke." He realized it was the first time he'd said the words out loud.

She gave him a small smile. "Love you, too, Daddy."

He breathed in her sweet scent, layered with a little bit of syrup after this morning's pancake breakfast.

Dropping from his embrace, she started toward her bedroom. "I'm going to get dressed. Millie, will you make my hair in braids?"

"Sure thing." As Millie walked past him, she brushed another kiss on his cheek. "You're a good man, Jake Travers."

Her belief in him made Jake feel as if he'd just won the lottery. When he got to the hospital, Vincent called him into his office and made a formal offer of employment. Jake had guessed it was coming and hadn't known how he'd feel about truly settling down. Then he remembered the way his daughter's eyes had lit up when he'd told her he loved her and how much she wanted him as a part of her life.

Didn't he owe it to her and to himself to really make that commitment?

His mind formed a picture of Brooke, Millie and him as a family, with a little brother or sister added to the mix. His heart began to race, but not in panic. What he felt was anticipation in a way he hadn't looked forward to the future in a long time.

Unfortunately, his mood didn't last. There had been an explosion at one of the silver mines north of town and half a dozen men were brought in with a variety of injuries. The intensity of the work tested his stamina and his focus. He lost himself in the familiar exhilaration of crisis medicine, so absorbed in what he was doing that he didn't give a thought to the clock.

This was his skill set, his training and where he was most comfortable. He kept working until all of the patients were stable and either discharged or admitted. Adrenaline kept him moving when his leg started to throb and his wrist ached. But his hand held up through the entire day, with none of the nerve pain he'd become accustomed to feeling.

At some point, he'd misplaced his cell phone, so he'd given the reception desk Millie's number and asked them to call and relay a message that he'd be home later than expected.

By the time he pulled onto his street, fatigue was starting to set in. That changed when he saw the fire truck in front of the house. He parked and ran through the front door.

Brooke was the first to spot him. "Daddy, you didn't come back," she yelled. "You left and we needed you and you didn't come home."

"I'm sorry, Cookie," he said, his hammering heart starting to slow at the realization that his daughter wasn't hurt.

He ignored Janis's disapproving stare and swung Brooke into his arms, hugging her tight. "I'm here now. What's going on?"

"Fairy Poppins got dead for a few minutes. I was bleeding and it killed her."

His heart took off once again.

"I'm okay," Millie called from the couch. Two large EMT workers blocked her from view. "Not a big deal. Sorry for all the trouble."

He put Brooke down and strode forward, elbowing one of the guys out of the way. The other had his hands in Millie's hair and frowned. "Excuse me, sir. We're working here."

"I'm a doctor." Jake nudged the man aside. Both EMTs were young and stepped back in deference to Jake. "Tell me what happened."

He'd been talking to Millie, but the taller EMT recited her injuries. "She has head trauma, a skin laceration. It doesn't look like a concussion, but that's a possibility."

"I don't have a concussion," she said, her eyes rolling.

He held up a hand, silencing the EMT. "Talk to me," he said as he spread her hair to examine the cut on the back of her head.

"Brooke cut herself. I'm not great with blood. I fainted, but luckily the edge of the counter broke my fall." She flashed a wan smile that he didn't return. "That led to more blood and I passed out again." She must have read the look on his face because she quickly added, "It was only a few minutes."

"Thank heavens we stopped by when we did." Janis had come to stand behind him, holding Brooke's hand. "This poor thing was scared to death."

Jake turned, noticing Brooke held Bunny in a death grip once again.

"You were 'posed to come back, Daddy."

"I'm sorry," Millie whispered.

At that moment, Olivia hurried into the house.

"What the hell," Jake muttered.

"Sorry," Millie said again. "I called my sister when Brooke's grandparents showed up. You weren't answering your phone. I wanted…someone here for me."

His gaze crashed into hers and he thought he read

the words she'd left unspoken clearly in her eyes. *Because you weren't.*

Olivia came forward and Brooke ran to her. "Aunt Livvy, Millie almost got dead like Mommy."

"Oh, sweetie." Olivia hugged her. "Millie is just fine."

Brooke gave a small nod. "I got a cut, too." She tipped her chin to show off the bandage there. "I bleeded a whole lot."

"It's a good thing you're so brave." Jake watched as Olivia met Millie's eyes. "You okay?"

"I'll be better as soon as people stop hovering over me." Millie's voice sounded thin and embarrassed, as if she'd done something wrong.

Jake didn't understand, but he hustled the two EMTs out of the house. From what he could tell, Millie didn't need stitches and he planned to keep a very close eye on her in case she had any post-concussive symptoms.

When he came back, Millie was sitting up on the couch, Brooke tucked in at her side.

He saw Janis down the hallway, carrying his daughter's small backpack, and walked over to meet her before she was within earshot. "I'm going to take Brooke home with me." She glared at Jake, as if daring him to argue.

Which he was happy to do given his mood. "How is that going to help?"

"You didn't see the look on her face, Jake. She was terrified. After everything that girl has been through, she needs stability. She needs to be taken care of by people who will put her needs first."

"I'm here, Janis. I'm in Crimson with Brooke doing my best to make this work."

She gave a hard shake of her head. "Not good enough. My daughter died trying to give Brooke a father. Stacy put everything in her life on hold. She dedicated herself to Brooke. She did it alone."

"Because she never, in four years, thought to mention to me that I had a daughter. That isn't my fault."

"No," the woman agreed after a moment. "But you hired a nanny." The fact that she put air quotes around the word *nanny* grated on Jake's nerves. "A nanny who passes out at the sight of blood. One you can't take your eyes from most of the time." Her gaze narrowed. "Don't think I haven't noticed. The two of you playing at whatever games you like. What kind of a role model are you for my granddaughter? That's not how Stacy would have wanted her raised. She would have wanted her daughter to be brought up in a stable, steady home." She took a breath and her tone softened. "I know that's not what you had as a boy, Jake. I've asked around town about your family."

"You had no right—"

"When it comes to protecting my granddaughter, I don't give a horse's patoot about minding my own business. That girl is my business. I believe you want what's best for her. John and I can give her a stable home. Tonight proves she belongs with us."

What tonight proved was that Jake's life was more damned complicated than he'd even imagined.

"Please, let me take her." Janis's voice broke and he saw tears swim in her eyes.

He blew out a breath. "She can spend the night with

you. That's as much as I can promise for now." But he knew he'd give more. He'd let Janis and John raise his daughter because it would be best for Brooke. As much as he tried, Jake didn't believe he would ever deserve to be her full-time father. She was worth so much more than he could give her.

Emotion tightened his throat. He turned before Janis could see his heart breaking. "Cookie," he said, coming to the couch but not meeting Millie's intense gaze, "you're going to spend the night with Nana and Papa. How does that sound?"

Brooke shook her head. "I want to stay here. So you don't leave and Millie doesn't die."

"I'm going to be just fine, sweetie." Millie hugged her hard. "Remember I'm taking my trip to California tomorrow. I'll be back to tuck you in at bedtime, though."

"Daddy needs me," Brooke said, her innocent gaze trained on Millie.

Millie smiled gently. "Of course he does. You'll always be there for him. Just like he will for you."

The words gnawed at Jake's insides as if Millie had chosen them for that very purpose.

She sat up straighter, lifting Brooke onto her lap. "But tonight you're going to have fun with your grandparents. I bet they'll even take you for doughnuts in the morning."

"Not exactly a healthy way to start the day," Janis mumbled from where she stood behind Jake.

Jake watched Millie's brow rise and her lips purse.

"We can definitely have doughnuts for breakfast,"

Janis amended quickly, "if that's what you want, Brooke."

Tipping back her head to kiss Millie's chin, Brooke wrapped her arms awkwardly around her shoulders. "I love you, Fairy Poppins."

"I love you, too, Brookie-Cookie." Millie helped the girl to stand. "Have lots of fun with Nana and Papa so you can tell me all about it when I get back."

Brooke nodded and gave Olivia, then Jake, a hug.

"I'll bring you a doughnut, Daddy."

As he put his arms around her, the fierce need to never let go engulfed him. He straightened and tapped one finger against her nose. "Can you guess my favorite kind?"

"The ones with chocolate icing," Brooke said without hesitation.

"How did you know?" He glanced at Millie, who shook her head.

"Silly, Daddy. Those are my favorites, too."

With that sugary lance to his heart, she took her grandma's hand and skipped out the front door.

MILLIE DUG HER fingernails into the couch cushions to stop herself from bolting into Jake's arms. He looked so stunned and alone as Brooke walked away.

Stop her! Millie wanted to shout. *Don't let her go.*

It was for one night. Millie knew she was overreacting but couldn't help but think there was more to it than that.

Jake turned, his gaze shuttered. "I'm going to get a flashlight and the first-aid kit and have another look at your head."

"I'm fine, Jake." She met her sister's sympathetic gaze and was comforted when Olivia nodded in agreement. "The EMTs said I was fine."

"They said possible concussion."

"You know that's not true."

Finally his eyes met hers. "Humor me on this, Millie." The tenderness in his tone undid her.

She gave a tiny nod. When he'd disappeared down the hall, Millie looked to Olivia. "I'm in trouble here, sis."

"You love him," Olivia supplied.

Millie choked back a sob. "How can I be so stupid? I'm just like my mother, falling for the guy who's my boss. The one I can't have."

"Why can't you have him?"

"Come on, Olivia. This is me. I've told you I don't stick in one place, I don't form long-lasting attachments. I will never have a man dictate my life. Not like she did."

"Jake isn't the type of guy who would want to run your life. The way it looks to me, you do that for him."

"He's also not the type of guy who settles down. And even if he did, it would be for Brooke. They need time. I don't want to get in the way."

"You don't get in the way, Millie. You help bridge the distance between them."

"I can't take the chance if…" She stopped as Jake came back into the room.

"I should go." Olivia stretched her arm around Millie's shoulder and squeezed. "I'm glad you're okay and I'm glad you called me."

"Can I stay with you tonight?" Millie asked as Olivia stood.

She saw Jake stiffen but kept her eyes on Olivia. "Of course," her sister answered slowly. "It probably makes sense since I'll be taking you to Denver for your flight tomorrow morning. I'm just going to step out onto the porch and call Logan. Come on out when you're ready."

When she was alone with Jake, Millie blurted, "I'm sorry. I know I've ruined everything."

"What the hell are you talking about?"

She started to stand but he blocked her, lowering himself to sit behind her. "I want to look at your head."

"It's nothing. I just… The blood… I feel awful that Brooke was scared." She put her fingers to her mouth, emotion welling. "She thought I was dead."

"It was an accident."

"That I should have prevented. I've always had that reaction to blood. If I'd told you and Brooke, she would have known not to be afraid."

"How did she cut her chin?"

His fingers massaged her skin, making some of the tension in her body fade. "She fell off her scooter out front. She was upset that you were late and…"

"Are you saying it was my fault?"

"I didn't mean it that way. I'd set up an obstacle course in the driveway. It's one of the things she loves playing at the preschool. She hit a patch of gravel and fell. I was fine at first, but you know how much blood there can be from even a little cut on the face. I brought her into the house to clean it up and just lost it. It was my fault, Jake. No one else's."

"Sometimes things happen for a reason."

She gave a harsh laugh. "You don't believe that." She turned to him, his hands falling from her head. "I heard you and Janis talking."

"She wants what's best with Brooke."

"So do you."

"That's the point. I'm not best for Brooke. I'm too into my work. Today was a perfect example. I love what I do. I worked my whole life for this career, and I thought I'd lost it. Now I have another chance."

"Does that mean you're going back to work for Miles of Medicine?"

His face went hard. "I told you I would try to be a father. Look at what came of my attempt."

"Because of me," she said on a half sob. "You promised me—"

"I never promised you anything more, Millie."

That stilled her, even as the pain in her heart swelled so savagely she feared it might drag her under. "That's true." *Men don't make promises to people like us, hon.* Her mother's words echoed in her head. *You need to learn to take what you can get and be happy for it.*

She stood, shrugging out of Jake's grasp. "I'm going to my sister's house."

"You don't have to go. You're safe with me. I won't touch you if you don't want me to."

Wasn't that just the problem? She wanted him to touch her almost as much as she wanted to breathe. She could easily push aside her dreams, bury anything she might need in life like her mother had done, just to stay with him.

"I'm leaving, Jake. I'll be in California tomorrow.

When I get back, I'll continue to nanny for you through the end of the month. But I'm staying with Olivia."

"No. Brooke needs you here."

"She needs you here more. Janis was right. You and I are just complicating the situation when we know this isn't going to last."

"How do you know we won't last?"

"Are you staying in Crimson?"

He looked away from her. "I got a job offer from the hospital."

Hope, damned hope, sprang forward in her heart. "Do you plan to accept it?"

He ran his finger through her hair, the unconscious gesture now so familiar and dear to her. "The agency sent a new contract. They want me to go to Africa. There's a huge need because of the drought plaguing the region near Nairobi. I'm good at that kind of medicine. I know I can make a difference there."

I need you to make a difference here. "What are you going to do, Jake?"

"I'm not like your father, Millie. Even if Brooke lives with her grandparents, I won't desert her or put her aside. I'll be a part of her life."

But not mine.

"Do what you think is best, Jake. It's your decision." She made her voice even, belying the emotions that tumbled through her. "This is mine."

Then she stood and walked away.

CHAPTER FIFTEEN

"She's not coming back."

"Sure she will, bro. Have a little faith."

Jake glanced at his brother Logan, sitting on the park bench next to him. Brooke called his name and Jake waved to her. She was on the far side of the playground, taking turns on the slide with one of her preschool friends who was also at the park today. Jake caught the eye of the other girl's mother. She waved and went back to texting on her phone.

"Are you afraid that the single-mom vultures will swoop with Millie not around to protect you?"

"I'm afraid of a lot of things." Jake tried to make the words sound like a joke but they held the ominous ring of truth.

"Aren't we all?"

Jake was surprised when his brother didn't try to lighten the conversation. "Olivia's pregnant."

That news broke Jake out of his sour mood. "I'm so happy for you, Logan." He slapped his brother on the back. "You two will make wonderful parents."

"If it's a girl we're going to name her Elizabeth. We'll call her Liz but I wanted to see what you thought of that?"

"I think Beth would have loved it."

Logan nodded. "I ran into someone I know at the hospital, heard they want you to work for them full-time. We'd love for you to stay in Crimson. Josh, too. Dad has ruled our lives from the great beyond for too long."

Jake didn't like to think of his father involved in any part of his life. "Janis and John are talking about leaving for Atlanta the first part of November. They want to take Brooke with them. The agency needs me in Africa."

"So that's it. You're leaving?"

Jake heard the disappointment in his brother's voice.

"I want to do what's best for Brooke." He dropped his head back, watching the clouds roll by in the bright blue Colorado sky. "I don't believe I'm it, Logan. I'm not cut out to raise a kid on my own."

"If you stay here, you won't be on your own."

"You know what a lot of people in Crimson see when they look at me? Dad."

"That's what you see, not the town."

"I don't want to, but I'm scared as hell that the parts of me that are like him are going to come out and Brooke's going to pay the price."

Logan shook his head. "I wish it wasn't like that for you. You took the brunt of his anger."

"Leaving you, Beth and Josh behind to deal with it when I was gone. I should have done more to make your life a good one. I can do that for my daughter."

"So Brooke and Millie are tossed aside while you move on with your life?" Now Logan sounded angry and Jake felt a matching temper flare to life in himself.

"I didn't create this situation. I'm just trying to deal with it."

"You're not dealing with it." Logan pressed on. "You're running away." He paused then added, "Like you did when you left Crimson the first time." He held up a hand before Jake could argue. "I'm not saying I blame you for going to college, for taking your chance. But you never returned, never tried to stay in contact. You can't forge decent relationships by popping in and out of people's lives, Jake. It didn't work with us and it won't work with your daughter. She needs more."

Brooke waved him over and Jake stood, unable to deal with this conversation any longer. "It's all I have to give, Logan."

By the time he had Brooke settled on the swing, his brother was gone.

Millie did return, true to her word, which should have meant something to him. But it wasn't the same. She barely made eye contact with him each morning as she arrived at the house. She made breakfast, prepped dinner and took care of Brooke's needs. She busied herself in the afternoons when Jake was available with preparations for the fall musical or her plans to return to California. Janis and John stepped in to help as he needed it, and he agreed Brooke would return to Atlanta with them.

A deep ache settled in his chest every time he thought of being separated from Brooke, but Janis tried to convince him that between Skype and phone calls, she and John would make sure he never lost touch with his daughter when he traveled. He'd turned down the job in Crimson and accepted the contract with the agency, wanting to believe he was doing what was best for Brooke.

He hadn't mentioned the plans to her yet. Brooke didn't like Millie staying with Olivia any more than Jake did and had become as clingy and emotional as when he'd first come into her life. He hoped this was just her way of adjusting and scaled back on his shifts at the hospital to spend more time with her.

Each time he did, his heart broke a little. He loved Brooke, but he wanted to do the right thing. No matter what Millie said, being with Jake wasn't it. If it was, why was Millie leaving after the musical?

He'd told her he wanted her to stay with him, that he wouldn't push her for anything she wasn't willing to give. But it hadn't been enough.

It killed him to be near her when all he wanted was to drag her into his arms. He imagined leaving with her and Brooke, venturing deep into the mountains, far away from family and reality. They could be together without the outside world crashing in making demands. Jake had never dealt well with the outside world—that was why he'd always kept to himself and continued his nomadic medical practice.

Was he running the way Logan had suggested? He preferred to think of it as keeping himself sane.

There was certainly no time to reason it all out in Crimson. His brothers and their wives had circled his household like a wagon train. He wasn't sure what Millie had shared with Olivia, but someone was always stopping by or insisting that Jake and Brooke come for dinner.

He was happy that his family had clearly made Millie one of their own, which also meant he had more time with her. Even if he had to watch her across a room or laughing from the other end of the table, he still felt her light travel through him. Sometimes he'd catch her watching him and swore her eyes held the same longing he felt. Then it would be gone and she'd look away.

He didn't blame her. He was making a mess of everything but couldn't see how to stop it.

Two days before the preschool musical, Josh and Logan insisted on a guys' night out. Since both of them were happily married, Jake didn't worry that the evening would turn into a late-night drunkfest, but he still arranged for Brooke to spend the night with Janis and John.

He planned to tell her about his job and the new living arrangements the next morning. He'd put it off as long as he could. He'd come up with all the reasons that this was for the best and how he'd still be a part of her life. Janis and John had agreed to a custody arrangement that would allow Brooke to spend at least a month in the summer and most school holidays with him. He'd explained his new schedule to his boss at the agency. She'd reluctantly agreed, although she was sorry to lose a doctor who'd been willing to travel anywhere in the world with no notice. That wasn't his life anymore. He was doing his best to make things work for everyone involved.

He only wished he knew how to keep Millie involved. He hadn't had a moment alone with her since she'd returned from California. Her sister and friends had seen to that. Jake got the distinct impression that they were protecting her from him but couldn't un-derstand why.

After all, Millie had walked away from *him*.

Thankfully, neither of his brothers brought it up over their dinner at a local hamburger joint. But when they moved on to beers at the Two Moon Saloon, both Josh and Logan were more than willing to tell him how badly he'd mucked up his life—as if he didn't already know.

"I told Sara book smarts don't translate to real life." Josh studied Jake over the rim of his beer bottle. "You never did have a lick of common sense."

"Shut it," Jake growled.

"Olivia's so mad she could spit," Logan added. He punched Jake harder than necessary on the shoulder. "I don't like it when my wife's upset. You know what I mean?"

"I know you both need to let it go." He took a long pull on his beer. "I didn't come back to Crimson to have you two harping at me."

Logan shrugged. "Remind us again—why did you come back? Especially since you're pulling out so soon."

The question threw him. After a few moments he answered, "Because I was scared and overwhelmed. I didn't know how the hell to be a father, what that meant. My only role model had been Dad. You know how that went."

"Bad and worse," Josh answered.

"The past can teach you something about what not to do," Logan agreed.

"We might not have been close, but you two are the

only family I have. It made sense to bring Brooke here. Somehow I knew if I needed help, you'd be there for me." He saluted the two of them with his beer bottle. "And you have been."

"So why are you leaving?"

"It's complicated."

"Lame," Logan mumbled.

Jake wanted to lay his fist into his baby brother's face. Before he could argue, his cell phone rang. The display showed John's number. He imagined Brooke wanted to talk to him before she went to bed. He answered and his heart hit the floor as John spoke.

"Call the police," he said, already out of his chair. "I'm on my way."

Josh grabbed at his arm. "What's going on?"

"I need your help. Both of you."

Without hesitation his two brothers stood. Jake would have been touched except for the ball of fear curling in his gut. "It's Brooke," he said, his voice shaking. "She's gone missing."

MILLIE STOPPED AT every storefront on the east side of Main Street while Olivia canvassed the other half of the street. Logan had called both Olivia and Millie as he left the bar. Millie hadn't spoken to Jake but knew he must be terrified.

Her stomach had been rolling for the past hour. She and Olivia had raced to Janis and John's rented condo when they found out Brooke had disappeared.

Janis, in between sobs, had told them that they'd tucked Brooke in for bed, but when John had gone to check on her thirty minutes later, she'd been gone.

They turned the house upside down then knocked on each door within a ten-block radius of the house. The police had arrived and started their own search. Neighbors joined in and pretty soon it seemed as if the whole town of Crimson was looking for little Brooke.

Jake had held himself together as he answered questions about his daughter. Millie had wanted to run to him, to apologize for walking out and offer him whatever comfort she could give. But the one time his eyes met hers, he'd looked right through her as if she was no longer alive to him. She'd forced away her own pain, concentrating all her energy on helping find Brooke.

Once Millie and Olivia finished talking to business owners and people on the street, they returned to Jake's house. The makeshift headquarters for the search had been moved there since Janis and John's place didn't have much extra room.

Jake was on his phone when they came into the kitchen. The police had asked him to stay at the house. In case any information came in on the girl, they wanted him to be available.

"No luck?" Katie Garrity asked. She'd closed down the bakery and brought snacks and coffee to the house to keep people going.

Millie shook her head and saw Jake glance her way. She took a step toward him then stopped as his phone clattered to the floor. He moved toward her then past her in a whirlwind.

She turned and saw an older man standing in the doorway to the family room, Brooke sleeping in his arms.

"I think this belongs to you," he said to Jake.

"Brooke." Millie watched as Jake reached forward to take his daughter from the man. He held her close, his shoulders shaking as tears streaked his cheeks.

Brooke snuggled sleepily into her father's chest.

"Silas Benton," Olivia said, walking forward. "How did you end up with this child? You didn't even answer your door when we came by your house."

Silas shrugged. "Found her curled up in a chair on my patio a few minutes ago when I took the dog for his evening walk." He looked at Jake. "I didn't know there was such a big hullabaloo, but I knew right off she was your kid. She's got your eyes, same as your daddy's." He rubbed a hand over his scratchy chin. "Of course, your dad's weren't near so sweet. Always red-rimmed with drink and sharp with temper." He put a hand on Jake's arm. "She looks like you, son."

"Thank you," Jake said, his voice hoarse. Millie saw him wipe at his eyes with the back of his hand before Olivia gave him a tissue.

Again, Millie wanted to go to him but stayed rooted in her place.

Brooke's head lifted. "Daddy, you said you wouldn't leave me."

He kissed the tip of her nose. "You're the one who left, Cookie." He made a broad sweeping motion with his hand. "Half the town was out looking for you to-night."

She glanced over his shoulder to where Janis was seated at the table, silently sobbing. "I heard Nana talking to Papa. They said I was going to live with them. They were making plans for me in Hat-lanta. I don't want to go, Daddy." Her voice rose as she clearly became agitated. "I want to stay with you. I want you to stay with me."

He gave her a tight hug. "I'm not going anywhere and neither are you. We're staying in Crimson, Brooke. You're going to be my girl forever. For as long as you'll have me. There is nothing more important to me than you. I'm sorry it's taken me so long to realize it." He turned to Janis and John. "I know you loved your daughter, and I love mine. Stacy asked me to take care of Brooke for a reason. I'm her father, and it's about time I start acting like it. You're a part of Brooke's life and you always will be. But she belongs with me."

Janis cried harder but nodded. John gave Jake a thumbs-up and came forward to hug his granddaughter.

A round of cheers went up, the loudest from Josh and Logan, who had walked in behind Jake. Millie felt tears spill down her cheeks. This was what she'd wanted from the start. This was the man she knew Jake could be, and it broke her heart even more not to be a part of his world.

Suddenly, the thought of how alone she was settled on her like a heavy burden. As family and friends surrounded Jake, Millie slipped out the back door and walked by herself to Olivia's house.

THEY SAY THE SHOW must go on, and the preschool musical was no exception. Millie stood behind the curtain the following night, putting all of the children in their places on the makeshift stage. She gave Brooke an extra hug as she adjusted one of her fox ears.

"I'm so happy you're here, Brookie-Cookie."

Brooke grinned up at her. "Daddy is, too. We're going to live in Crimson. Together. Forever. All of—" The girl broke off and clapped her hand over her mouth.

Millie figured she was worried about breaking Ms. Laura's request for silence before the show started. "It's okay, sweetie. I know just how you feel."

Brooke gave her a curious look but said nothing more. They listened as Ms. Laura thanked the parent volunteers and introduced the program. She made special mention that they were thrilled to have one lost little critter back and Brooke stifled a giggle.

Millie moved offstage as the curtain opened. The parents and family members in the audience watched with smiles and small chortles of laughter as the preschoolers sang and danced their way through the four seasons.

Laura crouched in front of the stage, mouthing words and encouraging the kids. Millie remained out of sight, lining up children for their entrances and giving quick hugs when they exited the stage. Only once did she have to step out when the beaver's costume came down over his eyes and the poor boy underneath started to wander the stage, hands out, as if he were playing a game of Marco Polo.

Brooke sang with gusto through the entire performance, occasionally waving to her family in the front row. Jake sat with his brothers and their wives plus Janis and John. She knew from Olivia that Brooke's grandparents were sorely disappointed the girl wasn't going to live with them, but they seemed to finally understand her devotion to Jake.

Millie took small comfort that she'd known Jake would make a wonderful father. She'd been secretly relieved to hear that Lana Mayfield had taken Jake's open position with Miles of Medicine and had already left Crimson. But someday he'd find a woman to marry, make a proper family and move forward. Likely he'd forget all about her, but she'd always carry with her the knowledge that she'd helped make him and Brooke a family. She may not have had a choice as to her own upbringing, but she was happy to have helped another little girl avoid her same fate.

The audience applauded as the last verse of the song ended. She whispered directions to the children about lining up, then stepped back behind the curtain again.

Laura Wilkes straightened and turned to the audience. She congratulated the children, which led to additional clapping and cheering from the parents.

"I also want to recognize our teaching assistant, Millie Spencer, for all the time and energy she's put into making our musical a success."

Another round of applause sounded as Laura turned and motioned Millie to join her at the front. Millie shook her head, but the clapping grew louder. Then Brooke walked over and took her hand, leading her out from behind the curtain.

Millie wasn't used to being the center of attention this way. Her knees trembled as she smiled and nodded at the parents in the audience. After being run out on the rails from her last teaching position, the change here was overwhelming to her senses.

As the audience quieted, Laura gave her a small hug. "You've been such a blessing to this preschool," she said, her voice gentle. "I wish there was something we could do to convince you to stay on in Crimson."

One of the boys from the class stepped forward and handed Millie a stack of letters, tied with a ribbon.

"Thank-you notes from the class," Laura explained.

"Read mine now," Brooke said, bouncing on her toes next to Millie. "I made it special today." She handed Millie a folded piece of paper.

Millie could feel color rise to her cheeks. "This is so nice," she said to Laura. "All of it. You didn't have to—"

"Read my letter." Brooke snatched the paper from her hand, opened it and held it up in front of Millie. The crowd fell silent. In bold, childish scrawl were the words *Merry Us*.

A sigh went up in the crowd, but Millie stood in confusion for a few seconds as Brooke stared at her expectantly.

"It should be an *A*," a voice from the audience said. As she turned, Jake walked up the few steps to stand in front of her. His smile was hesitant, unsure and so very sweet to her.

"So will you with an *A*?" Brooke asked.

"Will I—"

"Marry us?" Jake supplied. "Or more specifically, marry me?"

"Daddy, do it right." Brooke poked at her father's leg. "You have to do it right so she'll say yes."

He took a breath, as if to calm his nerves, and dropped to one knee. He slid his fingers into hers, and despite all of the people watching, Millie couldn't look away from his gaze.

"I love you, Millie," he said softly.

"Speak up," someone from the audience yelled. Millie was pretty sure the voice belonged to Josh. "They can't hear you in the back."

"I love you," Jake said more clearly, not taking his eyes from hers. "I think I loved you from the first moment you came shimmering into my life. You changed things. You brought back laughter and light and you helped me become the man I didn't know I could be."

"You were always that man," she whispered.

He shook his head. "It's because of you. It's for you. You deserve so much more than I can ever give you, Millie. But please let me try. I want you to be my wife."

"And my stepmom," Brooke added.

Jake drew his daughter to his side. "We're a package deal, Brooke and me. But we won't be whole without you in our lives. Please marry us."

Stunned, Millie looked out to the audience then to the preschoolers watching from the stage. She'd come to think of this place as home but never imagined she could feel as happy and complete as she did at this moment.

"You gonna say yes or no?" one of the boys asked. "'Cause if you don't want him, I'll marry you."

Millie let out a laugh. "Yes," she said, as Jake stood, picked up Brooke and wrapped them both in a tight hug. "I love you. I love you both. Of course I'll marry you, Jake. You're my heart and my life."

The crowd cheered again. Millie buried her face in Jake's shoulder, afraid that her emotions would get the best of her.

Laura Wilkes spoke again. "Let's celebrate our

preschoolers and this new engagement with cake and punch out on the back lawn."

This time the cheer went up from the children. Brooke wiggled out of Jake's grasp and led the charge out the door.

Jake wrapped both his arms around Millie and pulled her to the back of the stage behind the curtain.

"You're sure?" he asked, tipping up her chin. "You'll have me even though I'm the biggest idiot on the planet?"

She smiled and touched her hand to his cheek. "You're mine and you're not an idiot," she whispered and reached onto her tiptoes to kiss him. "We're going to figure this out together, Jake. I love you and there's no place in the world I'd rather be than at your side."

He deepened the kiss and her senses spun. She reveled in the heat of him around her and the love she'd always dreamed of having.

"Forever, Millie. You are mine. Forever."

Just then the curtain pulled back. Brooke stood there, a fork in her hand, icing smeared across her cheek. "Come on, you guys." She shook the fork at them. "Uncle Josh and Uncle Logan are going to eat all the cake if you don't hurry."

"Then let's go," Jake said, ruffling his daughter's hair, and the three of them walked into the future together.

EPILOGUE

One Month Later

"ARE YOU SURE you're okay to leave Bunny behind?" Millie bent forward to readjust one of the flowers that adorned Brooke's hair.

The little girl nodded. "He doesn't like weddings and ate too much pumpkin pie yesterday. I'll put him down for a nap and then we can get married." She giggled at the words she'd just said. "I mean you can get married. To Daddy."

As Brooke went to adjust her stuffed animal on the bed, Millie turned to Olivia, who smiled at the two of them from where she stood near the door, holding a bouquet of pale lilies. "Thank you for arranging all of this so quickly."

"It was my pleasure. I'm happy for you, Millie."

"But with your condition…"

"I feel great, hardly any morning sickness." Olivia patted her stomach, which was just beginning to round. "Besides, Sara and Natalie helped. Katie took care of all the food. It was a community effort." Her smile widened. "It helped that you and Jake wanted a small wedding. You're absolutely radiant."

Millie looked at herself in the mirror above the

dresser. She was getting married today. Her heart pounded as she tried to absorb the significance of that.

Josh and Sara had insisted they have the ceremony at Crimson Ranch, so she was in one of the guest bedrooms at the main house. It was Thanksgiving Day. They'd decided to hold the wedding on the holiday that was traditionally filled with family and food, keeping things easy and casual for everyone involved. Millie had been staying with Olivia and Logan since Jake had asked her to marry him because they didn't want to confuse Brooke with the change in Millie's status from nanny to future stepmother.

Like Brooke, her hair was adorned with tiny flowers, and the simple white dress with a lace overlay made her feel like a true bride. The engagement ring Jake had given her sparkled on her finger. The stone was a beautiful yellow diamond surrounded by a cluster of smaller clear diamonds. He'd told her he always wanted her to remember that she'd brought color and sunshine into his life. Every time she looked at the ring and what it represented, her heart sang.

"It's happiness," Millie whispered. "I look happy."

"You do, indeed. Even your mom noticed."

"I can't believe she came. I didn't think she'd make the trip."

"She loves you," Olivia told her. "She might not have been the greatest mom growing up, but she does love you."

Millie turned and walked toward her sister, reaching forward to give Olivia a swift hug. "I know your mom loves you, as well, even though the thought of me gives her hives." She squeezed her sister's shoulders. "I think Dad loved all of us in his own convoluted way."

"I'm glad you're staying in Crimson, Millie. You belong here. I always wanted a big family—"

"Me, too."

"Now we both have one." Olivia wiped at her eyes.

"Don't make me cry," Millie said with a laugh. "My makeup will run."

A soft tap sounded on the door and Sara poked her head in. "The guys are ready." Her gazed landed on Millie and she waved her hand in front of her face. "You look so perfect it's going to make me cry."

"No happy tears until the wedding," Olivia whispered.

"Right," Sara agreed. "I'll tell them you're ready to start?"

Millie took a deep breath and nodded. "It's time."

Sara closed the door again as Brooke came up to take Millie's hand. "Let's go get married so you can come home."

Millie couldn't agree more and followed the girl she loved like a true daughter into the hall.

JAKE WATCHED BROOKE walk down the makeshift aisle in the big Crimson Ranch family room. Furniture had been moved so that chairs could be set in front of the picture window overlooking the valley. A dusting of early snow covered the highest peaks, a sure sign the seasons were changing in Crimson. Jake stood before the window, flanked by Logan, who was serving as his best man, and Josh, who'd agreed to officiate the service. They'd been looking for an officiate when someone in town had mentioned the little-known Colorado law that allowed Jake and Millie to perform the marriage ceremony themselves or have someone in the wedding party do it. Josh had offered, which seemed like a perfect fit for the intimate gathering they wanted.

It was only family and close friends in the room, but his daughter dropped her rose petals with the pomp and circumstance fit for a royal wedding.

He couldn't imagine that a few short months ago he hadn't even known she existed. She'd turned his tired world upside down and made him want to overcome his fears to be the father she deserved. He would always be grateful to Stacy for allowing him the opportunity to be a part of his daughter's life and wouldn't forget what she'd sacrificed in the process.

Olivia came into view next. He heard Logan draw in a breath and glanced over to see his youngest brother break into an ear-to-ear grin at the sight of his pregnant wife. Jake was happy Logan had come through his grief over their sister's death and knew Olivia was to thank for it.

Then Millie appeared in the doorway and every thought other than her vanished. She gave him a shy smile as she walked toward him. The combination of her delicate wedding gown, the flowers woven into her hair and the way her skin shimmered in the light made her truly look like a fairy come to life. But Millie was a real woman and Jake could barely believe that she was about to become his forever.

"She's wearing the lotion I like." Brooke tugged

on his hand. "She's glittery, Daddy. Like when we first met her."

He lifted his daughter into his arms and gave her a hug. "She is beautiful inside and out. Just like you, Cookie."

"You got the ring, right?"

"It's right here," Logan said from Jake's side. He reached out for Brooke. "Come here, sweetie. You can help me keep it safe."

Brooke allowed herself to be transferred to Logan's arms. Jake concentrated on Millie walking down the aisle. When she got close enough he stepped forward and took her hands in his. "I love you," he whispered. "Now and forever, Millie."

"Forever," she repeated.

Josh cleared his throat from behind Logan. "You two are stealing my thunder. This may be the first and last wedding I officiate. Let me have a little fun here."

Millie laughed as she and Jake turned to his brother.

The ceremony was very personal for the two of them. Sara and Natalie each read a poem. Then Jake recited the vows he'd written for Millie.

He felt his palms grow damp as he looked into her eyes. Jake wasn't the kind of guy who talked about his feelings, but he wanted Millie and everyone in the room to understand exactly how he felt about her. "From the moment I met you, my life changed for the better. You are so much more than I ever expected. More intelligent, more caring, more beautiful. I want to spend the rest of my life building a life with you. I can't promise there won't be difficult times, but I will promise to stay by your side through every moment. Now and forever."

Millie's eyes shone with tears by the time he finished. "You may not say much, Dr. Travers, but you sure know how to make the words count when you do."

He took the ring Brooke handed him and slipped the thin wedding band onto her finger. "I don't ever want you to doubt my love, Millie."

She shook her head. "I wouldn't. I love you, Jake. All my life I've been looking for a home, for a place I could truly belong. I've found that with you. At your side, I'm so much better than on my own. I want you as my partner, my friend and my one true love. No matter what the future brings, we'll face it together. Now and forever."

Josh pronounced them husband and wife and Jake took her in his arms. This was where the two of them belonged, together with their family and friends, building the life they both wanted.

Now and forever.

* * * * *

We hope you enjoyed reading

A Soldier's Secret

by *New York Times* bestselling author

RAEANNE THAYNE

and

Suddenly a Father

by *USA TODAY* bestselling author

MICHELLE MAJOR.

Both were originally Harlequin® series stories!

From passionate, suspenseful and dramatic
love stories to inspirational or historical,
Harlequin offers different lines to
satisfy every romance reader.

New books in each line are available every month.

HARLEQUIN
SPECIAL EDITION

**Believe in love. Overcome obstacles.
Find happiness.**

Harlequin.com

Surely it was his imagination. Still… "Is something
wrong? Did something happen? Are you feeling okay?"

A wry smile flickered across her face. "Nothing
happened, Doctor. I'm feeling fine." She fidgeted with
the zipper tab on her parka. "What did you need to talk
about?"

He stuffed his hands into his jacket pockets to keep
from reaching out for her, cupping her beautiful face
highlighted by the afternoon sun. The last thing he
wanted was to spook her before he even got to pitch his
idea. "Ignoring each other isn't going so well for me.
How about you?"

Her shoulders sagged, and she stopped looking all
around. Instead, her attention became laser focused on

him. She shifted in her boots, the movement crushing into the powdery snow beneath them. A small tug of a smile while her cheeks turned red from the rush of cold that barreled through the porch. "Me neither."

Those two simple words powered through him, affirming what he suspected but had barely dared let himself presume. She was just as drawn to him as he was to her.

Nolan reached, touching her elbow lightly as snow flurries kept streaming from the sky. "What do you propose we do about that?"

Frowning, she swept snowflakes off her face while other snowflakes decorated her caramel-brown hair, making her look like some ethereal, fine-boned ice queen—with a steely spine. "I have no idea. But I'm open to suggestions."

Exactly what he'd been hoping to hear. "I suggest that we date."

Her eyes went wide in shock. An exhale billowed like smoke between them. "Date? The no-strings sort?"

Don't miss
The Cowgirl and the Country M.D.
by Catherine Mann, available October 2022
wherever Harlequin books and ebooks are sold.

Harlequin.com

SPECIAL EXCERPT FROM

LOVE INSPIRED
INSPIRATIONAL ROMANCE

*When a wounded veteran and his service dog seek work
at the Bright Tomorrows school for troubled boys, can
the principal—who happens to be the widow of his late
brother—hire the man who knows the past secrets she'd
rather forget?*

Read on for a sneak peek at
The Veteran's Holiday Home
by Lee Tobin McClain!

Jason stared at the woman in the doorway of the principal's office.
"*You're* A. Green?"

Just looking at her sent shock waves through him. What had happened
to his late brother's wife?

She was still gorgeous, no doubt. But she was much thinner than
she'd been when he'd last seen her, her strong cheekbones standing out
above full lips, still pretty although now without benefit of lipstick. She
wore a business suit, the blouse underneath buttoned up to her chin.

Her eyes still had that vulnerable look in them, though, the one that
had sucked him into making a mistake, doing what he shouldn't have
done. Making a phone call with disastrous results.

She recovered before he did. "Come in. You'll want to sit down," she
said. "I'm sorry about Ricky running into you and your dog."

He followed her into her office.

He waited for her to sit behind her desk before easing himself into
a chair. He wasn't supposed to lift anything above fifty pounds and he
wasn't supposed to twist, and the way his back felt right now, after doing
both, proved his orthopedic doctor was right.

Beside him, Titan whined and moved closer, and Jason put a hand
on the big dog. "Lie down," he ordered, but gently. Titan had saved him
from a bad fall.

"I didn't realize the two of you knew each other," the secretary said. "Can I get you both some coffee?"

"We're fine," Ashley said, and even though Jason had been about to decline the offer, he looked a question at her. Was she too hostile to even give a man a beverage?

The older woman backed out of the office. The door clicked shut.

Leaving Ashley and Jason alone.

"The website didn't have a picture—" he began.

"You always went by Jason in the family—" she said at the same time.

They both laughed awkwardly.

"You really didn't know it was me who'd be interviewing you?" she asked, her voice skeptical.

"No. Your website's kind of…limited."

If he'd known the job would involve working with his late half brother's wife, he'd never have applied. Too many bad memories, and while he'd been fortunate to come out of the combat zone with fewer mental health issues than some vets, he had to watch his frame of mind, take care about the kind of environment he lived in. That was one reason he'd liked the looks of this job, high in the Colorado Rocky Mountains. He needed to get out of the risky neighborhood where he was living.

Ashley presented a different kind of risk.

Being constantly reminded of his brilliant, successful younger brother, so much more suave and popular and talented than Jason was, at least on the outside…being reminded of the difficulties of his home life after his mom had married Christopher's dad…no. He'd escaped all that, and no way was he going back.

His own feelings for his brother's wife notwithstanding. He'd felt sorry for her, had tried to help, but she'd spurned his help and pushed him away.

Getting involved with her was a mistake he wouldn't make again.

Don't miss
The Veteran's Holiday Home *by Lee Tobin McClain,*
available October 2022
wherever Love Inspired books and ebooks are sold.

LoveInspired.com

LIEXP0822

Love Harlequin romance?

DISCOVER.

Be the first to find out about promotions,
news and exclusive content!

Facebook.com/HarlequinBooks

Twitter.com/HarlequinBooks

Instagram.com/HarlequinBooks

Pinterest.com/HarlequinBooks

YouTube.com/HarlequinBooks

ReaderService.com

EXPLORE.

Sign up for the Harlequin e-newsletter and
download a free book from any series at
TryHarlequin.com

CONNECT.

Join our Harlequin community to
share your thoughts and connect
with other romance readers!
Facebook.com/groups/HarlequinConnection

HARLEQUIN

Heartfelt or thrilling, passionate or uplifting—Harlequin is more than just happily-ever-after.

With twelve different series to choose from and new books available every month, you are sure to find stories that will move you, uplift you, inspire and delight you.

SIGN UP FOR THE HARLEQUIN NEWSLETTER
Be the first to hear about great new reads and exciting offers!

Harlequin.com/newsletters

HNEWS2021